The Ibis

The Ibis

BY

William Connell Cawthon

ISBN: 1-58500-114-7

About the Book

An epic historical novel, the story of Egypt's last wars before recorded history, culminating in the combining of the Upper and Lower Nile kingdoms, into a single nation ruled by the first dynasty in history, contemporaneous with the invention of the alphabet and the first introduction of writing, circa 3050 BC. Illustrated throughout by the author.

Figure 1: Narmer Palette, Upper Nile Side

Foreword

Time was legend and legend brought with it myth. A man was old from the number of summers he could remember. His grandfather may have related true incidents in his lifetime as well as his version of the stories his own grandfather told him, but there was no way to know that any of those tales were fact. And other men and women had the stories that they had received in the smae way. If the stories matched up then surely this was truth whether it be of flying beasts or men of preposterous size and strength, gods on earth.

Throughout almost all of human time all people could do to communicate was talk to each other and draw pictures. Some early peoples made little markers and clay envelopes to serve as evidence of barter but they had no way to leave a record of who they were, things they did or thought about, or such things akin to history. They made some things and left some highly enigmatic monuments scattered all over Europe and the Eastern end of the Mediterranean, but no real writing at all.

By about six thousand years ago, up in northeast Africa people had gathered into communities in what was called 'the black land' (later written as Kemet, now Egypt) along the Nile River. These communities likely began as expanded families; and as territories overlapped other, like-family groups would became tribal in nature, each with its chieftain. The properties were probably communal since the Nile washed out river's edge boundaries every year during its flood time. Life continued to be dependent on the Nile for its rich silt which supported elementary crops and for the fish and game that abounded within and near its banks. Feed crops permitted cattle which in turn led to stable towns with some type of governing disciplines, however primitive they may have been.

As the towns grew there would have been conflicts, even in the best of years for fishing rights, hunting rights and areas for cultivation and animal husbandry. And of course wives and husbands had to be found for each succeeding generation, something never in perfect balance within small communities. The feuding and fighting inevitably brought winners and losers. Losers were absorbed into the tribal realms of the winners and eventually accepted their rule. Of course with time and intermingling these little groups became larger and more homogeneous with increasingly powerful "high chiefs" presiding over groups of tribal chieftains.

Two such kingdoms grew to dominate the whole of Kemet, one in the South on the upper Nile; and one in the North near the delta. The capital of Upper Nile was first at El-Kab, then Nekhen; the Lower Nile federation's capital was Pe . Thebes and Memphis became capitals long afterward.

By about 3,100 BC these city-states had embarked on rather large building programs, including dikes and stone walls with parapets of sorts. They had houses with bounded, irrigated fields and stalls and stock pens for domesticated animals. They captured slaves and put them to useful work. Some slaves were the result of conquest among the tribes, but they also left pictures of slaves who came from Nubia and elsewhere, probably the Sinai peninsula and the desert country to the east.

Farther up the Nile, Nubia and beyond has only the civilizations of the lower Nile to account for even the existence of communities, kingdoms or any advances whatever in the making of their own history. Except for crafted articles and slaves brought back from hunting/raiding/trading expeditions these peoples might well have continued as simple hunter-gatherers unknown to history.

Not so for southern Mesopotamia where astronomy and geometry were already well advanced in places like Ur, Uruk and Eridu and early pictograms were yielding some sorts of messages...not writing as such, but still descriptive of things and animate objects for whatever reasons they wanted to depict them. Like the people along the Nile they could not yet leave a written historical record, nor could they express anything in writing related to abstract thoughts such as emotions, time-related identifications or social rules and laws.

The vastness of the deserts separating Egypt and the fertile, occupied parts of Mesopotamia was a formidable bar to regular contact between these developing civilizations though they were acquainted with each other. Both would soon have writing and therefore 'history'. However the cultures of the two areas were evolving along different lines, perhaps due more to environmental and topographic elements of their locales than differences in the people themselves. Except for means of telling each other (or us) about themselves each of these base generators of the civilizations of the world as we know them now were already quite advanced.

The Persian Gulf extended farther north than it does now and settlers had roamed down from the northeast to establish Ur, Uruk and Eridu along the Euphrates River, with Eridu originally a seaport. These and other communities of Sumer and Akkad had already amassed perhaps a thousand pictographic symbols and the wedge-shaped 'cuneiform' ciphers were soon to appear. Geometry of the ruler and compass variety and applications of fractions were at an advanced state. Astronomy applied to seasons and phases of the moon was well understood, and in Egypt a three hundred and sixty day calendar with twelve, thirty-day months was in use.The Sumerians had survived disastrous floods and were reaching farther out in their wanderings, north along the Euphrates toward Kish (near where Babylon later arose) in particular.

Masons, smiths and potters using wheels were craftsmen and copper alloys were in use at the same time gold and silver were being smelted. Although their economy had been based on farming and herding they had metals and crafted goods to trade with. Sumer had wheeled vehicles in local use for heavy hauling and war.

During this fourth millennium, BC people from in and around Ur in the far south migrated northward and westward in the green belt that bordered the Arabian Desert bringing established communities up to their culture, lore and trading levels. Up the Euphrates river and past the kingdom of Mari these Sumerians eventually reached the shores of the Mediterranean. Wandering bands walked along the sea, fishing and exploring, settling in protective coves. Sometimes they rowed, poled or sailed small boats close by the shores. Cretans were already sailing the eastern Mediterranean.

The towns of Sumer were not continually at war from such evidence as we have. For one thing the communities did not merge together as they did along the Nile and raiding parties would have had to be quite large to have any hope of completing a successful foray and getting back home with whatever loot they had managed to obtain. For another, such loot was not worth risking much effort over in those settled areas where the land pretty well provided for the needs of the communities, somewhat isolated as they were. So there was time for learning from the seasons and the stars; and a stability necessary for the lore and knowledge...accumulated generation by generation to be handed down...and to build huge temples from sun-dried bricks.

Though more unstable the communities along the Nile remained in place, century by century piling up their own legends of battles and the favor/disfavor of their god figures, be they bird, animal, sun or moon. Their 'high-chief-kings' did not live forever in some hereafter on earth though; it took the Mesopotamians to introduce the pantheon of gods which did not appear in any effective way in Egypt until hundreds of years after the first introduction of prose writing came about in the area we can call Lower Nile, not far from where Cairo is now.

And these northerners were doing their own exploring along the coastline and out into the sea. Jericho had been occupied for thousands of years; though it did not contribute much to advance civilization it was at least "there". With increasing contacts between the two major seats of learning and social structure, sharing of knowledge and crafts benefited both to the extent that it is difficult to know "who did what first" in many instances. It is safe to suppose that the practices of mathematics, astronomy and major temple building...temples to specific gods existed in Ur, Uruk and Eridu...emanated from Sumeria.

If so, early Egyptians were extraordinarily quick and enthusiastic learners and fanatic in their zeal for applications of their newfound knowledge. Their buildings, monuments and engineering achievements were simply phenomenal.

The first Egyptians with names and characteristics, feats and station in life were two men whose lives were intertwined and who left the incunabulum of history: a palette of writing. One became the first Pharaoh, Menes, sometimes called Narmer. The other, Th-T after his death became the god, Thoth, a powerful figure with the head of the ibis replacing his own rather handsome features from the only picture we have of him. Both men are portrayed on a large stone palette commemorating Narmer's defeat of the nameless northern 'King of the Plumed Crown'. Narmer's own picture wearing that crown is on the back of the palette...losers were not normally commemorated.

Narmer established the First Dynasty, not just in Egypt, the first dynasty known to have existed anywhere in the world. Th-T was a titular name, in Egyptian, 'Dhwty' (Tehuti)....the sacred ibis or the ibis-god, 'Thoth'. In time myths about Thoth grew until he had taken the shattered eye of Horus, the hawk-god and recreated it into the 'Sacred eye of Horus', composed of the fractions from one-half through one-sixtyfourth. For the world he had invented language, writing, mathematics, music and poetry, anatomy and medicine, in fact all knowledge. By the time the Grecian states had a mythology of their own he was Hermes, second only to God for he was 'the messenger of God'. The Romans renamed Hermes, Mercury but he was the same Thoth as the 'Ibis', a man titled, 'Th-T'.

What 'Th-T' really did was create 'mdw-ntr', madu-neter, the speech of the gods. He assigned twenty-odd ciphers to the consonantal sounds a human is capable of pronouncing and arranged them in an order from Ah to Tah that lasted for three thousand years. That order remained unchanged in Greek and Hebrew. He invented the Alphabet.

This is the story of the lives and times of Menhes of Upper Nile and Miqel of Sumer; and of the beginning of writing after the 'last war of pre-history' as it was recorded on the Narmer Palette five thousand years ago.

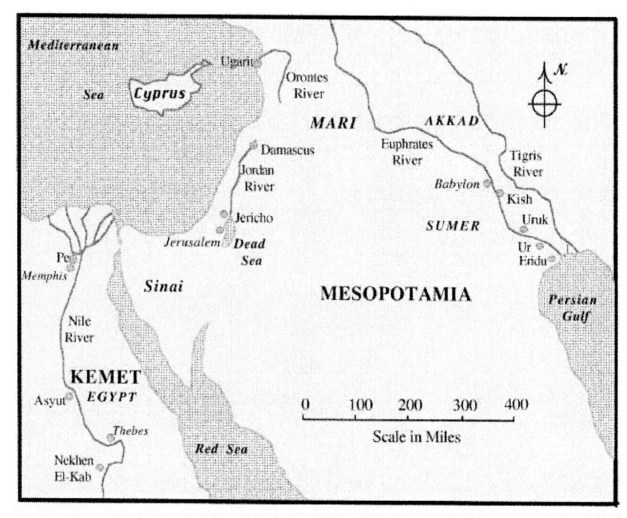

THE NEAR EAST

c. 3000 BC

Illustrated by W. C. Cawthon

Figure 2: Near-East Map

THE RIVER, NILE c. 3000 BC

Illustrated by W. C. Cawthon

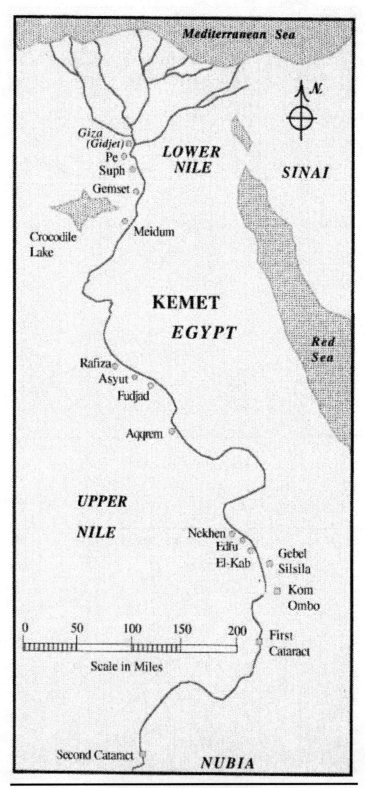

Figure 3: Egypt/Nile Map

Contents

ILLUSTRATIONS

GLOSSARY OF NAMES AND PLACES

Abb-Oth	High Priest, Kish
Abdala	Trader from Ur
Abgar	Senior Priest, Upper Nile
Addi-Hoda	Chief Prince of Nubia
Aff	Desert village between Thurn's and the Euphrates, home of Davri
Agga	Boatmaster and trader from Crete
Ahnpy	Captain of the Guards at Asyut
Akh-Loh	King of Upper Nile, Djo-Aten's grandfather
Akhuruk	Teacher of draftsmen at Ur, grandfather of Miqel
Akkad	Northern area in Mesopotamia
Alkhom	Djo-Aten's General at the Asyut Garrison
Aluba River	River entering the Euphrates north of Kish
Al-Ubaid	Temple at Ur
Amen	Moon god
Amen-Kha	King of Lower Nile, son of Hor-Amen
ANKH	Sacred hieroglyphic symbol for "Life"
Aqqrem	Village on Nile
Aqub	Village southeast of Huta on east bank of the Euphrates
Ar-Chab	Captain in Menku's armed forces. Father-in law of Menhes
Arpag	Farmer of Mu, pilgrim to Uruk
Assi-Rah	Prince of Nubia, son of Addi-Hoda
Asyut	Town on west bank of Nile in Upper Nile
Aten	Sun god
Athyat	Alphabet
Ayn-Far	High Priest, Uruk White Temple
Badjut	Senior priest, Lower Nile Temple at Pe
Bagh	Servant to Var-Lil, Ughada
Baldag	Shepherd of Uruk, father of Miqel
Batuk	Town on west bank of Nile, north of Nekhen
Bav	Town south of Quri, east bank of the Euphrates
Bodi	Miqel's sister
Bog	Hithabog
Catfish "Narmer"	Pseudonym for Menhes. Fish used with chisel on Narmer Palette for
Chad-Mar	Mar-Dug's name after becoming High Priest of the White Temple, Uruk
Coban-Bul	Servant to Mar-Dug, Uruk
Crocodile Lake Meidum	Enormous Lake and area in northern Egypt west of the Nile, near
Davri	Guide from Aff. Also Senior Priest, Ifn-Lot, Uruk White Temple
Djo-Aten	King of Upper Nile, called 'Scorpion'
Edfu	Upper Nile village near Nekhen
Edhmet	Port on Mediterranean Sea, east of Nile Delta

Eh-Buran	Robber, wanted in Uruk for murder
Ekhana	Daughter of Kalam-Bad, wife of Miqel
Ekhdur	Son of Menku, brother of Menhes
El-Kab	Upper Nile village near Nekhen
Enlid	Trader from Ur
Eridu	Port where Euphrates River entered Persian Gulf in southern Sumer
Ette	Miqel's sister
Ev	Hithabog of Oghud's tribe, hunting partner of Toq
Fudjad	Village, west bank of Nile between Aqqrem and Asyut
Fyd	Hithabog of Oghud's tribe, hunting partner of Toq
Gahnya	Wife of Baldag, mother of Miqel
Gand	Robber, Uruk
Gebel Silsila	Small mountain near the Nile in the Kom Ombo plain
Gem	Black Ibis in Egypt. Name Miqel assumed while in Lower Nile
Gemset	Town of west bank of Nile between Pe and Meidum v
Geval	Farmer of Mu, pilgrim to Uruk
Ghant-Ur	Chief Priest, Ur
Ghum	King of Upper Nile, beheaded by Akh-Loh
Gidjeh Plain	Giza, west of Nile and SW of Pe
Gurn-Thar	Senior priest, White Temple, Uruk
Hadu	Prince of Edfu Province, Upper Nile under Djo-Aten
Ham-Bal	Capital station of Mari, home of Qad-Rab
Hapi	Nile god
Hathuruk	Name given to Oghud's tribe of Hithabogs
Hel-Wyd	Senior priest, White Temple, Uruk
Hetti	Menku's wife, mother of Menhes
Hev-Ri	Chief Wizard, Asyut Academy
Hit	Village southeast of Aqub on east bank of the Euphrates
Hithabogs	Aboriginal hunter-gatherers scattered in small tribes along Euphrates.
Hor-Amen	King of Lower Nile
Hor-Djet	King of Lower Nile, father of Hor-Amen
Horus	Hawk-god. Chief god of ancient Egypt
Huta	Town east of Leb, north bank of the Euphrates
Ib-Seeg	Robber, criminal wanted in Uruk
Ifn-Lot	Senior Priest, Ifn-Lot of Uruk White Temple, called Davri at his desert
home at Aff	
Ikh	Town, west bank of Tigris, SW of Ughada
Ikruth	Village near Ugarit, south bank of the Orontes
Janna	Temple at Eridu
Jergil	Village, port, eastern end of Mediterranian
Jericho	Town on Jordan River, north end of Dead Sea
Kalam-Bad	Prince of Uruk, father of Ekhana
Kemet	Name ancient Egyptians used for Egypt..."black land"
Khafu	Oldest son of Menku
Ki	Son of Menhes and Meri-Lyt
Kish	Kingdom and city of Sumeria. Later abandoned for Babylon

Kmal-Dyl	Master Wizard of the Temple of Kish
Kom Ombo	Plain across Nile from Nekhen
Leb	Town south of Bav, east bank of the Euphrates
Luhinlil	God of the White Temple, Uruk
Lukh	Boy, guide from Salbat
Lvad	Hithabog hunter of Oghud's tribe
Magic Circle	Geometric construction for a value for "
Malbu	Fisherman, boat owner and guide at Huta
Malil	Friend of Miqel at Akhuruk's academy at Ur
Mar-Dug	Senior Priest, White Temple, Uruk. Later Chad-Mar, High Priest
Mara	Farming village on the west side of the Euphrates, NW of Uruk
Mari	Country of northwest Mesopotamia west of the Euphrates River
Meidum	Town on west bank of the Nile near Pe
Memshak	Fishing village west of Saqqut on Mediterranean
Menhes	First Pharaoh. Legendary Menes
MeriLyth	Queen of Egypt. Wife of Menhes and daughter of Ar-Chab
Men-Chad-Rez	King of Uruk
Mertud	High Priest of Upper Nile
Methwyd	Wife of Kalam-Bad. Mother of Ekhana
Miqel	Wizard of Sumer, son of Baldag
Mother of Heaven	Goddess of Ughada Temple ("Birdbeak" goddess) and Mari (Ushtur)
Mu	Farming village west of Uruk
Na	Hithabog hunter of Oghud's tribe
Naan	Boatman and protector of Menku's family at Crocodile Lake
Narak	Trader from Ur
Nebuty	nbty, the two ladies. Vulture and Cobra Standard of Nile
Nekhen	Capital of Upper Nile
Nekhbet	Vulture goddess of Upper Nile
Nubia	Country and Kingdom south of the Second Cataract of the Nile
Nura	Thurn's son
Nur-Bikh	Desert wilderness northeast of Kish toward Tigris River
Oghud	Chief of Hithabog tribe near Uruk
Ogtu	Robber, Uruk
Ombos	Area of hills west of Edfu and Nekhen
Om-Diph	Chief Priest of Lower Nile at Pe
Pe	Capital of Lower Nile
Pe-Diph	Region of Pe along Nile
Per-Qad	Senior wizard at Asyut Academy
Qadjus	Legendary wizard of Akkad, (Greek: Caduceus)
Qad-Rab	King of Mari
Qettrah	Queen of Lower Nile. Hor-Amen's widow and Amen-Kha's mother
Qom-Tur	King of Ur
Qumrif	Port, eastern end of Mediterrean Sea
Quri	Town south of Salbat, east bank of the Euphrates
Rabul	Senior wizard at Asyut Academy
Rafiza	Village, west bank of Nile north of Asyut

Rem-Chakh	High Priest, Ughada
Rif	Hithabog hunter of Oghud's tribe
Rom-Sha	Title for Captain of the King's guards, both Uruk and Kish
Rud	Village on Orontes, east of Ikruth
Salbat	Town east of Aff, on the west bank of the Euphrates
Saqqut	Fishing village, east end of the Mediterrean
Scorpion	Pseudonym for Djo-Aten, King of Upper Nile
Seb Seshat	Nubian Drawing Master, Asyut Academy. Hieroglyphics for "teaching scribe"
Sel-Abba	Prince of Nubia, son of Addi-Hoda
Shephset	Senior wizard at Asyut Academy
Sinai	Desert region east of Egypt
Sumer	Southern area in Mesopotamia
Suph	Town, west bank of Nile south of Pe
Tanis	Boy guide, Quri
Tehuti	Sacred Ibis. Transliterated hieroglyphic name for Thoth
Thar-Mes	King of Kish
Thurn	Shepherd living in the desert country between the Orontes and the Euphrates
Thuyi	General of Lower Nile. Loyal to Hor-Amen
Tylfar	Fishing village, eastern end of Mediterrean, near Ugarit
Toq	Hithabog, son of Oghud
Ugarit	Port, eastern end of Mediterrean Sea at mouth of the Orontes River
Ughada	City northeast of Kish on the east bank of the Tigris
Urba	General of Lower Nile. Loyal to Hor-Amen
Urnath	Priest of Kish, native of Ughada
Urunya	Wife of Akhuruk, grandmother of Miqel
Ushtur	Mari, 'Mother of Heaven'
Var-Lil	Senior priest of Ughada
Vashi	Robber of Eridu. Head of outlaw band at Mara
Vukhath	Senior wizard at Asyut Academy
Vedh-Ku	Son of Ghum, father of Menku, Grand father of Menhes, first King of Egypt
Wadjet	Cobra on Standard of Lower Nile
White Temple	Uruk temple
Zeti	Wicked god who stole the eye of Horus, name synomymous with "djet", serpent
Zuv	Hunter, Ugarit

CHAPTER ONE   "The Dissension"

Day came to the Nile as each day had always come with the huge red solar disk glowering over the shimmering waters of the Nile, rousing farmers, shepherds and fishermen to simple existence and pervasive fear: fear of everything unknown where almost everything was unknown; fear of starvation; fear of cutthroats; fear of neighbors' accusations to the high king or his hoods. It had been that way for as long as anyone knew and hope that it would change was yet another unknown thing. Hope was for the Nile's annual flood without which hope for sustenance vanished. Hope was for keeping one's head and for families having a strong man to provide whatever he could to extend living another day, another year perhaps.

At Nekhen, deep in the south Scorpion was King of Upper Nile, Prince of the vulture goddess, Nekhbet, Emisary of Aten, god of the sun. He ruled from the Second Cataract north to the village of Aqqrem, halfway down river toward Pe the capital of Lower Nile. He could claim the region to the south as far as the Third Cataract but he was satisfied to send slaving and looting parties there and let them return. With that he got what he wanted without having to set up garrisons or worry about revolt.

Aqqrem was another matter. There, there were repeated skirmishes with Lower Nile and continual threats of reprisal. Aqqrem was too close to Pe for Hor-Amen, King of Lower Nile and Prince of the cobra goddess to recognize it as part of Upper Nile. And it was far enough from Nekhen to make it difficult to hold on a permanent basis. The poor residents, mostly simple fishermen were buffeted as warriors overran their tents and dirt and reed-mat houses, first from the north; then from the south; then back again. But they made fair living stripping dead archers and spearmen of their armlets and weapons and trading them to whichever side was the enemy at the time. Most of the time it was easier than fishing so they did not complain too much.

Neither kingdom trusted them enough to conscript them into its army but both benefited sufficiently from the cheap recovery of arms lost in the almost constant forays not to destroy the thieving townspeople themselves. Occasionally Scorpion would have a few of them beheaded and place their heads on pikes in the village but the next day the pikes had been stolen so it made little impression on the villagers.

Scorpion was born, Djo-Aten and he succeeded his father as king when he was twenty-four. For several years he was confident in his inherited authority and ruled with a "live and let live" ease. Unrest as it always does began to appear throughout the farther reaches of Upper Nile until an almost successful coup about halfway to Aqqrem made him realize he needed to be more firm if he expected to keep his crown and his head. He took the name of the desert scourge when he was about thirty and began to install generals and garrisons from Nekken to Aqqrem, making each general a prince with sole authority for all matters in his province including worship of Aten. By now the significance of the sobriquet was lost neither on his people nor his enemies and he did his utmost to live up to it. He was old at forty-five. The struggle to control the fierce village chiefs to the north had been long and demanding and he had spent much of his adult life in the field, going out to subdue another three or four chieftains and rushing back to Nekhen to put down any idea of rebellion...rather to put down any idea of a successful rebellion. By then he was a tyrant of the first order and his enemies were everywhere. He trusted no one beyond the twenty or so 'Princes of Upper Nile' and they were more opportunistic henchmen than princes. Still, keeping alive depended on Scorpion's favor: the people would have gladly killed them if they were not surrounded by guards.

Many of the troops were from Scorpion's own towns and he pampered them lavishly, but approximately a third of his army was made up of expendable slaves, mostly Nubians. This gave him a tremendous advantage over Hor-Amen who was genuinely respected, absolute monarch though he was. Such slaves as he could bring in from the Sinai country were frightfully bad warriors, running away from his own troops before they could even reach the battlefield. In small skirmishes by the time Hor-Amen's club-wielders smashed their way through the phalanxes of Upper Nile buffer slaves they were so exhausted as to be relatively easy prey for Scorpions's swift, disciplined warriors.

The 'priests' of Upper Nile were a motley lot as could be imagined. Their remoteness from Sumer gave them little real knowledge beyond a few slates of fractions and geometric drawings. The original priests of Aten, the 'Sun-Wizards' had migrated to Nekhen during the glory days of King Ghum, a far more enlightened ruler. Nekhen was smaller then and the Upper Nile kingdom extended south past Edfu only as far as the First Cataract and no more than about fifty miles to the north. But an uprising led by Scorpions's grandfather, Akh-Loh of El-Kab ended with Ghum beheaded. The surviving senior priests fled north toward Pe as Akh-Loh moved into Nekhen.

Akh-Loh was uncouth, uneducated and ruthless. He trusted no one he could not absolutely control by fear or bribery, usually both. He appointed warriors to be senior priests and took the title, High Priest to himself. A few younger priests and priest-trainees remained, playing on the sheer ignorance of their superiors. They designed 'gods' that they would show Akh-Loh; these they lifted directly from their enigmatic slates to become birds, snakes and anything else that suited their fancy for gods. Akh-Loh sanctified every one of them and declared the death penalty for anyone who protested this utter nonsense. The Upper Nile standard honored the 'Vulture Goddess', derived from the vulture, Nekhbet. The sun, Aten was often engraved with a nose to look like a man; and the bull became a quite picturesque raging monster, pawing the ground over helpless victims in depictions intended to terrify the people.

By the time Djo-Aten's father was made king he realized he would be lynched if he tried to change anything related to sun and bull worship so he let things stand as they were. The proliferation of symbol icons continued unabated until Scorpion himself put a stop to it. He restored the rank of High-Priest and attempted to recruit a genuine wizard from Lower Nile for the job. There were no takers so he named an aged, senile priest named, Mertud High Priest of Upper Nile and had the little Nekhen temple restored enough to make a better appearance on feast days.

Beer was plentiful and feast days were rather frequent to keep non-warriors in line. They were little more than orgies with Nubian slave girls brought in in sufficient numbers to provide entertainment to the disgust of the men's wives. Polygamy was endorsed and mixed blood children filled the fields. Hapi, the Nile-god had behaved rather well most of the years Scorpion ruled so that there was enough to eat, further securing his hold on the White Crown of Upper Nile.

Following the rebellion that brought Akh-Loh to power one of Ghum's sons escaped to Meidum, a thriving town near the vast Crocodile Lake in Lower Nile. He traded his gold armlets and jeweled pectoral for cattle and eventually owned large herds and flocks establishing himself as a person of stature in Meidum. Hor-Amen's grandfather, the then king was unaware of this Vedh-Ku's heritage and he lived a long, peaceful life becoming even more revered than the provincial chieftain there. Nevertheless he passed on his dream of retaking Upper Nile to his sons and one of them, Menku began training his shepherds and cattlemen into an effective band of warriors. In time he started breaking out small herds and sending them with their warrior

2

handlers to villages well south of Aqqrem. In each of these the warriors set up stock pens and built houses to meld into the population of the town gaining friendly and respected acceptance. Their herds and flocks grew until these became prosperous strongholds, closer and closer to Nekhen.

There was an uneasy peace between the provinces of Upper and Lower Nile. Hor-Amen, king of Lower Nile, Prince of the Cobra Goddess, Wadjet, Emissary of Amun, god of the moon was content with the areas of his domain, relying more on commerce and occasional slave raids to the Sinai and into the western wadis and desert country to add to the abundant wealth of Lower Nile. He endowed the temple services with more than adequate provisions and exerted minimal influence on their teachings. The Amen-cult grew increasingly powerful with the king but remained aloof from the people much as was the custom in Sumer as well as Akkad.

At Nekhen Scorpion had been too busy with the 'feasts' and keeping his princes loyal to care much about expansion to the north. Furthermore the Nubians had begun to mount large raids below the second cataract, as in days long past. He rightly viewed these encroachments with alarm and repeatedly sent bands of warriors all the way to the third cataract for reprisal. The results were often fearful with entire war parties ambushed and slaughtered in these sorties. Finally to forestall a revolt he was forced to head an army that marched up the Nile annihilating whole Nubian villages on the way. The principal chieftain of the northern provinces of Nubia sued for peace with reparations of gold and lapis lazuli. He guaranteed a provisioned standing army of two thousand trained Nubian warriors to be made available to Nekhen and stationed at Edfu, south of Nekhen.

Djo-Aten had never heard of Vedh-Ku's escape: Akh-Loh boasted that he had destroyed every trace of Ghum's family. Menku attracted himself to the Aten-cult which still flourished in Lower Nile outside Pe-Diph itself. He furnished supplies to the scattered Sun-Temples and entered his sons in their academies until they were old enough to be warrior-herdsmen. Twice each year, before and following flood time he sailed up the Nile to visit his 'extension herds' and at each reviewed the warriors' proficiency with weapons. These extensions were split as soon as they were large enough to be self supporting and the spin-off group was sent to yet another village to repeat the cycle. Always the selected village was well beyond the last one established so that in time Menku was visiting within seventy-five miles of Nekhen.

The routine was invariable: Menku presented himself to the elders, "I am Menku, a peaceful herdsman from the crocodile lake come to visit my sons and kinsmen. I bring an ox for sacrifice to your god as an offering of friendship. My priests will gladly assist in the slaughter to obtain the blessing of Aten." The poor villagers ate mostly fish and game and the offer of an ox was beyond their wildest dreams. Menku was almost deified at each stop but he always humbly detached himself and went to see his 'sons and kinsmen'. The priests who accompanied him were accomplished wizards, descendants and proteges of the 'Sun Wizards' from the days of Ghum in Nekhen. Menku was something of a wizard himself, understanding the fractional mathematics and ruler and compass drawings very well and having a passing knowledge of the geometric design construction to yield a very accurate value of the relationship of the circumference of a circle to its radius. Though he did not perform the constructions any more he knew their meanings and why they were considered sacred. He had heard of Kish's Master Wizard, Kmal-Dyl and wished he and his Academy Priests at Meidum could arramge to meet with him.

Unfortunately some 'fractional dissidents', geometers from Mesopotamia had entered the academy and were spreading their views in a quiet but convincing manner. Without a giant

3

circle...a henge...or some other huge "drawing board" they could not be confuted except by faith in the sacredness of the ancient and sacred geometric construction for determining an extremely accurate value for 'Pi'.And only an intellect matching that of Kmal-Dyl could provide such a faith. The fractional method of determining the relationship was compellingly simple and their measure of pi was also extremely accurate. The differences were not measurable on any terrestrial plane so they resorted to star sightings, just as was the case with the sacred geometric construction.

The problem was no one knew either the antiquity or true origin of either method. And the relative ease of application of the fractional method compared to the tedious twenty-two steps of the so-called 'Sacred Circle' geometric method implied its general use in all but sacred matters. All wizards of stature agreed to this; what the fractional zealots insisted on, however was doing away entirely with the Sacred Circle. Legend had it that the Sacred Circle was from the speech of the gods, or even of God, Himself. This belief had been carefully transmitted from generation to generation in parallel lineages from times before memory. The 'General Consensus of Sumer and Akkad' for the exact twenty-two steps was not reached until somewhat later; nevertheless the basis was sound and accepted as such. Kmal-Dyl's influence on the 'Consensus' assured that.

The Sumerian approach called for the unchanged continuation of the teaching of the Sacred Circle construction with the fractional relation brought in for more quickly estimating areas of land involving circular sectors. This was complex mathematics for ruler and compass geometry and fractional computation to handle. Yet these were the only forms of mathematics available to the wizards or anyone else until arithmetic and algebra could be invented nearly three millenniums later.

One of Menku's sons, a strapping adolescent named Menhes alternated between wanting to become a wizard and his natural bent toward becoming a warrior-herdsman and following in the steps of his father. He was born when Menku was in his late forties and it was obvious to all he was his favorite child. Since his older brothers were at extension stations there was no sibling rivalry; in fact they were almost as fond of Menhes as Menku and his wife, Hetti were. When he was old enough Menhes accompanied Menku on his semi-annual tours during which he got to know the townspeople of Upper 3

Nile. By the time he was fifteen just about every father with an eligible daughter in any of the communities he visited wanted him betrothed. But Menku told all of them, that while he was flattered Menhes had chosen the priesthood. Though this was not entirely true Menhes gave a good account of himself before elders and priests alike.

Menhes begged Menku to let him set up a really large station at Edfu, farther up the Nile past Nekhen. The situation between Hor-Amen and Scorpion was steadily worsening and Menku knew full well that the time was approaching for him to move all his possessions out of Lower Nile and distribute them throughout Upper Nile before Hor-Amen banished the Aten sun worship cult for security purposes in Lower Nile. The differences between the sun priests and the moon priests were all ritual oriented as far as the wizards of either cult were concerned. But with Nekhen having once represented the center of the Sun Wizards, even though by accident the trivial divergences began to take on a nationalistic fervor in lower Nile. The more men of reason protested the more fanatics called for banishment of Aten in any form from the temples and tombs in Lower Nile.

Scorpion's excesses were frightening, not only to men like Menku but to the elders of the villages where he had stations. They discussed it with him during every visit. Menku had transferred his Meidum academy to a large extension station at Asyut about sixty-five miles north of Aqqrem and the priests were scattered throughout the other stations along the river in Upper Nile. To move such large herds and flocks up the Nile was not only out of the question logistically, it would attract the attention of Scorpion or his princes. They would surely feel either threatened or seize the opportunity for murder and confiscation.

Menku at length hit on a plan. He barged small herds down to the delta where he could find plentiful hardwood for boats. There his chief warrior-herdsmen bartered a single herd or flock for a single boat made to Menku's specifications. All the boats were exactly alike: long, sleek and heavily sailed for speed. Built from planks of acacia wood and with high bow and stern these one hundred and forty foot long 'ships' could be maneuvered with ease in the wide river and pushed off sand bars when they went aground. With rows of benches for oarsmen to supplement the sails their speed was equal to smaller wooden craft and far exceeded the papyrus skiffs normally in use on the Nile. Each could carry a hundred and fifty fully armed warriors and travel from a hundred to a hundred and fifty miles up river in a single day and night when the prevailing winds from the north were favorable.

Menku and his warrior-herdsmen told Lower Nile princes and their representatives that the boats were needed for trade from Crocodile Lake south throughout Lower Nile. Bartered goods were to flow to and from Pe. If war did not break out it was even possible trade could be reestablished with some of the northern centers of Upper Nile. Hor-Amen's eyes lighted up when he learned this might bring more of the gold from Ombos and the hills west of Edfu to Pe and Lower Nile. In recent years this gold flow had been restricted to a trickle as Scorpion sequestered more gold to bribe troops with.

There was no interference and by the end of four years Menku had accumulated a fleet of thirty vessels. Ten of the vessels did indeed ply the Lower Nile trade routes and their distinctive sails were seen at the Pe-Diph wharves on a regular basis. The others were assigned to the extension stations, one per station. They made bartering runs up and down the Nile for short distances keeping the barter at the village level, meaning very low value goods. All this was for the sake of appearance; Menku could ill afford any suspicion of militaristic motives.

At last Menku gave in to Menhes pleading and agreed to send him south of Nekhen. However instead of Edfu he sent him farther south to the Kom Ombo plain on the east side of the Nile across from Edfu and Nekhen. This huge plain afforded every advantage for herdsmen and warriors alike and it offered concealment and protection without the need for erection of stockades. Four boats sailed silently past Nekhen and Edfu in the black of night and on reaching a large stream that flowed through the center of the plain turned into it, oarsmen stroking hard as the sails were lowered. At selected landings the boats were beached and dragged ashore where with masts dropped they were covered with reed mats to look like rows of fishermen's hovels. Later other groups of four would sail progressively farther up the stream and receive the same treatment until sixteen boats were securely beached above flood levels and concealed.

Menhes was now a man of twenty-three. He was powerful and gracefully athletic and towered over the warriors he took with him. Skilled in the martial arts he was nevertheless studious and attentive to anything the Asyut Sun-Wizards could teach him. He was a severe disciplinarian, driving the training of his troops mercilessly yet he was fair and regularly broke the training routine with hunting parties and feasts for the warrior-herdsmen and the families they had brought with them.

Contact was maintained with the extensions in the north by small bartering parties that regularly stopped at the Nekhen landing. Their goods were mostly agricultural products and a few items of such village wares as crude pottery: goods normally seen in the Nekhen market yards. The traders were townspeople loyal to the Menku family and they were easily assimilated into the gossip gatherings of the temple yards wherever they stopped to barter. Information and the mood of the people was transmitted to Menku at Asyut and Menhes at the Kom Ombo station.

Menku and Hetti had moved to Asyut after the Nile flood subsided the year before. He left a trading house at Meidum and a camp at Crocodile Lake to continue appearances as Lower Nile residents. The staffs while small maintained Menku's practice of providing for many of the small temples of Aten in Lower Nile; and he planned to visit them at least once a year as long as necessary to establish his constituency there. One of the ships from the various Upper Nile stations was always on the water between Asyut and Pe-Diph, stopping at Meidum each trip. A few reed barges also carried cattle to the delta region and returned with grain and fruit for trade along the river. As far as Lower Nile was concerned little had changed except that the Menku family was now almost entirely involved in trading, leaving the production of cattle to the local herdsmen. Hired shepherds tended the small flocks that remained at the lake camp; except for domestic needs no herds were left there.

Kom Ombo was beautiful in the spring. Antelope abounded and flamingos fed along the river and in the shallow ponds left by creeks and streams created by the Nile's wanderings. Game of every kind was plentiful and the lush grass supported Menhes's growing herds. Papyrus and sedges furnished material for the ubiquitous reed mats of the Nile country and willows and shrubs in profusion allowed the weaving of ropes and making of baskets for every need. Roving bands of Nubian hunters were constantly in evidence but seldom gave any trouble to the camps Menhes set up.

To the north a protracted drought had begun and Menku hoped it would not spread to the sources of the Nile. Crocodile Lake, with no outlet evaporated away to at least a foot below its normal level; no cause for alarm yet but still news from the Euphrates and the Mari country south of the Orontes was bad. The upper winds had for some time shifted to the north and rains now fell regularly on barren steppes with practically none falling from the Persian Gulf northward up past Kish. Nor did much rain come to Akkad along the Tigris.

Hor-Amen was under some pressure already from the tribes in the delta counry north of Pe and he was sending priests of Amen there regularly to plead for the blessing of the Amen. They were received with surly silence though no one was attacked. Hor-Amen thought another year of this and things would become serious. Fortunately when the Nile flood came, though somewhat smaller than usual it was sufficient to satisfy the farmers and game was still abundant.

Menku was seventy now and Hetti insisted that he turn the management of Asyut and the stations north of Nekhen over to their oldest son, Khafu who with his family had stayed at Meidum and Crocodile Lake. Arthritis severely restricted Menku's movements to the extent that most of the time he had to be carried whenever he left the house but his mind was as facile as ever and it was hard for him to give up the idea of visiting the stations every year. Hetti, ten years younger than he was would have none of it but to satisfy him agreed to accompany Khafu on the next tour.

Khafu, now in his late forties was content to enjoy the rich life his father had provided and had no ambitions to become king of anything, not even a minor province. He was right as far as living went; kings, including his great grandfather often fared badly. And if they fell their whole family fell with them. He lived far better than most princes and he was a hard working manager. He shared his father's resentment of the beheading of Ghum but it was so long before his time he did not associate it with Djo-Aten. Menku had fired Menhes with the responsibility for avenging the wrong to his family from the time he was old enough to begin to understand such. As he grew to manhood he became obsessed with the dream of unseating the ruler of Upper Nile, whomever it might be.

Menku seized on this and began his long range strategy as soon as he was comfortable that Menhes would some day carry out his plans. With Menhes building a formidable army at Kom Ombo the pincers were forming nicely and the ships gave higher mobility than anything ever before seen on the Nile. The only better sailors were the men from Crete who stayed in the Mediterranean, the 'Great Sea'. Such deep-hulled open sea vessels were not only not needed on the river, they would have been a handicap with its changing courses and frequent, barely submerged sand-bars.

Menku redirected his attention to the priesthood, particularly the dissensions that kept arising over what he rightly regarded as trivia. These nit-picking arguments were not only occurring between the sun and moon priests they were getting worse between the fractional fanatics and the die-hard legendary 'Sacred Circle' supporters. At last he called in his chief wizard, the head of the Asyut Academy and told him, "Hev-Ri, I think you and I can speak frankly. I am weary of all this squabbling and I do not believe it will be settled on any factual basis in my lifetime. Do you think someone like Kmal-Dyl, or even Kmal-Dyl himself could settle it, even if only among the priests of Aten?"

"Yes, Menku. I do believe Kmal-Dyl could settle things down; not someone like him. There is no such as far as I know. It would have to be the Master Wizard himself." Menku smiled and said, "Then send for him. I have gold, lands or whatever else a man might want. All he has to do is name his price; I will meet it." Hev-Ri was less sure, "Even the powerful Ayn-Far and Ghant-Ur of Sumer have been unable to get him to leave Kish. And their kings have been willing to build a temple especially for him if he would consent to go down there. Furthermore we've received a bad reputation in Sumer. The wizards there have had more contact with the moon priests than with us and they regard Akh-Loh and his heirs as barbarians. 'Hithabogs' they call them." "What has Djo-Aten got to do with us?" Menku wanted to know. "Everything and nothing as far as the priests of Sumer are concerned. How could they know anything about you except that you have been a strong supporter of the priesthood and the academies and that you are a very rich man? The secrecy of your strategy to restore the throne of Upper Nile to your family is well kept outside our little circle. I assure you Kmal-Dyl will not come."

Menku did not like what he heard, "Then I suppose the only thing to do is for us to go to him. For me that is impossible of course. But you are young enough to make the journey and I would think you could pick two of the most respected fractional wizards and two of the most conservative senior priests of Aten to go with you." Sensing Hev-Ri's distaste for the idea Menku continued, "I will let you take one of the fast boats to the port of Saqqut on the Great Sea. Once there I am sure you can barter with a Cretan captain to sail you up the coast to Qumrif or Ugarit. You can go overland from there in a few days to the Euphrates and barter for a sailing skiff down to Kish. I do not think you would be gone so very long, do you?" "I suppose not." "Then why do you not want to do it?"

"I have no fear of the people along the Nile. We know them well enough. But the Mari desert is badlands; every gorge has its murdererous band and every oasis is likely to be a den of cutthroats." It was clear that Hev-Ri was truly alarmed. "Then I will send an escort of guards. Surely eight of our warriors can protect five priests. Make your arrangements and get back to me before you leave by the day after tomorrow." Menku countered. Hev-Ri shrugged his assent but still spoke again, "May I ask you one question?" "Say on." "After all this time why is this

7

suddenly so urgent? I'm not arguing with you. I'm just curious."

"Menhes is almost prepared to attack Nekhen. It will be only two or three years at the most before Scorpion will have broken the will of the last village elders we can count on. I want the battle to be staged at El-Kab, or between Nekhen and Edfu where a decisive victory would demoralize the rest of the Upper Nile army. It must be swift and final. I am physically unable to help Menhes in this uprising. But I do not want him to end up with a consolidated kingdom and a divided priesthood. That is a   burden I do not want to load on him or the poor people who have already suffered so much. And I do not want any more killing than is necessary to take the throne. If it were possible I would do away with only Djo-Aten, his family and his twenty or so princes."

Hev-Ri asked, "Will that make peace in Upper Nile?" "For a time perhaps. That really depends on whether Hor-Amen can hold onto his plumed crown...and his head...in Lower Nile. He is not much of a warrior and his princes will feel threatened the instant Menhes takes the crown of Upper Nile. Furthermore the moon priests are faring badly with this drought in the north. I would not put it past them to arouse the people against the Sun Wizards, meaning the entire Upper Nile kingdom.

"Menhes must make an alliance with the Nubian Prince who is supplying part of Djo-Aten's army with trained warriors. If he can he will have a force strong enough to defeat any gathering of princes in Upper or Lower Nile. I am not so ambitious for myself or for him to wish a full scale war on him, or anyone else. It would be a bloody affair and a lot of good people would lose their lives unnecessarily. But there has to be peace along the entire distance from the second cataract to the Great Sea. I think we can leave the Nubians alone to rule themselves. We do not need them as slaves and I believe we can prevent their raiding of our villages in the far south if we treat them with respect."

"What you are saying is that war is inevitable, Menku." "I cannot control that. Chances are I will not be alive if it comes. But there can be no peace with these continual bickerings over ritual and the supposed superiority of one set of worship icons over another. Scorpion has tried to contain the mess Akh-Loh left him. But worship in Nekhen and most of Upper Nile is reduced to gibberish and attempts to scare the people out of their wits with incantations to birds and snakes. You know all this, Hev-Ri."

Hev-Ri nodded and started to leave. But Menku was curious, "Where did all these ancient methods of geometric drawing come from: things like the 'Sacred Circle' and the 'Fractional Calculation' constructions'? They are legendary, this much I know but the legends are too consistent to be simple myth. And there are the names. What do they mean?"

Hev-Ri knew he had to respond, "Without a way to make a record all we have is the stories handed down to us by our mentors and our fathers, and of course the drawings themselves which do form something of a record I suppose. When I was a young man in training at Al-Ubaid, the temple near Ur I received what the senior priests there believed to be true. Each of the methods had an originator though now it is popular to talk of such things as the 'Speech of the Gods'. I will tell you what I was taught; that is all any of us has to go on".

"That is interesting, Hev-Ri. What about the Sacred Circle?" "I think that originated somewhere in the south, in what is now Sumer. There was a wizard who talked to God. No, I am not making this up; every accredited wizard I know believes that. The wizard carefully laid out about twenty steps to construct for pi with extraordinary accuracy. The basis of the construction has never changed I am told, even though there is general agreement among most wizards that the twenty steps handed down were originally twenty-two."

"What was the basis, Hev-Ri? I vaguely remember the construction but I never have known why it works." "It really is quite simple in principle. A rather tedious construction leads to a small circle, the Sacred Circle which is moved to the center of the basic diagram so it can be added to three. That gives the value for pi".

Menku still did not see what the problem was regarding the fractional dissenters, "I know the fractional method obtains a little circle that is probably about as good as the Sacred Circle, at least for any possible practical application we will ever have. Why won't the diehards give up?"

"The answer is partly just that. They, we are traditionalists. But there is more. That solution will likely never be duplicated if it is ever lost. And we do know, even if intuitively that it is a lot more accurate than the fractional construction. There have been in addition a small number of individuals over the centuries, all of them brilliant who have thought that the twenty-two step symbols could be used for written communication, recording what has happened for example. It would be the greatest invention ever created if it could come about somehow. Your name and mine; when we lived and where; what we thought and did...all such things would be a matter of record...maybe in stone or on clay pieces like we and the Sumerians use for barter now. As we do here the Sumerians already have many symbols they use to record trade and keep track of things. But no one has yet succeeded in writing anything that someone else can "read" if the person who recorded it was not present to explain it. There are many of us who believe that if such a system is ever invented it will be based on the twenty-two steps of the Sacred Circle construction. That is the real reason for holding on to it at all costs.

"Now that makes sense. Why can't the fractional people see that, Hev-Ri? They are certainly intelligent enough. We both know that." "They have their tradition too. It may be that those of us trained in Sumer do not want to believe that another ancient wizared originated fractional mathematics. But I don't think that is all there is to it. There is strong basis in the stories of Sumer to support that what their wizard exposed was known in lower Sumer before the Sacred Circle construction came into being.

"The fractions named for symbols representing the parts of the eye was a brilliant piece of work. We all use them. The fractional solution for the "pi circle' is even more brilliant but those who were contemporaries of the 'fraction wizard' passed on their legends that he stole that solution while he trained in Sumer and then claimed he received it from the Mother of Heaven. And that claim seems to be the origin of the extradinary fanaticism of so many of the fractional adherents, moreso in Mari than in any other place. The Amen priests and the Sun Wizards all hold that the transferred Sacred Circle is truly sacred". Menku questioned how such a myth could have survived among true wizards. "I am sure Kmal-Dyl never thought it would become a myth. He used a little story for academy instructors to teach as a memory device when training young boys. It is a rather charming fiction and is considered such in Uruk and Kish. Nobody expected anything like what has happened in Nekhen with Scorpion's crowd to pretend to believe it and force the people to bow down every time a hawk flies by or a cobra slithers into view. They will not even hunt the ibis anymore."

Hev-Ri returned to his house to find Seb, the drawing master waiting for him. Seb was a Nubian who had been taken into Menku's academy at Meidum when he was a child. He was as knowledgeable as any of the senior Sun Wizards but they never quite accepted him as one of them. Menku was extremely fond of Seb and would have installed him at the Asyut Academy but Menhes had asked Seb to come to Kom Ombo and head up the 'refresher' academy he had there. Hev-Ri trusted Seb as much as anyone in the Aten Service; he could be relied on to teach the young wizards drawing skills and the traditional works of Sumer and keep the fractional studies in perspective as extra learning, not as an alternative to truth.

Hev-Ri embraced him warmly, "My old friend, Seb. How is your health?" "I am as usual blessed with the well being I had as a boy running in the forests of Nubia, Hev-Ri. I hope you are as well." "I am indeed, thank you. What brings you to Asyut?" Seb grinned with his white teeth flashing, "I come to obtain Master Menku's permission for Menhes to marry the daughter of Captain ArChab. ArChab brought his family to Kom Ombo a few months ago and his daughter, Merilyth is very bright and very beautiful. Menhes wants her for his wife but insists that the Master and Madam Hetti know of his plans before he brings her into his tent."

"ArChab and Menku are good friends and I am sure there will be no problem. It is time Menhes was married. He has spent his whole life preparing for the throne of Upper Nile and his only relaxation has come from hunting and sailing. He needs to have a wife and children. He has no intention of being a sun wizard; though I must admit he would be one of the best of them if he did, don't you, Seb?." "He amazes me with his understanding of what we do. He has always been a quick learner. But now he is a powerful warrior and seems to be born to lead people. He has become quieter and more serious in the time he has been at Kom Ombo and his father should be very proud of him."

Hev-ri agreed but wanted to change the subject, "Seb, I have just left Menku and he wants me to take some priests to Kish and meet with Kmal-Dyl there. We hope we can settle the fractional dissension once and for all before Menhes starts his assault on Nekhen." "It needs settling, Hev-Ri. I have my hands full at Kom Ombo trying to keep the factions in line. I wish you success on your journey." "Thank you, Seb. Would you be willing to go with me?

"Hev-Ri, you know the laws of the temples of Sumer and Akkad better than I do. Their hithabogs and people with skin the color of mine would be put to death if they were found in the shadow of a temple wall. I wish it were not so. We have no such problem in the Master's service though I cannot say the same for Pe. I was once there and was treated like an outcast even when I was accompanied by our senior priests." "I suppose you are right. Things are changing in the south of Sumer but I am not sure Kish has accepted the changes yet. It will of course. You would be a great help to us."

"Actually I do not think I could go anyway. Menhes wants me to assist him with the alliance his father proposes with Nubia's Prince Addi-Hoda and we will try to set that up as soon as I can get back to Kom Ombo. Let one of your young wizards go in my place." "Since you trained them will you help me select the two best suited for these presentations to Kmal-Dyl?" "Of course, Hev-Ri. That is an easy decision on my part. Take Rabul and Vukhath . They are as conservative and as convincing as anyone you will find."

Menku and Hetti were elated that Menhes had found a wife and they both knew and liked Merilyth. ArChab was the most influential warrior-herdsman in Menku's service and was sure to be a prince in the new Kingdom of Upper Nile. The match seemed perfectly suited. Menku told Seb, "Go and tell our son we love him and are honored that he sent you to ask our blessing. We give it with joy and the wish for many children to bring them happiness when they are old as we are now."

Menhes took the gold and lapis bracelets and the gold ring Menku and Hetti had sent and gave them to MeriLyth as they stood alone on a bluff above the river watching an ibis drift slowly down to the water below. He gently placed a lotus blossom in her hand and pulled her to him as the last rays of the sun sparkled on the Nile. As a wisp of her hair brushed his face Menhes kissed her lips with a passion he had never known before and at last lifted her into his arms and carried her into his tent.

'NEKHBET', THE STANDARD OF UPPER NILE

Vulture from relief found beneath the Great Pyramid, Khufu.

Illustrated by W. C. Cawthon

Figure 4: Upper Nile Standard

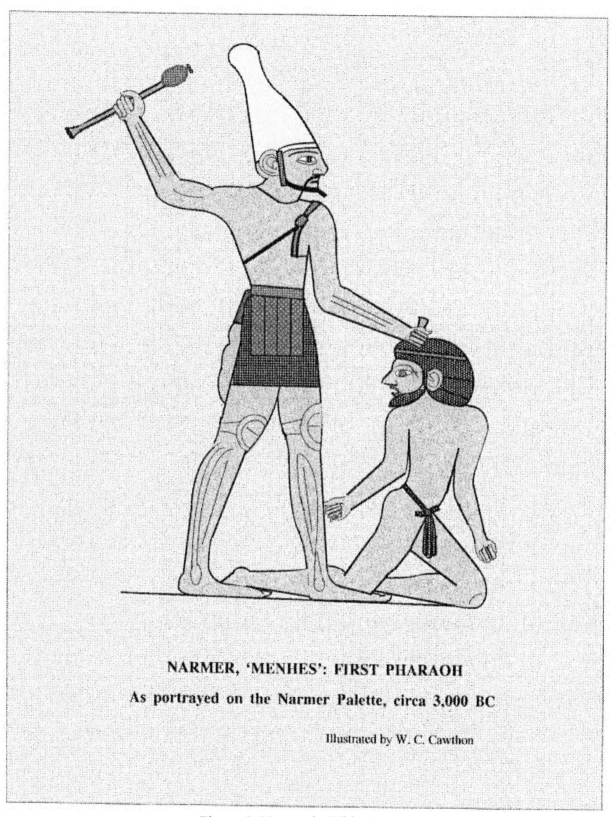

NARMER, 'MENHES': FIRST PHARAOH

As portrayed on the Narmer Palette, circa 3,000 BC

Illustrated by W. C. Cawthon

Figure 5: Narmer in White Crown

CHAPTER TWO   'The Alliance'

Djo-Aten called his generals to a meeting in El-Kab at the large stone granary, the same place his grandfather, Akh-Loh had plotted the overthrow of King Ghum so many years before. On the short jaunt to El-Kab from Nekhen he was joined by Abgar, the most senior priest in Upper Nile, second only to the aged High Priest, Mertud. Abgar had held all the power of the temples almost from the time Mertud had been appointed...even then Mertud was a doddering old figurehead. It was a good arrangement for Djo-Aten and Abgar: Mertud was easily manipulated and easier to quote on any issue of conflict of which he had not the slightest understanding. The death penalty was meted out in Mertud's name whenever 'Scorpion' or Abgar decided there was a hint of sedition or such a thing as a suspected disloyalty, however slight.

Abgar studied Djo-Aten's surly expression and wondered what reason there might be for such a conference, all the more why it was being held in rural El-Kab where the amenities of Nekhen were notably absent. "My Lord is in deep thought." he ventured. "I am worried, Abgar. Something is going on. I can almost feel it. Things are too quiet; there have been no protests for months and you, yourself have executed no wizards or priests lately." "Do you not think that is testimony to your absolute rule, Djo-Aten? You have worked hard all these years to achieve it and I think you have done a remarkable job. Do you think Hor-Amen may be up to something?"

"No more than usual. He has his hands full north of Pe in the delta country and will not likely be sending any more expeditions past Aqqrem soon in my opinion. No, it is something else. It has been three years since we subdued the last province, the towns around Asyut. Normally we would have had to keep on killing the hard-liners for a couple of years after subjugation but there the resistance simply melted. Or it appeared to melt." "I have people at Asyut, Djo-Aten. Nothing seems to be happening there. The Menku family has moved in from Crocodile Lake to their cattle station there but they are loyal to Aten to a fault. He has restored the temple, just as his herdsmen have done at every one of his stations along the Nile. Menku is old and he told me not long ago he had come to fear that Hor-Amen and his Moon-priests would totally ban the worship of Aten throughout Lower Nile. I know that has already occurred around Pe and I would not be surprised to see Hor-Amen trying to strengthen his hold with the drought they are having down there. We are glad to have the Menku's and the benefit of the trade they conduct with Lower Nile. Are you thinking we ought to cut that off?"

"Menku doesn't bother me much. He is very rich and I can take his possessions if I ever need them. No, I want the trade to continue. It is a source of information on what is going on in Pe, in all the towns of Lower Nile for that matter. Who runs the station at Asyut for him?" "His oldest son, Khafu and he is as old as you or I. He works hard but he thoroughly enjoys the good things of life that Menku's riches bring him. He gave me this gold ring; took it right off his hand and gave it to me. He showed me a little elementary academy they have set up to train priests for Aten. The day I saw it there was just a bunch of boys there, most not over ten or twelve years old."

"I said Menku doesn't worry me." Djo-Aten snapped. "What does worry me is the town and village elders all over Upper Nile. I have always relied on the feasts with a lot of beer to get them drunk enough to speak what was on their minds. Many times a few of the drunks would get too worked up over some wrong they felt I had inflicted. They lost their heads of course but I at least knew what they were thinking. Lately they seem to drink as much but there have been no protest beheadings for over a year. What do you make of it?" "Perhaps they have become wiser. Or more likely they are content with your rule. Hapi has been good and I know of no village where there is not plenty to eat. There will always be some people who will not agree with anything but they would have to be desperate to keep risking their heads for petty grievances."

Djo-Aten relaxed a little, "You may be right. You have always had a good ear for what the people are saying, aloud or behind my back. Nevertheless I want to find out what the generals are running into. They are soundly hated and I want to keep it that way for a few more years. Fear will do things for me that full bellies will not. To keep their own heads the generals and princes had better know the temper of their subjects. And their subjects are my subjects." On arriving at the El-Kab granary they found the generals all there. They were a fearful lot and most wondered if some or all of them would sleep with their ancestors that night. It was unlike the Scorpion to call such a meeting. The fact was that his own fear of rebellion was so great they had never been assembled in one place before, not even for battles. Some of them were always kept 'in relief': near the field but ready to defend Djo-Aten if there was a coup in the making. None of them trusted any of his peers enough to venture a guess as to the purpose of the conference and as a result there was a total, uneasy silence.

They were put at ease when Djo-Aten ordered beer and laughing, opened the meeting, "We have been needing to get together for a long time. Should do more of it if the distances were not so great and you were not needed out in the provinces so much. It gets lonely back in Nekhen. Women all over the place but not many men I can trust the way I do you." There was a rousing cheer and Djo-Aten, still smiling waved for silence.

"I have called you here because I am uneasy at the quietness that prevails throughout Upper Nile. Perhaps you are so thorough in your rule that there are no serious grievances. Yet I find that hard to believe. You have all been commanded to continue to instill fear by whatever means you choose. Why have there been no protest beheadings during the past year? Does any one of you have something you have not told me?"

There was some minor discussion but most seemed perplexed at the question. One of them asked if he could be more specific. Addressing the prince of the Edfu province, Djo-Aten asked, "Hadu, what is the behavior of Addi-Hoda's troops you have camped outside Edfu these days?" Hadu's slow response was, "Not very different from past years. They train just as hard as ever and never speak except to answer a direct question. The year away from their families is hard on them and none of them is old enough to remember when your father forced Addi-Hoda into this arrangement. But I would say they are good troops." "Do the Nubians still hunt the Kom Ombo? I gave Addi-Hoda permission for his hunting parties to go there to keep him from pulling back the troops at Edfu. Have any of your men seen them over there, Hadu?"

"There is some activity there, Djo-Aten. But you know how large Kom Ombo plain is. We cannot police it with the forces I have at Edfu and there does not appear to be any reason to try to do so. I can assure you that not a single hunting party has crossed the river to our side below the first cataract for the years I have been there. They may venture over between the first and second cataracts but there have been no incidents of their bothering any of the villages up that way. They are harmless as far as I am concerned." "Good. I am glad."

"Djo-ATen." "Yes, Hadu." "Why don't you ask one of the Menku's what goes on south of Edfu? They trade everywhere. Provide stuff the villagers want, pottery and wool mostly for the more remote places. Then they take grain and lentils back down river. They always stop at Nekhen I suspect; they certainly do at Edfu. The families at Edfu catch up on all the news of their relatives; all the gossip too I imagine. The Menku traders know more than we do about the comings and goings at the poorest levels." "It does not become a king...or a prince either...to wander down to the trade docks and chat idly with traders, Hadu. Surely you do not do that."

"No, of course not. But Abgar's junior priests do. It might be well for Abgar to bring you the information they pick up, for whatever value it may be. I have to advise you however that I doubt you will find much interest in whose lover ran off with someone's wife. That I am told is about the extent of the so-called 'news' they bring. Yet that is what the townspeople talk about and I'd rather they talked on that sorry plane than elevating the conversation to carping about what we are doing."

There was a round of laughter and Djo-Aten closed the meeting with, "Never forget that you are generals first. If you can get intelligent information in the manner you are accustomed to and if you can trust that information that is well enough. But if you cannot then use torture whenever necessary to save your heads and mine. The kingdom stands on the power of the king and a king who sits in the dark will not have a throne to sit on for long. That applies equally to princes. Now let's get on with the feast. Am I to believe this is all the beer there is?" and Djo-Aten in mock astonishment held up his golden cup for a trembling slave to fill.

Menhes called Seb to him early one morning, "Seb, it is time we approached Addi-Hoda. How do you think we should go about it? Did Father have any ideas on the subject?" "Only that he wished the alliance to be made as quickly as possible, Menhes and that I was to help you in any way you would choose." "Then let us get about it. I have thought a lot on the subject but I am not sure how to get to Addi-Hoda without his troops at Edfu learning of it and reporting to Hadu there."

"Prince Addi-Hoda is the ruler of my people, Menhes. He cannot be 'called on' as we might say one does with your father who is also a great and powerful man. His sentinels are everywhere and you can be sure his hunting parties have told him we are here at Kom Ombo. I doubt that he knows or cares much about such people as the Menku's, whether they are rich and powerful or not. As a ruler he was humiliated by Scorpion's father and now that he is old he hates being forced to supply conscripted troops to Upper Nile. And the troops hate it too according to our own trading party when we traveled to Asyut."

"Then what do you propose we do? I am prepared to do away with the troops and allow the continued hunting of Kom Ombo by the Nubians when I become king. In fact I will agree to stay below the second cataract with no slaving parties chasing his people down like pigs. If I need troops I will pay for them with barter that will be mutually advantageous and I will promise that. But I cannot promise anything if I cannot meet with him."

"Master, would you let me be your emissary? I know you trust me but will you trust me that much?" "Seb, I trust you with my life. You know that. You are my emissary. There, that's final. Now what do we do?" "I need to pick out a couple of our young Nubian trainees who have come here since we arrived. They will have close ties with their families and we can attach ourselves to a hunting party as it heads home. That will get us past the lookouts; after all I still have family there. Then I will petition the prince for an audience. That may take a few days but he will grant it; I know he will for he is a benevolent prince.

"I will talk to him as a native son. If he resents my being joined to your service I will try to tell him what your father has done for the people of Upper Nile and the priests and wizards of Aten. He is a deeply religious man and respects the beliefs of others, that is others outside his own domain. He allows no defection among his own priests. Do not worry, I was a little boy when I left, not a priest. If he talks openly to me about his hatred of Djo-Aten and the awful things he has done then I must trust him with your plan to overthrow the Nekhen crowd. That is a

15

terrible burden for me to carry and for you to share. He could order me killed in an instant if he feels he is being used. And you would be exposed to all out attack by Djo-Aten's forces. Without your brothers' support you would either become a renegade in hiding or be slaughtered, be assured of that. There is great risk here."

"Seb, do you really believe you can trust Addi-Hoda? Forget that you are a Nubian for a moment. You have cast your lot with my family for thirty-five years. Is Addi-Hoda the kind of man you would trust if he were an Upper Nile village elder, many of whom we trust now?" Seb answered simply, "Yes." "Then I trust him as I trust you. You will have to use your own best judgment as to when or whether to reveal what we are doing. Once you have revealed it then lay before Addi-Hoda what I propose to offer in the alliance. Ask him if he will pull back his two thousand troops at Edfu and let me deploy them where I think they are most needed. They will be decommissioned as soon as the capital is secure. Ask him if he has men who can effectively man our ships; we need every one of our warriors.

"If he agrees to these things send back a messenger to me and I will come to the second cataract alone to meet with him there. I can offer no more test of trust than that. I am not afraid. If I have not heard from you by the rising of the new moon I will know to mount the attack immediately to stave off disaster."

Seb bowed his head and wept. "After all these years must I place your head on the block to help you? It does not seem right, Master. Is there no other way?" "No, my beloved friend. There is not. I fear the Nubian troops would be decisive in a pitched battle at Edfu; and Edfu is where I will attack. Furthermore I do not wish the prospect of war with Nubia if I am successful in defeating Scorpion. That is not what I want for the people of Upper Nile; I want them free from Scorpion's murderous tyranny. What gain would they have if I then engage them in a deadly war from which there is no reward? We hold no malice toward Nubia. Let them live at peace with us. We will trade with them but we do not want them for our slaves. Our countrymen can provide for themselves as they always have."

Seb stood and laid his hand on Menhes' shoulder, "Then I will leave today. The journey is hard and I will have to move quickly to have a messenger back by the rising of the new moon. Nubian runners are fast and can run for great distances; I will get one back to you in time. I believe that or I would not attempt this mission. May Aten's blessings be upon you." "And on you, Seb. Take whatever you need. This ring will show my respect for Addi-Hoda. Give it to him. My great grandfather, the king wore it."

MeriLyth caught sight of Seb wearing only a loin wrap and walking out of the camp followed by two of the boys from the academy. Carrying only his spear and a small bag tied to his girdle he seemed to be in a hurry. She waved to him but he appeared not to notice her and as she came to where Menhes was standing she asked, "Where is Seb going in such a rush? He didn't even return my wave."

"He wants to go and see his family beyond the second cataract. I am sure he did not see you, MeriLyth." "Why is he carrying a spear, Menhes? Does he fear the Nubians?" "Of course not, my love. It is a long way and he plans to hunt to feed himself. He is using his sling for a girdle...did you not notice that?" "No matter. I do hope he will be safe. He is a good person, Menhes." Menhes held her to him, "You may never know how good he really is, MeriLyth. I hope more than you can imagine that he returns soon. A faithful old friend like Seb cannot be replaced, now can he?" "No. Of course not. I love you, Menhes. Is anything wrong? You look so sad and your eyes are red." "Just being sentimental I guess. I will miss Seb. And yes, I do worry about him."

No one, not even Ar-Chab knew why Seb had chosen this particular time to "visit his family". In fact no one could remember when Seb had ever mentioned having a family back in Nubia. But then Seb was so quiet that few people who knew him had any idea what he thought about. He seemed to like it that way and was proud of the trust the Menku family had in him.

Menhes called for Ar-Chab to hunt with him at the gorge below Gebel Silsila, the little mountain at the edge of the plain, and to come alone. When he got to Menhes' tent Ar-Chab hugged his daughter and asked, "Are you as happy as you look, child?" "I have never been happier, Father. How is Mother?" "Busy as always, MeriLyth. You will do well to take as good care of this man as she has of me all these years." She nodded and laughed as Menhes kissed her on the cheek and left with Ar-Chab.

On the way to the gorge he told Ar-Chab of Seb's leaving to attempt to arrange the alliance with Addi-Hoda. Ar-Chab was alarmed, "Surely you realize the danger to you this involves, Menhes." "No more than to you, Ar-Chab, you and all the people associated with us here at Kom Ombo as well as the rest of the stations and camps."

"If the alliance can be arranged let me go with you to meet Addi-Hoda, Menhes. I was born into the Menku service; your father entrusted your safety to me when you were still a boy. My life would be worthless to me if I failed you now; and your father would never forgive me, nor I myself." "No, Ar-Chab. Not even MeriLyth may know I am going: I do not want to frighten her and am not afraid for myself. This is something that has to be done. If Addi-Hoda should set up a trap...and I do not believe he will...then you must be here to launch the attack three days after the rising of the new moon."

"What do you want me to do in the meantime, Menhes? The warriors we have are ready now." "There is a trading party here. Before the sun sets today take one of the fast ships and rig the masts and sails. Put fresh pitch on the planking and load the barter goods the traders have with them into it; then drag it into the stream. They can leave their skiff at the landing; tomorrow have three or four of your men take the skiff upriver and let them do a little bartering with the villages near here. But when the sky is black tonight I want you and the trading party ...no one else aboard...to drift with the current past Edfu and Nekhen the same way we came here. At first light get under full sail and reach Asyut as fast as you can. If for any reason you think it is necessary put into a town and let the traders do a little bartering for appearances sake. You stay with the ship.

"When you get to Asyut let the traders take the ship down river a little way to make it look like they are heading for Pe. You must get to Father and Khafu and tell them everything; then you are to return here on one of the little reed skiffs as soon as possible. Do not risk being detected in one of the fast ships. On the third day after the rising of the new moon every ship and boat we have north of Nekhen will be loaded with the warriors at every one of our stations along the Nile and proceed upriver to reach the Nekhen landing by dawn of the fourth day after the new moon. There they will beach the boats and attack Nekhen from the north, driving Djo-Aten and his troops toward Edfu where he will think he has Hadu's forces and the Nubian regiment in reserve. We will attack Edfu at dawn of the same day."

Ar-Chab listened intently up to that point, then interrupted, "Menhes, what you say means you will attack without the alliance." "No, Ar-Chab. I hope to hear from Seb by the rising of the new moon telling me that I am to meet Addi-Hoda at the second cataract. That will take nearly three weeks to go and return using a boat between the first and second cataracts. In that case the initial assault will be delayed by exactly three weeks.

"A ship will be ready to sail from here as the new moon sets. That will allow time for Khafu to set back his invasion for three weeks. The attacks at Edfu and Nekhen will commence at dawn three weeks and four days after the new moon. If for any reason I do not return in time the battles will begin without me. Is that clear to you?" "May the gods forbid such a thing, Menhes. Who would be king if we succeed?"

"My father will be king, Ar-Chab. He can designate one of my brothers to take the throne. Khafu does not want it and I cannot say I blame him." "And who will lead the northern forces into battle, Menhes? Khafu is too old to stay in front of the warriors; he would be killed in the first few moments of the attack." "I have thought of that, Ar-Chab. We both know my brother Ekhdur is the most able captain in the northern service. But Khafu is the oldest son and I think my father will wisely let him make the choice. Do your best to lead him to that decision but defer to his judgment."

"I will do as you have commanded, Menhes. Are there any other instructions you have for me?" "There are some details we will have to work out, especially having our own ships and boats ready to launch within hours of our signal. I will also have to go over with you the disposition of your forces, club and ax men, spearmen and archers. I want the men with slings, the ones who are the most devastating in their accuracy to be interspersed among the javelin throwers. Let the archers come behind them and shoot over their heads. Then the spearmen and club and ax wielders will attack, routing the rest of Scorpions's forces. The Nubians will man one flank at Edfu with their archers and javelin throwers."

Menhes paused, then added, "Ar-Chab I have a personal matter to discuss with you." "I will listen." "It is MeriLyth and my mother and father; and your wife and other daughters if you choose. I want them taken to the Crocodile Lake camp while all this is going on. We can bring them back when it is safe. But they must be there before the rising of the new moon." "I will arrange that, Menhes. Do you think your father will go of his own will? He is a proud man and will not take humiliation lightly."

"That is a job you have to take care of when you are there, Ar-Chab. If Djo-Aten's forces do not surrender after we have conquered Nekhen and Edfu the first thing they would do would be to take Father and Mother hostage. That is a burden and a sorrow I cannot bear to think about. I believe Father will understand that. After all this entire strategy is his from before the time I was born. You must convince Father of his and our vulnerability if he is captured. Hor-Amen's troops have left the lake camp alone for a long time. There is no reason to think they will be nosing around there now."

Ar-Chab had one question he wanted to ask, "Menhes, what do you think our chances are if Addi-Hoda will have no part of your plan?" Menhes walked a short way before he answered, "I think we will eventually succeed. I believe we can defeat Scorpion at Nekhen, even if he is alerted and has a day to prepare for us. Any more warning than that and we will all be running to save our skins. He has a powerful army when you include the provinces, far more powerful than any we can put together as you know all too well. We must catch him by surprise. We missed the opportunity when he had all his generals drunk at El-Kab. Unfortunately we did not get wind of it until they had all left for their home provinces. Either way, Ar-Chab we are going to have a war in a very short time. If victory will be ours so much for the good. If not, so be it. We will fight like the men we are."

The long boat, lightly loaded as it was skimmed freely over the water. Oarsmen stood silently on the prow with long, flexible willow rods held out before them, sounding as they went. Pole men stood ready to shove the prow off any sandbars they might graze but there were no problems encountered as they held near midstream and took advantage of the swift Nile current.

There were no lights except a few fires kept going through the night at Edfu and Nekhen to tell them where they were. When the last of these disappeared behind them Ar-Chab helped the crew ready the sails to be hoisted at the earliest dim light of the morning.

A fair breeze sprang up from the southwest and the sails billowed into voluptuous bosoms straining the masts as the boat lurched forward. The prow lifted high and expert hands held the tiller oars to keep in the center of the river. It was noon before they passed anything more than crude reed barges plodding along between villages. A full sailed skiff was headed up river and as it approached one of the traders told Ar-Chab, "That's a Menku boat. I know it well. Anything you want to tell them?" "No, just shout your greetings and let's keep going. I want to see the Master before nightfall."

Farther on however one of Scorpion's beautiful barges sailed majestically against the current in full view. The sails were painted with the plumes of Nekhbet but there was no standard trailing from the mast. Ar-Chab ordered the traders to stand along the gunwales and hold up their wares...the cheapest things they had...to see if they would get a response. He kept partly hidden by the stern oarsmen as the Menku boat slowed out of respect for the king's barge. It appeared that the barge was returning from taking one of the generals back from the El-Kab conference to his province. It was obvious that there was no personage on board: the crewmen were sprawled all over the boat, most of them asleep. A burly warrior shouted from the prow, "Keep away from us with your sleazy goods. Do you think we are going to take that trash to the king?" He let out a coarse laugh as the others on board guffawed at his little joke. The Menku men pulled in their wares and sank humbly behind the gunwales as the ships passed a few yards apart. As soon as they were out of earshot Ar-Chab began to laugh and struck up a lusty song to amuse the traders. There would be no need to stop at a village this day.

After they landed at Asyut Ar-Chab went immediately to Menku's house and found Hetti fanning herself beneath date palms that arched over the front yard. She jumped up and ran to him, "Ar-Chab, what a pleasant surprise. Tell me all about my new daughter-in-law. Has she made Menhes happy?" "Hello, Madam Hetti. I think if you could see the two of them you would know the answer. They are very much in love." "Have you come to see Menku? He is resting now and I would rather not disturb him."

From inside the house Menku let out a roar, "Woman. Let me decide when I need rest. Ar-Chab, come in here; I want to see you." Hetti sighed, "Just like him. Go on in Ar-Chab. Can I get you some beer? Some food?" "Thank you. No, Madam. I will be going over to the academy shortly and plan to eat with the priests there."

Menku heard him and said, "You will not find Hev-Ri here. I have sent him to Kish with some priests to see a wizard there named Kmal-Dyl. Ever hear of him?" "Only from Seb, Menku. He told me about Hev-Ri's plans to go to Kish. Did he take Rabul and Vukhath with him?" "Yes, and two of the dissenters as well. You know we have these fractional fellows who keep the Sun Wizards stirred up all the time. I do not know who is right...maybe all of them...but I don't like all the hair-splitting arguments we keep having. By the way I sent a guard of eight warriors with them. Hev-Ri feared they would need them in the desert west of the Euphrates." Ar-Chab frowned, "I am sorry to hear that, Menku. It was the right thing to do of course but we are going to need every loyal warrior we can find in the next few weeks. That is why I am here now."

Menku spoke excitedly but softly, "Then the time has come?" With that Ar-Chab laid out everything he and Menhes had discussed except the matter of Crocodile Lake. He thought it would be better to leave that until morning when Menku would be fresh and less likely to argue

19

against going. Menku remained silent for a long time. Then he said with finality, "I want Ekhdur to lead the northern arm of the pincers. But I have turned everything over to Khafu and the decision will be his. You must help me make him think the decision is his, Ar-Chab. But now it is late and I am tired. Let's leave all this till in the morning."

The next morning Khafu came over and Ar-Chab repeated his conversation with Menku of the night before. Khafu listened until the end and looked pleadingly at his father, "Father, you know I am no warrior any more, if I ever was one. I am not afraid to die but it would calamitous for me to be killed early in the battle without a designated general to take over. Why should I not step aside now and let Ekhdur take the troops into Nekhen and push Scorpion and his forces toward Edfu where Menhes can deal with them? Let me command our fleet of boats. I can deliver the warriors with competent certainty and contribute to Menhes' victory that way."

"That is a noble gesture, Khafu. I am proud of you as I have always been. You will command Ekhdur to lead the forces of the northern pincer. Bring him here so Ar-Chab can relay what Menhes' plans are and he can take over from then on." As Khafu left to find Ekhdur Ar-Chab asked to have a few more moments of Menku's attention. Hetti was muttering that it was time for his nap and Ar-Chab knew it was then or he would have to wait another day to broach the subject of Crocodile Lake.

Menku nodded for him to continue and Ar-Chab carefully explained Menhes' concerns for his family's safety. Menku had a fit of coughing and exploded, "Am I not a man! Must I be treated like a woman or a child? Ar-Chab, I am astonished at you for bringing such a message as this." Ar-Chab bowed humbly but refused to be put off, "Forgive me, Master. You know Menhes would not offend you for his life. It is the alliance, or the possible lack of it that poses the problem we are concerned with. It is all a matter of timing; and the distance between here and Kom Ombo precludes timely communications." Menku was taken aback by Ar-Chab's authoritative insistence. "Forgive my outburst, Ar-Chab. You are right. Menhes knows what he is doing. Say on. I will listen."

"It hurts me deeply to tell you the risk Menhes is taking by going alone to meet Addi-Hoda. He is as my son too. He is unafraid for himself and he is no longer a brash young warrior. He has all the responsibility of a king and the concern for his troops and subjects that demands. If Addi-Hoda should go against the alliance and warns Djo-Aten we will face a slaughter unless we attack on the date I have given you, both from the north and from the south. There will be no time to warn you if that happens. Menhes concedes that we might then be locked in a long war with Djo-Aten giving him time to rally his huge forces in the provinces. Menhes, as do I believes that some of the provincial generals would seek to capture you and MeriLyth for hostages. He can not accept that sorrow or that burden: your lives against the lives of so many warriors if we have to retreat and go into hiding."

Menku began to weep, "What have I brought on my son? Perhaps Khafu is right. I should have left well enough alone. I am an old man and this is an unbearable thought. The alliance was my idea. It has never occurred to me that Addi-Hoda would not accept it." "Do not be hard on yourself, Menku. I have discussed this with Menhes and he knows that the alliance is essential for the assurance of a first strike victory. He would have sought it without your prompting I think; he had to. None of us underestimates Scorpion's strength. You yourself have said that another two years and there could be no revolt. But Menhes has laid his plans cautiously and though the attack will be daring he believes he can get our warriors out with minimal casualties if Scorpion does not suspect anyone could be so audacious."

Menku agreed, "I will go. When will it be? I must have Hetti get the servants together."

"When I return I will send MeriLyth here with her sisters and her mother. You can all go to Crocodile Lake at your convenience any time before the rising of the new moon." Menku smiled and grasped Ar-Chab's hand, "Assure Menhes of it. It will be done."

MeriLyth left without knowing of Menhes expected meeting with Addi-Hoda though she of course knew with certainty of a coming battle at Edfu. Menku had agreed to explain the risk of her being taken hostage and what that would mean in lost lives. She thought her heart would break when the boat left the landing without Menhes. Her father had reminded her she would be the queen of Upper Nile when she returned and she resigned herself to the hurts she must learn to bear with such an awful burden at her age. It was not the life a young wife would have wished for.

The moon became more full each night and Menhes kept lookouts with signal fires going to alert him of any messenger from Seb. Day by day there was nothing until one morning just before dawn Menhes was wakened by the sound of a gasping runner outside his tent. He sprang up and ran out to find a Nubian prostrate on the ground begging for water and heaving as if each breath were his last. Menhes bent down and asked him, "Are you here with a message from Seb?" The runner could scarcely speak but he nodded and Menhes held a water skin to his lips. In a few minutes he revived enough to talk, "Prince Addi-Hoda say he meet you at second cataract. Nine days you count. You come alone. Do not delay. Prince not wait." "Is there any more?" Menhes asked. "I tell you all I have to tell you, Master. I go home now." Menhes agreed but insisted that he eat something and take some bread and cheese for his return. Though reluctant the runner accepted and then set out trotting into the grass of the vast plain.

Menhes called Ar-Chab and told him of the message and that he would leave immediately. Ar-Chab was to dispatch a boat for Asyut with instructions to delay the attack three weeks according to the plan he had given Ekhdur and Khafu. A light reed boat had already been constructed just above the first cataract and with good fortune he could arrive at the second cataract in eight days. He took only a spear and sling to provide game in case the boat capsized with the provisions for the journey.

The first cataract was reached just before sundown and Menhes found his boat crew waiting there. A thunderstorm thrashed their camp during the night with flashes of lightning so intense and rapid that trees stood out as if in daylight. Menhes and the crew were soaked and shivering from the violent winds that swept and whirled around them until the storm ended as quickly as it began. As Venus hung alone near the horizon, the only heavenly body to be seen they went down to where the boat was tied to inspect for any damage. There was none but what bread they had brought was a sodden paste and had to be thrown out. Menhes was not bothered; they could always pick up such rustic food at one of the villages by the river.

Most of the way up the Nile the wind carried them along fast enough to make good headway. On the days when the wind fell and the sail hung limp the voyagers all took turns with the oars. Sometimes Menhes stood with the tiller oar; sometimes he stroked with the others. When they were not rowing they amused themselves bringing down birds with their slings. At night they camped short distances from villages where they could get fire and roast whatever game they had.

The crew had been provided with bags of low value jewelry, some of it made at Nekhen: ivory beads and copper bands; some bits of gold worked into tiny ivory amulets; horn and woven hair armlets and the usual collection of awls and needles for the women. After they bartered at the first villages where they camped they had pottery to trade at the later ones. They passed by the towns where Djo-Aten's troops were stationed, trading only at tiny fishing communities where there was no danger of elders who might be too inquiring.

When they were within a day's hike of the second cataract Menhes went ashore. He was sure by now that Nubian lookouts were reporting back to the prince that he was on the way and it was mandatory that there be no cause for Addi-Hoda to suspect he might have any supporting warriors within summoning range. He stayed close enough to the river to keep his bearings but used the sun to take shortcuts between bends in its course.

By late afternoon of the eighth day after his departure from the Kom Ombo station Menhes could hear the thundering waters of the great cataract. He quickened his pace as he walked through some low bushes near the river banks only to find himself surrounded by a band of fierce Nubian warriors. One of them addressed him, "You are grandson of Vedh-Ku?" "I am Menhes, son of Menku, son of Vedh-Ku." The warrior motioned him to come with them and they set out trotting in a direction away from the cataract. Menhes wondered where they were taking him but had no choice but to follow.

After they had gone about three miles they came to a ledge of rock from which the cataract could be seen in the distance. There a lone hunter roasted a pig on the fire before him. The spokesman for the Nubians raised his hand and pointed to the fire, "We stay here tonight." They ate without a word spoken and lay down afterward to sleep. It went without saying that there would be more warriors watching them from the brush and small trees scattered beneath the ledge but Menhes knew to ask no questions, not even to look around before he too rested by the fire.

At the exact moment that the sun cleared the horizon a shout came from the trees nearest the ledge and ram's horns signaled the approach of Prince Addi-Hoda. Menhes stood and peered at the retinue which seemed to spring out of the earth. Just before the blasts of the horns there was nothing there but shrubs. Now there must have been fifty warriors with their spears held high trailing a very tall, erect old man, ostrich plumed banners waving on either side of him. As he came nearer Menhes could make out the jeweled ivory and plumed crown he wore. His gold armlets glittered in the sun and the buckler on his sword girdle was also worked gold. Eight or nine equally tall warriors who walked immediately behind him, separate from the rest of the party were similarly bedecked except they wore no crowns.

The warriors stopped short of the ledge and the guidons fell back as Addi-Hoda strode toward Menhes, alone. Without a sound he raised his right hand and, smiling lowered it for Menhes to see that he wore the ring Seb had brought to him. Menhes spoke first, "Lord Addi-Hoda. I greet you with good wishes from my father, Menku of Meidum and Asyut." "And how is the great prince of Crocodile Lake my friend." "He is well and hopes you are in good health." "I am and as you can see I have brought my sons who extend my life with happiness." At that Addi-Hoda raised his hand again and Seb quickly emerged from the group and came to where they were standing. He embraced Menhes and then stood respectfully to one side.

The prince began, "Seb has told me of your plans and your wishes for an alliance between the Menku's and the kingdom of Nubia. By my wearing of this ring the alliance is forged. We are as your own warriors and will be a friendly nation to you when war is done. Let the region between the first and second cataracts be yours and we will share the open hunting of the Kom Ombo in the future." "Menhes placed his hand on Addi-Hoda's shoulder and said, "It is good. May our gods be our witnesses."

Addi-Hoda invited Menhes to eat with him and introduced his sons, one in particular who was to go back to Kom Ombo with Menhes. As he came to where Menhes was sitting, Addi-Hoda said, "This is Sel-Abba, my son. He commands the army from which the Edfu detachment is taken. When you attack another troop of equal number will be just above Edfu, held in reserve for your disposition. Sel-Abba has picked warriors who can bring a dove down with their slings and pierce a running hare with their javelins. I think you know our warriors are all expert archers, Prince Menhes." "Their reputations extend throughout Upper Nile, Prince Addi-Hoda. They will be the difference between taking the day and death for the Menku forces."

Menhes asked Sel-Abba, "Such a large force as you will hold in reserve until we cross the river, how will you deploy it so Hadu's people are unaware of it?" Sel-Abba flashed a wide grin, "I will review them before Hadu, Prince Menhes." Before Menhes could protest, he went on, "For more than thirty years, ever since Ar-Quhn trapped our father, the prince when most of the Nubian army was putting down an uprising far up the river we have been changing the troops at Edfu at this time of the year. Our fresh forces are due to take over at Edfu sometime before the next new moon. They will leave from a station near here tomorrow morning and be in place at Edfu before you attack. It is the troops that are there now which will have marched away only the day before...those are the reserves Father spoke of." "Just a fortuitous circumstance, Prince Menhes but I think it augurs well for your success." Addi-Hoda interjected.

Menhes looked at Seb, "Will you be going back with me, Seb? I must leave now." "Yes, Menhes. The prince has granted permission for me to return to the academy and I have promised to train a number of young Nubians to be drawing scribes every two years. If Prince Addi-Hoda wishes for us to turn them into Sun Wizards we will do that too." Seb laughed. Addi-Hoda roared with laughter, "Prince Menhes, this Seb would make us all Sun Priests I think. My gods will make me very small indeed if I listen too much to him. Nevertheless we are grateful for the training he gives our scribes. We are able to have better houses and docks along the river now that they can draw up plans for us before we begin building."

Menhes stood and raised his right hand in salute, "May your gods keep you tall and straight, Prince Addi-Hoda. And may this alliance last to the grandchildren of our grandchildren."

Addi-Hoda returned the salute, "It will be so. We have spoken it."

ADDI-HODA'S 'STANDARD OF NUBIA'

Illustrated by W. C. Cawthon

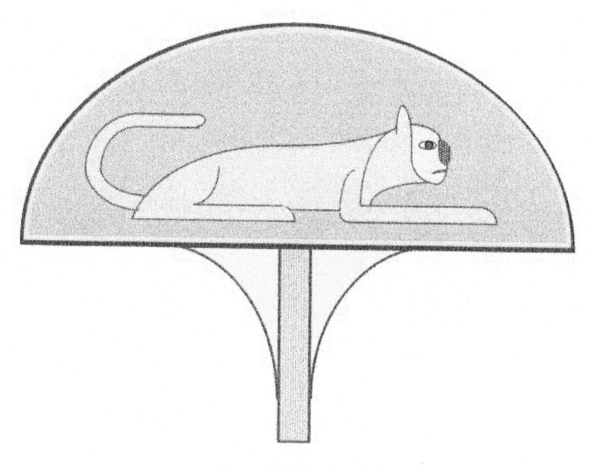

Figure 6: Nubian Standard

24

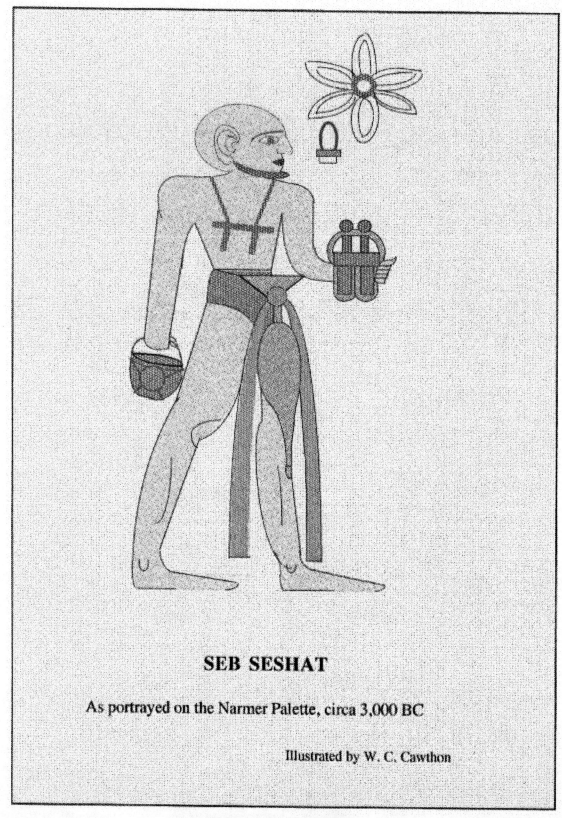

SEB SESHAT

As portrayed on the Narmer Palette, circa 3,000 BC

Illustrated by W. C. Cawthon

Figure 7: Seb Seshat

CHAPTER THREE 'Sun Wizards at Kish'

The Menku fast ship with Hev-Ri and his party aboard stopped briefly at Pe to deliver some woolens and a number of pieces of pottery Pe traders had previously ordered from the Asyut station. The Kish-bound party got off the ship to stretch and get something to eat before going on down the Nile into the delta region at the edge of the Great Sea. Hev-Ri had brought Rabul and Vukhath with him as Seb suggested and in addition had persuaded Per-Qad and Shephset to join them. The latter two were among the more reasonable of the fractional dissidents but both were outspoken and Per-Qad tended to be argumentative.

Hev-Ri had warned the priests to make no references to Aten while at Pe to avoid conflict with the dominant Amen priests there. "We do not have time for dogma confrontations and I do not want to be hauled before Hor-Amen as a heretic. Let's just get some beer and cheese and be on our way. As they stopped before a food stall in the trading yard above the landing a heated discussion was going on among some priests from a little temple near the river. They were quite young and one insisted that the Ankh he was waving around proved fractions were sacred. The others just as hotly held forth that the Ankh led to eye of Horus and that that was all that was sacred except the Sacred Circle itself.

Before Hev-Ri could stop him Per-Qad was in the midst of it stoutly supporting the Ankh waver. An older Priest of Amen was passing and walking up to Per-Qad demanded, "Who are you? Where do you come from? You sound strange to us; are you one of the Aten infidels?" Hev-Ri spoke to cut Per-Qad off, "We are simple drawing scribes returning from a visit to Meidum to our homes at Saqqut on the Great Sea. We caught passage on this trading vessel which stopped here to off load a cargo. My friend meant no harm and we all know we are not able to argue these points with such learned men as Priests of Amen." "These are not Priests of Amen and from the sounds of it they never will be. Now be gone, all of you before I call the guards down for the commotion you have raised." The young priest-aspirants scattered before anyone could get their names and Hev-Ri and his band of 'the unlearned' moved quickly back to the boat with orders to get under sail.

Hev-Ri was furious, "When we reach Saqqut I am of a mind to send you back to Menku, Per-Qad. If you cannot control yourself better than that what am I to expect when we have an audience with Kmal-Dyl?" Per-Qad promised to behave himself but Hev-Ri still had doubts about the wisdom of having such wizards on this trip at all.

They were in luck at Saqqut. A small sailing vessel from Crete was unloading its cargo there. With a bank of oars such a light ship could make progress in calm waters without use of its sails and in the waters east of Cyprus ships were about as apt to be facing a headwind or becalmed as they were to have favoring breezes. Smaller ships stayed close enough to shore to run into the first available haven in any kind of a storm.

Hev-Ri approached the master of the ship and negotiated passage to the mouth of the Orontes, far up the coast for him and his party of twelve. The master told him, "This time of the year we are usually safe to sail at night. Are you afraid of that because if you are I cannot take you there. I have to get back to Cyprus in three weeks and I have only one load of cargo to lay off between here and the Orontes. Unless I can make a fast trip up there I cannot afford it." Hev-Ri wanted to know, "How long will it take?" "With good winds and only one stop I can make it in four days but I would count on five, maybe even six to be sure. That is all I can spare anyway. If we run out of time I will have to put you ashore down the coast from the Orontes." That sounded fair enough so when the cargo was unloaded the crew rowed away from the docks and hoisted the sails in the open waters of the Mediterranean.

For the first leg of the voyage the master set his course in what amounted to East-by-Northeast expecting to sight land by the following evening. None of Hev-Ri's party had ever been on the open sea before and as would have been expected they almost immediately became seasick to the great and continuing amusement of the seasoned sailors. The crew finally had to tie ropes around their waists and tether them to the oarsmen's benches to keep them from rolling overboard as they stayed bent over the gunwales most of the night. The Cretan crew's language was unintelligible to the Kemet people so most of the jocular insults went unnoticed.By morning none of them cared anyway. The fact was they didn't care much whether they lived or died if only the ship would stop its lurching and rolling long enough for them to get their stomachs back down where they belonged.

At daybreak the master told them to eat some gruel or they would be sicker still. Hev-Ri volunteered to try it and managed to keep part of it down though he was sure it was the foulest tasting mess he had ever eaten. One by one the others gave it a try and by noon they began to feel almost human again. As the sun began sinking into the horizon a crewman in the bow sighted the faint outline of the shore and the ship was steered straight away from the blackness of due South. The waters were fairly calm and riding the waves under full sail they moved rapidly up the coast, reaching Tylfar in the early afternoon of the third day. Tylfar was the destination of the cargo and all hands were glad to get their feet on solid ground again.

The warriors located some fishermen grilling perch on a fire at the seashore and persuaded them to provide a meal of fish and bread to the Asyut party. They wolfed the food down and wondered whether any of them really wanted to get back on the ship when, late in the day the master came looking for them. "The sky is clear and the boat is unloaded. There will be fair sailing tonight I think. Come get aboard." There was no satisfactory alternative so all of them waded out to the ship and tumbled into the stern as the oarsmen put out to sea.

A squall caught the ship in the early morning hours of the fifth day. The sails were dropped instantly and the crew jumped to the oars with the master standing in the bow sniffing the wind and calling for soundings every few minutes. They were too far at sea to head for shore when the storm cloud first obscured the stars. It was on them in what seemed like moments. Yet they were too near the shore to risk running with the wind so all that could be hoped for was the difference of the smell of the surf from open water. That was unreliable at best and in a night squall little to go on except when one had nothing else. The squall subsided soon enough and with the air cleared of clouds the moon shone bright on the churning sea. Soon the dim light of fires off the starboard bow could be made out and the master slumped back and ordered the crew to hoist the sails.

By noon the ship was gliding smoothly up to the Ugarit landing. Ugarit was not much of a town but it was the closest port of any consequence to the banks of the Orontes and was their planned point of debarkation. The travelers, now more seasoned waded ashore and left the crew to take on water and provisions for the run to Cyprus. They had plenty of time to get there and Hev-Ri wondered why the master had been in such a rush to put them off at Ugarit. As it turned out he was headed back down the coast to try his luck at bartering some bronze knives and utensils he had brought along to improve his fortunes compared to trading at Cyprus. A band of hunters who planned to hunt along the Orontes was gathered at Ugarit. They were glad to have the Nile party walk along with them, more curious as to who they were and what they did than anything else.

Most senior wizards had come from or been trained in southern Sumer and could manage the polyglot dialects that sprang up along the rivers of the fertile crescent. The crescent formed a northern arc which eventually encompassed the languages from the Jordan across to the Persian Gulf and up through Anatolia to the northwest to form the broad category of what eventually would become Canaanite speech. The argot of the hunters was no exception and, except for the Menku warriors the two groups were soon communicating rather freely.

Hev-Ri explained that they were going to Kish to visit the temple there, that they were priests from Upper Nile. The hunters nodded; they knew of the Nile from sailors who frequently visited Ugarit. Vukhath questioned them regarding what they would be hunting since there was ample game and fish along the coast and there were small farms and flocks around Ugarit. The leader of the hunters, a man named Zuv answered, "We look for meat and skins, deer maybe. Maybe lions. Good lion skins can be traded to desert tribes for jewel stones and sometimes they also have silver. Deer skin is soft and has many uses. The ships bring pottery and bronze they will trade for whole deer skins. And the meat is very good." The hunters were an amiable lot and the distance to Ikruth on the south banks of the Orontes seemed short.

At Ikruth Zuv knew a man who had a fairly large river boat, large enough to accommodate the priests and warriors of Asyut. The owner was willing to take them to Rud at the bend in the river where it turned toward its source many miles to the south. They would stay the night at Ikruth and leave with the boat and its small crew the next morning. Although a sail was rigged to a rough mast held in place by ropes there were oars and poles to allow the boat to move under any conditions they might encounter.

One good thing about it, sailing up a river did not induce seasickness and the journey with the prevailing winds from the great sea would take no more than two days, stopping to camp at night. Zuv had talked a local herdsman into trading a goat for a Nubian amulet Rabul was wearing. The goat would be needed to carry their water skins and provisions as they crossed the desert to the Euphrates; and its milk would offer refreshment as well. Cheese, parched barley and cakes of dates and figs would keep them from going hungry between villages since they would carry no fire and raw game left a lot to be desired. The boat owner's son, Gelvi had always wanted to go to Kish and persuaded his father to let him be the guide for the party if they in turn would show him the temple there.

After spending the night at the tiny settlement of Rud they began the trek across the desert expecting to reach the Euphrates by sundown of the fifth day. The terrain was rocky and scored with small stream beds where water normally flowed to the Orontes. But now they were dry and there was little hope the drought that began over a year before would soon end. Gelvi was a cheerful boy who Hev-Ri estimated to be about seventeen years old.

As they walked out of the brush and twisted trees that grew along the river and looked out over the forbidding 'badlands' Gelvi explained, "We want to keep moving today; it is a hard day's hike to the first place I know of where there is water. We are going to walk along some of these dry beds until we get to a rocky flat. When we have crossed that it will be sand and gravel most of the way to Thurn's place." "And who is Thurn?" Shephset inquired. "Thurn is a shepherd who left Ikruth when I was little and went to this place where there is a spring- fed pond. There is grass there and he will have a fire going. Thurn comes to Ikruth every year on his way to Ugarit with his wool and whatever lambs he has to trade. He has a son as old as I am called Nura and he fishes off the boat with Father and me while Thurn goes down to Ugarit. We have a good time together; there are not so many my age around here."

Hev-Ri was listening, "Gelvi, is Thurn's family the only one in this whole area of desert?" "Oh no, Master. There are two other families at Thurn's; they are all shepherds. Nothing much grows there now except some little gardens they keep down by the pond. They grow enough grain and beans and lentils to make out until they can trade for bags of such stuff at Ikruth and Ugarit. There are other places like Thurn's but they are far off the way I am taking you to the Euphrates. We are going the shortest way. It is rough country but we will get there faster this way." Rabul grinned, "Are you taking us to Thurn's just so you can see Nura?" Gelvi laughed, "I don't think you want to sleep in the badlands without a fire any more than I do, Master Rabul."

When the party was in sight of the pond at Thurn's Gelvi ran ahead to tell them who was coming. He feared the families there would panic if they saw a band of spear-carrying warriors approaching without warning. Thurn and Nura came out to greet him and walked back to join the others.

"Welcome to our city in the wilderness." Thurn called out, "As you can see there is little here but we will share what we have with you. Where do you come from that you would be walking in this forsaken country?" Hev-Ri stepped forward and introduced Thurn and Nura to the rest of the group, "We come from Asyut in Upper Nile. Are you familiar with the nations along the Nile?" "People in Ugarit speak of them but we do not know where they are. You must tell us about these strange places. Come and I will kill a sheep. The others who live here will want to hear from you too. Nura. Gelvi. Go fetch a fat sheep for me."

Hev-Ri gave Thurn's wife an ivory bracelet that was carved with the Nekhbet the Upper Nile standard, . He explained to her and the rest of the families what it meant and where 'Nile' was. They wanted to know where he was headed and he told them Kish. Thurn looked disturbed, "Master Hev-Ri, that is a long way and you must go through Mari country." "We know that , Thurn. Do you see that as a problem?" "It may be. Sometimes travelers stop here who have made the journey that way without anything happening. Sometimes they stop here on the way there and we never see them again."

"What kinds of things happen, Thurn?" Per-Qad asked. "The Mari people are a bad lot I am told. They have gangs who ask people questions. If they are not satisfied with the answers they get they kill them. That is what the desert people say about them. They do not harm such folk as we are. What would they get from us? But rich people and noble ones like you sometimes do not fare so well."

Per-Qad persisted, "Is there not some way to avoid them?" "Gelvi can take you only as far as the

Euphrates. Neither he nor Nura has ever been farther than that. Nor have I. But at Aff which is two days from here there is a man who has made his way to Kish and back many times. And other people have gone with him. His name is Davri and they say he knows every place where the Mari people stop travelers and that he knows the ways around them. Your warriors will not do you much good if they stop you. They have large bands of warriors roving the countryside on both sides of the Euphrates. This is all I know but you will do well to take Davri with you I think." Hev-Ri responded, "If he is at Aff we will try to persuade him to go with us, Thurn. Thank you for the information. Now let's enjoy this food and get some sleep. We must leave at daybreak."

Four warriors went ahead with Gelvi and four trailed the priests for protection as they left Thurn's. They made slow progress the first day but still reached the campsite Gelvi had told them about before nightfall. It was desolate enough to explain why Gelvi chose not to spend a night without fire and Hev-Ri was thankful that Thurn had insisted on giving them a horn of oil

29

and fire to take with them that day. The place was strewn with rocks and there was no water; nevertheless it was slightly elevated, giving a good view in all directions. A few twisted pines managed to survive and there was plenty of wood to get a good fire going.

The forward warriors and Gelvi had killed a couple of hare and some ground squirrels with their slings, enough for fresh meat that night before they stretched out to sleep under the desert moon. The warriors rotated guard duty throughout the night but nothing bothered them with the fire. They had tramped a wide circle earlier to send some vipers slithering off and following Gelvi's advice built the fire and slept on a ledge of rock that appeared to afford no further crevices for venomous snakes to creep out of.

They were only too glad to get on their way when morning came and reached Aff by mid-afternoon. Along the way one of the small deer that roamed the countryside came to a place where a trickling spring still poured water. As the party approached downwind Gelvi saw it first and crept silently behind a rock where he motioned one of the guards to join him. A flash of the guard's javelin disabled the deer and in minutes it was gutted and slung over his shoulder for the short distance that remained to reach Aff. It would be a good gift for the little community and show friendly intentions. Gelvi was permitted to take the deer and go on ahead to be the first to arrive since he was known there.

After introductions and satisfaction of the elders that their purpose was merely to spend the night in a friendly environment, Hev-Ri asked the man who seemed to be the most senior of the group, "Gelvi's friend, Thurn told us we might find a man named, Davri at Aff. May we inquire if he is here now?" The man he addressed was named Grig and he answered, "Why do you wish to see Davri? Are you friends of the priests in Mari country?" "We have come from Asyut in Upper Nile and are on the way to Kish to visit a wizard at the temple there. We know no one in Mari or the surrounding country." Grig pressed his query, "How may we know this?"

At that point Gelvi asked permission to speak and when Grig motioned to him to come forward said, "These men came to Ikruth with Zuv, the hunter from Ugarit. My father and I took them to Rud in our boat and when we got there my father permitted me to go with them and guide them to the Euphrates if they will let me go to Kish with them. They speak the truth." Grig smiled, "Then welcome to Aff. Yes, Davri is here." Davri was standing with the other elders and stepped up beside Grig with his hand raised, "What did Thurn tell you about me? I know Thurn well." Hev-Ri raised his hand in response, "He said you might be willing to guide us through Mari country to Kish, that you had made the trip many times."

Davri studied the group for several moments, then asked, "Who is it you wish to see in Kish?" "The wizard, Kmal-Dyl. We need his help in some matters of geometry at our academies in Upper Nile." "Master Hev-Ri, do you know Kmal-Dyl?" Grig asked. "I met with him as a young man when I had finished my training in Sumer. I have not seen him since. None of the others with me knows him." Davri spoke again, "Do you believe he will see you? He is an old man now." "Yes, Davri I believe he will. Our master is Menku of Kemet. I am sure Kmal-Dyl knows of him and in addition I have friends in Ur and Uruk who are friends of Kmal-Dyl." Davri asked, "Who are your friends in Ur and Uruk, Master?"

"Ayn-Far, Chief Priest of the White Temple at Uruk and Ghant-Ur, Chief Priest of Temple Al-Ubaid at Ur." Davri at last smiled warmly, "I know of the Menku family and l know Ayn-Far and Ghant-Ur well. I will accompany you after we have talked and you have eaten with us here tonight. With that he turned to Grig and said, "Prepare a feast for us, Grig. Bring out a wineskin for our guests. We must eat well before we start such a long, hard journey." Grig bowed and went with the other men to get things ready as Davri had commanded.

As they sat around the fire Hev-Ri was curious, "May I speak to you alone, Davri?" Davri waved his arm and the herdsmen with him left immediately. Hev-Ri nodded to the others from Asyut and they went over to another fire where Gelvi was talking to friends of his. "What is on your mind, Master Hev-Ri of Asyut?" Hev-Ri measured his words, "It is not appropriate for me to pry into your personal affairs, Davri. Yet we will be placing our lives in your hands if I am to believe Thurn. How is it that you know all these people? Aff is a remote settlement in a vast desert. You are obviously not a simple herdsman by the way you speak and by the deference these people show you. Would you be willing to trust me? Who are you? Where do you come from? If not I will ask no more." Davri looked into the fire as if he had not heard the questions. At length he said, "Since you and I are both senior wizards I will dispense with the formalities and speak to you as an equal, Hev-Ri. My own training began in Eridu when I was a young boy. Ayn-Far is served by a senior priest named Mar-Dug...he will succeed Ayn-Far as High Priest of the White Temple...and he took me to Kish with him soon after I became a drawing scribe. He was there to meet with Kmal-Dyl; this is many years ago. I was permitted to join the meetings where they discussed the desirability of achieving a consensus for Sumer and Akkad regarding the sacred nature of the twenty-two steps of the 'Sacred Circle' construction Some were using twenty steps, some twenty-one but Mar-Dug tried hard to get agreement on his and Kmal-Dyl's twenty-two steps. Are you familiar with all this?"

"In Upper Nile I am known as one of the Sun Wizards, Davri. Has the consensus been reached yet?" "I think so. If not it will be shortly. Ayn-Far is not well and insists that it must be formalized before he dies. Kmal-Dyl is respected throughout the region and has put his stamp on it. Are you aware why it is so important, Hev-Ri?" "It is not the twenty-two steps themselves that is important as I understand it. They want a standard construction everyone will accept and adhere to throughout the world of wizardry." "That is correct and that is as much as Ayn-Far seems to want for now. What would make you travel so far to see Kmal-Dyl and why now, Hev-Ri?"

"From what Thurn told us you must know all about the dissidents, the fractional people. This is not to imply that Thurn is a wizard, Davri. But he did say you know how to avoid the disputatious questioning of the Mari bandits. From that I have assumed that the Mari bands are fractional wizards since there is no such fanatic zealotry among the Sacred Circle advocates. At least there is none that I have ever known about." "Again you are correct. They are zealots and they are mean, not just regarding the constructions but for the Mother of Heaven as well. All of us with other views are ready to agree that they will have their day when we finally achieve the kind of universal acceptance of the twenty two steps. "Kmal-Dyl thinks it will take some kind of drawing field twice as large as anything we have envisioned before to prove what we believe we know."

Hev-Ri was startled, "There has been no henge that large anywhere, Davri; I mean a two hundred Sumer cubit one. It would take trees larger than the biggest cedars in the Jordan country or stones as big as a house to make the gates for such a henge. I doubt that it can be done with bricks, what with settling over the years it will take to work out the angles, sighting the stars. To even think of what Kmal-Dyl is talking about is beyond my imagination. Where would there be such stones and how could they be moved?" Davri laughed, "Those are all problems that keep the pot boiling for the fractional people. Their point is that such accuracy has no real purpose: that the gods don't care; why should men?"

"Maybe they are right. I just don't know. The dissension however is upsetting to all of us, particularly to Menku who is also old and wants some kind of settlement before he dies to keep the academies from splitting apart when he can no longer command peaceful co-existence in Upper Nile. That is what we are on the way to see Kmal-Dyl about. Menku and I believe all our priests will listen to what he says. By the way Per-Qad and Shephset are fractional priests, among the more reasonable ones but they can still generate a hot dispute, especially Per-Qad. We want them to hear Kmal-Dyl in person in the hope that they will calm the others down back at Asyut."

Davri was concerned, "That may make it very difficult for us when we pass Mari country. Are you absolutely sure you can trust these men, so sure you will stake your life on it?" "I believe in them or I would not have brought them with me. I have known both for a long time and in my opinion neither would give up the life the academy service affords if it came to a real showdown. Menku is not a wizard though he knows a lot about what we are talking about. He wants reason to prevail, not forced obedience so there will not likely ever be such a showdown at our academy, which is what lets men like Per-Qad strut around in a superior way pointing to their 'difference'."

Davri was obviously less than satisfied but did not press the issue. "It is regrettable, all the more so since none of this has anything to do with what the real aim is." "Will you explain that, Davri?" Davri commented simply, "With all our wizardry... some of it genius to be sure...we cannot record anything except trade transactions. You and I will die with no one even remembering our names by the time Gelvi is a grandfather.

"You people in the Nile country have a calendar but you still have to reckon time in moons when you want to forecast something, something as simple as when you will return to Asyut. You cannot mark it down so someone else can 'read' it and understand it if you are not there to tell him what it means. We have perhaps a thousand symbols already in Sumer and for what? So traders can keep track of their barter and describe that they traded a sheep or a girl. But they cannot name the girl or the man who traded for her. They cannot record when the man lived in relation to when someone else lived.

"We can communicate only with words which means we cannot expand what we are doing any further until someone, somewhere invents a system of recording things. Kmal-Dyl has worked on it for years, as have wizards before him. It will take someone of his intellect to solve the overwhelming problems we face. I know they always begin with the sounds of our speech. They say that there must be a way to record symbols people will recognize as sounds; that when the symbols are combined somehow, if they are pronounced aloud the result will sound just like what someone has said. I cannot even begin to think how it might work." "Nor I, Davri." Hev-Ri laughed, "But what has that to do with the Sacred Circle construction?"

"Kmal-Dyl and Mar-Dug believe that someone, some young genius can be brought up to work on nothing else and with a good foundation he might accomplish the presently impossible task of sorting it all out. They think that twenty-odd symbols are all that will be needed for basic communication. Kmal-Dyl has explained this much to me and if he is right, the only thing we have that is widely known and accepted as a well remembered order of things is the twenty-two step Sacred Circle construction. That is what our 'war' is about."

Hev-Ri let out a low groan, "I think I can predict what will happen wherever men live together if this yet-to-be genius is not successful, Davri. At least I am sure of it throughout the Nile country." "What is that, Hev-Ri?" "The priests will divide into various persuasions and excite the people to worship things that are not sacred, things like birds and snakes; stars and the sun and the moon; animals and perhaps even the temples themselves. We are already into that in Nile now but the excuse is to keep the peoples' minds occupied with icon-gods and preclude their interference in the serious work we have to do at the academies. If so small a thing as the fractional dispute can cause so much dissension, imagine what it would be like if priests had so little to do the temple services would not be supported by the kings. I think they will invent more gods to frighten the kings to keep them ignorant and they can probably accomplish that." Davri broke in, "I think it would be unlikely for that to happen in Sumer, Hev-Ri. Yet human nature being what it is there is little reason for me to say that. Let's just hope such a future young wizard succeeds."

The next morning Davri led the party quickly to a high point from which he pointed out the general area they would be going through that day. They would take a well traveled path to the town of Salbat on the west bank of the Euphrates just above where the Euphrates turned eastward. He estimated arrival there by the middle of the afternoon and told them he would be able to obtain a boat to float down the river. "The river is at flood and is about as high as it will be this year. That is still lower than normal but the current is swift enough for us to cover the distance from Salbat to Quri in a day. It is another day from Quri to Bav which is on the far bank where the Narku River flows into the Euphrates. After we leave there we will continue for two more days down the river in the boat. We will spend the night at Leb and the following day we should be in Huta. That is where I will have to get information on what lies ahead between Huta and the Aluba River near Kish. I cannot tell you exactly how long the whole journey will take. Maybe it will be six or seven days; maybe it will be two or three weeks before we get to Kish. I hope we will not have to go across country to the Tigris to avoid the Mari mob but if we have to we will. Are all of you sure you are willing to take these risks that threaten your lives?"

"Davri." "Yes, Rabul?" "Are you not in the same danger we are?" "Yes, Rabul." "Then why are you willing to take this trip with us?" Davri laughed, "I live in danger wherever I am. I am not well liked by the people of eastern Mari and they can come get me here or in Kish as well as wait for me to travel through the country where they operate. They know that I guide people to and from Kish. Beyond that they know very little about me. It is to your advantage and mine that they do not even know what I look like. But I know the places where they most often attack from, whether the river is at its highest or at its lowest level. I think I will get through safely and you will be safe with me. That is all the assurance I can give you."

After Salbat at each place they stopped Hev-Ri spoke to the elders, pointing to Gelvi as their guide. Davri took a spear and stood silently with the Menku warriors. If anyone recognized him they gave no hint of it. Hev-Ri told the same story each time, "We are priests from the Nile country on our way to Kish to ask for help for our poor temples at home. We are a peaceful but poor people and have no gifts to offer the High Priest at Kish. Have you been there? Are they friendly?" The elders of these tiny settlements were good hosts and invited them to their fires and fed them before they returned to their boat and continued down the river.

When they got to Huta Davri told the other priests to stay in the boat and, again carrying his spear went in to the town with Hev-Ri and four of the warriors. Hev-Ri was to ask for 'his friend', Malbu. If Malbu was there he would speak with him. If he was not they would be on their way, not troubling the town for anything except a little oil for their fire pots.

Malbu walked up to Hev-Ri and embracing him warmly invited the party, including those who had stayed in the boat to his tent, a short walk down the river. He was a fisherman and lived there with his wife. Once away from the elders, Malbu spoke, "Master Davri, I am always glad when you come here. Are you headed for Kish again?" "We intend to try to get there, Malbu. Hev-Ri, let's walk down by the river with Malbu; the rest of the party may want to stretch out and relax awhile."

Davri smiled, "You can trust Hev-Ri, Malbu. Tell me the news." "Things are quiet between here and Aqub so you can use your boat for another day, maybe two. You will be safe in Aqub as long as they do not know who you are." Looking at Hev-Ri Malbu asked, "What sort of priests are these and why are they going to Kish, Davri?" "I will let Hev-Ri answer that. One piece of information you will wish to know: two of the priests, Per-Qad and Shephset are fractional wizards. Hev-Ri trusts them and I prefer to have them with us rather than sending them back alone and having to wonder what they might be up to."

Hev-Ri explained the pertinent factors of their trip to Malbu, just as he had done for Davri. When he had finished Malbu turned to Davri, "Davri, this means that two of the dissenters, trustworthy or otherwise know what you and I look like. Except for knowing you I am worth nothing to them, but in spite of the good reason for their visit to Kmal-Dyl these two men can cause untold problems in days to come with what we are trying to do to get people through Mari country.

"I suggest we do this: Let me take one party made up of four of the warrior guards and Per-Qad and Shephset while you take the rest of the group to Aqub. You leave tomorrow morning; I will keep the others here to fish for a day and then follow you there. I have my own boat so we will get there within a day of when you do." Hev-Ri appeared alarmed but Davri was interested, "What might this plan gain for us, Malbu?" "If you find that things still look good below Aqub wait for us and we will go on together to Hit. If you have any question about what lies ahead go on without us and I will decide what to do after I get to Aqub. We will meet you in Kish in that instance."

Davri pondered over this and then commented, "That assumes we both make it to Kish. There is a better chance of one of two groups making it than for a single, larger party. With that I agree. But if you are stopped by the Mari what happens to you?" "We will not be captured. We may be killed but we will not be captured." Hev-Ri, startled asked, "Why do you say that, Malbu?" "If your two fraction men were tortured would they not admit to their origins? Then they would be forced to tell why they are going to Kish and who it is they will see there. The guards do not speak as I do so it will be obvious that I am the guide but I am not one of 'their' guides. They will know that I am somehow connected with Davri and I do not care to think of the torture I would suffer for that."

Davri lowered his head and spoke to Hev-Ri, "Do you understand what Malbu is saying?" "I think so and I don't like it. My master has entrusted me with these men's well being and they themselves have trusted me as I must trust them. To send them to an uncertain end, such that I might never know what happened to them would make it extremely hard for me to return to Asyut to face Menku. Furthermore there would be nothing to talk to Kmal-Dyl about assuming we get to Kish."

Davri said nothing until Hev-Ri shrugged and held out his hands, palms up, "Hev-Ri, I cannot ask Malbu to take the risk of being caught with me. I am sorry you have brought these men even though I do understand they are the real purpose of your journey to Kish. You will not make it alone; of that much I am certain. If you want to continue we will have to accept Malbu's plan. Otherwise we turn back now. There may be no cause for concern by the time we get to Aqub. In that case our fears are unfounded and we will all go on together; except for Malbu who will return to his home here."

At Aqub Davri, as a simple boat owner with a party of hunters going to Hit asked for someone who could tell him what the prospects were for finding lions in the desert east of Hit. One of the elders told him that a hunting party had come back from there two days before and found no lions though there was some other game in that area. When he returned to the boat Hev-Ri asked, "What did you find out?" "There are no Mari gangs around Hit right now, just a few hithabogs hunting in the general region. The bogs won't bother us so we will wait here for the others and let Malbu go on back to Huta. We might as well do a little hunting while we wait."

The reunited party sailed on past the Hit landing to a protected inlet some distance downstream where they put in for the night. Davri felt there were good prospects of clear sailing all the way to Kish and got a fire going to cook the birds they had killed the day before. Two of the guards were posted as lookouts several hundred yards from the fire. As the moon dropped out of sight one of them came and stomped out the fire and then shook Davri to waken him, "There is a large boat with maybe twenty men on it coming up the river toward where we are. They are going very slowly but they will be where they can see our boat very shortly. They may have already seen the fire." Davri jumped to his feet and the two of them got everybody up. He gave orders quickly and in a low voice, "Every one of you get your spear and whatever other weapons you have. We may have to fight our way out of this. Follow me."

He led them up a draw to some large stones where they could be concealed and still see and hear what was going on. They watched as the boat landed and the men came ashore. One who appeared to be the leader spoke, "They can't be far. May just be some hunters but I want to know before we go on to Hit; they could be priests headed for Kish. Looks like there might be a dozen or so of them." Davri whispered to Hev-Ri and Gelvi, "Mari priests. They are almost far enough away from their boat for us to make a run for it. When we get to the water we must get both boats far enough out so they can't come after us. It is chancy at best but that is the only alternative to a bloody fight we have. Gelvi, crawl over to the others and tell them. You take four of the guards and Rabul and Per-Qad and push their boat out into the current as fast as you can get it there. I will take my boat with the rest of us and we will land downstream a short distance where we can decide what to do next. If they catch us we all fight together."

In a few moments Davri gave the signal and they crawled silently back down toward the river until they got to where their fire had been. Then they broke into a run as the Mari group heard them and ran to catch up. Gelvi reached the Mari boat first and began pushing it out into the stream as the Menku warriors splashed into the water behind him. The other group was just as frantically shoving Davri's boat off the bank when the first member of the Mari band got to the water's edge. Before he could raise his spear to throw it one of the Asyut warriors pierced him with his javelin and he fell into the shallow water. Several others ran into the water and had to be beaten off but both boats caught the current and moved to get out of range in a hail of spears.

Rabul took a spear through his heart and died instantly. One of the warriors in Davri's boat had a deep slice in his thigh but managed to get the blood stopped by the time the sails were raised. After a short chase along the bank the Mari party gave up and the boats sailed for about an hour before Davri cut to a gravel beach and Gelvi pulled in beside him. Hev-Ri jumped immediately into the the Mari boat and bent over Rabul, "Poor Rabul. Did he take long to die, Gelvi?" "No, Master. He just fell down without a sound. By the time we could tend to him he was dead. I am sorry." Hev-Ri stood up and looked around, "Where is Per-Qad?" No one knew what had happened to him but he was not with them. Davri walked over to Hev-Ri, "This is bad. He may be all right, Hev-Ri. He will likely have a chance to talk if he did not fight with them; they will probably let him live if he tells the truth. I presume he can give a good account of himself as a fractional wizard." Hev-Ri stood with his hands on his hips, "Per-Qad is a senior wizard and knows all we know. He is only a wizard and cares little about the Mother of Heaven or Aten or Amen for that matter. If they let him live what will happen then?"

Davri answered, "Unless he can escape sometime in the future...if he wants to escape...he will have to live as one of them. As for me I will assume that he will do all he can to save his life. That is natural and would be expected. He can identify Malbu and me and knows the purpose of your meeting in Kish. We are going to get to Kish as quickly as we can. We have enough water and a little food they left in their boat; that is all we have and we have no fire so we will run for it." Hev-Ri asked, "Is there no alternative, Davri? Must we think Per-Qad deserted us?"

"If I want to live there is no alternative. The risk is too great to even assume Per-Qad is dead. When I have delivered you to Kmal-Dyl I will leave for Uruk. Ayn-Far and Mar-Dug will take me in and I will live at the White Temple until I know what happened to Per-Qad, if that is ever knowable. Men-Chad-Res is King of Uruk and his warriors may be able to learn more about all this in the next year or two. You will have to stay in the temple at Kish until the river Tigris reaches its lowest level. You can get to the Tigris in four or five days through the desert from Kish. Its current will not be so strong by then and you can navigate upstream to Ughada. There you will turn back toward the Euphrates to come to Huta where Malbu can help you; that is of course if Per-Qad has not betrayed him."

Kmal-Dyl was pleased to see Hev-Ri but terribly upset by Davri's account of the disastrous run-in near Hit. "Davri, I have feared this for years. You may be known now and that means for some long period of time we will have to forgo any more ventures to the northwest except to go far north and then over land to the Great Sea." "That is true, Kmal-Dyl. I will be at the White Temple for at least the next year or two, or until someone from here can definitely find out what happened to Per-Qad."

Hev-Ri asked Kmal-Dyl what sort of ventures were undertaken from Kish that required travel through the Mari country. Kmal-Dyl was tired and said, "Davri, you tell Hev-Ri about that while I rest. But I want to talk to you before you leave for Uruk so come back later today if you will."

Davri suggested they get something to eat and find places for the warriors to sleep. Then he began to describe what by now was part legend, part knowledge about the 'ventures to the northwest' Kmal-Dyl had referred to."Long ago, before the temples of Sumer were built wizards set out to look for a place where they could build a really large henge for the little circles and for a calendar to know the days and seasons. What they sought was a grassy plain on a bed of rock that would be soft enough to dig permanent trenches in. They knew they would need massive, very hard stones for the gates and for sighting the stars against. These stones would have to stand much higher than a man for them to be used effectively as sighting lines to the heavens. They would also require tall trees to establish their points of reference until the stones could be put in place. No such place exists anywhere we have ever been, not even along the Nile I am told.

"The story is told that a very great many years ago these first wizards left Ur to go along the north shore of the Great Sea, returning eventually to report that there was no such place there. In time others went back and sailed westward over the Great Sea. They were driven off course and passed through a gate into a region of the sea where there was no more land but somehow they were blown ashore far north of the gate. There they found what they were looking for and built a henge. Most of them died and the rest had to resort to hunting and gathering to survive.

"Over the years they were assimilated into the roving tribes of hunters and gatherers but two of the original wizards with the help of some of the local savages repaired the boat that had brought them to that land and went back out on the 'sea which has no bounds'. The wind carried them south and they found the gate again whereupon they sailed through it and let the wind take them where it would. They were almost dead of thirst and starvation when they landed at Crete. They died there but not before they had told their story to a local wizard who related it to travelers from Ur he met at Ugarit. Eventually one of those travelers was my grandfather's grandfather."

Shephset asked, "Davri, has anyone ever gone back there to see if this is true?" "My grandfather said that another party left Ur before he was born with plans to find the great henge. They were to go to Cyprus, then to Crete and from there proceed to the 'great gate' where they would wait for for a second party which would leave Ur two moons later. The first party would then sail through the gate while the second party waited for a third to arrive before they too would sail through and out on the boundless sea. It was thought that in this way the steps could always be retraced and a line of communications set up between Ur and the great henge country."

Hev-Ri broke in, "I have never heard these legends, or myths or whatever they are before, Davri. Do you believe these stories?" "My grandfather did, for his father told him when the last party departed; at that time my grandfather was old enough to remember it." "Has anyone heard of them since?" Vukhath wondered. "There was a rumor that they never found it, that the first two parties were both shipwrecked in another land in the sea, a land of mists and green fields like no place else in the world. By then the floods that destroyed so much of Sumer and Akkad even before my grandfather was born had reached the stage that there was no travel possible to the Great Sea from Ur for many, many years. There has never been any more word from them." Shephset broke in, "Then what you are telling us is that these ventures from Kish are still searching for those lost wizards, is that it? I am surprised that we have not heard of them in Asyut."

Davri laughed, "No, Shephset. We are not chasers of myths, whether we choose to believe them or not. The risks are too great and the time too long to be worth pursuing to anyone in the priesthood I know. Furthermore there is no king or High Priest who would authorize such expenditures of provisions and effort anymore. Our 'ventures' amount only to a continuing search in the lands north of Crete and perhaps somewhat west of there for such a site. Up to now we have found nothing and the kings are tired of supporting even these limited voyages. In fact I believe Ayn-Far intends to send Mar-Dug far east of the Tigris to see if there is such a land there. I will have to talk to Kmal-Dyl about that this afternoon so I can report to Ayn-Far when I reach Uruk."

Davri then drew Hev-Ri to one side and said, "Hev-Ri, I will be leaving for Uruk tonight. I am not safe even in this temple. There are some Mari priests in the town of Kish, how many we never know. They will learn I am here all too soon I fear. I wish you well on your return journey and hope that we will see each other again. When we do, will you remember that my name will be Ifn-Lot? That is what I am called in the south of Sumer. The priests there know of no 'Davri'."

After Davri had told Kmal-Dyl of his plans to go to the White Temple in Uruk and take up residence there as 'Ifn-Lot' Kmal-Dyl sighed, "I wonder what will become of all we have worked so hard to accomplish now, Davri. There is not much I can do to convince Shephset of the rightness of retaining the 'Sacred Circle' construction but I will try. As for Per-Qad I hope he has stayed loyal to the Menku's, yet I doubt it. Do you think he intentionally deserted Hev-Ri's party?" "Yes, I do, Kmal-Dyl. I looked back for him and he was nowhere near us when we got to the boats. There was no cry from him and it was not likely he fell when we ran so hard. Per-

Qad is younger than Hev-Ri and Rabul and should have outrun them both."

Kmal-Dyl frowned, "Do you think the Mari gang knew you were leading them here?" "No. If they had suspected I was in the party they would never have abandoned their boat and come looking for us with such carelessness. When I gave the signal to run we could see their leader and it may be that Per-Qad recognized him. I have to believe I can be identified now and that makes me useless to you until we learn with certainty what happened to Per-Qad."

"What about Malbu, Davri?" Davri winced, "I trust Malbu got back to Huta. It is a small village and there is not much likelihood the Mari priests will go there looking for him since it is not in their area. Nevertheless Malbu is exposed and can help only if someone is going north from Aqub. I suggest you try to find out what he is doing from the next party that comes through Aqub. I would like to know whatever you learn of Per-Qad whenever there is passage from here to Uruk, Kmal-Dyl." "That will be done of course. Good luck, Ifn-Lot." Davri smiled and left through a side gate to get away from Kish before the light of morning. He was sure he could safely find a boat at the next village below Kish.

CHAPTER FOUR 'The Academy at Ur'

The wizard, Miqel was born near Uruk. He was the son of Baldag, a shepherd whose fascination with the pageantry of the stars stemmed from nights tending his flocks. Miqel's mother, Gahnya was the daughter of Akhuruk, a teaching scribe in the fields of astronomy and geometry. It was not difficult for her to convince Baldag that Miqel should follow in his grandfather's footsteps. After eight summers with his father and mother Miqel was sent to live with his maternal grandfather and grandmother at Ur. There he began the long and arduous training and education in becoming a geometer and learning the secrets of the moon and the stars.

First he had to learn to make his rudimentary equipment and Akhuruk gave him his own small piece of obsidian to serve as a knife. Taking the gut of a newly butchered lamb Miqel struggled to make 'compass strings'. These had to be stretched and dried, then chewed to a soft pliability and were to be regarded as his most valuable possessions until he could progress to pieces of cane with edges made evenwhich would serve as ruler and square. Urunya, his grandmother patiently guided his hands and soothed the cuts that inevitably resulted from handling the razor-sharp obsidian.

In the mornings Miqel would follow Urunya about her chores. Depending on the season these ran from happy searches for figs and grapes and berries and venturing down to the Euphrates in the hope of capturing a fish, to the onerous cultivation of food crops and tanning of hides which provided clothing and shelter. In all these times there were many other children, some near his own age. And in spite of the hard work aspect of it all they chased and ran and wrestled in the sun as they went from one task to another, each with a sense of adventure and newness before the boredom of tedious repetition could spell maturity with the passsage of years.

Urunya, twenty years younger than Akhuruk already seemed old with gnarled hands and leathery skin. Her teeth were good but badly worn from use as tools, notably gnawing hides for soft garments to supplement the woolen cloth she wove or obtained from Akhuruk's teaching. Compared to the primitive existence of the hunter-gatherers of the past she had a good life and was happy with it. But sleep came easy after each day wore itself out before she could possibly accomplish all that was needed for much more than survival.

Urunya understood all too well how hard it was to be the wife of a scribe...even one who could teach...who had not risen to the service of Ur's king or at the grand Al Ubaid temple outside Ur. Akhuruk had devoted himself to teaching the very young to prepare them to enter such service and be provided for from the communal bounty. In the long afternoons he tutored at his little "academy in the sand". In the evenings he searched the stars and marked what the moon was doing to tell when and what to plant, when and what to reap. In the mornings he hunted for fowl and small game or slaughtered and butchered whatever sheep he had bartered for as 'tuition'.

When Miqel and his new and very best friend, Malil had advanced beyond the almost endless inscribing of interlinking circles in the smooth, flat sand of the academy, using their thongs and sharpened reeds for styluses. Akhuruk gave them flattened strips of scarce wood for their squares which they slaved over until they were able to satisfy Akhuruk that they were usable as rulers and squares. After a seemingly unending process Miqel and Malil learned the value of protecting their squares, even wearing them hooked to their fiber girdles giving them the appearance of grownup scribes. One day while they were hunting berries by a small creek that flowed near the tents where they lived they paused to rest in the shade of a large bush close to the waters edge. Lying on his back and looking up into the sky Malil boasted, "I will go into the service of the king I think. And I will throw the lots; and read the pegged liver to tell the king what the gods want him to do each day. And he will be glad and will give me all I want to eat and I will not have to drag the hoe in the ground to plant barley anymore." Miqel responded, "I think that I shall have an academy like Akhuruk's, only much bigger, with stone trenches to follow the stars and the moon; and stone columns to tell when the sun begins another year. And my academy will be in the White Temple at Uruk and the priests will tell me what the gods want me to find with my square and my compass." "But the priests will make you do their work," Malil protested, "and if the gods are angry you will not even have enough to eat."

"I don't care. Maybe I will even become a priest and then both you and the king will have to do what I tell you to do. I may even be the high priest of the White Temple. Wouldn't that be grand?" But before they could continue with their musings Urunya came looking for them, calling, "Lazy little boys will be hungry little boys if they do not get back to the tent with berries before Papa Akhuruk comes home." Miqel hollered, "We are over here. Come and see the berries we have found. Papa will be glad and he will let me stay up with him to search the face of the moon tonight...don't you think?" "I think you will fall off to sleep before the sun lets the moon get very high in the sky. That is what I think", Urunya laughed, gulping down a handful of their berries.

Three years passed and Miqel and Malil had become unusually proficient, using their string-compasses and squares to make figures in their smooth white sand 'blackboards' at the academy. The string compasses had by now been made into different lengths for easy choices in making the basic geometric diagram. The elementary diagram, a collection of interlocking circles with lines connecting the intersections was the basis of all the ruler and compass geometry known to the world at the time of Akhuruk. From the basic diagram all the mathematics they knew could be constructed, including layouts for the signs in the heavens for the times and seasons. Each fledgling geometer had to learn and overlearn this tedious process until it was engraved on his mind.

In late summer when Miqel and Malil achieved this milestone in their education Akhuruk rewarded them with time off from their classes. Miqel wanted to go home to Uruk and visit his parents and younger sisters and invited Malil to go with him. They were to return to the academy when the second new moon appeared following the day when light and dark were equal. A trading party was leaving for Uruk a few days later and it was arranged for the two boys to accompany it until they could locate the tent of Baldag and Gahnya.

Even before Miqel had left Uruk the great river's flow had begun to slow. Rainfall had been so sparse that the land was parched at any distance from the Euphrates and simple trench irrigation could no longer be practiced. This lead to the increasing numbers of sightings of hithabogs, the still aboriginal remnants of ancient settlers. The 'bogs' as they were called normally avoided cultivated settlements where people lived in tents and houses and cleared land for planting. They relied on game and gathering fruits and nuts; communities made this precarious if not impossible for them. Furthermore some village chieftains from time to time captured bogs and enslaved them so they were more than a little frightened and highly antagonistic toward people such as Akhuruk and his peers.

For all that the hithabogs were, among themselves a rather gentle people who endured privation and fearsome odds against survival as they pursued a pristine freedom rapidly disappearing from the lands of Mesopotamia. These were very small wandering bands whose members...mostly related to each other by common ancestry and intermarriage among close kin...lost most of their offspring to death before illness or wild beasts could do the job with chilling effect. Few of the smallest bands lasted more than four or five generations before famine or disease wiped out nearly all of a tribal family.

Inured to hardship though they were starvation forced them to scavenge near communities along the river and to risk encounter with the hated Sumerians, fear notwithstanding. They could revert to savagery with little provocation whenever they felt their families and freedom threatened and this lead the Sumerians to fear them as much as they themselves were feared.

It was such a time as this that Miqel and Malil prepared for their difficult trek to Uruk with the trading party. Now the route was lengthened by traveling up river as much of the distance as possible, perhaps bartering with someone to pole a reed skiff for the group, perhaps not. With the Euphrates at considerably lower than normal level walking along its edge introduced so many obstacles that it was often easier to trudge through the marsh grasses between the stretches of desert. The desert was less to be feared than being surprised by venomous snakes, wild dog packs or the dreaded hithabogs in the still soggy areas of the tall grass.

The more circuitous route could cover sixty or more miles and take anywhere from four days to a week unless a river skiff could be arranged for. And that was by no means assured at any time, much less so now with bogs and robbers threatening isolated wanderers. The bogs did not take to water travel very well. They would use reeds to get across a stream only when they could not possibly ford it. Unlike the short distance between Ur and the seaport of Eridu, there was no 'highway of commerce' to be traveled between Ur and Uruk.

Toq, at nineteen summers was the only living son of Oghud the tribal leader of a band of some thirty bogs which had hunted over an extensive area north and west of Ur and Eridu from before memory. Skirmishes with other bands on the fringes of their territory had decimated the once much larger tribe before Toq was born. Oghud had seen his first three sons and Toq's mother die in a single battle before he and the remnant of his band escaped by night. Toq's mate was pregnant and nearing the time of delivery, a time she dreaded knowing full well that with the continuing famine the child could be snatched and eaten by the other women before it drew its first breath. They had lost their babies in the same manner struggling to survive hard hunger as tribal justice succumbed to savagery that bordered on insanity. Toq could not stay by her side with the endless hunting for scraps of garbage or an occasional bird or pig he and the other men found in their foraging. The men usually went out in three's since this afforded them some protection against ferocious wild dog packs that roamed in the vicinity of cities. Armed with clubs and crude spears three of them could keep a pack at bay long enough to kill a dog or two for the pack to turn on and devour. Fire at the campsite kept such dangerous animals away from the women and remaining older children.

Toq's hunting partners were Ev and Fyd, strong, fast runners, though both were several years older than he was. They had hunted and gathered together since Toq's older brothers had been killed in the fight with the northern bogs. Fyd could sling his club, circling like a planing propeller with almost unerring accuracy at any hare that leaped into view within fifteen or twenty yards, killing or stunning it long enough for one or the other of the runners to capture. Sometimes he could get close enough to one of the larger river birds to accomplish the same result, but game had become so scarce and scattered that sundown usually found the trio with little to take back to camp except their own empty bellies.

They had taken to downwind stalking of shepherds on clear, moonless nights when their chances of grabbing a lamb or goat before the sheepdogs roused were at least fair. Ev would crouch with shouldered spear to, if necessary impale the dog while Toq and Fyd ran on the flock. Shepherds took the loss of a single animal rather than leaving the flock in a hopeless chase where they were invariably outmatched by the speed of the poaching bogs. Even this method of obtaining food had to be exercised with caution however. An occasional report of such activity disturbed the shepherd's community but was no more than the normal loss to roving lions or birds of prey such as large owls. Repeated raids would bring out a band of villagers to find and attack the bogs' campsite and Oghud's tribe was too small to defend itself from a well organized and armed band of villagers.

The trading party to Uruk had gathered wares and prepared for the journey weeks before the time of departure. Gold trinkets and amulets; copper and gold arm bands, some with embedded pieces of carnelian; ivory and shell necklaces and copper-alloy knives were all bagged in leather pouches. Barley loaves, dates and goat cheese along with goatskins of water provided for brief desert crossings. Goats carried the heavier bales of wool and woven goods and gave milk along the way. Most traders would take their own dogs for protection, not only at night but to scatter snakes in grassy areas and sound the alarm at any scent of bogs. This party numbered eleven men with eight dogs and five goats before adding Miqel and Malil. The leader of the party, Enlid was a friend of Akhuruk's and glad to have the boys along to run ahead with the dogs seeking small game for food along the way. They would scarcely get beyond the barley fields before the first stand of marsh grass made the going hard for 'day one' out of Ur.

Enlid had already eliminated the possibility of obtaining a large reed boat from the Ur landing. Such boats which would have normally been for hire stayed close to Ur ferrying grain and animals and their owners across the river; or going no more than a few hours upriver for fishing, returning well before sundown to avoid going ashore at some remote place where bogs might be lying in wait. There was always plenty of business tending to the needs of groups from beyond the river bringing their offerings to the great temple of Al Ubaid. In fact Enlid would likely join such as he and his party neared Uruk for the White Temple there drew worshipers from considerable distances all year round.

On the day for leaving in the still dimness of predawn Miqel and Malil stood shivering in their wool tunics outside Enlid's reed house. With bags of parched barley tied to their rope girdles they were ready for travel and eager to set out. Miqel was sure Gahnya and Baldag would be proud of how tall he had grown during the more than three years since he had seen them. Malil was excited at the prospect of Uruk and the storied White Temple; he had never been more than a few miles from Ur, not even as far as the gulf at nearby Eridu. Enlid came out and called for the rest of the party and they quickly assembled for the first leg of the trip, beginning with the required 'checkout' at the temple yard.

The little band walked to the gate of the temple and showed their wares to the scribe and guard there, explaining what their mission was and where they were going as well as when they expected to return. If they were very long overdue it was possible that a search party made up of friends would be organized to rescue them if perchance they had been attacked by bogs. Usually however for a trip to a place as large as Uruk bands would meet each other along the way and news of their safety would be sent back to their families.

The sun was up with not a cloud in the sky. This would be yet another scorcher of a day, better spent in the relative cool of tents and reed houses than slogging through steamy marshes and stinging sand. But trade was trade and this was their living. Many considered it was a better way of life than tilling the soil or tending sheep and for some it led to the accumulation of wealth and influence at the temple. Enlid was not one of them though he did manage to extract a decent living for himself and his large family. And he thoroughly enjoyed the give and take of barter, regaling his friends with stories of the 'deals' he had made through the years.

Miqel and Malil were perhaps a hundred yards ahead of the others, running with the dogs when they flushed a large hare. Malil stunned it with a sun hardened clay 'stone' from his sling. He could sling fast and well for his age and had sometimes knocked larger, slower birds out of the air when he was at home. They dispatched the hare and would save it for the dogs until late in the day if the dogs had not found enough rodents to satisfy them. Otherwise the hare would serve as fresh meat for their own evening meal.

By the time the sun got to the top of the sky the grass was getting taller and the dry trail grew fainter. Overhead an eagle rode the thermals, flapping its wings only when something made it decide to change direction. Suddenly it plummeted toward the ground and grasping a fleeing ground squirrel in its huge talons it headed back upwind toward its nest. Far off to their right vultures circled up from feeding on carrion, probably the past night's kill by a lion. It was close enough for discomfort and Enlid called the boys to bring the dogs and stay nearer the trading party for fear the lion might still be lurking in the vicinity.

They came to a place where the grass had been beaten down and discovered a bloody trail running for several yards off the path to the freshly dismembered head and hooves of a wild goat. This was not the work of any wild animal; every member of the band including the boys knew they had chanced on the spot where bogs had been hunting. Enlid knelt down and rubbed the earth with his hand. Breathing heavily he stood up, "They were here earlier this morning. From the looks of it there must have been at least three of them. With something as big as a goat for food I hope it is safe to guess that they have headed back to their camp and we will not see anymore of them during this trip."

As a precautionary measure Miqel and Malil were placed in the center of the party and Abdala and Narak, the two strongest traders took their dogs and moved thirty of forty paces ahead, eyes steadily sweeping the terrain. The dogs began barking excitedly and Miqel shivered as he gasped, "Bogs?" "What is it, Narak?", Enlid called. Abdala was first to answer, "Just a harmless snake. We can handle two or three bogs any time, but a lion could be another matter. We will stay ahead if you will bring two more dogs up here. I want all the warning we can get until we find a place to build a fire and bed down for the night. Is the torch still smoldering?" "Both torches are fine. We will have no trouble making fire with this dry grass but some of us are going to be up all night feeding it the way this stuff burns", Enlid shouted.

Toq had told Ev and Fyd that their best plan would be to trail the lion whose roaring had started them moving in the dead of night. Though accustomed to hunting in almost total darkness they had long since eaten their dogs and only stark hunger could have lead him to such a foolhardy decision. If the lion was a small one they could surely kill it with spears but not even insanity would make a man hunt a big cat in the dark. Fyd grumbled, "Why Toq want to feed Fyd, Ev to lion?" "Lion feed Toq, Fyd, Ev with what lion not eat if lion kills goat. We get to lion before vultures do. We will find leg, find shoulder to eat", answered Toq, continuing, "Keep lion roar far away; follow wind. Lion not know we here until sun give light. Then see lion." Ev and Fyd nodded and began a slow dog trot, silently stalking the lion; behind them Toq sniffed the air for anything else worth chasing.

The lion's roaring turned to fierce growling and the snorts and screams of a wild pig rent the air; the lion swiftly killed it within two hundred yards of where the three bogs had frozen in their tracks. "We wait for light", Fyd observed. Toq and Ev agreed.

After they rested, happy that the lion had enough to eat and would not come near them the

43

stars faded into dawn's faint glow and they moved cautiously toward where they had last heard the lion. First one and then the other moved out, then stopped and knelt with his spear at the ready while the next moved forward to repeat the action. This would overcome surprise and avert total calamity: two spears were ready to cut the air in an instant if the forward hunter was attacked. Instant death was less to be feared than mauling. The forward hunter's eyes searched for holes that could twist an ankle or snap a leg in the speed of a chase. A seriously injured hunter knew all too well the agony of forced abandonment. This universal tribal law was accepted for there was no other way a tribe could survive but for at least part of a hunting party to return to the camp with whatever food had been found. Three heads popped back in unison with wide open nostrils sniffing the breeze. "Goat", Ev whispered, "not far." The other two nodded and the three sprang forward in unison, Toq and Ev with spears raised, Fyd ahead swinging his club on the run. A wild goat meant there was no lion hunting where they were now or there would have been no wild goat to sniff. Caution left behind they came within Fyd's range by the time the goat was aware of them. It bolted too late; Fyd's club completed its arc breaking the goat's neck before either Toq or Ev could let their spears fly.

Within seconds they had disemboweled the goat, lapping up its blood with their hands and gorging on its entrails. Then they stood and looked for a spot to carve up the remains for easier carrying back to camp, dragging the carcass as they began moving through the knee deep grass; finding nothing they stomped down the grass in a small circle. Their flint knives cut off the head and hooves which they left on the spot.

Elated they turned to go back to camp, jogging to cover the distance of more than twenty miles before the sun would begin to sink out of sight into the half-glow of dusk.

CHAPTER FIVE   'Journey to Uruk'

Enlid and his party continued their progress without knowing they were moving in the general direction of the main bog hunt area. Late in the day they reached a trickling stream with low tamarisk bushes and stunted willows along its banks. Wood was scarce in the region of Ur as was stone. Bricks and clay ware provided substitutes for stone but wood was almost a precious commodity. Except for willows and palms there were few uncultivated trees left close to Ur. The trees at this campsite would have been cut long ago if they could have served any purpose other than firewood or clubs. But it was a sheltered site and certainly suited the trading party's purpose.

Not too far away a curl of smoke rose and drifted slowly in their direction. The barking of dogs told Enlid that in all likelihood another traveling band of pilgrims or traders was camped there. He and Abdala and Narak approached the source of the sound with their own dogs, careful to avoid detection until they were more sure the other group might be friendly.

They were relieved to hear voices shouting in a Sumerian dialect they recognized as originating from the area northeast of Ur. Enlid called out, "Friends from Ur and Al Ubaid come to greet you. Hold your dogs and we will hold ours. We are camped near here and wish you no harm."

A large man approached with his right hand raised high and a dog tightly reined in with his left. "Come near and share our meal with us. There is plenty for all." He was truly a giant of a man and wore the long skirt of fur with its pelt decorated border that signified a leader of stature. "I am Kalam-Bad. We have priests from the White Temple and their scribes with us."

"We are grateful but we have food. I am Enlid and these are Abdala and Narak. Let us bring the others and we will share your fire and give you the news of Ur." "It is good that you do that and we will tell you of Uruk as it was before we left two moons ago." Kalam-Bad turned back to his party as two priests walked up. They wanted to know who was in the Enlid party before consenting to stay the night in their company. "Time to find out while we eat with them but they do not look like robbers and it is clear they have left Ur only today or at most yesterday", Kalam-Bad observed.

The Ur group was elated at the good fortune and most especially Miqel and Malil who would have run straight for the other camp if Enlid had not ordered them to proceed slowly with the others. "We must give them time to see that we do not threaten and we want to be sure that Kalam-Bad is what he says he is. He has been traveling for a long time and judging by his wet furs must have crossed the river only hours ago. If they are from Uruk that would seem an odd way to get to Ur." As they walked up to the camp Abdala and Narak and the other men were relieved to see what was obviously a group of star-watchers and that Kalam-Bad and four or five men armed as he was were there for protection and service. They had been somewhere where game was more plentiful for they had live geese and pigs and smaller game far beyond their own needs.

The Uruk party gathered around and they all exchanged greetings, right hands high in gestures of friendship. The priests identified themselves as Mar-Dug and Ifn-Lot of the White Temple service, their specialties being geometry and astronomy. "We have been out in the plains beyond the rivers where there is much stone. Atop a great flat stone mound we have found the place to build our gates and trenches to better know the times of the moon and the sun in their travels. We need many men to help us and are on our way to Al Ubaid and Eridu to offer gifts to their gods and to ask their priests' support", Mar-Dug, the older of the two offered. This at least explained their appearance and the reason for the recent river crossing.

Enlid hastened to introduce Miqel and Malil who were standing wide-eyed in awe of the priests. "These two young ones are training for the service and are on the way to see the White Temple at Uruk. Enlid informed them; and taking Miqel by the hand he pushed him forward, continuing, "The father of this one is a shepherd who lives near Uruk with the boy's mother and sisters. Both Miqel and Malil have been studying with Miqel's grandfather, Akhuruk at his academy at Ur."

"I know of Akhuruk and his academy", Mar-Dug, smiling and moving closer to Miqel and Malil went on, "and if these two have learned their lessons well they will most certainly be welcome at any temple in our country. How far have you got in your studies?" Malil answered that they had mastered the basic construction while Miqel on one knee took his sling and a stick and started to draw circles in the damp sand. Mar-Dug frowned, "It is not good for one so young to claim mastery; few really comprehend all of it in a lifetime. What is this you are drawing, young 'Master'?" Miqel was stung by the slur in Mar-Dug's voice and annoyed that Malil had been so brash, more for the embarrassment this could cause Akhuruk than for himself. "I will show you quickly and you can judge if Papa has taught us well", he exclaimed.

He continued for the few moments it took him to complete enough of the basic diagram to show the the signs for reading the stars, making rather good straight lines with his stick to indicate the answers he would explain. Mar-Dug waited and Ifn-Lot bent over to study the figure carefully. "What do the lines tell you", he asked, "and what would you do next?" "The lines tell me that if I draw a little circle from the top or the bottom of the center circle that just touches it I can repeat that circle all around Bull ten times...exactly." "Go on", said Ifn-Lot.

"And if I draw a square like this", sketching in a square around the circle and drawing the line that touched the left 'sign', "I will have made the Sacred Golden Section". Miqel stood up with his head bowed to wait for any further censure from Mar-Dug. Mar-Dug and Ifn-Lot both smiled and Mar-Dug said he wanted to meet this Akhuruk who taught so well, thinking to himself what Akhuruk already knew: that here indeed was a truly gifted child. "But we must get on with supper before there is no light to see what it is the bearers of burden have prepared for us. Come, you two will eat with us and we will hear of you plans." Clapping his hands, Mar-Dug summoned a small, stooped older man who was busy over the nearest fire, "Coban-Bul, here are two more aspirants whose bellies are empty from the long day's travel. Have you any goat cheese they can nibble on while you cook their hare?"

"I have goat cheese and also figs that have dried in the sun for my master's friends", Coban-Bul softly offered, "would the Master like some too?" "No, I think I shall wait for the fish you caught as we crossed the river. Ifn-Lot, if you wish you may join them." "A thousand thanks, Master." And Ifn-Lot sat down with Miqel and Malil to the cheese and figs while they told him of what they wanted to do with their lives.

Malil repeated his ambition to serve the king and "'cast the lots and read the liver' just like the wizards do" "Ever the presumptuous one, but then perhaps you will do just that my young friend", Ifn-Lot laughed as he turned to Miqel, "and you?". Miqel swallowed hard and did not really want to answer fearing Papa would scold him when he returned to the academy and told him of their experience; but tell him he must. Better from him than to have Mar-Dug or Ifn-Lot condescending to him. Papa was a great man even though he did not directly serve the king and was not a priest. "Come, come. Surely you must know by now what plans you have to live by", Ifn-Lot chuckled.

"I think I would like to have my own academy", Miqel began, "not like Papa's but one inside the walls of a temple so that I could go out like you and build the trenches and the gates to learn the secrets of the moon and the stars." "Well said, young master", came from Mar-Dug who had been standing behind him. This time there was no slur in his voice and Miqel smiled at such a rare compliment from one so eminent. "What will 'Papa' teach you when you return to Ur?"

"We will go back to make a new diagram with the dividing angles all through it so that we can learn the secrets of the circle. I think that is what comes next, don't you, Malil? Papa has told us we could not do that until we truly understood the basics." Malil answered that this was so and Mar-Dug told them, "The circle and its secrets does come then and after that will be the circle and the square and how they can be measured. This is most difficult and there are few if any who ever achieve it. Even those who claim they do will never agree that anyone else's way is correct. This is a mad thing for the Chief Priests to contend with these days. Perhaps it will be that your henge of gates and trenches or some other great monument only you can build will yield the true answer. No one knows of a certainty now. If you persist in pursuing that goal be warned that it is a hard and lonely life; you may wish that you had gone with Malil and lived at a king's pleasure, raising a happy family beside the quiet walls of a temple."

Miqel would turn these things over and over in his mind for years to come. This was a heady conversation for a young boy and indeed it had been many years since Mar-Dug had even spoken to a child, much less counseled one. But now Coban-Bul was calling and the sun had gone into its final red-phase before there would be night. As they walked over to get their food Ifn-Lot asked them if they knew what day this was. "This is the 'day that the sun and the stars are equals, when the night and the day have the same time'", both responded almost in a single voice. Mar-Dug and Ifn-Lot nodded with enjoyment at their relaxing visit with the boys and determined that they would see more of this young Miqel after Akhuruk could teach him the secrets of the circle.

The weary bogs with their goat arrived to find turmoil in the camp. Another hunting party had traveled eastward toward Uruk and overtaken two lone pilgrims with what to the bogs was a bounty of offerings. The pilgrims were no match for the hunters though one put up a fight until a blow to the head from the lead bog's club left him unconscious and bleeding profusely. The other pilgrim escaped while the bogs were scurrying to catch the game set free in the melee. The bogs thought the pilgrim was dead; it had not been their intention to kill, only to take the food and get back to camp quickly. When Oghud learned what they had done he was livid at their thoughtlessness. If the pilgrim died there would most certainly be a large party of armed men from Uruk who would run down every bog in that part of the country, slaying them without mercy. Lvag, leader of the party became enraged at what he took as ingratitude and challenged Oghud. "You tell us go get food or we starve. Wives hungry. Eat own babies before we find food. Eat mice and lizards. No berries now and figs and grapes too close to strong men's houses. You do not find new place for us to hunt where gods smile and there is plenty."

"We stay here where our fathers hunted", Oghud responded. "When gods give rain river grow big. Birds and deer come back. Berries and nuts give food and strong men will leave barley where we can find it. Now you go back and find if man is dead. If he does not live you watch for men who hunt for us. You come find us so we can run away."

Some of the band sided with Oghud while others thought Lvad was right. As the hunters fingered their clubs and knives Toq and his party appeared. The distraction of their report and the goat meat they brought quieted things for the moment but the matter was obviously not settled. Lvad squatted off to himself, sulking and gnawing on a raw bird he had grabbed out of a child's hands. Toq announced that he and Ev and Fyd would go and find the pilgrim's fate, inquiring if

47

it was near enough to reach the spot before total darkness came. Oghud told Lvad to go with them but he did not even answer until Fyd, towering over him said, "You go." He lunged at Fyd slashing the air with his flint knife. Fyd sidestepped and came down hard with his club catching Lvad on the shoulder with a glancing blow. Lvad writhed in pain and fell to the ground as the others gathered to see if he would get up. Instead he rolled over on his back and exposed his neck signifying his defeat and waiting for Fyd's mercy, or lack of it.

Oghud knelt down and gently lifted Lvad's arm to find a broken collarbone. Lvad did not let out a whimper but the fear in his eyes told Oghud that with a limp right arm he was now defenseless. It would heal of course but Lvad would be severely incapacitated for some time to come. Nevertheless his arm was bound close to his body and Oghud ordered him to go with the search party. They were to set out immediately.

Toq's mate looked pleadingly into his eyes, hoping that with food for the time being he would somehow save their unborn baby from cannibalism. He never returned the glance but left her a choice piece of goat meat and trotted over to Ev and Fyd. "We go now. Lvad lead. Ev watch Lvad." And turning to Oghud, "Father, we find hurt man."

Before dawn Enlid and his party left Kalam-Bad's group and took up their journey toward Uruk. In parting Ifn-Lot promised Miqel that he would speak to Akhuruk regarding Miqel's future; and Miqel and Malil bowed for Mar-Dug to touch their heads as a blessing from the gods. Miqel and Malil then took their slings and the dogs and moved out in front of the band as they had the day before, only a little closer this time at Enlid's insistence.

The grass grew more sparse and finally faded out as they came to a stretch of desert sand. It would be shorter to head straight for the next bend of the Euphrates than follow its sinuous path through the marshes. No more running back and forth now for there would be little in the way of game to hunt most of this day. The dogs would find some rodents but there was nothing of interest to the humans, nor would the goats have fodder until they could find another stream or a pool that had not completely dried up. Enlid thought there was a good likelihood of finding such however and drove the goats at a good pace cursing the hot sand as he went.

The only living things the boys saw were some small birds and an occasional hawk, diving now and again for a lizard or a small snake. A couple of ducks did fly over but they were far too high for even a man to think of slinging a pellet at them. Here and there a tamarisk or other small shrub struggled to survive near what had been a salt pond before the drought came and the sand blew over its bed. It was all tiresome and boring and Miqel and Malil returned frequently to the group for company as much as for a drink of water, their usual excuse. Enlid was amused but he had a train of men and goats to think about and men and goats were grumbling at the fierce heat. "Winter comes soon and surely there will be rain and cool nights", he said, as much to himself as to Abdala who walked beside him. "It should rain before we return to Ur, don't you think?" "I do not think anything but hot", Abdala laughed, "but I tell you the goats will give curdled milk tonight!" They both chortled and began to discuss how far to go before turning back to the river if they did not find a stream. Looking up toward the sun Abdala allowed that they had a bit farther to go before they would have to make that decision. Enlid nodded. Miqel and Malil had been listening and groaned beneath their breath before struggling back in front of the group, dragging the reluctant dogs along with them.

The wind in their faces rose somewhat and the dogs let out low, rumbling growls. Enlid and Abdala moved up ahead of Miqel and Malil, taking the dogs' leashes as they did. They could see nothing but were coming to the top of a small rise and perhaps that would give them a view of what was disturbing the dogs. Near the crest Abdala motioned the party to stop and he and Enlid cautiously inched their way to where they could just see over the ridge. A lone figure stumbled aimlessly across their path perhaps fifty or sixty yards in front of them. His long white skirt flapped loosely as if tattered and from what they could see that he had: no water bottle, no bag of food, no nothing. "That is no bog but what would a person be walking alone in a stretch like this", murmured Abdala, "do you think he has been robbed perhaps?"

Standing on the top of the rise with his dog held back Enlid called out but there was no sign of recognition; the man simply stumbled on in the direction he had been going. Enlid signaled for Narak and the three of them rushed down the slope toward the wanderer. As they neared him he fell headlong in the sand; struggling to get back on his feet he fell again and lay facedown and still. At that Abdala began to run and reached him before Enlid and Narak could catch up with him. He rolled the unconscious pilgrim over and gasped as he saw the bloody mess on the side of his head. "Robbed and left to die", Enlid guessed, "wonder how many others there were in his party. Do either of you know him; he does not look like anyone from Ur that I have seen." "If we do not get some water in him we will never know", Abdala answered and then shouted, "Miqel, Malil. Quick! Fetch a water skin and bring it here."

Abdala cradled the poor pilgrim's head on his knees while Enlid poured a little water on his lips. He blinked and smiled weakly, opening his lips for more water. Then closing his eyes he seemed to pass out again. Taking a linen kerchief from his head Narak began to bathe the wound, shaking his head in disbelief that the pilgrim could have survived at all, much less wandering alone in the desert. The pilgrim opened his eyes again and began to sit up, haltingly murmuring, "Could I have more water? I was about gone when I heard you and I think I just gave up. I have been trying to find the river since last night." "The river is not far and we will probably have to camp there tonight anyway. Can you walk if we give you a staff?" Enlid was worried. They had no poles for a travois and they could not carry him very far. But neither would they leave him. "Let me try, but first have you a little cheese or fruit? I have not eaten since yesterday morning and the heat has drained my strength." By then the rest of the party had gotten to where they were and Abdala hastened to open a pouch and hand him a cake of raisins and a ball of cheese.

He revived enough to get up on one knee and with help he stood. Suddenly he grasped his head with both hands, "May the gods be merciful. The pain!" "Take it easy, friend. You have a bad wound there", and Abdala offered his arm for support. "What happened to you and why are you alone in this forsaken desert?" "I till the soil and my friend and I were on the way to offer of the little we had to the god of the White Temple when bogs fell on us yesterday. I was left for dead but I think my friend escaped. If so he might have made it as far as the river; but he had nothing more than I have. The bogs took everything, even our goatskins. They steal I know but I have never known them to try to kill one of us before."

"How are you called?", Enlid asked. "I am Arpag of the village of Mu." "Where is that?". "It is toward the setting sun from Uruk, two days of walking for a strong man. Water came to us as a stream from the great river all the years of my life; but these past two years we have had less and less water and some have starved as our crops have failed." "What will you do now if you go to Uruk with us?" "My friend and I wished to find work to bring food home to our families. We thought if the god accepted our offerings he would lead us to work and grain."

Lvad lead the search party straight to where the pilgrims had been attacked. Though the sun was down the moon gave enough light to see that there had been a scuffle but nothing more. There was no sign of the downed pilgrim nor was there any way to follow the trail at night or know if his friend had returned to rescue him, or what was left of him. "Lvad, you sure this is place? No man here." Fyd got down on all fours and sniffed the ground, "I smell blood. Maybe blood of man." "This is place. Man was here. He lie still. We do not feel him for life. We run off to camp."

Toq and Ev snorted in disgust at Lvad's stupidity but there was nothing to do now but wait for daylight. They first had to find a safe place to sleep and water to drink. With no fire each would take his turn to guard against any hungry beast; lions could travel far and they had not forgot the one they stalked the night before. They walked into the wind until they smelled water and jogged to an old irrigation ditch close to the river.

"Maybe we find turtles in rushes here when sun gives light. Place is good. We rest here." Toq scooped up water in his hands and drank deeply, splashing his head again and again to cool off. "Lvad, you sleep now. Fyd, you watch awhile. Then I watch. Then Ev watch till light comes."

At first light Ev roused the others. "See turtle I find. You find more. We eat." They all waded into the water feeling along the muddy bottom till Fyd shrieked with pain, holding up an angry turtle firmly clamped to his finger. Fortunately it was not a very large one and pain and indignity were all he suffered. Soon with enough to eat they could start the search for the pilgrim they were compelled to find before returning to Oghud.

Retracing their steps to the site of the attack they began trailing the lone pilgrim. In spite of his seemingly aimless wandering he had gone farther than they expected but there was no indication that the other pilgrim had come back. There was just one set of tracks which would be quickly lost in the blowing sand if he had not fallen so often.

At daybreak Oghud called the other two hunters of Lvad's party, "Go back where you find man Lvad hurt. Send Lvad back to camp. If man is dead we will run toward place where sun sets and find new place to wait. You and Toq and others go find food. We must get food or all will die." The hunters, Nah and Rif nodded and set out immediately. They quickly arrived at the place to find tracks going in two directions. "Man has moved. Tracks go out; come back. We follow tracks that go toward sun?" Rif looked at Nah for assent and they picked up the trail to overtake Toq and his band and relay Oghud's message.

They came upon the bogs shortly after they had arrived at the place where Enlid's party had found the pilgrim. Lvad was protesting further pursuit, "Man lives. We go back now. Many men go toward river. They not look for us." Fyd did not agree, "See. Man fall down here. Maybe die. Maybe many men find him; go for others. Come back. Kill us all." Before the argument could be settled Toq caught sight of Rif and Nah coming over the ridge. Nah reported Oghud's orders and Toq promptly dispatched the humiliated Lvad back to Oghud and the women. "We do what Oghud says do. These people do not go far yet. We find them. We know what do then." The remaining band of five began tracking with extreme care. They must not be seen under any circumstance but most particularly not until they knew the fate of the pilgrim. Fyd went a considerable distance ahead of the others, still always in sight so that he could signal back when he saw anything.

After a couple of hours they came to the swampy area near the river and knew that the group must be setting up camp for the night. The sun by now was low in the sky and a plume of smoke already rose not more than two miles upriver. Toq called Fyd back to decide how they would proceed. Watching the smoke drift lazily out toward the water, Fyd was uneasy. "If move closer dogs know we here. Do not like. We wait. Wind change maybe." Toq stood up to get a better view of the area between them and Enlid's camp. "Not good. Soon no light. Must see man Lvad hurt. Not stay night here. Not get close to see from here." At this point Rif spoke up, "We go up river side. Wade under trees. Hide in rushes maybe. We see then. Dogs not know."

Enlid and Abdala had managed to help Arpag to a spot where the rushes gave way to willows growing along what had been the banks during times of normal water level. The area was strewn with gravel washed down by the Euphrates and there was an inviting campsite in a shallow draw well back from the water's edge. The usual tamarisk was dry enough for keeping a fire going all night and the party set about preparing the evening meal. Though the wind blew off the desert the place was much cooler than they had been experiencing out in the sand and they were relieved to wash off and make themselves comfortable. "We are close enough to Uruk that I think danger is past for all of us, Arpag. Would you not say so, Enlid?", Abdala spoke, trying to reassure Arpag.

"Yes, I would believe that is true. Still I am carrying some gold and jewelry that I will be most relieved to get into a trader's hands in the safety beside the White Temple walls. Just to feel secure, Narak will you stand the first watch? I will take the middle and Abdala can hold out till we get moving at dawn." With the goatskins refilled and soaked the cooled water was more than welcome after the intense heat of the day. Abdala was particularly grateful, "I think trading and traveling in the summer is getting too hard for me. Maybe in a couple of years or so I will stay in my cool reed house by the river during the long summer days; fish a little at night. And do my trading in the winter months so my wife and I can barter for our needs the rest of the year. We do not need so much anymore."

Not far upriver an escaped murderer, Eh-Buran sat quietly with two of his robber band in the reed boat he had sequestered only hours before. The boat was moored to a stump at a convenient dry landing while he waited for Ib-Seeg, another criminal the king of Uruk wanted in custody very badly. He was to bring a report on what size party was camped where the smoke came from. Ib-Seeg waded alongside the boat and leaned toward Eh-Buran, "Traders with wool and woolens. I heard one say he had gold and jewelry. Beyond that I do not know what they have but four of us could take the lighter stuff and be back on the water before they could do much. They are not very well armed; the dogs are the only ones we need to worry about I think." "I want your report. Not what you think", snapped Eh-Buran. "Is there a place where we can float in and tie up quietly enough that the dogs will not know we are there until it is too late?" "To be sure there is. But they are encamped a little way back from the water. I would rather catch them in the desert sand where we leave no marks and no one to get to Uruk and tell the king what happened. I have counted them: there are nine men and two young boys. If we lose any of them there will be trouble I tell you." "Hold your tongue or I will cut it out! We are not here to ask for gifts. If I do not get back with something to barter for food and women our little band up north will slit all our throats. We have not taken much lately and they are restless. What say you to that?" "Ugly I know. What do you want us to do?" "Wait till the moon is down. Then we will float very quietly a little way past them and tie up in the rushes. Then we will wade back to where they are and start killing before the dogs attack. Have we enough mutton to throw to the dogs?" "Plenty of mutton even for the eight dogs I counted. Are we to use spears or clubs?" "Both. We will start with spears. Kill the boys first; I do not fancy chasing two lively youngsters in the dark. Go for the men's shoulders. We can finish the job with clubs when they cannot fight back. It will look like bogs did it."

Toq and Fyd had led the others wading toward the camp, scarcely rippling the water as they went.

When they got to where they could just make out the members of the party Fyd touched Toq's shoulder and nodded ahead a little way. The shadowy figure of Ib-Seeg was backing quietly into the water and coming toward them. All five bogs moved into the rushes with their heads barely out of the water to wait and see what would happen. Ib-Seeg had no thought of

51

being watched and was smugly satisfied that he had enough to report to Eh-Buran as he made his way toward where the boat was.

Toq touched Fyd and motioned for him to follow Ib-Seeg, pointing to where he and the others were as a soundless message that they would wait there. Fyd moved with the stealth only a bog could have mastered and listened as Ib-Seeg and Eh-Buran talked. Then he silently moved back to Toq and the two of them waded back downstream a short distance so they could talk. "Four men in boat with much food. They rob and kill. Others wait for them far away in north country. They will kill all these men and other men will say 'bogs kill.'" Toq frowned, "Bad men. Bad men. Man Lvad hurt lives. Now all die. Then tribe die." Motioning the others to come near he told them his plan and they moved back to where they had waited before.

Eh-Buran's boat made not a sound as it drifted past the watching bogs, out of sight in the rushes. A short distance away one of the robbers tied the boat to an overhanging willow and all of them got out and waded back past the bogs toward the camp, pieces of mutton and spears held high over their heads. Just as they were ready to make their dash into the camp a long hideous shriek, "Ahyeeeiieeahee" rose in unison from the five bogs and the dogs came tearing into the water, slashing, snapping, biting arms, faces, throats before a single spear found its mark. Abdala, Narak and Enlid brought torches as the robbers fought frantically to maintain their balance and move into deeper water. The roiling water was red with their blood and Eh-Buran sank dying with a slashed jugular.

The bogs noiselessly got to where the boat was tethered and untying it poled it with all their strength into the mainstream of the Euphrates. There the current swiftly took them miles away before the men at the camp had any idea of what had been happening. They took stock of what was on board and found food for days for such a small tribe as Oghud's.

Ib-Seeg and the other two robbers were dragged before the fire and given the chance to confess or be beheaded forthwith. Ib-Seeg spoke, "We are poor outcasts and starving. Do with us what you will." "Liar!", Abdala screamed, "you are fat and drip with oil. Let us dump their carcasses into the great river for the fishes to eat." "No, Abdala. We will bind them and deliver them to the king at Uruk. He will do to them whatever seems right to him. We are not priests or leaders either in Ur or Uruk and do not want to face the king for taking such matters into our own hands." Enlid reasoned. Abdala slumped down on the ground and agreed, "You are right, Enlid. But at least let them live off their own fat until we get to the White Temple. No food for such as these."

Ib-Seeg wallowed on the ground, pleading for a quick death there and then. The others wailed and begged for the same. The torture they were sure awaited them far outweighed any fear of dying at the hands of such people as these. But all they got was a shaking of the heads of the assembled traders. It would be done; they would be delivered for the king to decide.

Miqel and Malil trembled with mixed fear and excitement, never knowing how near they were to death moments before. Aside from the bogs the only real beneficiaries of the evening were the dogs. They had a feast on the retrieved mutton the robbers had brought. Only one formality remained before heading for Uruk. As was the custom for the times Eh-Buran's head was severed from his body and stuck on his spear to be carried to the king as certain evidence that whomever he was he was indeed dead.

The hour was late and there was still most of a day's travel to get to Uruk. Half the party stood guard while the rest slept as best they could after the events of the night. Their turn on watch would come before a hurried departure at earliest light.

CHAPTER SIX   'King of Upper Nile'

After a day of walking and trotting Menhes and Seb found the boat and crew waiting for them. They rested for the night and set out for Kom Ombo the next morning. Sailing with the current they made good time and arrived late on the twentieth day after the new moon. The numerous small craft that took Sel-Abba's forces to Edfu brought them to a day's walk above Edfu and they would march into the Nubian camp the next day. On the twenty-second day after the new moon Hadu would be expected to review his new troops and the 'relieved force' would march upriver on the next day.

Menhes found Ar-Chab and told him of the successful meeting with Addi-Hoda. He asked if everything was ready for the attack. "All is ready here and in Asyut. Your father and mother took MeriLyth and her mother and sisters to Crocodile Lake and are safe there now. Khafu will have all the northern boats ready and Ekhdur will attack below Nekhen at dawn five days from now." Menhes told him of the the two thousand Nubians who would be their relief forces above Edfu, then asked, "What about our own boats, Ar-Chab?" "They are already uncovered and fresh pitched. They will be put in the water each night and pulled back up on the banks each morning to be sure they are watertight."

"I want the Nubian relief forces brought down in our boats to the point across the river from Edfu as soon as we have landed and attacked. That will take thirteen of the long boats. Three hundred of your warriors will remain at the landing in two other long boats. Five skiffs will stay with them and five more will tie up and wait behind us on the Edfu bank. These will be used for messages to Khafu and Ekhdur. I expect to signal across the river for anything we need to move the troops into battle; otherwise one of us will send a skiff across.

"Send a skiff to Asyut today; Ekhdur's plans appear to be complete from what you tell me. Khafu is to seize the three royal barges and everything that floats they find anywhere near Nekhen and tow them away just as soon as their troops have landed. I want the barges towed to join the reserve boats across from Edfu where I can see them. Then we will know that Djo-Aten has no way to escape except toward El-Kab or Edfu. Ekhdur already knows to drive him away from El-Kab if he goes there, which I think he will. As for any local boats near Edfu your crews will tow them away just as Khafu's crew's do at Nekhen. I cannot afford to have Hadu escape. You are to send this message to Khafu. Repeat it back to me and then get the skiff underway."

Ar-Chab returned from dispatching the skiff and Menhes then said, "Now, Ar-Chab I want to talk about what happens if we cannot sustain the attack. We have too many families and village elders who are loyal to us to simply fight to the death. They would all be executed as you well know. If we must retreat our forces will be the last to board the available water craft. We will fight until Ekhdur's men have crossed the river and the Nubians have joined them. Then we will cross and start marching for the first cataract. Ekhdur is to take his men and boats back down the river and start evacuating the families at as many of our northern stations as possible. They will sail on past Aqqrem and make their way to the Crocodile Lake camp. I do not think the Scorpion will emerge from our assault strong enough to do anything in Lower Nile territory for a long time. I am quite certain this will not be necessary, Ar-Chab but if I die and the battle goes against us you are to carry out these plans."

In spite of the feverish activity time hung heavy for Menhes and Ar-Chab during the next three days. On the third day traders were sent to Nekhen and Edfu with some valuable Sumerian amulets saved for the purpose. As expected the priests heard about them and rushed out to barter at both trading yards. The traders stayed until late in the afternoon before taking their boats downstream as if they were returning to Asyut. At sundown they turned around and sailed back to where Menhes was waiting.

The crew chiefs reported that everything appeared normal at both Nekhen and Edfu. Hadu had returned from seeing Sel-Abba off with the Nubian troops who had been relieved only the day before. A poor thief was being executed at Nekhen and Djo-Aten had appeared briefly, glowering at the gathered crowd before returning to his house. The crew chief thought he looked drunk but could not be sure from the distance at which he had observed him. There had been no signs of extra security at either place though there were the usual large numbers of guards and army troops in evidence, many of them milling around in the trade yards.

As darkness fell over the Kom Ombo the boats were silently pushed into the water and placed at landings close to where the attack troops for each boat slept. During the night skiffs came in to report on the number of fires burning at the villages above Edfu and below Nekhen. Nothing unusual had been noticed anywhere and by the time there was light enough to see by troops were debarking near the Nubian camp above Edfu.

Sel-Abba with eight of his captains had been brought to the Kom Ombo landing the night before. His was the first boat to land at Edfu and he immediately joined his troops, spreading the word that they would attack at sunup. Ekhdur's troops were marching on Nekhen and Khafu's boats were busily rounding up every craft of any sort along the river including the three royal barges. There were minor skirmishes as crews and owners protested the taking of their boats but they were rapidly put down and the boats towed to the other side of the river. Of course dogs began barking and soon townspeople and guards came running to the water's edge to see what was going on.

Menhes landed with his main force and signaled to Sel-Abba to form his left flank as Ar-Chab deployed his troops according to the battle plan Menhes had given him. The Nubians circled wide to the west, coming at Edfu's main garrison on a dead run. As Hadu's troops heard the shouting they began to run in confusion and met Ar-Chab's center thrust force head on in an open barley field just outside the town. They had no time to form an effective line and as the Menku warriors' clubs came down in hammer blows in hand-to-hand fighting the field was littered with corpses within minutes. Just as swiftly the warriors fell back and regrouped and the Nubians moved on the field to pick up the surviving stragglers. Hadu had retreated with his personal guards to the royal post below Edfu and was frantically forming a battle line when Menhes attacked with his right flank forces from the east, marching up from the river.

Again the maces swung with telling effect as the opposing armies closed and again the Menku warriors fell back quickly as Hadu's support troops began their counter attack. Now the Nubian slings began felling the leaders of the charge and the javelins took out the secondary men. A veritable rain of arrows suddenly flew from the western end of Hadu's line and his screaming men, fell where they stood. Trying to turn and run others were hit by another shower of arrows and now at last they could only return to face Menhes forces' spears, clubs and swords.

Hadu lay dead beneath the bodies of six of his personal guardsmen and all but three of his captains were either dead or dying by the time Ar-Chab's center forces swept across the field and through Edfu itself. The townspeople had fled at the first shouting and the few defenders who had hidden in the houses and tents were quickly rousted and skewered or beheaded. Menhes had moved on down past Edfu to the southern garrison and attacked it before the captains there could make a battle formation. The Nubians followed and drove Hadu's troops back toward Menhes's onrushing, mace-swinging flank which overran them.

In wide arcs the Nubians joined the Menhes forces and they descended on Edfu to trap what was left of the royal troops between them and Ar-Chab's warriors. The standards of Upper Nile, drenched in blood were trampled in the dirt beside or beneath the bodies of the guidons.

Quiet spread all across the town as the Menku forces regrouped down by the river to count their casualties. Ar-Chab had lost seventy of his mace men and had sixteen spearmen so severely injured as to be out of combat for the rest of the day. Menhes could count fifty-three missing mace and swordsmen and had twenty-two injured spearmen. Sel-Abba had not lost a man and his warriors were busily retrieving their javelins and arrows.

Menhes went to the water's edge where a skiff sailed up and landed. Khafu stepped off and after they had embraced Menhes told him the battle for Edfu was over. Khafu had remained in the Nekhen vicinity long enough to learn what Ekhdur had encountered and the results were similar except that Djo-Aten had escaped with a large force toward El-Kab. At the south garrison of Nekhen...its largest and best trained...the troops there had not attacked by the time Khafu had left and he could not see it from the river.

Menhes could only surmise that Nekhen was being abandoned and the Scorpion would regroup at El-Kab. He signaled for the boats with the Nubian reserves and his own relief warriors to cross over below Edfu. Khafu lead these forces to the landing above Nekhen where they would march on El-Kab in another pincers movement with Ekhdur's forces to drive Djo-Aten into the open fields. Menhes now marched his three forces in a wide line toward Nekhen, again with the Nubians far to the west to intercept any flight to the desert.

Ekhdur circled to the west and came on El-Kab from the North as the southern relief forces were reaching it from the East. The south garrison troops had marched to El-Kab without a fight which provided Djo-Aten with a formidable force at El-Kab to defend him. The onrush of the two Menku forces breached the royal line and Djo-Aten, taking command himself ordered a retreat toward Edfu, not knowing what had happened there.

Ekhdur ordered the southern relief forces back into their boats to sail upriver and land where Menhes could see them and wait for further orders. He then formed a long line and began a slow but relentless pursuit of Scorpion as his forces headed south. His men would take cover then run forward to just out of javelin range. They would then again take cover to prepare for a counterattack by Djo-Aten's troops. None came so they kept repeating the action, driving the royals inexorably toward Menhes' forces on the way down from Edfu to meet them.

As the morning wore on Djo-Aten let the mace wielders...about a thousand in all...fall back from his main forces and prepare to engage Ekhdur's troops as a further delaying action. He then moved the army toward Edfu at forced march expecting to join with Hadu's troops there and counterattack. The Scorpion still had no warning that he was driving toward another more powerful force and his troops marched with banners flying and the Standard of Upper Nile carried high.

Ekhdur's troops charged the mace swinging royals and again breached the line they had formed. The isolated west flank attempted to counterattack Ekhdur's center column but were driven back by javelins and fell into a broad retreat to regroup with the east flank about a mile to the south. The royals' center column had been all but destroyed in hand-to-hand fighting with the Menku warriors. Those who survived were surrounded and driven back toward Nekhen under guard.

The South Garrison warriors fought well but clubs and maces were no match for the javelins and slings of the forward center column Ekhdur commanded. Had he held the Nubian reserve troops at Nekhen their archers would have decimated the South Garrison detachment in minutes as they tried to escape the javelins. That was not the strategy however. Ekhdur's object was to force Djo-Aten to continually divert more of his main forces to protect his rear while he with no reserves marched into the advancing Menhes allied army.

Abgar, the priest walked beside Djo-Aten as Menhes had expected he would and they were to be taken alive. The second detachment from the South Garrison was made up of spearmen for spear-thrust combat; the javelin and sling forces stayed with Djo-Aten and Abgar and the remaining hand fighters. With each breach of the royal rear line more prisoners were taken but Ekhdur's own losses were mounting and he desperately need to regroup. His troops had been fighting since dawn without food or water and as the day began to end he had the horns blow the signal for retreat. The Menku army fell back about a half mile and waited for the response of Djo-Aten's forces. Suspecting a trap Djo-Aten pulled his own rear guard closer to his main corps and closed ranks in preparation for nightfall.

This was better than Ekhdur could have hoped for. The distance to Edfu was too great for the armies to meet that day with anything less than exhaustion; it was Menhes' plan to stop and set his line to wait for the royal army to march against his center column between the wide-swung Menku and Nubian flanks. With Ekhdur in pursuit it would have been suicide for Djo-Aten to try to flank Menhes. All the boats on the river were in the hands of the Menku army and reserves could be landed quickly and effectively at the optimum points at any time. If the royals turned to flee into the desert the two Menku armies would be joined in a sweep and the forces against Djo-Aten would be absolutely overpowering.

Djo-Aten had sent runners ahead toward Edfu after he left El-Kab. They were to carry orders for Hadu to march overland to meet the Nekhen forces at a point roughly two thirds of the distance between Nekhen and Edfu. The Edfu Garrison troops were to be brought down along the river banks to drive off any landing forces there. As night came these runners stood before Menhes' campfires in abject dismay. Learning of Hadu's death and realizing the battle would be over the next day they gave Ar-Chab the messages they had received from Djo-Aten in return for their lives.

Menhes called Sel-Abba and Seb to him and told them of the capture of the runners. "Sel-Abba, do you have two men who would run to meet Djo-Aten this night with a message? They will risk their lives if they do; you know that. I will not order it. They have to be willing to do it. But it will save many lives tomorrow if Djo-Aten believes Hadu's army is camped where we are now and waiting for him." Sel-Abba returned to his reserve troops and came back with two tall warriors who were willing to run in the night to Djo-Aten's camp and deliver the message that the forces were at Edfu and that Hadu was there with them.

Ekhdur's losses were reported to Khafu who sailed the long boats toward Edfu and brought back sufficient reserves to allow full columns when light would again appear the following morning. He also took the same message to Ekhdur that the Nubians were to deliver to Djo-Aten. Ekhdur prepared to launch an all out attack at dawn and under cover of night moved his forward forces to within a mile of Djo-Aten's army.

The Nubian runners were received by Djo-Aten who had ordered that any messengers would be brought directly to him. As he sat by the fire with Abgar they told him that Hadu waited for him below Edfu. The selected runners did not know that Hadu was dead but since Djo-Aten and Abgar would themselves be dead the following day they unwittingly told the truth.

Djo-Aten called his captains and laid out his plans for the morning. They were to march southwest so that when they met Hadu his army would form a northeast pincer line anchored at the river. The Nekhen forces would swing toward the center forming a reinforced V-shaped line for Ekhdur to march into. The two royal armies would close the jaws around the Menku forces and crush them.

At early light Ekhdur's horns blew and his army moved forward with a roar, shouting and screaming at the top of their lungs. Just as swiftly Djo-Aten's forces fell back with minimum resistance. Now Ekhdur was sure Djo-Aten had believed the message he got the night before. He quickly split the rear guard line and drove through it with his center column, engaging the two divided forces with his flanking warriors as he headed directly toward Djo-Aten's main army.

Djo-Aten ordered his rear guard to retreat and beat back Ekhdur's center column to form a cohesive line. He then retreated across the entire front and began his southwest march, heading directly toward the Nubian west flank. Menhes' guidons raised the Standard of Upper Nile and the banners of Hadu's armies. Djo-Aten's forward runners were again received; unbelievably they were the same two Nubians sent to him the night before. Menhes began the diversionary northeastward march when he was barely in sight of Djo-Aten's east flank, leading Djo-Aten to believe it was Hadu carrying out his orders.

What Djo-Aten now saw clearly was the Nubian force, Menhes' west flank. They were moving to the southeast and the Scorpion had no reason to believe they were not loyal to him. He began his sweep to form the west jaw and when his army was in place began the counterattack on Ekhdur's rapidly advancing army. Ekhdur's forces swung hard toward the river where they joined Menhes main army and advanced on Djo-Aten's center.

Now the Nubians attacked and Djo-Aten's forces began to move back toward the northwest, immediately encountering Ekhdur's west flank. They tried to breach the center in hopes of encircling Ekhdur's army only to find that the royal army itself was caught in the pincers of the two Menku armies. Again the javelins and hail of arrows of the Nubian troops threw Djo-Aten's troops into disarray and Ekhdur's spearmen moved in to drive them against Menhes' mace and sword forces.

There was no hope for Djo-Aten as he came to realize he had marched into a huge trap. The desert was closed off to him and a powerful, intact army lay between him and the river. His forces were being slaughtered from front and rear, and javelins and arrows continued to tear at him from his flanks.

At last the royal guard was surrounded with its two hundred picked warriors defenseless. Djo-Aten bravely raised his hand and ordered the Standard of Upper Nile lowered to the ground in humiliation. He and Abgar kneeled and bowed their heads as Menhes walked forward to where they were. He told them to rise and ordered Djo-Aten to hand him the crown of Upper Nile which he put on his head. He took the royal sword and buckled it to his hip without a word. Then he directed Sel-Abba to strip the gold armlets and the king's ring from Djo-Aten's arms and hand. These were to be taken to Addi-Hoda when his troops returned to Nubia as free men.

Djo-Aten asked if he might speak. Menhes granted him permission. "Who are you, My Lord?" "I am Menhes the son of Menku, son of Vedh-Ku who was the only son of Ghum, King of Upper Nile to survive the ax of your grandfather, Scorpion. These are my brothers, Ekhdur and Khafu. This is Sel-Abba, Prince of Nubia, son of Addi-Hoda." Djo-Aten fell prostrate to the ground, "Let me die like a warrior, My Lord. I ask no other mercy except that you spare my family."

"For the sake of your warriors who fought well and bravely I will grant your wish." With that Menhes swiftly took a peg and drove it through Djo-Aten's skull with his mace as Seb stood behind him. He then ordered Ar-Chab to behead Abgar.

Turning to the assembled victorious armies he shouted, "I am Menhes, King of Upper Nile,

Lord of Nekhen, Emissary of Aten. You are free of Scorpion and Abgar. You will never again be condemned by a priest without a hearing before the King." There was a shout and the warriors began to prepare for the feast of victory. Boats from Kom Ombo were brought to a nearby landing with provisions and beer for the celebration.

Menhes however first went with Ekhdur, Khafu, Ar-Chab and Sel-Abba to where the wounded warriors were being treated and then to the wounded prisoners to allow them the same treatment, such as it was. Mostly all that could be done was to try to stop the bleeding in open wounds and bathe and bind the injuries. Menhes spoke to Khafu, "Send the boats to Kom Ombo and bring the families to claim their dead. Tomorrow the people of Nekhen and Edfu can do the same for Djo-Aten's troops. I am sorry that the dead warriors who came with you and Ekhdur will have to be buried where they fell." Turning he saw Sel-Abba and asked, "What is the custom of your country when warriors die in battle, Sel-Abba?" "They are burned on a pyre, My Lord." "Then let your warriors attend to them in the morning, Sel-Abba. I will be there for the rites."

Ar-Chab asked what was to be done with the bodies of Djo-Aten and Abgar. Menhes thought a moment and said, "As for Abgar, if he has a family let them tend to it. Djo-Aten's body will be placed on a pyre on one of the reed barges. His oldest son will light the pyre and the barge will be allowed to float down the river until it sinks where it will. He was a king."

The next morning Menhes gave orders for the day, "Sel-Abba, take your troops back to the Edfu Garrison. There is food and shelter there. Following that I wish you would come to Nekhen and we can decide what we will do next. As for the warriors who have been at Edfu for a year let them return to their families. They can take the armlets and ring to Prince Addi-Hoda and report the outcome of the battles." Sel-Abba agreed that this was good and left immediately.

"Khafu, send Seb to our father at Crocodile Lake and tell him I am king now. He will want to know as soon as possible that you and Ekhdur are well and what our casualties have been. He and Mother must stay there until we can secure the northern stations all the way to Aqqrem. That will take some time but I do not know how long. MeriLyth and her mother and sisters must also remain there until I am sure Nekhen is safe for them.

"Take command of all the boats we have. I will wish one of the royal barges sent to Edfu to bring Sel-Abba to Nekhen. Ar-Chab will sail with the captains to Nekhen before you and Ekhdur and I arrive in Djo-Aten's personal barge. I want our long boats to deliver three thousand of our warriors to the Nekhen South Garrison where they will remain stationed for the time being. "The remaining warriors will cross to Kom Ombo to wait for you, Ar-Chab. After Nekhen is put in order you will lead them to the villages south of the first cataract with Sel-Abba's forces to secure Upper Nile from Nekhen south to Nubia. That will be a short campaign I believe and I will want to discuss it with you before you leave. I do not wish to start slaughtering people all over Upper Nile just because they served Djo-Aten. We were all forced to do that. His generals will be put to death, of that I am sure. They are common cutthroats and thieves.

"I wish your counsel, Ekhdur regarding the troops and priests at the outlying garrisons, both the ones to the south and those to the north. We will discuss this in days to come. "Khafu, if anything happens to me before I have established a full kingdom, our father is to be named Regent with all the powers of a king until he designates a ruler for the people. Now I think it is time for us to move on to Nekhen."

When Ekhdur's troops got to Nekhen they found pandemonium. During the night deserters from Djo-Aten's army had stolen back to El-Kab and told the news of his defeat. When word got to Nekhen before daylight the townspeople had stormed the temple and dragged the priests into

58

the trade yard where they were beaten; some had died from the injuries. The High Priest, Mertud was tied to a stake where he writhed in utter bewilderment as to what was going on.

As the warriors began to establish order they learned that Djo-Aten's family had escaped to the El-Kab granary and a detachment was sent to bring them back to Nekhen. On arriving at El-Kab they found bodies piled in the temple yard there and the heads of the Scorpion's six sons skewered on pikes, grotesquely arranged in a neat row. The bodies of his wife and daughters lay with those of senior priests from the temple, each with a spear through the heart.

Menhes was told of the murders when he stepped off the royal barge and turned to Ekhdur, "This will happen at every village and town if we do not swiftly bring order to them. Since we have all the boats we must send a force to Batuk. That is the next town to the north and Djo-Aten's forces will not yet know of his defeat. Do you know how many troops are at Batuk, Ekhdur?" "I do not, Menhes. But our traders were there shortly before our attack on Nekhen. Seb, do you know where they are?"

Seb ran down to the river and came back with one of the Menku traders who had his boat tied up there. The trader reported that there were no more than three hundred royal warriors at Batuk. It was an outpost for the North Garrison force at Nekhen. Menhes ordered Ekhdur to send three long boats, each with a captain and a hundred and fifty men to Batuk before the end of the day. "Send Djo–Aten's barge with his banner aloft ahead of the long boats. Let it stay off shore until the royal troops assemble at the river bank, which they will have to do for the king. Have your Captain of Guards call from the barge and tell them of Djo-Aten's defeat. They are to surrender and move back to the trade yard, leaving their weapons at the riverside. If they will not surrender sail downstream far enough to get the troops landed and march on Batuk and take it."

Menhes went on through the town to survey the damage and find the mood of the people. Everywhere he went he was cheered though no one knew who he really was. He decided to go on to El-Kab and bring the villagers from there to Nekhen where he would take his seat as king the following day when Sel-Abba and Ar-Chab would be there. He wanted the burials and funereal proceedings completed before he declared a feast to celebrate with the people of El-Kab and Nekhen.

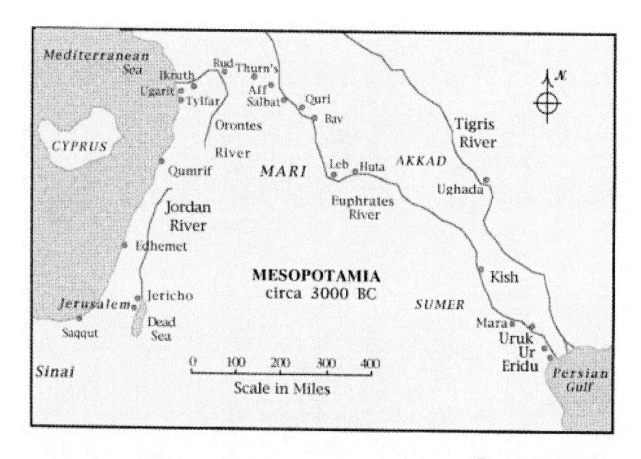

Figure 8: Map of Mesopotamia

BIRD GODDESS

Egypt, circa 4,000 BC

Illustrated by W. C. Cawthon
Figure 9: Bird-Beak Diety

CHAPTER SEVEN 'Rout at Mara'

Before sunup the robbers were forced to drag Eh-Buran's body out into the river a short distance and let it sink rather than leave it for the vultures. Then with their arms bound at the elbows they were tethered to each other, Ib-Seeg leading the way and carrying Eh-Buran's head firmly skewered on the end of his spear. Enlid and his grim faced party filed out on the long walk to Uruk.

When they reached the first fields, still some distance from the city the local farmers and their families came running to know what such a band of traders was doing with prisoners and a dead man's head on a spear. When they learned this was Ib-Seeg and the head was that of Eh-Buran it was all Enlid could do to talk them out of killing the prisoners on the spot. Questioning a shepherd among them Abdala learned that the gang was large and notorious for robbing and killing on both sides of the Euphrates; the king had sought to bring them to justice for some time. By the time they got to the White Temple a mob of shouting families surrounded them.

The commotion brought the temple guards on the run, spears ominously lowered for attack. Enlid stepped forward and raised his right hand to the captain of the guards, "We are peaceful traders from Ur. Last night our party was attacked by these men who intended to rob and kill us. Our dogs saved us and killed the leader of the gang whose head we have brought to present to the king as is the custom of Ur." "You have done well. Come with us to the temple and I will report this to the king and the high priest." The captain ordered his guards to take the prisoners and escort Enlid's band to the gates.

The king of Uruk stood with his arms folded while he received the captain's report; he then sent a messenger to call for the high priest before addressing Enlid directly. In a yard outside the walls of the temple there were brush arbors where scribes recorded what traders and pilgrims had brought to the city: food for the temple and the king's retinue; gold, silver and jewels for the treasury; arms for the king's guards and items for barter with traders, both local and from other domains. Miqel and Malil were fascinated with all the bustle and the wealth of goods in evidence. But they were awed by the grandness of the White Temple, its walls rising precipitously to great heights above the flat terrain of the city. Before they could take it all in the high priest came and stood by the king. After a brief conversation the king ordered Enlid and Abdala to come before him and state their purpose in coming to Uruk and to show cause for such a disturbance.

Enlid spoke for the party, again explaining their peaceful intent and giving an account of the attack. The king, Men-Chad-Rez, turned to the prisoners, "So, Ib-Seeg you have come to me at last. And I see you have brought me the head of your leader." "Mercy. Mercy, my Lord. We were starving wanderers intending to beg for food from these armed merchants when their dogs attacked us before we could greet them peacefully."

"Liar!" Abdala could not contain himself, "you had mutton to bribe our dogs and spears to kill us in the night. A scream in the darkness is all that saved us." "Silence!" Men-Chad-Rez turned to the high priest of the White Temple, "We know Eh-Buran all too well do we not, Ayn-Far?" "So we do. So we do. It is a shame that the dogs have denied us the pleasure of taking him alive. But it is just as well. These others will likely sleep with him and their fathers before another sun passes over us."

Men-Chad–Rez thought a moment and turned back to Ib-Seeg. "You will now tell us why there were only four of you. Eh-Buran's gang has many members; where are the others now? "I know of no gang, my lord. I tell the truth. The three of us met this Eh-Buran only two days ago when we were starving in the desert. He gave us water and told us to join him in foraging and begging for food. We found an abandoned reed boat and floated down the river until we saw smoke from this party's fires and thought to beseech their help." The other robbers nodded that this was true.

Raising his hand Men-Chad-Rez directed the captain of the guard to cut off the great toes of the prisoners. He and Ayn-Far stood in the shade of an arbor while the screams of the prisoners went unheeded. Ayn-Far called two priests who, following whispered instructions ran toward a group of tents at the edge of the barley fields. The prisoners were brought limping and stumbling back to the arbor and Men-Chad-Rez again spoke, "Ib-Seeg, you and Eh-Buran once lived in Uruk with your families before you killed a priest while you robbed the temple's treasury. Who are these others with you?"

One of the robbers seized the opportunity, "I am Ogtu and he is Gand. We are fishermen from Eridu. Eh-Buran and this man seized our boat and made us serve them for many days." A guard's staff slashed across his eyes and both fell to their knees. Men -Chad-Rez ignored the outburst, "Ib-Seeg, you will tell the truth now. Now!" Just then the two priests rushed forward with a young boy. When he saw Ib-Seeg he ran to him, "Father, Father. Where have you been? Why are you bound?"

"No! No! My lord, this is just a child. Do what you will with me but spare him. Please. I beg of you. Please." "The truth or the child's head on a pike. Now!" Ib-Seeg wept as the child was wrenched from his arms. "These are as I am, members of Eh-Buran's gang. The others are stronger than we are; even Eh-Buran was afraid of them. They number fifteen and are led by Vashi of Eridu who would have killed us if we did not find meat by today. They are a day by boat from here and are waiting north of the village of Mara in a stand of willows and palms. They may have already started down river looking for us; they don't trust us. They are well armed with swords and spears and have another boat."

Ayn-Far now spoke, "This sounds to be true. If it is or is not, who is to say?" Men-Chad-Rez ordered Ib-Seeg to be lashed to a post near the temple wall and given only water . The boy was to be held in full sight at the top of the wall, ready to be thrown down if it turned out that Ib-Seeg had lied. "Captain, you will take sixty armed guards in two parties. With thirty men you will go to Mara by land; the rest will sail up the river past Mara. You will gather more men from the fields around Mara and when you are ready to attack you will light three fires as a signal for the boat party to turn back to join you at the robbers' camp. You are to stay in sight of the river. If the robber-gang has left the lair the boat party will drive them to shore near where you are. Capture as many as you can but kill them without mercy if they do not surrender. Bring their heads here." Then to Ib-Seeg, "If they do not return with news that you have told the truth by the setting of the sun two days from now, the child will die before your eyes. Your torture will commence at that hour. If you have spoken truth the child will live and you will be given a swift and merciful death."

As Ib-Seeg and the boy were led away guards were summoned to behead Ogtu and Gand at sunrise the following day, Ib-Seeg to witness. Their heads would be mounted on pikes and placed alongside the speared head of Eh-Buran on the parapet of the temple facing the yard where they stood. "We will wait now, Ayn-Far. It is time to welcome our travelers from Ur. Let your servants prepare a sheep and bread for them and we will hear more from them in the morning." With that Men-Chad-Rez dismissed the crowd and walked to his own reed-roofed brick house not far from the temple wall.

Arpag's friend who had been standing at the edge of the crowd rushed to him and grabbed him by the shoulders. "How is it that you have returned to life, Arpag? I heard the bogs tell one of them called Lvad he had killed you so I just kept running all the way to the river." "I lay there for a long time, Geval. Then I too tried to find the river but these men from Ur found me. If they had not I would be dead." Geval explained that the danger of Eh-Buran's gang had become so great the captain of the guards did not want to organize a search party to hunt down bogs at this time. The king was alarmed that the bogs were becoming dangerous but considered one incident insufficient cause to throw the whole city into panic. "I do not know if you and I will find work here, Arpag. The people have enough for themselves but they are not inclined to send food to remote villages such as ours. If we bring our families here perhaps they will feed us but that is not assured; and that does nothing for the other farmers at home."

Ayn-Far joined Enlid and the Ur group for the meal that had been prepared for them. He wanted to know about Ur but before he could ask Enlid recounted their evening with Kalam-Bad and Mar-Dug. "That is good news indeed. So they have found the place for the secrets of the circle. Do you think Al Ubaid and the temple of Janna at Eridu can spare men and materials for the work?" "You will have to wait for Mar-Dug and Ifn-Lot to tell you that. I do not know. The temples have many priests but not so many workers anymore since the drought has forced longer hours in the fields with less yield from the crops. Perhaps when the rains come they will then be able to help."

As the fires burned down to flickering wisps of light Miqel and Malil were already sound asleep and Abdala was dozing off. The aged Ayn-Far wished them well and returned to his stark room in the temple. A guard was posted with the party until Enlid could dispose of his gold and jewelry.

Daybreak brought the grisly business of beheading Ogtu and Gand. Ib-Seeg collapsed in terror but was held up by the shoulders and forced to watch as their eyes were first gouged from the sockets and then at last their heads were hacked off with sharpened stone axes. It was not a clean severing as a sword would have performed but blow by blow until the spurting corpse reluctantly gave up its head. As each head fell to the sand a cheer went up from the crowd which included children as well as the men and women from the city and the surrounding countryside.

Miqel longed to talk to Ayn-Far but he and Malil had to first find his parents. Furthermore no children were permitted into the temple or even to address the High Priest unless he bid them to speak. Baldag had brought the flock back to just outside Uruk where he and Gahnya had planted barley and lentils and leaks. Their tent was as Miqel remembered it but he was surprised to find Baldag busily erecting a house of reeds large enough for the family including Miqel. Gahnya rushed out of the garden when she heard Miqel's call, "Oh, Miqel you have grown so big. Your father will be so proud." His two younger sisters peeked out from behind the tent flap and Gahnya called to them, "Ette, Bodi, come see your brother. Miqel, who is this you have brought with you?"

"It is Malil, Mama. He lives at Ur and attends Papa's academy. He and I have completed our basic work and Papa has let us come and visit until the second full moon after the next 'day when the sun and the stars are equals'." "Ette, run and fetch your father from the field. We must prepare a feast for our wizards and hear all about their schooling and their travels." Gahnya hugged Miqel and taking him and Malil by the hand led them to the tent where she broke a cake of raisins giving each half while she poured horns of goats' milk for them.

Baldag came running and lifted Miqel high above his head, laughing at how much harder it was to do than when last he had seen him. He greeted Malil and when Miqel explained their visit asked, "And how are Papa and Urunya?" "They are both well and send you good wishes. I must tell you about the great priest from the White Temple we have met; and he knows of Papa."

"I will hear all about these things. But now I must get back to the field. The time of rains comes soon and if the rains come this year we want all the food out of the fields and the garden before we lose it. Miqel, you and Malil can help your mother and your sisters and then later this day we will take the sheep to pasture." Baldag left them and Miqel and Malil went down to the garden with Gahnya while Ette and Bodi stayed to milk the goats.

With Arpag and Geval reunited Enlid and his party began trading with a gathering crowd of local merchants and traders from other locales. Scribes under the brush arbors in the trade yard kept count by markers and talismans as goods and produce were exchanged. Men-Chad-Rez watched the proceedings to insure that part of all trades was set aside for the city of Uruk and the maintenance of the White Temple. He was also there to settle any disputes that might arise; and there were plenty of disputes, some just haggling, others more serious.

Men-Chad-Rez approached Enlid, "Since you are the leader from Ur tell me how you wish to divide the gold armbands and crescents these criminals wore. They will serve as a reward to your group for the service you have rendered to us here in Uruk." "Let the pieces Eh-Buran wore be given to the White Temple so that the god will favor us on our journey back to Ur. We would give two armbands to Arpag and Geval to barter for sheep and goats they can drive back to their village; they lost their offerings for the temple to the bogs. For the remainder we will trade them for barley and lentils if such are to be had here." Men-Chad- Rez thought that was good and invited Enlid into the great temple for cheese and bread with Ayn-Far .

Ayn-Far wanted to know more about Mar-Dug, "Did he appear well? Has Coban-Bul seen to his needs with care?" "Yes. Coban-Bul is most devoted to him and Kalam-Bad and his warriors were protective just by their appearance; I would not want to engage even one of them in a fight", Enlid laughed. "They are indeed giants among men. That is why Prince Kalam-Bad was chosen to accompany Mar-Dug on this expedition so far away from us. I am getting old and my duties will soon fall to Mar-Dug. My eyes no longer give me assurance that what the wizards propose is right in the search for the secrets of the circle and the square. Do you know what I am talking about?"

"I listened to Mar-Dug and Ifn-Lot question the two young boys from my friend Akhuruk's academy who were with us yesterday. I do not pretend to understand it but Miqel, son of Baldag who lives here in Uruk drew a diagram in the sand and his skill and knowledge greatly impressed the priests. Mar-Dug wishes to know him better when he has completed the course on the Secrets of the Circle under Akhuruk. I do not know what that means but Mar-Dug planned to talk to Akhuruk about it." "You know more than most. This Miqel must be astonishing for Mar-Dug to have talked to him at all. It is not the way of our senior priests to waste their time with children, or for that matter men who cannot comprehend what we do. Where is Miqel now? Was there not another boy with him

"The other boy is his friend, Malil and he is also very bright. They will be staying with Baldag the shepherd for many days before returning to Akhuruk's academy. Malil wants to follow in your service, Men-Chad-Rez". "I will send for them after you have gone but not until we have dealt with Eh-Buran's gang. I hope the captain will bring Vashi and that band in alive so we can make a spectacle of them to discourage others from getting similar ideas of revolt against the law and the temple." Men-Chad-Rez glanced at Ayn-Far, "Enlid, it is time for us to go and let this holy man get some rest before the day is spent. I have other duties to perform but I do wish you to stop at the gate tomorrow before you leave. Ayn-Far, will you be there to bless their travel?" "I will be there. And thank you, I do need rest."

Captain Rom-Sha and the king's guards came overland to Mara with his troops late in the afternoon. The village elders gathered to ask his purpose in being there and when told sent for twelve strong farmers to go with him. These brought clubs and a few spears with them and were eager to engage in a good fight. According to the elders Eh-Buran's gang had been terrorizing the village off and on for some time but lately it had been worse. The villagers could not defend against the swords the killers carried. Their grain had been stolen in broad daylight and even young women had been taken recently; their fate was not known.

The boat from Uruk had sailed well past the supposed hideout of Vashi and his band. There was no visible activity there but a large reed boat without sails was tied to a willow at what looked like the site Ib-Seeg had described. Looking back toward Mara they caught sight of three plumes of smoke and immediately moved back downstream to a point a little way from the robbers' lair. The main force debarked leaving five men to take the boat and make for the place where Vashi and his men had tied their boat. They were to seize that boat and tow it to the Mara landing and to wait there for the king's guards

Rom-Sha's strategy was for the two raiding parties to converge on Vashi from opposite directions, preventing flight or ambush in case they were spotted too soon by lookouts. The king's boat had attracted the attention of an unseen lookout as it sailed past. He rushed to Vashi, "Why would a guards boat with thirty or more armed men be sailing upstream just now? Do you suppose the people of Mara got a message to the king that we were in this area?" Vashi stirred uneasily, "Did they see you?" "No, I was well hidden, but they did not seem to be looking for anything either." At that another lookout burst into the grove, "Something is going on at Mara. If you look you can see smoke from three fires that were set only moments ago. The people of Mara have nothing to cook; we have seen to that. What do you make of it?" "Head for the boat. We will cross to the other side a little distance down stream before anybody can reach here from Mara. If the sailing boat comes back we will already be gone. We take the women with us."

Rom-Sha split his force into two groups, with the farmers and twelve guards accompanying him on a march along the river. The remaining guards set out to attack the camp from the east, a few hundred yards from the river. The landing party from the boat did not arrive in time to intercept the gang before they got to their boat. By the time Rom-Sha got where he could see them they were heading for the opposite bank.

Fortunately the boat crew had spotted them and was swiftly sailing after them when Rom-Sha shouted for them to come back. He and his combined forces waded out to the boat and boarded, "Try to get between them and the far bank. They have no sail and the water is too deep at midstream to use their poles. They are already being carried down stream but the wind is with us. Even loaded as we are I believe we can catch them in the water."

Vashi and his band immediately caught the significance of Rom-Sha's maneuver and their plight. They had brought five women from Mara with them and now shoved them to the stern of their boat where they were in full sight. Vashi shouted,"If you attack us we kill the women." Two of the farmers recognized their wives and pleaded with Rom-Sha for their lives. Rom-Sha hesitated and then commanded the boat to move ahead, "Vashi, we know who you are and who you have with you. Ib-Seeg has told us everything and waits for you at Uruk. Ogtu and Gand are dead, their heads beside that of Eh-Buran on the White Temple wall. Give up and you will be returned to Men-Chad-Rez for a quick and decent death."

Vashi raised his sword to kill the first hostage but before he could act a spear was rammed through his heart by a robber standing behind him. "We will do as you say. Some of us have killed no man and do not deserve death." The other gang members broke into fighting among themselves and the women tumbled overboard and began to sink. Rom-Sha's boat moved among them and dragged them, wet and frightened but uninjured into the boat. "Head for shallow water" Rom-Sha commanded, "Women and farmers wade ashore and join the king's guards at Mara. We can handle this now."

The boat turned back and bore down on the reed skiff where the gang continued struggling. Rom-Sha called out, "Stop fighting or no mercy for anyone. Ib-Seeg will tell what is truth. If some deserve to live Men-Chad-Rez will decide that at the temple. I will take either you or your heads back to him tomorrow. Move toward the bow of your boat. Leave the dead and your weapons in the stern." There was hesitant murmuring but the remaining robbers slowly complied.

By now both boats were miles below Mara and the sun was low in the sky. The guards' boat pulled alongside the skiff and attached a mooring line to tow it to the west bank of the river. A decent spot for landing appeared and Rom-Sha with his contingent of guards and prisoners waded ashore. They left the bodies of Vashi and three other robbers in the skiff for the boat crew to tow to Mara. The dead could be dealt with later. The wounded had to be tended to so they could be brought before Men-Chad-Rez the next night.

At Mara the villagers, led by the armed farmers originally assigned to Rom-Sha rushed out to greet the victorious guards. The elders demanded the right to take the prisoners and deal with them then and there. But Rom-Sha ordered them to stand back and hold their peace. "Men-Chad-Rez will see that justice is done. Select two from your number to go back to Uruk with us. They will tell the king what Eh-Buran's gang has done to the people of Mara and identify which of these thugs deserve torture...which deserve a quick death." The elders agreed that this was reasonable and dispersed the crowd as Rom-Sha gathered his troops for the return.

By the time they got to the landing the boat crew had attended to the beheading of the bodies of Vashi and the three other robbers who had died in the fight on the river. The bodies had already been dumped at center stream in the Euphrates and the heads mounted on spears to be taken to Men-Chad-Rez. Even with two boats there was not room for all the members of the assembled party. Rom-Sha detailed a guard of eight to take the prisoners back to Uruk in their skiff. The robbers' weapons were moved to the guards' boat; these, especially the swords would be worth a fortune.

The thieves sullenly crawled aboard, eyeing each other with suspicion and loathing. Nevertheless every murmur was instantly quashed with the shaft of a guard's spear across the eyes. Escape from the sailing vessel was hopeless with its armed guards and the two elders from Mara only a few feet away at any time. Rom-Sha and the remaining guards would return to Uruk in the royal boat.

The sun had set and the chief of the boat crew put in to shore at a sheltered inlet he had noted on the trip upriver. The boats were quickly emptied and the parties began to settle down for an uneventful night. There was so little food in Mara that Rom-Sha's guards could not have hoped to feed the villagers from their travel rations. It was better to leave them to take care of themselves now that they would be free from Eh-Buran's marauding thieves. The two elders were glad to have even the meager meal the guards offered. The prisoners got water, nothing else.

At the faintest sign of light the boats headed out into the river and floated with the current to make landing by mid afternoon. Once more a large crowd assembled as the party walked briskly toward the temple. Men-Chad-Rez was waiting and Ib-Seeg, still lashed to a stake in the sun was relieved to see that they appeared to have found he had finally told the truth.

The spears that impaled the heads of Vashi and the three thieves were stuck in the ground and Rom-Sha ordered the prisoners to prostrate themselves before Men-Chad-Rez who spoke, "Well done, Rom-Sha. You and your troops will be rewarded. Who are these others you have brought?" The elders from Mara stepped forth and identified themselves, explaining they had come to witness against the remaining eleven members of the gang. Men-Chad-Rez stepped before each of the prisoners in turn, asking the same question each time, "Death or torture and death?" Rom-Sha pointed to the robber who had killed Vashi and the elders asked for leniency for him since he had saved the women of Mara from murder. The king ruled, "You shall have the death of a soldier, a spear through your heart. You may then be buried by your family." "May the gods bless you for your mercy, my Lord." the prisoner responded. He was taken immediately to the place of execution but allowed to speak to his family before he died. The others were sentenced in accordance the wishes of the elders bringing to an end the scourge of Eh-Buran.

Ib-Seeg embraced his son and then as promised was swiftly beheaded with his own sword. His head joined the others on the temple parapet, macabre testimony to anyone tempted to follow in Eh-Buran's footsteps.

CHAPTER EIGHT 'The Far Meadow'

On the morning Enlid and the trading party left for Ur Baldag and his family arrived at the gate of the temple to see them off. Enlid agreed to take a goat from Baldag and deliver it to Akhuruk and Urunya and promised Miqel he would tell them all that had happened, especially about Mar-Dug and Ifn-Lot.

Men-Chad-Rez and Ayn-Far sent their greetings to the king and High Priest of Ur and Al-Ubaid along with bags of millet which were laid on the back of the goat for Akhuruk. Men-Chad-Rez spoke first, "May the gods protect you and prosper your work. The people of Uruk thank you for what you have done and wish you well." Ayn-Far nodded and placed his right hand on the forehead of each of the travelers to add his own blessing.

When they had gone Men-Chad-Rez called Baldag to him, "Your young son and his friend have apparently impressed Mar–Dug and Ifn-Lot greatly according to Enlid. When Mar-Dug returns from Ur and Eridu I will send for them and they will have an audience with Ayn-Far and the priests of the temple service." Malil wanted to speak but Miqel motioned for him to be quiet. Ayn-Far smiled at them but did not speak. After expressing their appreciation Baldag and Gahnya took the boys back to the tent.

Miqel and Malil spent their days gathering reeds for the new house which from their tent was across an irrigation ditch that flowed from the nearby river. There were a number of new reed houses being built at the same time, all being rushed to completion before the expected rains would begin in two to three weeks. As reeds close by were depleted the searches grew longer and longer; but there were other boys and girls helping their fathers and the gatherings were times of laughter and horseplay. Both Malil and Miqel were good marksmen with their slings and everyday they brought back fowl or turtles for meat. Sometimes there was time to catch a few fish for Ette and Bodi to grill.

Baldag would have liked to make the foundation and lower wall for his house with sun dried bricks but with the drought he could not afford to barter for them; and there simply was not time to make his own bricks by hand. The floor of smoothed sand would be covered with straw mats, the same as the curtains against the wind and dust. He and his family would be comfortable and flooding was unlikely even if the Euphrates rose past the normal levels of recent memory.

As he tied the bundles of reeds and wove them into a tightly thatched roof Baldag had Miqel and Malil dismantle Gahnya's oven. It was next to their tent and the bricks had to be toted across the ditch and carefully set in place for the baking of barley loaves. Gahnya supervised with a critical eye, leaving nothing to chance. She had learned the already ancient secrets of an effective oven from Urunya and certainly could not afford to have half-cooked or charred bread from careless construction. The main fuel was goat dung which must not be wasted. The fact was that nothing could be wasted whether in times of plenty or of scarcity; providing for a family's needs always came with maximum effort, even moreso during the shorter days of winter.

When the house was complete Baldag killed a sheep in celebration and invited friends to share their meal. The rebuilt oven worked to perfection with Miqel and Malil proudly taking credit. Neighbors brought dates and honey to make this a real feast the youngsters would remember. It was late in the day when the skin of wine was emptied and the fires had died down. As the guests returned to their tents and houses Baldag called his family together, "It is time for me to take the sheep to the far meadow where I hope there will be enough grass to fatten them. Miqel, you and Malil will go with me and I will show you the signs in the stars and how they are read to know when the moon will be full." Then to Gahnya, "We will leave in the morning and return twelve days after the next full moon. That will give Miqel and Malil time to return to Akhuruk by the second full moon."

Baldag was comparatively well off with a flock, which though small...only twenty sheep and four goats...was more than enough for his family. He also tended another dozen sheep for a friend who was slowly recovering from a snake bite. His two dogs knew which sheep were Baldag's and kept the flocks apart so there would be no question of ownership when lambs were born.

The far meadow was up the river from Uruk; driving a flock was slow and the animals had to be kept near water which meant following the meandering twists of the Euphrates. It normally took three days to get there but the land was so dry around Uruk that there was little grass left anywhere closer; the far meadow was Baldag's only alternative in the fall of the year. It was a lonely place and Baldag was glad to have Miqel and Malil for company with little fear for their safety. Vashi's gang was dead and there had been no reports of other robbers operating in that area. Bogs sometimes hunted between the Tigris and the Euphrates but most of them were known to be some distance to the east. The faster current of the Tigris brought more wildlife to its banks though it discouraged human settlement with its raging spring torrents making irrigation channels exceedingly difficult to maintain.

The goats were loaded with the shepherds' tent; skins for sleeping during the cooler nights ahead; two burning fire pots with enough oil for a week; quantities of cheese, unleavened barley loaves and lentils as well as dates, figs and raisins. They would be well fed even before they found game and fish which could be counted on in some measure for most of the days they would be there. Sticks and small logs sufficient for fires could be gathered along the river as they traveled. Baldag mused that young boys were particularly good at that chore.

Gahnya wished they could have stayed at home; there would be little more time to visit after their return before the young 'wizards' had to go back to the academy. But sheep were sheep and had to be fed. She and Ette and Bodi would card and weave the pile of wool left from the spring shearing. Much of what they wove would be for personal use but there would be some for bartering to obtain pottery, knives and copper products.

Miqel and Malil speculated on their visit with Ayn-Far and Mar-Dug which Men-Chad-Rez had promised on their return. Miqel spoke first, "We will get to see the inside of the White Temple and the works of the priests there. There will be paintings and drawings on the walls according to Papa; he saw it once." Malil commented, "I want to see the swords of Eh-Buran's gang. Enlid said some of them even had gold and jewels on the handles; they must have been stolen from princes like Kalam-Bad." Miqel answered, "No one knows how many people they killed or who they killed for that matter. They say it has been two years since they killed the priest and robbed the temple and they have been robbing and killing during that entire time. Perhaps we can learn where Vashi and his men came from."

Miqel looked up and caught sight of a low flying heron, "Look, Malil. Let's see if we can bring it down with our slings." They both started to run and Malil was first to release his shot. The pellet caught a wing causing the heron to drop several feet before it could recover. By then Miqel's sling whirred and the heron fell to the ground. Malil quickly killed the stunned bird and hung it on one of the goats for the evening meal. "Good work, boys.We will eat like kings if you keep that up," Baldag laughed, slapping their backs as they ran to get ahead of the flock. The dogs panted beside them, occasionally darting back to retrieve a wandering sheep.

With only a couple of hours remaining before sundown Baldag started to move the flock toward the river's edge to find a decent place to spend the night. Miqel and Malil ran ahead looking for pieces of driftwood for a fire, and for a stream or shallow area along the river bank where the sheep and goats could be watered. They had not gone far when they found a creek that was still flowing with enough water for their needs and a small grassy plot that would be perfect for bedding down. While they waited for Baldad they went down stream a short way and stripping, splashed into the water for a cooling swim. Baldag would do the same but only after he had tended to the flock and got a fire started.

After the heron was cooked and eaten the boys quickly fell asleep; Baldag waited for the moon to rise and for the sheep to settle down under the watchful eyes of the dogs. The night was peaceful with no sound except for the occasional screech of an owl and the 'ribbet-ribbet' calling of frogs.

In the morning as Miqel and Baldag placed the supplies on the backs of three of the goats Malil milked the remaining one. Their breakfast of cheese and raisins was hastily washed down with milk while the dogs moved the sheep to the far side of the creek, nipping at the heels of a balky ram that did not want to leave the water. As Miqel and Malil trotted ahead and called the dogs to them Baldag put out the fire. 55

They were approaching a bend in the river and he wanted to cut diagonally across to save walking and intercept the main stream by nightfall. They rested among a few palms while the sun was high, then continued their slow, uneventful plodding toward the far meadow.

They were less fortunate the second night, ending up sleeping in the sand near the bank of the river. Miqel and Malil managed to lure fish to the shallows with a few bread crumbs and netted four nice ones for their supper. Fresh fish was always a treat but one they had not enjoyed much during the long drought. The people had fished the Euphrates extensively to supplement the meager crops and produce from the gardens around Ur and Uruk. Eridu was better off, being on the gulf but even there only the boat people caught much in the way of edible-sized fish. Without a reed skiff at Uruk's landing it had been a waste of time to try for fish there. Baldag was amazed at the boys' proficiency in the art of fishing and praised them lavishly for it. They promised to do more of it when they got to the far meadow and Baldag intended to encourage them.

The night was hot as the travelers spread skins out on the sand for pallets to sleep on. Malil and Miqel were laughing at each other's imaginative descriptions of what saw in the constellations that shown so brightly in the heavens. "There. There is a pig." Miqel pointed to some stars near the horizon. "No, it is not. It is a turtle with a funny tail. And it crawled all the way from the other side of the sky this very night." Malil giggled. Baldag broke in, "Another night I will teach you the names of the star clusters but for now get to sleep. We have got to make the far meadow before sundown tomorrow and there is still a long way to go."

Long after the moon had set two scorpions squared off in mortal combat. The larger scorpion had come upon the smaller one skittering across the sand in search of food and immediately chased it. The smaller one finally turned and put up a fierce struggle before being flipped on its back with the other's stinger driven home in its abdomen. A third scorpion watched briefly and then shuffled away to get out of range of the victorious fighter. In so doing it came to where Miqel was sleeping and proceeded to crawl awkwardly across his leg. The creepy sensation caused Miqel to jerk his leg away which was all that was needed to make the scorpion feel threatened: it curled its tail under and penetrated Miqel's calf with its burning venom.

Miqel screamed, "Father, Father! I am bitten." He moved to the fire immediately but too late to know what had stung him so severely until Baldag grabbed a faggot and caught sight of the scorpion rushing away toward its nest. The pain was awful. The instant Baldag knew Miqel had been bitten by a scorpion he ran back to the fire and grabbed Miqel's leg to find the area around the sting already puffy. He carefully inserted the point of his knife and then began to try to squeeze as much venom out of the wound as he could before it entered the bloodstream, letting the blood flow freely to flush it out. It helped some but the wildly burning sensation was enough to bring a man to his knees and could cause serious consequences in a child. Miqel tried to be brave but the tears flowed as Malil stood by patting him on the shoulder in a futile attempt to soothe. Spasms seized the calf muscles and began moving up the leg, even as Baldag pressed the tip of his knife blade against a red-hot coal and then cauterized the spot against infection, lying across the struggling Miqel to hold him down in the process.

After about an hour the knotted muscles began to relax a little and Miqel fell into a fitful sleep; nevertheless all three moved closer to the fire to avoid any further trouble from these scourges of the desert country. Baldag hoped Miqel would be able to walk the next day, deciding to let him use the shepherd's crook when he waked up. As the shore birds began to chatter Baldag rose and gently stirred Miqel. "Try to stand up, Miqel." Malil jumped up and helped him to his feet but the muscles in Miqel's calf were cramped and he at first had to lean on the two of them to stand. They walked him slowly around the fire as the tension relaxed. "Sit down, Miqel; Malil and I will get everything ready to leave. Eat these dates and I will bring you some milk and the curds from yesterday."

By the time the goats were loaded and the sheep started to mill around Baldag Miqel was hobbling well enough with the help of the crook to set out. After walking for a while and with the heat from the blistering sun he returned the crook to his father, "I think I need to grow some more before I am ready for such a long crook, Father. And you need it; I would not be much good at chasing a sheep with it right now, would I?" Baldag smiled, "No, I think not but you must learn to use the crook when we get to the meadow. You are a big boy now and must take your turn looking after the sheep. That applies to you too, Malil." Both boys beamed as they went ahead of the flock again, Miqel's limp notwithstanding.

Baldag hoped to find water in the large pond at the upper end of the meadowland toward the river. A spring fed creek normally flowed into it at one end and though its flow would have abated there was still a chance that it would have been flowing after the past winter. There just had to be grass there, parched though it would be. As they came to the top of a rise there before them it lay...whitened by the sun, but grass, beautiful grass. And the pond, glittering as a soft breeze blew over it, shrunken to a third of its normal size, but there. Baldag was ecstatic and so were Miqel and Malil. They would have water without having to drive the sheep and the goats to the river everyday; and there was enough grass to fatten the sheep throughout their planned stay.

The flock was herded to a spot near the pond's outlet to the river where they could drink without fouling the upstream water. Miqel grabbed a waterskin and limped to the creek where he filled and soaked it to get it cool for the dusty travelers. The dogs frolicked in and out of the water, seemingly caught up in the momentary euphoria until Baldag, wanting to return the flock to the meadow put them to work. He climbed back up to the slope they had just come down and began to pitch the tent against a stone outcrop he had used over the years for shelter from the wind.

"How is the leg, Miqel?" "It is still sore, Father but not so bad I can't help out. Let me get the fire going this time and then I will fix our supper. We did not take any game or fish today but there is plenty to eat here." Just then Malil came running up with a large hare he had killed while the sheep were being watered. Baldag skinned it in short order and it was soon roasting on Miqel's fire. "While this is cooking I think you boys had better go down by the river and gather

72

as much firewood as you can, enough for tonight and tomorrow at least. We need to keep a fire going for the time we will be here and save the oil for the journey home." They got to their feet and headed for the river bank as fast as they could go. A few large pieces of driftwood would carry the fire and their cooking could be done on the sheep dung they gathered daily. It was a little scary each time anyone far from a town or village had to extinguish the fire in the oil pots. For if the fire went out it meant someone had to find such a community to get more. That in itself was dangerous for villagers were justifiably suspicious of all strangers and their dogs attacked before an intruder could be recognized as peaceable.

The days were long and for the boys often boring. At first they stayed in the shelter of the tent during the hottest part of the day and soon ran out of anything to talk about. They used their slings to make compasses and practiced their lessons, but without straightedges the figures did not come out very well. Except for showing Baldag how the construction worked these were just exercises that quickly lost their appeal. Baldag was fascinated yet not prepared to undertake the laborious and painstaking work necessary to comprehend the meanings.For the most part the dogs managed the sheep letting them roam throughout the meadow during the day then waiting for Baldag to drive them down for watering before sundown.

After they had been there a couple of weeks a light rain fell during the night. Fortunately Baldag was on watch and hastily fired up an oil pot which he placed in the tent to preserve the fire. The cool breeze that followed was the most refreshing experience any of them had had since the prior winter and Baldag let the boys sleep late the following morning. When they rose he sent them out to find more and larger pieces of wood before they could get soaked if the rains continued. These they brought back and covered with skins to keep the precious fuel dry. Miqel and Malil with Baldag's coaching built a small, crude oven against the outcrop adjacent to the tent so they could bake in addition to roasting, grilling and boiling their food over the open fire. It was good that they did for the first rain was just the beginning of longer and harder rains that fell, soaking everything including the tent for several days in in a row. Everything had to be cooked over dung and that meant it was mostly boiled fare which soon became tiresome.

The boys spent more time fishing which also brought the opportunity of downing an occasional duck that wandered too close to their favorite spot in a stand of rushes stretching along the river bank not far from the meadow. With additional rains however the creek rose to a torrent and the pond began to creep back over the thin grass that had sprung up in the silt that was the old bed. Even more rain had fallen in the north and the Euphrates grew wider. As the current grew more swift Baldag kept Miqel and Malil away from the river unless he was with them and that was neither often nor long at a time which translated to no fish except the spindly little packages of bones in the pond.

The rains ceased as quickly as they began leaving clear skies and cool nights. Miqel and Malil stayed up with Baldag each night until the moon had climbed well up in the sky. He began to teach them the locations of the constellations and their names and to show them which sign the moon rose in and in which one it set for that time of the year. "The year begins with the Ram and there it is. Can you make it out, Malil? Do you not see that it does look like a ram, Miqel?" "Oh, yes. But should not the Bull be next to it and Fishes on the other side?" Miqel wanted to know. "They are. You are not looking high enough. Do you see those bright stars over there? Now point your finger at them and move it down and to the left; see the other bright star? Close your eyes a little...squint just so and the Bull will jump right out at you." Malil became excited, "I see it. I see it. Don't you see it, Miqel?" "I think so. Yes, I do; I really do. Isn't it wonderful!"

From there on around, up and down in the sky Baldag pointed out each 'sign' until they were back to rhe Ram. The following night Baldag told them, "Now we will divide the heavens into the seasons. We are just past the beginning of autumn which follows the summer. Before the Twins get to where the Bull is tonight we will head back home so you boys can be at the academy when the moon is full like Papa said. That is how I know when to begin driving the flock back toward Uruk." Malil asked, "How do you remember where the Bull was, or any of the signs from one month to the next?" "I chose the spot where we are standing, down here in the meadow so I can sight across the center tent pole to the heavens. Look that way now. There is the Lion straight up from the tent pole; do you see it?" "I do. But how do you know where the Bull is supposed to be?" Malil wanted to know.

Without a word Baldag walked up past the tent and out on the rock ledge as Miqel and Malil followed. He knelt down in a shallow depression and motioned for them to come near. "This notch I have made in the stone years ago is where I could see a very bright red star rising early one evening." Then carefully turning around toward the other side of the depression, "This notch is where that same star set that same night. Now, what does that tell you?" The boys looked at each other and back at Baldag shaking their heads without understanding. "If I use my sling to draw half a circle, right from where I am standing and it just touches the two notches then I can divide it in two. From the center of the half circle to that halfway point...see the line I drew there?...it has to be pointing due South would you not agree?"

"And the line connecting the notches runs from West to East, does it not?" Miqel wanted to know. "Surely it does. What is important is to know which sign is nearest to the east line when the new moon first appears. Then I can know when 'the day the sun and the stars are equals' comes, in the spring and after the summer." "That's how your Papa knew when to tell us to come back to the academy isn't it, Miqel?" "I am sure it must be. And that is why the priests dig the trenches and build the gates. Do you not think so, Father?" "I know that is at least partly why they do it but I don't know enough to explain all that to you. Nor do I need to know so much. This little spot here is all I need to tell the seasons and the day to go home. It would tell me which direction to go if I did not already know it. Something else tells me it is time for young boys to be asleep. We will talk more about this tomorrow."

Early the next morning two young wizards burst forth with unbounded energy. Baldag could not imagine what had brought about such a frenetic display, "What in the wide world are you two up to?" "We want to build a 'star-trench' of our own and I know just where to do it." Miqel proclaimed, "That is if we have your permission." "Before I promise anything are both of you prepared to stay up all night and watch the star you select move all the way from one side of the sky to the other? Don't answer yet. It takes several nights of searching and watching in order to find a star that is not too hard to follow; there are myriads of stars, you know. Once you have decided on a star and know how long after the moon first rises before that star will rise you cannot take your eyes off of it for more than a few moments all night or you will lose track of it. You must count on wasted nights during which that will happen."

"We are prepared, Father." "All right then. Now tell me where you want to make your star-trench?" "At the far end of the outcrop there is a large rock that stands apart, separated by about six or seven cubits of sod between it and the ledge. We could dig a three cubit deep trench there inside the arc of the half circle." Miqel explained. "Let's go have a look after we have had something to eat and you have finished your chores. Miqel, get the fire going while we still have coals; then run down to the creek and fill this goatskin with water. Malil, it is time to milk the goats and mash the curds from the last couple of days." In the entire time they had been gone never had chores been done so quickly. With breakfast over both boys looked at Baldag with that expectant look that demands a response. "Well, let's go see the site of your trench."

Baldag bent down and fingered the sod, "I guess you two can dig this. But it is going to be hard going and slow I fear. There is clay in it and digging with nothing more than sticks is a problem in any soil. Start out by digging the trench only one and one-half cubits deep; and you must dig a drainage ditch down the slope or you will be swimming after the next rain." "I found an old limb yesterday down by the river when we were gathering firewood. Where it broke off the tree left the end with a big, flat part and it is so dry it is as hard as this rock. We were going to burn it but after last night I think we can use it better to dig with, don't you, Miqel?" "Yes, I do Malil. Let's get it and start digging so we can pick a star tonight."

After insuring the death of Ib-Seeg and Eh-Buran and getting away with their boat the five bogs made their way back to camp where Toq reported to Oghud all that had happened. "Man Lvad hurt lives. We try to steal goat from traders. Thieves get there first; they say they kill traders and little boys. Then Uruk men blame bogs. We yell so dogs bite thieves. We steal thieves' boat with all this food. We bring food to families." "This good," Oghud began, "did traders kill thieves?" Fyd spoke, "Dogs kill one. Traders grab others. Hear one say, 'Kill all'. Did not stay. Stole boat. Came to camp." By then men, women and children were tearing at the food, eating it raw until they could hold no more that day. Toq's mate fainted and he lifted her gently and carried her to the fur she had been sleeping on. There she gave birth to a boy, safe for the time being at least.

After resting the hunting parties set out as usual. Days passed with very little in the way of meat being brought in and Oghud was worried. Lvad's injury seemed to be healing and he was getting surlier each day. It was obvious that the pain was gone, his mood was one of hateful resentment for the humiliation he had suffered. Some of the tribe had sided with him before and he was a big, strong man, someone to contend with unless Oghud could clearly reestablish his leadership. And that, more than anything else demanded seeing after the tribe's needs on a day to day basis.

The bands of hunters had covered the areas around Ur and Eridu to the extent that their wide ranging forage expeditions there most often lead to frustration; they did not find enough to feed themselves, seldom bringing anything of substance back to the camp. This had resulted in farther forays toward and past Uruk, even north of Mara. Oghud called Toq to him and asked, "You at Mara. What you see across river?" "Some birds, some reeds, shallow spots. Maybe fish and turtles there. Place where water flows to river from big grass field. Maybe men with sheep come there sometime." "How you cross river there?" "Not cross there. Go far away from Mara. Water not much deep there. We use reeds to cross."

Oghud thought for a while before speaking, "Go. Take Fyd. Take Ev. Take Lvad." Toq was taken aback at the idea of being burdened with Lvad and answered, "We go there. Not take Lvad. Lvad no good." "Lvad catch fish and turtles. Take Lvad." There was finality in Oghud's voice and Toq obeyed. Fyd and Ev were so strong in their opposition that Oghud had to repeat his orders to them before they grudgingly gave in. Lvad had no choice but to go, particularly with Fyd standing over him, "Up, Lvad. We go. You go. Now."

The four bogs cut across country, avoiding Uruk and stopped at the river below Mara only long enough to catch a few turtles to eat. They then traversed a wide arc around Mara, not wanting to be detected by the newly aggressive farmers there, finally coming to the place Toq had spoken of late on the third day. Fyd asked, "We wait here till sun tomorrow?" "We wait. Get reeds now. Tie so we stay on top of water. Lvad, find fish. I tie reeds for you." Toq began pulling reeds as fast as he could and Fyd and Ev followed. Lvad waded out a short way into the stream and then slowly moved back toward the bank, head down looking for fish. When he spotted one in the shallow water he swiftly speared it, flipping it up on the bank with a single motion of his good arm. It took him perhaps an hour to get enough fish for the four of them, but he kept at work without complaining; Toq even began to feel that Oghud might have been right. With no fire the raw fish still satisfied their appetites before the sun set, leaving them to sleep beside their bundles of reeds.

During the night rain fell and the soaked bogs had to move to higher ground though there were no sheltering trees anywhere near. The cooler breeze compensated for their wet misery and at dawn they were more than ready to get to the other side where they could see some herons and a duck or two flying in out of the reeds. It was agreed that Fyd would be the first to go into the water, followed by Ev, Lvad and Toq in that order. If the current was too swift in the deeper water Toq could push Lvad's bundle of reeds toward the far bank while Lvad held on with his one good arm. They lashed their spears, knives and clubs to the reeds and Fyd started across. He kept himself upstream from the bundle and with his right arm tightly locked around the reeds kicked furiously as the midstream current swept him farther and farther away from the others. At last he could touch bottom and waded safely up on the bank, waving the others to do the same. Ev took his turn without incident except that he was carried a long way past Fyd. As he walked back to where Fyd was Lvad and Toq began to wade out to where the water was only chest deep.

Lvad looked terrified but was so afraid of Toq he gamely wrapped his good left arm around the reeds before Toq realized this would put him downstream from the bundle and make his kicking against the current ineffective. Not wanting to be laughed at Lvad took a deep breath and pushed off into the swift current. Toq shouted, "No, Lvad. Wait!" too late. Lvad's bundle immediately shifted in front of him and as he tried to kick for the bank he had just left began slowly turning. The harder he kicked the faster he spun in the water as the others watched helplessly. Toq pushed off and began kicking toward Lvad to try to catch him and stabilize his motions, but Lvad somehow managed to roll under the bundle of reeds. In his desperate attempt to get his head above water he lost his grasp on the reeds and after a few seconds of wild flailing vanished below the surface.

Toq was already around a bend in the river from where Ev and Fyd were and had to get to the bank as fast as he could for his own safety. By the time he made it the other two had run the distance and pulled him out of the water. Without a word they watched Lvad's bundle disappear in the distance, then retrieving their weapons lay down to rest for awhile. Fyd was the first to speak, "We hunt now. Maybe kill bird." The others nodded and they looked back along the banks to where several herons were fishing in the shallow waters. As they crept forward Ev's spear was the first to fly and a heron flapped a useless wing against the water. Not a sound was made while Toq and then Fyd threw their spears. Three herons were pulled out of the water and voraciously eaten in minutes.

Clouds rolled in from the north and a steady rain began to fall forcing the bogs to head back down the river in search of a stand of palms they had seen that would provide fronds to shed the water. "It is time for rains. Maybe get much rain before cold time comes." Fyd observed with water pouring off his scraggly hair onto his face. "Water bring berries and figs. Berries bring birds. Maybe hunting not so hard some time", Ev puffed as they struggled up a slippery slope.

Soon they came to a sharp bend in the river and found a low bank which had washed out years before at flood time. There some stunted palms struggled to grow, bent low with a few fronds almost touching the ground. The bogs quickly constructed a makeshift shelter and climbed under it to wait out the rain. When it finally let up they took a look around and decided to hunt from there, returning at night as they got their bearings in this, to them wholly new area. The next few days took them progressively farther up and down the river. Only short distances from its banks the vegetation ran out as did their prospects of finding food beyond. There were no villages in the vicinity which was good and not so good: there would be no dogs to fear, but there would be no crops or livestock to steal either.

With the rain coming almost daily a creek began to flow just below their shelter. One morning a small deer came to drink from the stream and Toq spotted it before it knew they were near. He crawled slowly toward where it was, but slipped as he rose to throw his spear. The startled deer leaped away and headed down river. Ev and Fyd had been watching and all three took off in pursuit. They jogged for a 60 couple of hours, not trying to catch up with the frightened animal, only to keep after it until it would be too exhausted to run any farther.

The deer bounded across the swollen creek above the pond in the 'far meadow'. The bogs pulled up sharply as they heard Baldag's dogs chasing their deer which was already tiring. "Dogs catch deer for sure. Bad. What we do now?" Ev looked at Toq. "Maybe man get deer. Maybe we get sheep. Maybe we get goat." Toq responded.

Miqel and Malil had begun digging their trench with a vengeance, slowing noticeably as the sun beat down on their heads. Hours later they had little to show for the effort they had expended. Baldag laughed as he looked up the slope toward where they were, "I told you you would need patience. Stop for awhile and run down to the creek for a swim. You will feel better." There was no arguing with his wisdom and the appeal of the cool water was greater than the ambitions of wizardry right then so they dropped their sticks and ran down to the creek. They were heading back to where Baldag had herded the flock when the dogs, barking wildly raced past them, running along the creek. Baldag assumed they were chasing a hare and stayed where he was.

"What do you suppose they are after?" Malil wondered as they ran behind the dogs. "I see it. It's a deer! It must have been running a long time. Look at its tongue; the dogs will catch it. I know they will." Miqel panted, "Let's slow down a little. We can still keep sight of the dogs and bring it back to Father when they have killed it."

From a distance the bogs could see the boys but could not hear them, nor could they see Baldag. "Maybe we get to deer before boys get to deer." Toq started to run with Fyd and Ev following close behind. As the creek narrowed the deer again jumped it, this time gaining a little distance on the dogs; they had to swim across. But the deer continued along the creek, away from the trotting bogs and still outdistancing the dogs.

A young lion in its first year out of a pride had gone hungry more days than it had captured something to eat. The smell of goats had lured it toward the meadow but with the rains the flocks had been kept close; a man and dogs were more than it wanted to fight. As the dogs ran off the lion began stalking the flock until it caught the scent of the deer. Cutting across the meadow it reached the creek and ran along it keeping sight of the deer.

Now the bogs began to run in earnest. And the boys, who had not seen the lion, sensing a quick capture started to run as fast as they could. Neither of them had taken time to figure out what they would do if they caught the deer; they had no weapons of any kind and even a small deer was more than the the two of them could handle. To be sure the dogs would kill it but this was a savage scene they had never witnessed in their young lives. The excitement spurred them on until suddenly the deer once more leaped the creek and was on the same side they were. The dogs leaped in and out and were closing fast when they caught sight of the lion about the same time as Miqel and Malil saw it.

The deer stumbled and fell to its knees exhausted and the lion charged. With a vicious roar it was on the deer's back in a great bound and tore its throat open instantly. Then with low growls it stood over its prey daring anyone to take it away. The dogs rushed in and one was sent flying, its shoulder ripped open with a slash of claws. The other ran around the lion in circles, barking and snarling, darting in and out but the lion continued to stand over the deer trying to reach the dog without chasing after it.

Fyd jumped the creek first and seeing the boys shouted, "Go back. Go back. Lion hurt you. Lion kill your dog. Go back." Miqel, startled stopped where he was but Malil ran straight at the lion, tears streaming down his face at the wrong of it all...dead deer, ripped dog and what looked to him to be no more than a very large cat. As he got within a few feet of the lion, it gave a single leap and bowled him backward to the ground. Its hind claws instinctively disemboweled Malil as it tried to get past his arms to his throat.

Fyd's spear shot like an arrow and went through the lions body, impaling it to the ground. He jumped the creek and rushed to pull Malil away just as Miqel reached him. Miqel tried to fight Fyd off, thinking he was going to kill Malil when the lion let out a low, guttural growl. Fyd stepped over Miqel and smashing the lion's head with his club killed it.

He knelt down over Malil as Toq and Ev got to where he was. "Boy hurt bad. He die I think." Toq looked down and nodded, then looked at Miqel who was holding Malil's head and weeping. "Oh, Malil. Why didn't you stop? Don't die. Please don't die. Father will know what to do." Toq put his hand on Miqel's shoulder, "Little boy, friend hurt bad. He rest now." and gently laid Malil's head on the ground.

Malil tried to speak but fainted from the loss of so much blood before he could say anything. His eyes glazed and Toq closed the eyelids over them so Miqel would not see them turn white. Fyd picked up the mangled body of the would be wizard and asked Miqel, "Where Father?" Baldag had heard the commotion and was walking in their direction to see what was going on. Miqel looked up and, seeing him ran to him, "Father, Malil is hurt. Please do something. Please don't let him die."

Baldag ran until he saw Fyd hesitantly walking toward him with Malil's body still in his arms. "What are you doing with that child. Put him down! Put him down, do you hear me?" "Fyd not hurt child. Lion hurt child." Fyd protested as Baldag tried to snatch Malil away from him. Miqel nodded, crying so hard he could scarcely speak, "It's true, Father. This man killed the lion." Baldag motioned for Fyd to put the body down so he could look at it. Standing up he said, "Miqel, my son, your friend is dead. I am sorry but let me look at you. Are you all right?" After the shock of what his father had said subsided enough for Miqel to speak he answered, "I'm not hurt. What will we do?" "First I must find out what happened. Let us all go back to the fire. You, Fyd? You carry boy?" Fyd spoke, "I Fyd. This Toq. This Ev. We chase deer. I carry boy." Baldag turned to Toq and Ev, "You Toq? You Ev? You carry deer to fire?" Toq and Ev silently picked up the deer as Baldag went over to look at the bleeding, whimpering dog. Lifting it to his shoulder and taking Miqel's hand he called the other dog to him and started to walk slowly back toward the fire, leaving the lion with Fyd's spear still stuck through it.

Malil's body was covered with the hide he had used for sleeping and protection against the rain during the time they had been at the meadow. Miqel sat down beside it, overcome with grief and unable to comprehend the swiftness of change that had come to that day's happy beginnings. The bogs nervously stood back and Baldag had to coax them to come and sit down with him at the fire, "I am Baldag of Uruk. I am a shepherd. The one who is alive is my son. The other one was his friend from the city of Ur. We wish you no harm and are grateful for what you did.

Come and have some cheese and raisins with me. There is water in the skin there if you are thirsty."

The bogs looked at Toq as he took the goatskin and drank from it, then sat across the fire from Baldag. Ev and Fyd did the same. Baldag called Miqel, "Son, come and sit with us now. Go into the tent first and bring some cheese and raisins and the rest of the barley loaf for our guests." Miqel, with his chin on his chest limply rose to obey. Then he came and sat down by Baldag. They were silent for a long time. The bogs devoured the food, passing the bread back and forth and grunting that it was good. It was a new taste to them, bread baked in an oven was something they did not know.

Finally Baldag spoke, "Where is your camp? How many are you?" Toq responded, "We hunt in land other side of river. Our fathers hunt there before us. We not many. Oghud my father. He lead tribe." "When did you cross the river. How did you cross it? Are there others of your tribe on this side?" Toq, continuing as the spokesman told how the four of them had been sent to search for food across the river when there was not enough in their normal hunting grounds. He gave an account of the crossing on bundles of reeds and Lvad's drowning. When Baldag asked why they had never hunted there before Fyd explained that there had always been plenty until the rains stopped for so long. He related as simple fact their being forced into stealing and even cannibalism and their fear of the men of the cities and their dogs.

Baldag grimaced as Fyd spoke. Then Fyd asked, "Little boys come from Ur many days ago? We see boys like them with traders by river at night. Thieves say they kill them. These boys?" "Why yes. Miqel and Malil were with traders from Ur when a gang of thieves tried to kill them. How did you know about that?" a startled Baldag answered. Toq picked up the story, "We look for man Lvad hurt. Lvad stole man's food. Man with traders and little boys. We hear thieves say they kill men and boys and dogs and steal goats. Blame bogs. We yell and run away. Dogs bite thieves. We steal thieves' food from boat. Much food for tribe."

Baldag thought about what they said and Enlid's account of the mysterious scream that had saved all their lives. He began to realize that had it not been for these bogs Eh-Buran would still be making his murderous raids on villages and travelers. "You have been mistreated by men like me. The lack of rain has made us do things that we would not normally do, much the same as it has done to you. I think the king would like to reward you for what you have done. Now that the rains have begun perhaps we will all have plenty after the cold season is over. Toq, would you come to Uruk with me? Just for a few days."

Ev looked at Toq and then at Fyd. It was Toq who spoke, "Tribe hungry. We find food. When sun shows face we cross river. Go back to tribe." Baldag continued, "Let Fyd come with me. I will give you a sheep. You and Ev take the deer and the sheep back to the tribe. Tell your father about all this. Tell him Fyd will be at the camp in a few days. Tell him he need not fear us anymore." Fyd nodded and Toq looked at Ev who also nodded. He turned back to Baldag, "We do what you say. What you do with little boy that die?"

Miqel, who had been very quiet during the conversation pleaded with Baldag, "I think Malil would like to be buried where we dug our trench, Father. There are stones up there and we can cover him with them so jackals or wild dogs won't dig there when we are gone." Baldag agreed and the Malil's body was interred without ceremony at the end of the outcrop.

The bogs skinned the lion for its pelt; Fyd would be entitled to were it. The carcass was left for the dogs; the injured one was up, hobbling on three legs but tore into the meat as ravenously as the other one. Baldag gutted the deer and grilled the entrails over the fire for their supper. The next morning Toq and Ev with their sheep and deer headed back up river to make a sturdy little

79

reed skiff for the crossing, not only for the added weight of the animals, the river was flowing much faster after the rains.

Baldag decided that it was time to herd the flock back down to Uruk: Miqel would have to leave for the academy soon enough. He was glad to have Fyd going with them; with only one healthy dog it was quite a task for a lone shepherd to drive the flock and the goats down the river.

Miqel liked Fyd and Fyd enjoyed taking him teaching him to spear fowl on the way to Uruk. He also let Miqel practice bringing down small game, particularly hare with his club. Miqel was fascinated with the way Fyd threw the spinning club with such devastating accuracy. The time passed quickly and they were at the river landing across from Uruk by noon of the third day.

CHAPTER NINE   'The White Temple Plan'

At the the Uruk landing Baldag gathered his flock and proceeded toward the gate of the temple to tell Men-Chad-Res he was back. With Fyd to help the return trek had gone smoothly but there was much to tell both in the temple yard and at home.

Miqel ran ahead to the reed house to tell Gahnya they were home and bring her the sad news of Malil's death. Holding Miqel tightly in her arms as he breathlessly spurted out all that had happened to them at the far meadow Gahnya listened intently until Miqel came to the part about Fyd accompanying them to Uruk. "Your father has brought a bog here? Here! The king will be furious. In my life no bog has ever been allowed in the city." "But Mama, Fyd is a kind man and he is good. He and the other bogs saved Enlid and all of us from Eh-Buran on the way here from Ur. And Fyd kept the lion from killing me at the far meadow. I want him to stay with us. I want him to take me to Ur and live with Papa and Urunya. He can do so many things and he is so strong." Gahnya sighed, "We will wait and talk to your father about all this when he comes back from seeing the king."

As they neared the temple gate yard Baldag left Fyd with the flock and walked alone to where the king stood watching a bartering session that been in progress for some time. After a few moments Rom-Sha motioned Baldag to step forward and Men-Chad-Rez greeted him warmly, "My friend, Baldag. How were things at the far meadow after the rains? Are your sheep fat and ready for the cold times that come?" "They are that. The rains revived the grass there and brought game to the river. We have eaten well."

Ayn-Far came close and asked, "And how are our young wizards? Did they get to learn the signs in the stars? Were you able to teach them the ways of following the stars and the moon and setting the times of seasons?"

Baldag turned to the king, "With your permission I will tell you our sad news and bring you more knowledge about the capture of Eh-Buran's gang than we had when I left." Men-Chad-Rez nodded, "Say on." After Baldag recounted Malil's death and Miqel's rescue by Fyd he went on to tell the source of the enigmatic scream that had awakened Enlid's party to defend themselves. When he was through Men-Chad-Rez, troubled spoke, "Where is this bog, Fyd now? I am concerned for his safety here in Uruk unless we can inform the people of all these things before someone kills him out of fear."

Baldag waved for Fyd to approach them. Fyd looked in terror at Rom-Sha's armed guards as he came and fell prostrate before the king. Baldag reached down and touched his shoulder, "It is all right, Fyd. These are our friends. The king and the High Priest wish to meet you." Shaking visibly Fyd stood and spoke, "I Fyd. I not harm men of Uruk. Bogs not harm men of Uruk." "I know that is true, Fyd. Do not be afraid. Go with Baldag to his home until I can talk with the other men here. Then I will call you. Rom-Sha, detach two men to go with them and protect Fyd through the night." Men-Chad-Rez raised his right hand in salute and Baldag led Fyd back to the flock for the walk to the reed house and an uncertain welcome from Gahnya.

Miqel ran out out to greet them and took Fyd by the hand, "Mother, this is Fyd. Fyd, this is my mother and these are my sisters, Ette and Bodi." Fyd smiled at the little girls, "I Fyd. I not hurt you. Not be afraid of Fyd." Nevertheless they hid behind Gahnya until Baldag came up, then ran to him, each grabbing a hand for security. Baldag hugged them and walked over to embrace Gahnya, "What Fyd says is true. I think you will be glad he came with us; he has been so very good for Miqel. Has Miqel told you the news? It has been very hard for him."

"Miqel has told me the news. It is all so sad. What did the king have to say? Does Ayn-Far object to your bringing Fyd here?" "No," Baldag began, "Men-Chad-Rez and Ayn-Far understand. They want to speak to the people before we are called back and told what we are to do."

Ayn-Far went back inside the temple and called Mar-Dug and Ifn-Lot to him. They had recently returned from Ur and Eridu with little more than empty promises for help at some future time in establishing a large henge beyond the Tigris. Ayn-Far told them, "I have sorrowful news for you. One of your young geometers, the one named Malil is dead. The other, Miqel is at home with his parents here in Uruk but plans to leave as soon as possible to go back to Akhuruk's academy in Ur." Mar-Dug spoke, "That is indeed sad news; even worse it is very bad news, for Malil was obviously very gifted and we have not seen any others as bright as these two in my days as a priest." Ayn-Far nodded, "Nor in my days."

Ifn-Lot looked at Mar-Dug, "It would be a terrible blow to our works and hopes if anything should happen to Miqel. I talked to his grandfather and am inclined to agree with him that his like has not been seen in Sumer. Malil was quick to grasp the meaning of things but Miqel has insight far beyond his years, perhaps beyond any of our years." Mar-Dug agreed, "Did you get to spend any time with him, Ayn-Far?" "No, the matter of the gang of thieves had to be taken care of first; and before Men-Chad-Rez could call the little wizards back to us they had gone up to the far meadow with Baldag. Miqel and Baldag returned only today. By the way, they brought a bog back with them. It seems he and some other bogs saved Enlid's party and then rescued Miqel from the lion that killed Malil. The bog seems devoted to Miqel."

Mar-Dug continued, "Ifn-Lot and I visited Akhuruk and his wife, Urunya when we were on the way back from Eridu. They have very little, living almost hand to mouth with what Akhuruk can barter for his teaching. The Al-Ubaid temple contributes nothing though many of their most knowledgeable scribe-priests have trained under Akhuruk and give high praise to his methods and disciplines. I wonder if we could convince him and Urunya to come here; Baldag's wife is their daughter and Baldag has done quite well as a shepherd. We could give him room here in the White Temple to serve for his academy and I am sure some of our priests would help build a reed house for them. They are getting too old to be living in a tent, a rather poor tent at that."

Ayn-Far expressed his doubts, "I do not know if he would come. Gahnya once told me of her father's disappointment that he was not taken into the service of either the temple or the king when he applied here over twenty years ago." "Yet Miqel's apprenticeship will last only another three or four years...if we allow it to go on even that long...before we call him here. Miqel will need the teaching and exposure to the best minds we have and in my opinion there are none to match them in either Ur or Eridu. What will Akhuruk do after Miqel has completed his academy course?", Mar-Dug argued. Ayn-Far seemed convinced, "I think a lot will depend on Men-Chad-Rez. He is far more diplomatic than his father was and he can authorize better terms than we can to attract Akhuruk here. Let's wait until he is ready to call Miqel before us and then I will present your ideas to him."

Toq and Ev had arrived at the camp with the deer and the sheep and told Oghud the story of all that had happened to them: of Lvad's death and of Fyd's agreement to accompany Baldag and Miqel back to Uruk. Oghud clapped his hands to his face, "I never see Fyd again. Why you let Fyd go? Fyd good man. Men kill Fyd. Lose Lvad. Now Lose Fyd." "No, Father. Man Baldag good man. He send Fyd to camp. King wants see Fyd. Give Fyd food for camp. Baldag promise." Ev agreed with Toq but Oghu would not be consoled. Finally Toq told him, "Fyd not return at new moon we go get Fyd. Fyd strong. Fyd run fast. Men not kill Fyd."

Oghud pondered the situation for a bit then said, "No. Fyd come. Fyd not come. Oghud not fight king. Toq, Ev take Rif, Nah. Go back to meadow. Hunt game. Bring to camp." That made sense and Toq agreed to leave the following morning, though still wondering how they would cross the rain-swollen river with anything as heavy as a deer or a large pig. Their struggles with the deer and the sheep on the flat reed skiff they had rigged took all the strength they could muster. But the rains had continued and from farther north the river kept on rising. Still they would try. Oghud could not be placated by promises.

At Uruk by the time the evening meal was finished clouds had gathered to obscure the setting sun. A soft rain began falling and Fyd spoke to Baldag, "I take dogs. I watch sheep. You sleep now." Miqel looked up, "I will go with Fyd." "You will come into the house and sleep, young man!", Gahnya snapped. "You have had a long day and there is no need for you to lie out in the rain. We don't want you to be sick these few days you have left to visit with us, do we?" Fyd smiled, "Miqel good boy. Do what mother say do. Miqel, Fyd go catch fish when sun come back." Baldaag grinned at Gahnya as she resigned with a shrug. Miqel was happy: Fyd could catch fish where no one else would even try. Fyd, the dogs at this feet settled down with the sheep as the guards took up their positions nearby.

Late the next morning Rom-Sha came to Baldag's house and learning that Fyd and Miqel were fishing walked down to where they were. As Baldag walked along with him he asked, "What do you the think the king will do?" "I do not know. Men-Chad-Rez was at the temple early this morning with Ayn-Far and Mar-Dug. They came out to the yard a little while ago and talked back and forth but I could not hear them. Mar-Dug seemed to be pressing the king on some matter and Ayn-Far kept nodding and agreeing with him. Finally the king sent me here to bring you and Miqel and Fyd before him. They are waiting in the yard now."

Fyd and Miqel were wading in water that came up to Miqel's waist, happily scooping fish up onto the shore. They had already caught about a dozen fish when the guards spotted Rom-Sha and Baldag. One of them called to Miqel, "Your father is here with the Captain. I think you and Fyd had better come on out of the water now." Fyd lifted Miqel to his shoulder and the two of them, laughing approached Baldag, "Father, look at all the fish we caught. We can have a feast, don't you think?" "Yes, Miqel but for now we must go see the king and your friend, the priest Mar-dug. "Oh, is he back? Is Ifn-Lot with him? I like them. I wish Malil were here." "They both came back while we were at the meadow. Hurry up now. You need to get a dry tunic before we see the king. Your mother would be very unhappy if I took you there looking like you do now. Fyd, you must cover yourself with the hide you left at the house this morning." Rom-Sha left them to report back to the king that there would be a slight delay.

Men-Chad-Rez thanked Miqel and Fyd for the fish they brought him. He was pleased at their affection for each other and looked at Mar-Dug, "I think your plan might just work out after all." Then addressing Baldag, " The priests have some things they want to talk to you about. Listen carefully. I wish you to agree with them but I will not demand it. When they have finished come back here and we will eat these splendid fish together. Fyd, you stay with Rom-Sha while they talk. Do you understand what I am saying?" "I stay. I do what King say do."

Toq and his newly constituted hunting party reached the river above Mara early in the morning of the second day out of camp. He surveyed the torrent with skepticism, finally deciding to cross from a sand bar that had been isolated by the high water. He and the bogs hastily fashioned a raft from some palm logs that had washed down, tying them together and supplementing the logs with reed bundles for added buoyancy. The four of them pushed in unison and then tumbled aboard for their wild ride. Several miles downstream they managed by kicking furiously to beach the raft near where the palm shelter had been set up on their earlier hunt. They dragged the raft far enough up on the bank to prevent its being swept away if the water continued to rise. Then, being exhausted they rested.

Water birds had followed the fish down from the north and were more plentiful than they had been for several years. No one had hunted the huge area east of the river this far north of Uruk in recent times. When they were ready to return to camp the fowl would provide additional food but for now they were in search of bigger game. Deer, wild pigs and goats ought to be out there somewhere Toq thought and Ev agreed, "Find deer. Maybe find goat. Goat give milk maybe. Keep goat. Not kill." The experience with the lion argued against splitting up by twos, yet there was a lot of country to cover and not much time if the tribe was to have food. It was decided that Toq and Nah would hunt together and Ev and Rif would head out in a different direction. They would return to where the boat was at night; with trees there any game could be strung up out of the reach of predators while they hunted.

Ifn-Lot came to the gate to meet Baldag and Miqel as they entered the temple with Ayn-Far and Mar-Dug. "So glad you are back. Miqel, I am sorry about Malil's accident; I know you miss him." "Yes, I do. Thank you." Miqel was restrained by the overpowering massiveness of the temple walls. He had never been closer than the temple yard with its stalls and pens and from there he could not see beyond the gate. Ifn-Lot suggested, "Miqel, why don't you come with me and we will see the temple and places where we watch the stars. There is much to see and while we are gone Ayn-Far and Mar-Dug can visit with your father." "I would like that very much. May I, Father?" Baldag of course agreed and Ifn-Lot and Miqel disappeared through a low passage off the courtyard. Baldag was left wondering what there was for him talk about with such eminent priests.

They went up a few steps to a small, starkly furnished apartment where Ayn-Far invited them to sit down. Low stools were brought and Mar-Dug was the first to speak, "Baldag, we have been discussing Miqel's future with Men-Chad-Rez. I have been to Ur and visited with Akhuruk and Urunya. I know it has been some years since you have seen them. Are you aware how poor they are?" Baldag was taken aback by the implication of the blunt question, "Why no. Urunya has sent messages by travelers from time to time saying things were good at the academy and that they had plenty. I send a sheep or goat to them occasionally but we never knew they did not have enough. Does Akhuruk not receive an allowance from the Temple Al-Ubaid? I believe he did once." "They are proud people. No, neither the temple nor the king provide them with anything. The old king saw to it that the tuition-barter provided for them very well. But since he died seven years ago his son has cut back the allotments to the temple. Though Akhuruk has attracted a number of scribe-trainees their parents can furnish very little; he and Urunya are living from day to day." Baldag looked down at the floor, embarrassed, "With the children and my flocks to attend to there always seem to be things we have to do each day just to keep going here. Gahnya meant to visit them but since the drought she has been working hard to get enough to eat out of the garden and fields."

Ayn-Far leaned toward him, "Baldag, it is not our purpose to criticize you or Gahnya. There is no way you could have known. Akhuruk and Urunya get by. I do not think Mar-Dug intended to imply that they are hungry. Gahnya once told me that Akhuruk was bitter at Men-Chad-Rez's father and my predecessor as high-priest for denying him a position in the service of the White Temple. That was more than twenty years ago and he has never been back to Uruk since." "I know that is true. He is getting old though. Gahnya and I have talked of bringing them here when Miqel has completed his training at the academy. She thinks Urunya could convince Akhuruk to come; that is not certain but perhaps he will."

Mar-Dug gave an assuring glance to Ayn-Far, "Baldag, we think Miqel is the most gifted child we have seen for a long time, if ever in our contacts with the temples of Sumer. That is why we went to the king first before talking to you. He must be protected and educated to the utmost limit by the best geometers in the land. Do not consider this lightly for it will be a hard and lonely life for such a bright, happy boy to embark on. We are at a crossroads with the square and the circle and there are emergent doubters regarding the 'Sacred Circle' construction itself. If some person with overwhelming intellect does not arise to clear all this up soon we fear there will be chaotic bickering all over Sumer. That could lead to war among the cities as they try to defend the credibility of their temple services. Some of our friends have been to far away towns and cities along a river called 'Nile'. They seem to be combining into two kingdoms, one in the delta area and the other farther up the Nile toward the wild land of Nubians. The king of the Upper Nile alliance is called, 'Scorpion' and he has put together a sizable army to enforce his sovereignty there. He has conscripted slaves from Nubia and we are told he has the village chiefs at near fever pitch over whether their 'sun god' priests can survive the lower kingdom's worship of the 'moon god'."

Baldag was alarmed, "Miqel is just a boy. Surely you do not think the powers of kings and countries rest on his small shoulders. And what does all this have to do with Akhuruk and Urunya?" Ayn-Far broke in, "We want to bring Akhuruk's academy here. The king will provide for him and we can furnish facilities within the temple that are better than anything he has now. I have talked to some of the young priests and they will build a reed house similar to yours for him and Urunya. They really are too old to be living out their lives in a tent in the heat of this land." "I suppose it would be hard for him to turn that down. Gahnya can influence her father and mother to some extent since she is an only child. Still I can give you no assured answer as to what he will do. I really think Miqel will have more to do with it than we do. Their lives are very much wrapped up in his from what Enlid told me."

Mar-Dug studied Baldag, "Men-Chad-Rez has said he will not force you to do what we ask. In fairness I will tell you we tried to get him to do so; that is how important we think it is to have Miqel here where we can watch over him and help him in his studies...if that is needed. Akhuruk is unquestionably a great teacher." "Normally it is a decision I would make alone. However in this instance unless Gahnya agrees fully it will be impossible to sway Akhuruk to move. One more thing. Are you aware that Miqel wants Fyd to go to Uruk with him, not just for the trip but to live there?" Ayn-Far was disturbed, "Is Miqel safe with a bog? I know the stories about what he and the others did. But these are not people such as we know. They seem honest enough from what dealings I have ever had with them but they have animal-like tempers and ways of dealing with adversity. I hear they have resorted to cannibalism during the drought."

Baldag was quick to respond, "What you say is true insofar as any of us has ever observed. The only reason there are any bogs left at all is that they have somehow survived while communities grew up in their hunting and gathering areas. My grandfather told me that tribes do not live long as a rule; whatever survivors there are, usually young women get taken over by other families or other tribes which are also small. My grandfather said that the bogs we see around here were once a fairly large group, perhaps sixty or seventy men. They hunted in the north, far past Mara until an invading, more powerful tribe killed most of their hunting age men and drove them down to this poor country, poor for hunting and gathering at least. Their chief, Oghud lost all but one son; I met the son at the meadow. His name is Toq. Fyd is a man such as you and I and I suspect Toq is too. They have a very limited ability to communicate, yet they get along expressing themselves rather effectively. Most of our suspicions spring from mutual fear. Men-Chad-Rez was right when he feared for Fyd's life in our peaceful city. Some of our men would kill a bog as if he were a wild pig or a marauding lion that endangered our stock."

"What do you propose we do? I am sure Miqel can be convinced to let Fyd go back to his freedom.", Mar-Dug protested. Baldag was not so sure that was the answer, "Before Miqel and I knew Fyd I have thought about this for a long time. I doubt that there are more than thirty bogs in their whole tribe. Why should the king not designate a territory for them where they could live the ways of their ancestors while they learn herding? They abhor farming. That is obvious. But they have in the past kept some goats, eating them only when they were starving with this long drought. Maybe a part of the king's flock could be set aside for them to tend. They could be given grain and produce from our fields as payment for their work. That way they would be less dependent on wild game without being told they were not allowed to hunt anymore."

Ayn-Far thought there was merit in what Baldag proposed. Convincing the king might be difficult for him and Mar-Dug: they had been drawn into the temple service as boys and had not dealt in community matters much; this was the custom of senior priests. "Baldag, your grandfather was a prince like Kalam-Bad under Men-Chad-Rez's grandfather. My father told me about him, what a great man he was. What happened that your father did not join the king's service?" Baldag winced but answered, "There was a dispute over a woman my grandfather wanted my father to take for his wife. My father ran off to Ur with my mother and did not come back until the king died. My only brother died while we lived in Ur. My grandfather took my father back and came to love me. He taught me many things but he never once spoke to my mother. When he died his title was not passed on to my father and he became a shepherd just as I am." Ayn-Far was quiet for a bit, then said, "I think we have made this a difficult time for you, Baldag. I am sorry for any personal hurt we have caused you. Let Mar-Dug and me have some time to think these matters over. Do not offer your proposal for the bogs to the king yet. We will discuss this again later today."

Ifn-Lot took Miqel into an open court where scribes were drawing in the sand and on the surrounding walls. Miqel walked up to a finished work on one of the walls and studied it intently as Ifn-Lot waited to see what he would say. "What do you think that is, Miqel?" "I believe this is the 'Sacred Circle'. Papa has a drawing of it on a slate he keeps in his tent at Ur. All those lines that cross each other are not in the basic diagram." Ifn-Lot beamed, "You are correct. Do you see this little circle up at the left? We call that the 'eye'." Then with his finger he traced an arc past the vertical line of the diagram; it just touched the bottom of the 'eye'. "The 'eye' rides the back of the serpent to the door. You will be learning all this from your grandfather. But remember there are many steps in constructing the 'Sacred Circle'...twenty-two steps in all. And they are difficult to understand." "Papa told me that before we left to come home. He said that I would have to learn about the circle and the square before I would know what it meant and that I would never really grasp it unless I could relate all this to the crossing lines of the 'Sacred Circle' diagram." "Akhuruk is very wise. You will be weary of retracing these steps over and over again in the coming years, Miqel. If you lose your desire to comprehend their meaning you will never complete the course. Most young people give up." "Oh no! I will never give up. I want to be a real wizard like you and Mar-Dug. And I must learn quickly so I can begin work on the 'circle and the square'." "I think you will. I do think you will. But now let's go up to the back corner of the temple parapets. I want to show you the wall where we track the stars before we have to get back to the others and Men-Chad-Rez."

Walking along the brick parapets Ifn-Lot showed Miqel the copper plates with finely scribed marks designating South and East and West. He showed him a pole mounted in a socket and pointed to similar poles mounted at other locations on the walls, one diagonally across the temple on the far corner, "These are the posts for the times of the moon and the seasons. From where we stand if you look past that farthest pole on a certain night the right side of the moon will appear to just touch it as it rises from the East. That will tell us it is the beginning of the time for planting when the cold times are over." "This is so grand compared to Father's marks at the far meadow. Malil and I were digging a trench to follow the stars and the moon the day he was killed by the lion. We planned to set up rock gates to let in the sun on the 'days the sun and the stars are equals'.", Miqel told him. "Look below us to the far yard. Do you see the two gates there? They will let in the sun on those days when its rays shine through this notch in the wall right here."

Then Ifn-Lot, noticing the shadow of a pole on a mark on the floor where they were standing said, "It is time for us to join your father and Ayn-Far and Mar-Dug. We must not keep the king waiting and I am hungry for some of the fish you and Fyd caught this morning." When they got to Ayn-Far's apartment Ayn-Far was just standing up to conclude their meeting, "Here is Miqel now. Come with us, Miqel and we will go see what Fyd has been doing. Do you suppose the king let him cook the fish?" "He would do it. Fyd can do anything. He can even knock a bird out of the air with his club, can't he, Father?" Baldag grinned and nodded to him as he winked at Mar-Dug. Mar-Dug shrugged and took Miqel's hand, "You love Fyd, don't you?" "Oh, yes I do. I think he is as strong as Kalam-Bad and he is almost as big as Kalam-Bad, don't you think so?" Ayn-Far chuckled, "Well, almost, Miqel. Almost." Baldag noticed Ayn-Far was limping and seemed to be in pain as they climbed back down the steps to the courtyard where Rom-Sha was waiting with Fyd.

"Fyd, Fyd! You must see the temple and all the things Ifn-Lot has showed me. I will tell you all about it when we get home. My grandfather knows all these things too and he will be glad you were here.", Miqel bubbled, running over to where Fyd stood silently. Fyd looked at Baldag and then at Rom-Sha before answering, "Fyd not know these things. Fyd know to hunt. Fyd know to fish. Miqel know all these things. Baldag know all these things. Fyd cook fish for king. You eat now."

Men-Chad-Rez sat down and the others sat in a semicircle before him as Fyd brought the fish. "Have you and Baldag come to an agreement, Ayn-Far?" "About the academy and Akhuruk, yes. Baldag must talk to Gahnya before we decide how to approach her father but he believes she will try to help us.", Ayn-Far answered. "Miqel, your father will tell you about the things we are discussing when he talks to your mother. Thank you for the fish. It is very good." Baldag put his finger to his lips and Miqel remained silent, only nodding to Ayn-Far that he understood.

When they had finished eating Mar-Dug spoke to the king, "There is a matter we would like to discuss with you while Baldag talks to Gahnya." The king raised his hand and Baldag, bowing motioned to Miqel that they must leave now. Miqel called Fyd and they left the others to talk.

Men-Chad-Rez rose, "It is my intent to reward Fyd with enough food to help this Oghud and his little tribe until game is more plentiful south of Mara. But that is enough. The Hithabogs are a fiercely free people and they fear that we will enslave them as much as our people fear that they will kill our children." Mar-Dug rose now, "If we do not do something soon there will be no bogs to be concerned with in this part of the country. They say Oghud is is quite old and after a terrible fight with another tribe many years ago is left with only this one son, Toq. Toq is younger than the other hunters but his hunting party is fast and strong; he may take over the tribe

87

without a struggle. If not there will not be enough of them left to survive.

"And that means a rogue band of bogs preying on farms and stock, even children if they are unprotected." Men-Chad-Rez looked alarmed, "I think I am beginning to see what you mean. I will listen." Mar-Dug went on, "This was not meant to alarm the king. But we are truly concerned. Do you remember your grandfather had a prince in his service who was Baldag's grandfather?" "Yes. It was a great sadness to my father that Baldag's father did not enter his service. He ran away to Ur as I recall." "Baldag's grandfather took him back and proceeded to bring Baldag up in the tradition of the service though he of course had no title. He is a deep thinker and loves the country with a passionate pride, even though he keeps to himself and his family and to tending his sheep. He has a proposal that will serve our purposes very well I think and we implore the king to weigh it carefully."

With that Mar-Dug and Ayn-Far laid out Baldag's plan and then Ayn-Far elaborated, "I am a sick old man. My time will come soon I think. I know it is the king's plan that Mar-Dug will replace me as High Priest of the White Temple. In his time there will be chaos among the wizards of Sumer if a strong leader does not emerge, one so brilliant they cannot contest his word. It may be that Miqel with his gifts will be that wizard; we certainly hope so. It is my plan that Ifn-Lot will serve as master tutor to Miqel even while he learns under Akhuruk. He will devote his life to insuring that everything we know to teach him Miqel is given every opportunity to learn. That may mean he will have to travel to Kish; the greatest of today's wizards lives there. More, he will need a servant and guard for the rest of his days. We think Fyd could be trained to be that servant: there is no question that he is strong enough and expert enough with weapons to be a guard. Miqel has begged Baldag to let Fyd go to Ur and live with his grandparents there while he finishes his training. Incidentally Miqel does not know anything of what I have just told you."

Men-Chad-Rez walked slowly back and forth while he thought about all they had told him. He was a deliberate man and not given to quick or rash actions. "I will let you know my decision at the rising of the sun tomorrow. Until then think of how all this can be implemented. Your proposals are rather complex and will be difficult to explain to the princes of Uruk and their people. Go to Kalam-Bad now. He is back from a trip up north where I sent him after your return from Ur. I am sure he can offer guidance in these matters."

The hunt had gone well for Toq and his party. They had killed two deer and a large pig and taken three wild goats alive. Toq decided it was time to get back to camp and the four of them began to look over the raft. Ev spoke first, "Take two goats. Put deer on goats. Ev take goats. Nah help Ev. We go cross river. We tie goats other bank. We bring raft back. Toq, Rif take pig. Take goat. Go place raft land. All take pig, goat. All cross river." The other three bogs nodded. The sun was low and they needed to hurry. Ev and Nah pushed off and were immediately caught in the fast flowing current. The terrified goats wrestled with their captors causing the logs to shift. The reed bundles kept the raft afloat but it would take repairs before they could recross the river in it; and Toq was the only one who knew how to tie everything together. The river was wide here and their shouts could not be heard so there was nothing to do but for both parties to wait out the night.

Toq guessed what had happened from watching the wild flailing on the raft and he and Rif began gathering reed bundles and plaiting reed strips in cords for the next morning. They were up with the sun and watched as Ev and Nah finally shoved off with the rickety raft. Rif threw the pig across his shoulders and Toq loaded the goat with bundles and tugged it along as they trotted downstream, steadily losing ground against the fast moving raft. At last Ev and Nah were able to maneuver the raft toward a low embankment where it crashed and broke in two. Neither was hurt but both were angry and by the time Toq and Rif got there they were in no mood to try again. "Tribe hungry. We fix. We go.", Toq snapped. Neither moved. So Toq and Rif began the laborious work of tying it all back together, this time with greater care. In time it was ready to try and again Toq spoke, "Tribe hungry. Boat fixed. We go!" Ev got up and Nah sullenly followed him as they all climbed aboard and pushed off. A few miles downstream the water had overflowed the banks at a wide bend in the river and the raft shot through the break, careening wildly and landing upside down. The bogs managed to get free but the goat and pig vanished. In a few seconds it was all over.

There was nothing to do but go back to where the other goats were tethered and trudge back to camp. They managed to take a couple of herons on the way but it hurt to have lost the pig and goat. Arriving at camp Oghud was elated until Toq told him there would be no more hunts across the river as long as the water was at such high levels. Oghud slumped to the ground. "No game here. No berries now. No figs now. Not much raisins. Not much dates. 'We starve now." Toq looked at his father with pity, "Where Fyd? He not come? Man say Fyd come. Man say king give Fyd food." "Fyd not come. Man lie." There was finality in Oghud's voice. Toq walked away. Oghud called, "Where Toq go?" "Toq get Fyd. Fyd come here. King not give food. We take food. Take sheep. Take goats." And Toq was gone, trotting swiftly toward Uruk, angry in the belief that they had been betrayed.

Men-Chad-Rez appeared in the temple yard as the sun began to shed its first light. Ayn-Far and Mar-Dug came up to where he was standing and the king asked, "Have you seen Kalam-Bad? What did he say?" As he spoke Kalam-Bad, jovial as usual came over, "I will answer that. The proposals of our priests and Baldag are good. I will talk to the other princes but do not expect any opposition we cannot handle among ourselves. Let the king not trouble himself with the matter of telling the people. We will do that." "Good, Kalam-Bad. I have made the decision that we will proceed as Ayn-Far has asked. Rom-Sha, bring Baldag and Fyd here. Do not bring Miqel now. Baldag can talk to him later."

When Baldag strode into the yard with Fyd behind him Men-Chad-Rez addressed them, "Fyd, I promised to reward you for the brave acts you and your friends have done. You will be given four goats and three sheep to take to your tribe. The goats will be loaded with grain and lintels, enough to feed your tribe for a moon. Baldag, you will explain your plan to Fyd. You and Rom-Sha with twelve guards will accompany Fyd to a point within half a day's walk from the camp. There you will wait for Fyd to convince the tribe's chief, Oghud and his son, Toq to come and meet with you. If Fyd believes Oghud will listen then bring him and his son to me and I will make the promises we propose. If Fyd does not like your plan, let him take the goats and the sheep and go back alone, free to do as he has always done. This is my command. You will obey." "We will do as the king bids. Fyd, come with me and Rom-Sha. I will tell you what the king has said. We must go and get ready for you to go back to your tribe today." Fyd smiled and followed. Rom-Sha went to assemble the guard troop, saying he would be at Baldag's house shortly.

Mar-Dug walked after Baldag to tell him the rest of what Ayn-Far had told the king. Baldag was astonished at first but agreed that if Fyd could convince Oghud and Toq of his plan he would convince Gahnya that it was necessary for Fyd to live with them. "I am sorry for my son. He thinks this is what he wants, yet one day he will be a man and the loneliness of a wizard will be a hard life for him. Still the gods give to whom they will. It is not for me to say you have not decided rightly." Mar-Dug understood and walked slowly back to the temple to tell Ayn-Far that

Miqel would be their instrument. There would be so little time for him to be a boy anymore.

Gahnya listened while Baldag laid out the rest of Ayn-Far's story then burst into tears, "Oh, what a monstrous thing to do to a child. Poor, poor Miqel." Baldag held her close to him, "Gahnya, I think your father would say we must let Miqel have the chance to do this. When he is a man he will be able to decide if he wishes to continue as a wizard. For now it is the king's command. Will you try to make the best of it?" "You know I will obey. I also know it is right. Just let me be a mother for whatever time we have. I will not stand in his way."

Outside Fyd sat stoically while Baldag carefully revealed what the king had said, including the fact that he could go back to his free ranging ways as a hunter if he chose to do so. Fyd repeated each part of the plan in his own words to be sure he knew exactly what Baldag was trying to tell him. At last he stood and placed his on Baldag's shoulder, "Fyd know what you say. Fyd like what you say. Fyd do what you say. Fyd keep boy safe." "Fyd, do you think Oghud will agree to this?" "Oghud good man. Fyd tell Toq. Toq tell Oghud. Maybe Oghud come. Maybe Oghud not come. Fyd come. Maybe Toq come."

Rom-Sha was waiting as Baldag finished his discussion with Fyd. Baldag left his crook with Miqel and told him to look after his mother and sisters while he would be gone. He explained that Fyd had been rewarded by the king and had to take the sheep and the goats back to his tribe but that he would return in a few days. Miqel liked that.

The party set out to make camp where Oghud was to come and meet them. They walked at a brisk pace with Fyd guiding since no one knew exactly where the bogs were camped. Usually they moved from one locale to another over the years. But during the extended drought the place Oghud had selected offered enough water and there were trees and a sheltering ledge of rock for protection so there seemed to be no reason to move on. They had been there for over three years.

With the sun at its zenith they stopped to rest by a newly flowing creek where willows were again showing life and offering welcome shade. A light breeze was blowing toward them and suddenly Fyd tossed his head back and sniffed. A moment later he rose to his full height and sniffed again, muttering, "Man." "What is it, Fyd?", Baldag came over to where he was standing. "Fyd smell man. Man not far." He began trotting into the wind looking out past the trees and the banks of the creek toward an undulating stretch of sand. Baldag and Rom-Sha started to run after him and Rom-Sha signaled for the guards to follow.

Fyd stopped running and shouted, "Toq? You Toq?" The creature running toward them stopped just as suddenly and called out, "Fyd? You Fyd?" Then both began running as fast as they could. As he got closer Toq saw the armed guards and, sensing a trap turned and started to run away. Fyd called, "No, Toq. Toq not run. Men not hurt Toq." But it was to no avail. Toq was frantic like an animal frightened by a much superior predator and he ran until it seemed his heart would burst. Fyd never stopped though the others fell far back, jogging to try to keep in sight. At last Fyd reached him and pulled him to the ground. "Toq stop now. Fyd bring food. Men want talk. Men not hurt Toq." Baldag and the guards stopped short a reasonable distance away until Fyd would be able to calm Toq enough for them to talk to him. Rom-Sha sent the guards back to where they had left the animals and told them to wait there. He and Baldag sat down in the sand until Fyd convinced Toq to come over and talk to them.

"Toq know Baldag. Baldag father of boy. Baldag good man.", Fyd spoke softly. Toq, still panting looked down at Baldag and Rom-Sha, then back at Fyd, "Man tell truth?" "Man tell truth." Fyd smiled and Toq held up his hand to Baldag who rose and came over to him. Each man put his right hand on the other's shoulder and Baldag said, "Toq, come back to the trees where there is shade and water. I want to talk to you. This is our friend, Rom-Sha. "Rom-Sha,

Toq's father is the tribe chief." Toq raised his hand to Rom-Sha but did not come close to him. Nevertheless he did follow them to the creek. Once there he and Fyd both dived in, splashing and laughing like children. Baldag and Rom-Sha were satisfied to lean down and drink, throwing water in their faces and down their backs.

Baldag, through Fyd mostly, explained why he had come and that the guards were his and Fyd's protection, that they did not threaten Toq or any other bog. Toq sat silently throughout the explanation until Fyd spoke, "Toq do what king say? King good man. King tell truth. King send food for tribe." Toq answered, "Toq try. Toq tell Oghud. Fyd come. Toq, Fyd tell Oghud. Men stay." Baldag nodded and he and the others remained seated while Fyd and Toq herded the goats and sheep off to their camp.

"How long do you think we will wait here, Baldag?", Rom-Sha asked. "As long as it takes I suppose. My guess is their camp is almost a day from here. Fyd had not planned to stop here long and he knew we were not to go closer than a half day from the camp. We might as well see if there are any fish in the creek. Tell one of your guards there is a village not far from here where he might get some fire for us." A couple of guards were promptly dispatched to find the village and the rest of the company stretched out in the shade.

By the next day the guards were beginning to get bored and Baldag suggested they might be able to do a bit of hunting. They might find some game and fresh meat grilled on the fire would taste good. Rom-Sha liked the idea and the guards split up into four parties, one remaining at the creek and other three heading generally toward the river. They were under orders to be back before nightfall.

As they began to straggle into camp, empty-handed in all cases Baldag looked up and saw three figures approaching from where they had first seen Toq the day before. He and Rom-Sha walked a little way toward them and determined that it was Toq and Fyd with a much older man, presumably Oghud. Oghud held up his hand in greeting and Baldag and Rom-Sha responded, waiting for the bogs to come near without a word. Together they walked silently back to the camp. Though this was a tiny and weak tribe, Oghud was as much a king to the members of his tribe as Men-Chad-Rez was to the princes and people of his own domain. Courtesy implied waiting for him to speak.

Oghud sat down and nodded as water was offered, motioning to Toq and Fyd to drink also. He looked straight at Baldag, "You friend Fyd. You friend Toq. You friend Oghud." Baldag responded, "We are friends, yes." "You friend king? King friend Fyd. King friend Oghud." "The king is my friend. The king is Fyd's friend. The king is Oghud's friend." A long silence followed. "Oghud old. Oghud go back to tribe. Toq, Fyd go see king. Tribe do what Oghud say. Oghud do what king say." With that Oghud rose abruptly and walked away. Turning, he smiled at Baldag and raised his hand.

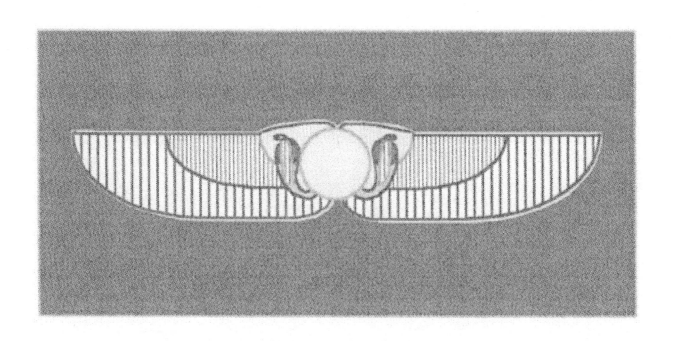

WINGED ORB OF EGYPT

Illustrated by W. C. Cawthon

Figure 10: Winged Orb of Egypt

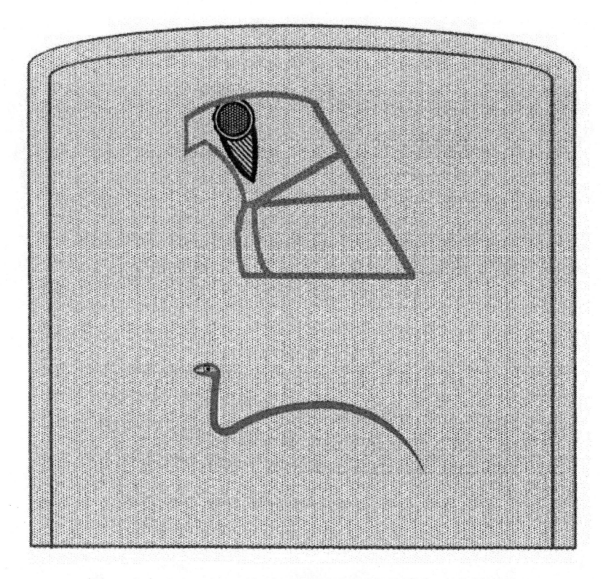

**Horus' Head and 'djet' as portrayed on the tomb stele
of Zet, the fourth Pharaoh. c. 3,000 BC**

Illustrated by W. C. Cawthon

Figure 11: Horus' Head & djet

CHAPTER TEN   'Return of the Sun Wizards'

A few days passed before Hev-Ri saw Kmal-Dyl again. He brought Vukhath and Shephset with him and asked for an audience. After explaining the situation at Asyut Hev-Ri told Kmal-Dyl that the dissension was not particularly serious there but that it bothered Menku enough to send them to Kish. He also spoke of difficulties in Lower Nile and Menku's fears that there would be heightened emphasis on strict obedience to whatever beliefs one had. There was so little difference in the rituals and creeds between the temples of the sun and those of the moon that he suspected they would polarize along the lines of those who held to the Sacred Circle and those who opposed it.

Kmal-Dyl at first seemed amused. Then he asked Shephset to explain why he believed the Sacred Circle construction should be abandoned. Shephset spoke of the known accuracy of the fractional solution and said, "Master, I do not believe we are as unreasonable as the priests who come from southern Sumer are. There may never be a monument large enough to employ the accuracy of the Sacred Circle construction and it is certainly a long, drawn out method for obtaining the relationship of a circle and its radius. As for its "sacredness" many of us hold that these legends are myth. Even if we grant there is substance to them we question what good can come of it all. Young wizards waste a lifetime trying to learn applications for it when our wizards have gone on to useful employment in a few years."

Hev-Ri and Vukhath remained silent, waiting for Kmal-Dyl's answer. At length he spoke, "There is logic in what you say, Shephset though I deplore the zealotry with which some of your fellow wizards try to force us to comply with your reasoning. What I think has happened is that such fanaticism has obscured their ability to listen to reasonable wizards who oppose them. Can you accept that?" "I think I follow what you are saying. Yes, I suppose there is some of that, especially since it cost Rabul his life. Maybe Per-Qad too."

"How much do you know about the work we are doing with the Circle and Square and with our efforts to create a set of phonic designated symbols for writing, Shephset?" Shephset seemed perplexed at the question, "I do not think anyone in Kemet knows so much about those things, Master. Perhaps if we knew more we would think differently. Why would the Sacred Circle be essential to writing and why cannot the fractional construction be used for the work on the circle and the square?" Kmal-Dyl appreciated Shephset's candor, "These are hard questions to answer, Shephset, mainly because there are no absolute answers for either.

"For symbols to use in writing we have no other construction set that is so universally applicable as the Sacred Circle. Whether you practice it or not all of your wizards know it. The only thing we know of with enough steps and general acceptance for wizards everywhere to be able to remember is the Sacred Circle construction. Even that does not make the problem simple to define by any means. I have struggled with it for over twenty years and am not close to assigning sounds to readable symbols which would make sense to everyone who understood the application. I think about twenty-two ciphers will be required. That is all I am really certain about now. "The circle and the square is something else again. We can and do use the same steps in a derivative construction to get the same accuracy we get with the Sacred Circle. "For now that is good enough but in the future I think it will give too great an error in measuring very large circular areas to be acceptable. Before you start thinking that the fractional solution will work on the squared circle pause to remember that the Sacred Circle is many times as accurate as the fractional circle and yet is really not accurate enough."

Shephset would not be put off so easily, "Then why do your wizards say they will use the fractional unit for the squared circle, Master?" "We are seeking yet another standard dimension, Shephset. What is going to be required is an absolutely enormous triangle, a pyramid if you will, so that sight angles to the stars can be made in the way we erect the gates at a henge site. This is where we think the fractional circle may be used to create this third, direct-conversion dimension."

Shephset was not prepared for such advanced views but he had listened intently and intelligently, "I believe I understand up to this point. I do not know where you are going with this line of reasoning however." Kmal-Dyl responded, "Shephset, almost anything I say about the circle and the square is speculative at best. However the need and hope for a system of writing is very real and the Sacred Circle construction's twenty-two steps with nearly universal acceptance is truly essential to that."

Shephset grinned, "But you have not worked that out yet either?" "True, Shephset. But I have worked on this for years and am convinced I have made rather good progress toward some sort of writing, albeit rather combersome. I hope I have the years left to complete this work."

Hev-Ri at last spoke, "I think we have learned a great deal today. I doubt that we can contribute much of anything to these advances you have talked about, Kmal-Dyl. The priesthood at Nekhen has fallen into cult worship under the Scorpion and his gang, particularly a man named Abgar who is effectively the High Priest. At Asyut we resort principally to training young drawing-scribes in the constructions we already know. Things are little if any better in Pe." Kmal-Dyl asked, "What about the land southwest of Pe, the area on the west side of the river? I have heard that it might be possible to build the great henge or a pyramid there."

Hev-Ri pondered the question and then, brightening, "You must be referring to the Gidjeh Plain. There is stone near the large flat area that could be used for the gates, but it would have to be cut out of the hills. Who could do that? And the desert sands keep blowing in all the time so I fear the trenches would be filled every year. There would not likely be any lasting value to a henge there even though there is plenty of room and it is flat. I would suspect you have just as good sites in Sumer except for the lack of stones."

Kmal-Dyl was obviously disappointed, "We might yet build the great henge there someday. I do wish we had heard back from the work that legend says was done past the gate at the end of the Great Sea. Perhaps they did build a great stone henge in some strange country. We are planning a lot but really accomplishing little more than you are at Asyut: just teaching and looking for some genius to tell us where to turn next.

"Shephset, Vukhath. Are you able to get on with the business of wizardry now? Can you stop arguing for awhile and perhaps help us think of some answers to these imponderables?" Both were embarrassed but nodded and smiled in agreement, wondering what they could ever contribute to overcome such obstacles as Kmal-Dyl had discussed. Hev-Ri rose and said, "We have burdened you, Kmal-Dyl but we are grateful for your explanations. My master, Menku wishes that you could come and settle in Asyut with us. He can give you anything you could ask for I think."

"I am honored, Hev-Ri. Tell Menku that. But I am old and have much to do here. I sometimes wish that when I was younger I had gone to live in Uruk. Still our High Priest, Abb-Oth and the kings I have served under here have given me everything I needed or wanted all these years. And we do have good communications with South Sumer so perhaps we will make some headway yet. I wish we could go on talking but I am tired now. What are your plans?"

"We have to get back to Upper Nile. I plan to ask Abb-Oth for help, a guide perhaps. We do not know when we can leave but I am sure we will see you again before we do." The three wizards from Asyut left quietly and went to the temple yard to get something to eat.

Not knowing that Menhes had taken the throne at Nekhen Hev-Ri could not know that Asyut was still in the hands of Djo-Aten's followers, and would be for sometime to come. There was no further news from Hit and it could only be assumed that he and his party could not return the way they came. There was little for them to do at Kish after their meeting with Kmal-Dyl and temple life was boring with no duties to perform as the days became weeks. Gelvi was especially homesick and decided to join a hunting party that was headed for Hit, figuring he could get home from there. The drought was threatening to make things harder for Gelvi's father and he knew he would be needed. Hev-Ri tried to talk him out of it but in the end let him go.

If the priests were bored the Menku warriors were becoming even more restless and Hev-Ri knew he had to start the journey somehow regardless of the risks any plan posed. He went to Abb-Oth and requested his help to persuade the king to assign a guide across the desert to the Tigris as Davri had suggested. Abb-Oth did not like the idea of talking to the king, "The king is good to us, Hev-Ri but he does not take an active interest in the temple as his father did. He is surrounded by people who tend to the affairs of the city and will not allow himself to become entangled in our problems.

"He is probably wise to do that, considering how near the borders of Mari are. The ruler of Mari would like to add Kish to his kingdom and that is a greater threat to Kish than anything priests and wizards pose. Any guide you might get from the king's service could just as easily be a Mari sympathizer as someone loyal to the temple." Hev-Ri wished he had never let Menku talk him into coming to Kish. "What can we do, Abb-Oth? We cannot stay here indefinitely and though I have no reason to fear Per-Qad I do not know if he is still living. We surely do not want to face the band we ran into at Hit again."

Abb-Oth agreed, "To be sure. However I have a priest here who was born in Ughada on the Tigris. He sometimes goes home to visit his family and the temple where he trained there. The High Priest at the Ughada Temple is a friend to the wizards of Sumer and will help you get across to Aqub from there I think. Are you up to the hardships of travel across the desert to the Tigris?" "What choice do we have, Abb-Oth?"

Abb-Oth smiled wryly, "None I can think of. Let me do this. I will call Urnath...he is the priest I just mentioned, the one who is from Ughada...and you can talk to him. If he is willing to make the trip now I will send a message to Rem-Chakh, the High Priest at Ughada, asking him to help you. I believe he will arrange provisions and a guide for you to cross the desert to Aqub from there. That will be a harder trip than from here to the Tigris I fear but at least you will be safe from the Mari gangs. Do you have anything to barter with, Hev-Ri?"

"No, Abb-Oth. We lost all our provisions and things we brought with us at Hit." "Then we will have to furnish you with some items of ivory and copper, maybe an amulet or two for you to give Rem-Chakh for the guide. You must have trading goods or you will never get back to Asyut, my friend."

Urnath was willing to take them to Ughada if they would wait for a few weeks until the Tigris reached its lowest flow. He knew a boat owner who had taken him to Ughada before from a small fishing village almost due east of Kish. "The boat will just about hold us and the Tigris is too treacherous except for the brief time when it slows down a bit. Ikh is not much of a place but we can get some fresh food there and we will be ready for it. Your warriors may be able to bring in some game according to hunters who have been that way recently but they say it is scarcer than usual; and 'usual' is not very plentiful in that part of the desert. Why don't you and your fellow wizards do some instructing while we wait? You could pick up some items for barter that will make life a bit easier, especially after you leave Ughada."

Hev-Ri liked the idea of having something to do and so did Vukhath and Shephset. The weeks went by quickly enough and early one morning they walked out into the wilderness east of Kish. The terrain became more barren with each day they walked and the sun was searing in the hottest part of each day. Each morning their only goal was to keep going until the sunset brought the cooler night.

By the end of the fourth day the desert looked endless and there was no sign of anything that even suggested a river. Vukhath asked Urnath, "When do you think we will get to Ikh?" Urnath was plodding along and sweating profusely, "Don't you just love the desert, Vukhath?" "Be serious, Urnath. How much farther do we have to go?" "It is hard to measure distances here and we have not come to the next landmark, which is less than a day from Ikh. However to answer your question, if we are not in Ikh by tomorrow night we will be there by noon of the following day."

Vukhath let out a sigh of relief and went back to where Hev-Ri and Shephset were walking with the Menku guards, "Urnath says we are not more than a day or a day and a half from Ikh." Then addressing the guards, "Are you fellows up to doing a little hunting before we bed down for the night? I suspect that you are as tired as I am of dry barley crusts and cheese." They laughed and said they would like that if Urnath thought there was any kind of game around there. They came to an area where some scrub brush and a few spindly trees grew out of rough gravel. "A long time ago the river broke out of its banks and flooded down here." Urnath explained. "The landmark I am looking for is a short way from here. Let's take whatever shade we can get and then look around for game of any kind that may be wandering around here. There are normally hare, sometimes a pig or a wild goat; they come here for the little water hole at the end of this draw. At least it will be there if the spring has not dried up."

They walked along the shallow bed until they found a short stretch of wet gravel. Urnath took his staff and started to dig with the others joining in and in a few minutes water began to seep into the hole. Urnath looked up, "This is good. Not only will we have some fresh water but there are bound to be some animals that come here regularly." The guards spread out and in an hour brought back two hare and a wild pig. By then the priests had got a fire going and they sat down and had their first cooked meal in four days.

With rising spirits they came on the landmark shortly after they set out the next morning. It was a large stone tilted awkwardly to one side. It was the middle of the afternoon when they first saw Ikh and the Tigris. The men from Asyut were astonished at how wide the Tigris was there. Urnath approached the village with caution as the guards walked beside him with their spears. There was nothing to fear from the villagers but their dogs could be a serious threat. Two young boys came running out to meet them and when they saw it was Urnath ran back to get the elders who were all glad to see him. They welcomed him and his party to Ikh and as was the custom killed a sheep to feed them.

Urnath's friend, the boatman was willing to take them to Ughada for three bronze knives and said he could leave the next day. The current was slow enough to make the journey upstream in less than two days if the wind was with them and he could be back home by nightfall of the third day. The trip to Ughada was comparatively easy though the reed boat rode deeper in the water than the Menku men were comfortable with. Fish were plentiful for the one night they spent on the banks of the Tigris so they arrived relaxed and for the first time since Hit they were actually optimistic. Ughada was completely unexpected. It was larger than they thought it would be and surrounded by a low brick wall. The temple rose above well appointed brick houses and even the reed houses down by the river were built in a way to provide maximum comfort against the heat, with reed mats arranged to give ventilation and privacy. There were no tents in the town...only on the outskirts...and awnings covered the stalls in the temple trade yard.

The travelers went directly to the temple and asked to see Rem-Chakh but were informed it would be three days before he would give an audience. There was some kind of ritual going on, something to do with praying to the Tigris god for rain. There was nothing for them to do but walk on out to the edge of town to the tents of Urnath's family.

For three days they fished and hunted for herons and other fowl that nested along the river, becoming acquainted with some of the townspeople in the process. The people had never seen anyone from the Nile country before and were fascinated to hear about it. They could scarcely believe that there were so many towns and villages with temples and that there were two nations there, not counting Nubia.

The men of the town became incredulous when Hev-Ri tried to describe the Nubians to them. Urnath assured them that their skin was quite black and that they were tall, handsome people from what he had heard from travelers in Kish. Descriptions of the cataracts and the annual flooding, the green fields and fast sailing vessels brought more questions; in fact almost everything the priests told them elicited another round of questions. It was all good natured. The Ughadans were a peaceful people.

Rem-Chakh was a pleasant man, not more than fifty years old Hev-Ri thought. He wanted all the news from Abb-Oth and Kmal-Dyl and wondered why the men from Asyut would be taking such a circuitous route to go home. Such wizards as there were at Ughada were concerned mainly with making plans for buildings and the rather primitive wharfs at the rivers edge. They were really drawing-scribes and did not participate in the activities the priests were involved in. Rem-Chakh was not a wizard and knew only vaguely about anything beyond the most basic diagrams and signs, which he had to know to follow the seasons and designate special days for the temple and the king of Ughada.

Urnath gave Rem-Chakh the message from Abb-Oth which was nothing more than that these were friends who wanted to visit Ughada before returning to the Nile and that they would need whatever help he could provide to get them across the desert to Aqub. He asked Hev-Ri, "Is your king a good man? does he provide for your needs?" Urnath's eyes told Hev-Ri to dodge the question so he answered, "The Nile is a very long river, Master. We live a great distance from the capital of Upper Nile which is at Nekhen. Our master is a very rich and powerful man who has academies and temples at his herding stations. We never see our king and know of him only by reputation. We know as much about the king of Lower Nile as we do of our own king, though we've never seen him either. Our master has a camp at a huge lake in Lower Nile and we sometimes go there. We have been to Pe, the capital of Lower Nile but I have never been to Nekhen."

"This must be a very strange land indeed." Rem-Chakh marveled, "To what gods are your temples dedicated?" Hev-Ri continued to speak for the group, "In Upper Nile, the god of the sun, Aten. In Lower Nile, the god of the moon, Amen. Some of us from the Upper Nile academies are called the Sun Wizards." "How odd. What do you call the god of this great river of yours, Hev-Ri? Are there no temples to him?" "His name is Hapi. No, Master. There are no temples to Hapi though the people do offer gifts to him in the temples of Pe I think. That is not the custom in Upper Nile."

Rem-Chakh pursued his thought, "You say you receive your living from this Nile, a gift from a god you call Hapi but you do not pray to Hapi? You do not worship Hapi at all?" "No, Master. We do not."Urnath interrupted, "Master." "Yes, Urnath?" "The wizards have academies in the temples of Nile similar to those you have to train the young drawing-scribes here in Ughada. Some of the wizards in Nile are priests just as they are in South Sumer at the White Temple and Al-Ubaid for example. They do not always participate in the rituals of worship however. Hev-Ri's academy is not even located in a temple. Am I not correct, Hev-Ri?" "That is true, Urnath."

Rem-Chakh asked, "Do your people not worship the 'Mother of Heaven', Hev-Ri?" "We do not know who she is, Master. How may we know her?" Urnath sensed Rem-Chakh's annoyance and responded, "Hev-Ri, you know signs of the heavens as well as anyone. The Mother of Heaven gave us these signs, did she not, Master?" "Of course, Urnath. Everyone knows that in all of Sumer and Akkad. It is so strange that they seem not to know it in Nile."

Hev-Ri hastened to interject, "The signs we know and respect that it was given long before the memory of anyone any of our grandfathers have known. There is a legend that there was once a small statue which told the story of the signs in our land. It was somewhere in Lower Nile I think. It was of a woman and her arms were raised above her head, which was the head of a bird. Or it looked like a bird though it had the eyes and hair of a woman. No one has seen it for perhaps a thousand years; we cannot know how long. But the legend is persistent in Nile. Perhaps this is a statue of the Mother of Heaven but if it is we have lost it and do not know her."

Rem-Chakh relaxed and smiled, "Urnath, I think you and Abb-Oth have some educating to do over in this country of Hapi's. You must send some missionaries there I think." "I will speak to Abb-Oth about it when I return, Master. Might one of your priests accompany these men back to their academy at Asyut instead of just leading them to Aqub? What do you think, Hev-Ri?" "If the Master will permit that we would welcome such a priest. And I can assure you he will be listened to in Upper Nile."

Rem-Chakh offered, "Then it will be done. I will send Var-Lil with you. He is a senior priest here and responsible for the rituals of worship to the Mother of Heaven. Would you like to see the statue of her in our sanctuary? It was carved from a great stone that fell from the sky long before our grandfathers lived." "We would be grateful, Master and yes, we would like very much to see your sanctuary and the goddess who stands there."

The sanctuary was large with high timber columns supporting a roof of hewn beams. An opening in the roof lighted the goddess which towered above an altar, still streaked with blood from the sacrifices of the morning. There was absolute silence as the men studied the grotesque features of the statue's head: it was like a thick disk with a deep notch between what looked like a bird's beak and the neck. The eyes were where a bird's eyes would be but they were human eyes and scallops of paint or dye along the top and back of the disk were clearly meant to be a woman's hair. The Mother of Heaven's arms were raised and palms turned toward the face with fingers arced as if she held spheres in her hands. Her breasts were thin and drooped toward her waist which itself was tiny compared to her shoulders.

Urnath smiled at the Sun Wizards' astonishment, "What do you see, Shephset?" "I see arms like two tails of the scorpion in the heavens. Is that what I am supposed to see?" "Very good. Yes, that is what it represents I think though I fear the people of Ughada would sacrifice us to their goddess if they heard us talking this way. She is very real to them." As they left the sanctuary, Vukhath asked, "Urnath, you say the people really do worship this goddess, whatever her name is. It sounded to me like Rem-Chakh is just as committed to the reality of her existence as they may be. Is that not true?"

Urnath chuckled, "Perhaps so but likely not, Vukhath. In Ughada there is nothing much that goes on relating to wizardry in the Ughada temple but the priesthood brings a good living and the support of the king. All Rem-Chakh has to mystify the king with is the drawings of the scribes and the signs in the stars at night...and this weird goddess figure. He will follow the rituals all his life and demand total compliance from the priests who are trained here in this temple. He never takes priests from Uruk, or Kish for that matter. They might unsettle the 'rituals' for the Mother of Heaven and the Tigris god."

Shephset spoke up, "This is what we fear is beginning to happen at Pe. It appears that the moon god, Amen will become an object of worship with sacrifices and all the rituals that go with that sort of thing. There may even be statues to Hapi someday in their temples. The king of Lower Nile, Hor-Amen is threatened by the beginning of the effects of this drought you people over here are experiencing and they say he is pushing the priests to bring the people into awe of Amen."

Urnath became serious, "There is danger in Kish of the same thing, only it will be the Mother of Heaven we will have to worship if such comes to be. This is actually why Abb-Oth keeps sending me over here to placate Rem-Chakh and try to keep him from sending his 'missionaries' to Kish. If the drought makes things too desperate around Kish and the king begins cutting back on the provisions for the temple service there I would not be surprised for another stone-that-fell-from-the-sky to show up in Kish with a devoted cult springing up to worship it. There are priests in Kish who resent the authority of Kmal-Dyl and the influence of the wizards. They would be only too glad to put us in our places."

Var-Lil was more than happy to go with the Menku wizards. Contrary to what Hev-Ri had feared Var-Lil had little intention of paying more than lip service to his role in the business of proselyting for the Mother of Heaven. He was a man in his mid-forties and could best be described as fat and jolly. He knew so little of mathematics, and cared less about the subject that all he received depended on his adroit manipulation of the rituals to instill dread in the farmers and herdsmen that made up the population of Ughada. Furthermore Rem-Chakh had agreed he could take his man-of-all-burdens, his servant, Bagh with him on the journey, to "lighten the cares of the way". Hev-Ri was thankful for Bagh's company for it meant he would take goats and provisions they could carry, along with oil pots for fire crossing the desert. This was much better than traveling on goat cheese and dried fruits with flint-struck sparks if there was anything they could find to burn and cook game over.

The walk to Aqub took six days but there was no grumbling this time. For one thing the priests and warriors felt relief that they were actually heading toward home and would reach their first familiar territory at Aqub. For another Var-Lil kept up a lively banter and asked a thousand curious questions about the strange lands of Nile. He most wanted to see Nubians and expected Seb to be something of a god. Hev-Ri hoped Seb would get back to Asyut while Var-Lil would be there.

At Aqub the elders remembered them and were quite friendly. Nothing was said about the Hit experience and it could only be assumed that they did not associate it with Hev-Ri and his party, if they had even heard about it. The Euphrates was flowing so slowly the water scarcely seemed to move. There were three or four good sized fishing boats tied up at the landing and Hev-Ri wanted to negotiate passage to Huta on one of them. Since it was not a long run from Aqub to Huta arrangements were quickly made and they approached Huta late the next day, pulling in below the town at Malbu's fishing pier where they got out of the boat to walk up to his tent.

Malbu recognized the party from a distance and came out to greet them. Shephset ran to where he was and asked, "Have you heard anything from our friend, Per-Qad?" Malbu was pained by the question, "Only rumors, Shephset. How have you and the others made out at Kish? What happened to Davri?"

The rest of the party came up and Hev-Ri told Malbu all that had come about since they had last seen him. "What are these rumors, Malbu?" "Hunters from around Hit say there is a new priest who has a band of his own and that he is terrorizing the countryside west of Hit. I believe there is truth to what they say but do not know if it is Per-Qad or not. And I do not want to go down there to find out. I intend to go on eking out a living here with my fishing and some boat work up river. But that is all I intend to do now. Without Davri I am through with the wizards of Sumer and Kish. I like my head on my shoulders where it belongs."

"I hope the rumors are wrong, at least the part about Per-Qad. Will you take us to Salbat, Malbu? I think we can get to Thurn's from there all right." "Yes, Hev-Ri. I will take you there and I can arrange a guide who will take you all the way to Rud if you need him. Gelvi knows that area but anyone unfamiliar with the route can get lost in a day and miss Aff and Thurn's entirely. It is a dangerous thing to try to traverse the desert without someone to lead you." It was too late to leave for Salbat that day so they went into the town and shared a meal of fish Malbu provided with the villagers there.

When they got to Salbat Malbu introduced them to a young boy about Gelvi's age who it turned out knew Gelvi and wanted an opportunity to visit him and learn all about his journey to Kish. His name was Lukh and he was fascinated with Var-Lil but most of all with his servant, Bagh and the fact that he brought his own goats across the desert. Bagh ignored him, being too busy taking care of the needs of the priests and warriors to bother with a boy. Var-Lil's talkativeness easily made up for Bagh's taciturnity and they got along well.

Lukh led them straight to Aff and then on to Thurn's where they were again received with warm friendliness. Thurn wanted to know what had happened to them and particularly wondered where Per-Qad was. Hev-Ri told him about their narrow escape at Hit and how Davri had returned to Uruk to stay there for an indefinite period. Thurn wanted to know about Malbu and was relieved that he was safely back in Huta. Gelvi had stopped for a couple of days and stayed with Thurn and his family but he had not seen Malbu when he picked his way up the river on whatever boat that would let him ride. Nor had he heard any rumors about Per-Qad so Hev-Ri thought it better to leave them unsaid. Again Var-Lil was invited to visit on his return trip as they set out for Rud.

They were in luck again when they reached Rud. After they had rested and washed up in the Orontes they saw a familiar boat coming up the river. It was Gelvi and his father bringing some hunters up to Rud. The hunters would stay for two weeks so the boat was ready to leave immediately for Ikruth. Gelvi was so glad to see Lukh he forgot to greet Hev-Ri and the others he had traveled with months before.

Hev-Ri grinned at him, "Have you forgotten us so soon, young friend?" "Oh no, Master. It is good to see you again. I wondered if I ever would when I left Kish. You are not angry with me are you?" "We were never angry with you, Gelvi. We were just concerned for you safety. Did you have any troubles getting home from Thurn's? He told us you stopped there for a couple of days." "Not really, Master. I know that part of the desert well. It was lonely at night though. Do you know any more about what happened to Master Per-Qad?"

Hev-Ri looked at the others first and said, "Malbu has heard some rumors, Gelvi but we do not know what to make of them. My best answer is that we do not know." Gelvi took Lukh down to the water to introduce him to his father while the Asyut party gathered up their things to board for Ikruth.

Gelvi persuaded his father to take the priests and warriors down the coast from Ikruth to Ugarit. The boat had to hug the coastline and the progress was slow but it was only a short distance to where they would say goodbye. Hev-Ri gave Gelvi and Lukh each an ivory amulet from Kish, one of the ones Abb-Oth had provided and Var-Lil gave them armlets of horn and carnelian from Ughada. The boys beamed and Gelvi asked, "Master Hev-Ri. If I can get to Nile someday could I visit with you at your academy?" "Most assuredly, Gelvi. In fact I am sure Master Seb would be glad to teach you what we do there. He is the teaching scribe at the academy and the one Var-Lil most wants to meet. Is that not true, Var-Lil?" "I think Hev-Ri is twitting me but yes, I do want to meet Seb Seshat. He must be a very accomplished man."

They all said their goodbyes and Hev-Ri set out looking for a sailing vessel that would get them back to Saqqut. There was nothing due from Crete for weeks but a barge was going down the coast two days from then so they decided to go as far as they could and see what would take them to Saqqut from there. The water was relatively calm and this time only Bagh was sick. He had been so frightened when he saw the Great Sea that Var-Lil had to threaten him to get him to board the ship. There he lay in the stern with his head covered except when he got so sick he had to lunge for the gunwales. By the second day even Bagh had his sea legs and the barge was stopping at villages each night so the trip was not bad at all. Around noon of the sixth day the ship reached its destination, a small, unimpressive seaport called Jergil.

The Asyut bound party began to wonder if they would have to walk along the coast to Saqqut, a very long way and blocked by the "sea of reeds" in the northern delta region. The elders were cordial enough but there was little to eat except fish and bread. Bagh made some fresh curd cheese from the goats' milk but there was so little of it it served only as a spread for the rough barley loaves available at the pier.

By a happy turn of fate a fast, small Cretan ship landed at the Jergil pier on the fifth day they were there. It was delivering pottery from Cyprus for traders heading inland to the Jordan and on down to Jericho. Hev-Ri rushed down to the pier to talk to the ship's master to try to negotiate a trip to Saqqut. The captain told him, "I am not going to Saqqut this trip. I have to go west of there to Memshak and leave a consignment of copper ingots. Then from there I will head up the river for Pe. My ship is one of the few on the Great Sea that can negotiate the Nile currents."

Hev-Ri wondered what he had for Pe and the captain answered, "I have some woven goods, linens and woolens for a merchant whose boats come there. Let me think a moment. His name is Minka I believe. The Pe traders know who he is." Hev-Ri let out a whoop and the rest of the group came running while the captain wondered what was going on. Hev-Ri explained who they were and that they expected to catch the Menku traders at Pe and go on to Asyut's trading station from there. The ship's master welcomed them aboard and they were at the Pe landing before sundown of the fourth day.

Var-Lil could not believe what he saw. The city did not look like towns and cities he had ever seen before. And the temple was so small. The lush greenery of the delta country had been an experience for him already but he was simply not prepared for the informality of Pe. "Besides herding all these cattle and flocks what do the people grow here?" He wanted to know. Hev-Ri informed him that the usual barley and lintels were grown there along with leeks and onions, figs and dates. Acacia logs were brought in from down river for fashioning into wood products of all types and there was a good sized stoneworking and ivory carving craft center there. "But are the priests always allowed to mix with the people in the trade yards? We cannot do that in Ughada you know. Can the people go into the temple here?" "Yes, the priests go wherever they want to.

No, the people cannot ever go into the

emple unless the High Priest orders them to or invites them in; and that is very seldom", Hev-Ri answered. He inquired around to see if the Menku traders had been there recently or were expected soon and was greeted with silence.

Finally one of the guards who had drifted off to talk to a corporal from the king's service came back with the news that Menhes was king of Upper Nile and there was war between him and the loyalists below Nekhen. The people of Pe were ordered not to discuss these things with anyone from Upper Nile so that Hor-Amen would not be drawn into the conflict. Since Menhes was a Menku his traders had been forbidden to come to Pe anymore and that was the case all the way to Aqqrem. There was no hostility toward the Menku's; it just seemed prudent to keep out of the affairs of Upper Nile until they could be resolved.

Hev-Ri called his little group together and told them what had happened, asking for their thoughts on what to do next. Vukhath spoke first, "Hev-Ri, I believe we still have a small camp at Crocodile Lake. There should also be a little outpost at Meidum if Hor-Amen has not forced Menku to shut it down. Why don't we see if we can get passage to Meidum. We can always get to the lake from there and then I am sure we can get back to Asyut in a short time; our traders are always going in and out of there."

Hev-Ri asked the others, including the warriors what they thought and they all agreed that though it meant a further delay in getting home it was the only prudent alternative they seemed to have. They were fortunate to have enough barter items left to trade for a passage to Meidum if a boat was available or going that way. Var-Lil was assured that he would be given enough trade goods to get him back to Ughada; after all the Menku men had been stranded with nothing but their weapons and the clothing they wore when Abb-Oth and Rem-Chakh provided for them. They decided to stay at the Pe landing and see what turned up there.

Several dull days passed, dull for everyone but Var-Lil who kept the local people entertained with his tales of Ughada and the Tigris. He was obviously not associated with Upper Nile and his small stock of amulets and beads were so different that he almost always had a crowd of traders and priests around him offering their own things in trade. He would bring items of ivory and gold for Hev-Ri to appraise before he traded and he began to accumulate a rather valuable bag of armlets and small items of jewelry which delighted him no end.

It was over a week before a boat arrived from Meidum with skins from Crocodile Lake. The traders knew of the camp at the lake and were happy to find paying passengers for the return trip. It was Var-Lil who made the arrangements with Bagh watching intently at a discreet distance. Bagh brought the others to the boat where they said nothing until they had sailed up the Nile for hours.

Hev-Ri at last asked the young owner of the boat, "What do you hear from Nekhen?" The young man answered cautiously, "We have heard little except that a man named Menhes has murdered the rightful king of Upper Nile and taken the crown for Nekhen and Edfu." "But he does not control the rest of the kingdom. Is that not true?" Hev-Ri explored, equally cautious. "I think he may have taken some towns between here and Nekhen, Master but which ones we do not know. You are aware we cannot trade with Upper Nile anymore by orders of King Hor-Amen?"

Hev-Ri nodded, "We learned that at Pe when we returned from our long journey to countries beyond the desert. We are drawing wizards and have been visiting great temples which are made of bricks in lands far to the east of the Great Sea. Were you born at Meidum?" "No. I and my brothers here grew up in Aqqrem but there was so much fighting there between the north and south armies that we left two years ago to work out of Meidum. It is safer there now. I am called, Naan. We traded for a man named Menku for awhile but he moved to Asyut and we went out on our own with this boat he gave us. You have no doubt heard of Menku? This Menhes is his son and they say his other sons led the northern armies that took Nekhen."

Shephset asked, "Do the armies of the dead king come past Aqqrem anymore?" "No. But they have taken everything in Asyut and killed all the people at the Menku station there." Vukhath was so horrified he spoke without thinking, "Then our master, Menku is dead!" The young man looked fearfully at the warriors who had raised their spears ominously when they heard Vukhath's outburst, "Who are you, Masters? Menku is not dead. He and his wife and the wife of Menhes are at Crocodile Lake. We would not harm him. You must believe me. Spare us, whoever you are."

Hev-Ri spoke to calm him, "We will not harm you. How do you know about Menku at Crocodile Lake?" "We go there to his camp to see that they are safe. Ekhdur and Khafu told us to provide for their needs and we trade to the north so no one suspects we are from near Asyut. Khafu sent us to Meidum when Menku moved back to the lake." "Did you have family in Asyut?" Hev-Ri asked. "Yes. They are dead now I think." "I am sorry to hear that. I am Hev-Ri. We were priests in the academy at Asyut until a few months ago when we left to go to the city of Kish on the Euphrates. I suppose our families are dead too but we cannot go back to find out now. We will go to Crocodile Lake where Menku is and determine what we will do from there."

The grieving party fell silent for the rest of the trip up the river. Var-Lil was bewildered by it all but could offer no comfort so he too said nothing. They landed at a secluded inlet a few miles north of Meidum and the young brothers told them they would lead them directly to the camp. No one would know that they were there.

CHAPTER ELEVEN   'The Move to Uruk'

Baldag, Fyd and Toq, accompanied by Rom-Sha and the guards walked into the temple yard at Uruk a little after noon the following day and presented themselves to the king. Toq stepped forward as Oghud's emissary and Men-Chad-Rez raised his hand in greeting. Toq walked straight up to him and placed his hand on the king's shoulder, then stepping back he spoke, "I Toq. My father, Oghud. Oghud not come. Oghud say king talk. Toq, Fyd hear king."

Men-Chad-Rez asked Baldag if Toq and Oghud understood the proposal and was told that they did and that Toq and Fyd were there to begin its implementation. Men-Chad-Rez then addressed Toq, "There is an area down river from here where a stream of water has flowed all during the drought. A short distance from the river is a stand of date palms and willows and there are fig trees. There is also grass enough for the animals you will need at the camp. You and Fyd will be taken to look at it. If you like it for a campsite I will give it to your tribe and Oghud can bring the rest of your people there. You will be protected but you will be free to hunt and gather the things you eat as you always have. Your hunters will go with Baldag and other shepherds like him long enough to learn to herd and shear and tend sheep and goats. Grain and other crops will be provided as wages for those who work as shepherds and your women can learn to weave wool and flax and tan hides for trade. You tribe will become self-sufficient and will not need to fear starvation when drought comes again."

Toq appeared puzzled and Baldag asked Men-Chad-Rez for permission to explain to him and Fyd what the king had said. He took them aside and when Toq had repeated everything to indicate he understood he returned to Men-Chad-Rez who waited for him to speak. "Toq hear King. What King say good. Toq go where King say." Men-Chad-Rez asked Kalam-Bad to take Toq and Fyd and show the new campsite to them since it was in his area of authority.

As Baldag approached the reed house Miqel ran out, "Father, where is Fyd? Won't he come back? Won't I see him anymore?" Baldag laughed and lifted him off his feet, "You must learn to be patient if you wish to become a wizard. Fyd will be back soon. He and Toq have gone with Kalam-Bad to look at some land the king has offered the bogs for a campsite." Just then Gahnya walked out and Baldag told her all that had transpired during the past two days. "Where does that leave us? What are we to do now?" she wanted to know. Baldag thought a moment and said, "I think we should go talk to Mar-Dug before it gets too late today. The new moon will rise very soon now and we need to plan the journey to Ur carefully. It is all quite complicated and everything must work out or we will have made your father and mother very unhappy I fear." Gahnya nodded and turning toward the house called out, "Ette. Bodi. Milk the goats and fix some curds for our supper. There are some fish we can grill when we get back. Miqel, gather the flock and bring the goats up for Ette and Bodi. Put some fresh dung on the fire and cook the two barley loaves I just made; the oven is already hot. We should not be gone long."

Mar-Dug came out to the temple yard and motioned Baldag and Gahnya to an empty arbor where they would be cool while they talked. He was concerned at the swiftness with which solutions for all these details had come about and particularly wondered how Gahnya was taking it. "Gahnya, I think we men have involved you without taking much time to talk to you about what we plan. I know Baldag has explained everything to you but I would personally like to hear your thoughts before we proceed any farther." Gahnya was surprised at his candor; it was not necessary for a senior priest of the White Temple to consider the feelings of anyone, much less the wife of a shepherd. "I am as Baldag. I concur in what it is the king has commanded.

Moreover I am quite prepared to help in every way I can. I wish that Miqel could be just a happy boy and grow into a man such as his father. We have had a joyful life with our family but as Baldag has said the gods give to whom they will. It is not for me to go against their wishes".

"You have spoken wisely. It must be hard for a mother to give up her son at such an early age. I think it was for my mother; there were years when I did not see her. And she died without my really knowing her except as a child. Yet I think she wanted me to be a priest and would be pleased that I am to be considered for the High Priesthood someday soon." Mar-Dug then went on to outline what he thought they should do regarding the trip to Ur and the meeting with Akhuruk.

"Baldag, I want Kalam-Bad to go with us. He can take three or four of his warriors along for our protection and I will take the servants to make the journey easier." Baldag interrupted, "I did not know you planned to go to Ur." Mar-Dug continued, "I think it is necessary that I go and that Ifn-Lot accompany me. Akhuruk likes Ifn-Lot and I believe he will trust him. Coban-Bul can teach Fyd much of what he will need to know to be a proper companion and servant to Miqel. You know of course that Miqel's selection places him on a level with the young princes. He will not have many moments to call his own but he will not be distracted by menial tasks either." Gahnya leaned forward, "Shall I accompany you?" "Yes, but I do not think it is really necessary for Baldag to go. Your daughters can stay here with him and he can tend to his responsibilities here. There is no reason to add the hardship of such a journey to his cares. Do you agree, Baldag?" Baldag frowned, "This is a most unusual thing. Yet if Gahnya is willing to go I will stay here until you return." "Let's hope it all works out for the best, Baldag. I will tell the king what we plan. Gahnya, you should be ready to leave at dawn the day after tomorrow. We will provide all the provisions necessary. Just bring whatever clothing you and Miqel will need to go and return. If Akhuruk chooses not to accept the king's offer we will have to bring Miqel back here alone for his education. I hope very much that Akhuruk will come back with us." With that Mar-Dug returned to the temple and Baldag and Gahnya walked quietly back to their reed house.

Baldag called Miqel to him, "My son, you will be going to Ur in two days with your mother and Mar-Dug. Kalam-Bad will go with you and of course Fyd will be by your side the whole journey. The king wishes your grandfather to move the academy here and take his place in the service of the White Temple. Your mother and I do not know whether Akhuruk will be willing to do that; he and Urunya may wish to stay in Ur. But your mother and I want you to come back here either way. Ifn-Lot will watch over your education but we all feel that you will benefit from your grandfather's training; he is a great teacher." Miqel asked, "If Papa and Unya do not come here won't I see them anymore?" Gahnya pulled him to her, "We will go and see them from time to time. But let's hope that they will move here and you can see us and them on a regular basis. Whatever Papa decides you must accept his wishes, Miqel. The king has commanded that you are to study in the White Temple here."

The following morning Kalam-Bad returned to the temple yard with Toq and Fyd and walked up to where Men-Chad-Rez sat, "We have seen the land and Toq wants to talk to you." The king smiled and gestured to Toq to speak. "Land good. Toq, Fyd like land. Toq go camp. Bring Oghud new camp. Bring tribe new camp. King good man." Men-Chad-Rez sealed the agreement by placing his right hand on Toq's shoulder and giving him a small copper amulet to take to Oghud as a sign of possession of the land. Kalam-Bad gave him a necklace of crocodile teeth and carnelian on which to hang the amulet. It would serve as protection for Oghud and future chiefs: a promise that the people of Kalam-Bad's domain would know of the king's decree and not interfere in any way with the tribe's freedom. Toq beamed and lay down, prostrate before the king. At that Men-Chad-Rez lifted him to his feet and pronounced, "Toq is the son of Oghud, Chief of the Tribe of Hathuruk. Whoever harms Oghud harms the king. Let the people know that this is true. I have spoken it."

As Toq left to return to his newly named tribe Men-Chad-Rez told Kalam-Bad of Mar-Dug's planned visit to Ur the next day and that he was to accompany him. "It is good. I wish to take my daughter, Ekhana to Ur; she has never been there and it will be a fine experience for her." Ekhana was almost eleven years old and the only child of Kalam-Bad and his wife, Methwyd. She was a beautiful child; it would not be long before she would be betrothed to the son of another prince of Uruk as was the custom and Kalam-Bad was determined that she should be as learned as possible before that. He and Methwyd had taught her the elements of agriculture and animal husbandry and she had been briefly apprenticed to a jewelry craftsman to learn the values of various metals and stones.

Mar-Dug was at the temple gate before the sun rose the next morning. He waved as Kalam-Bad, Ekhana and four warriors approached and smiled to find that Miqel was already there with Fyd and his mother. Kalam-Bad had told Ekhana of Fyd's assignment to Miqel but she was still apprehensive as he walked up and towering over her spoke, "I Fyd. Girl not be afraid of Fyd. Fyd show girl how fish." Ekhana giggled in embarrassment and Kalam-Bad guffawed, "Ekhana, you must learn from Fyd. No one I know can catch fish the way he does. Is that not true, Miqel?" "Oh, yes. Fyd can do everything, Ekhana. Wait till you see him kill a hare with his club."

Kalam-Bad told Mar-Dug that they would spend the first night at the place where Eh-Buran had been killed. Fyd had told him it was a good place to camp and that there was water and shelter there. Coban-Bul and his servants herded goats with the provisions and fire-pots to make the trip as pleasant as possible; there was even a small tent for Gahnya and Ekhana. As they set out Fyd, holding the leashes of two of the dogs took Miqel and Ekhana in front of the group until they were separated by about a hundred paces. Then he let the dogs roam free to see if they would stir up any small game.

Miqel and Ekhana raced after the dogs for awhile until they came on a fig tree loaded with ripe fruit. Ekhana began gathering figs eagerly, "We will take these to your mother and my father, Miqel. They will like them don't you think?" Miqel's mouth was too full to answer but he grinned, nodding in agreement. Just then the dogs began barking furiously and the sound of Fyd's whirling club caught their attention. A wild pig dropped with a broken neck and Fyd called out, "Miqel, Come see." Ekhana put down her figs and they both rushed to where Fyd was standing with the pig held high for them to see. Miqel looked at Ekhana, "Didn't I tell you? Fyd can do everything!" She grinned and touched Fyd's arm. He reached down and swept her up on his shoulder and started back to give the pig to Coban-Bul, letting her down at the fig tree to collect her gift. Miqel ran ahead excitedly calling to his mother to come and see what they had found.

The party had followed the river, staying only a short distance from it now that it had risen past its normal level. When they reached the former campsite it was flooded, however there was plenty of area still sheltered by trees farther up on the bank. As a result of the rains tamarisk was everywhere and it afforded some privacy for Gahnya's tent. Fyd spoke to Kalam-Bad, "Fyd go find boat. Fyd come back." Kalam-Bad wanted to know what he was talking about but decided to send two of the warriors with him without further questioning.

After the bogs had abandoned it weeks before the thieves' boat had washed ashore and jammed behind a bed of rushes some distance downstream. It did not appear to be damaged however and to the warriors' delight still contained the thieves' swords and several excellent slings. The three men struggled and heaved; finally freeing the reed skiff they began slowly poling it back to the camp site. Kamal-Bad was both surprised and elated; with the skiff they could reach Ur by the following afternoon and complete the formalities of presenting themselves to the king of Ur well before sundown. Mar-Dug was less sure and Kamal-Bad ordered the warriors to take the boat upstream a short way and let it float back down in the rushing stream to assure Mar-Dug that it was safe. When it was tied up again he was satisfied and returned to where Coban-Bul was preparing the pig for their meal. "I see we will have a feast tonight, Coban-Bul. Do you think there will be enough for all of us?" "Yes, Master. There will be enough; look at these fish Fyd and Miqel and Ekhana caught while the warriors were testing the boat. We will eat well this night."

It was fortunate that the skiff was a large one since the entire party, goats and all had to get aboard. Although it rode somewhat low in the water there appeared to be no danger when it was launched very early the next morning. The skiff had barely left the bank when the midstream current of the Euphrates caught it and the bow lifted sharply out of the water. Two warriors with poles rushed forward and called for Fyd to bring the goats to the front to stabilize the craft. With that the skiff was manageable and the passengers settled down to enjoy the sights with a gentle breeze blowing in their faces.

About half way to Ur four or five crocodiles drifted out to see what was going on but did not bother anything, though they did scare the wits out of Miqel and Ekhana. Fyd laughed uproariously, "Fyd come back. Fyd kill monsters. Make good hides. Teeth make fine beads." Kalam-Bad smiled, "Not this trip, Fyd. Perhaps another time. We must get on to Ur today."

Shortly after high noon the farms surrounding Ur came into view and the warriors began steering the skiff toward the bank. Temple Al-Ubaid loomed in the distance and Miqel was quick to point it out to Ekhana. "Have you ever been inside the temple?" she asked Miqel. "No. But Ifn-Lot and Mar-Dug have been there. Ifn-Lot took me through the White Temple at home once. It is very beautiful and very, very large." Ekhana was duly impressed and Miqel continued to tell her of the wonders of the White Temple until they came to the Ur landing. Fyd leaped into the shallow water and taking one of the plaited ropes began to pull the skiff to beach it. The warriors plunged in beside him and in a few minutes the boat was safely on the gravel at the landing.

A guard detail from King Qom-Tur's service approached them with spears lowered and a corporal ordered them to stay where they were and state their purpose for landing at Ur. The giant Kalam-Bad stepped forward, "I am Prince Kalam-Bad of Uruk. These are my guests and I wish to see the king." The corporal was unmoved and pointed his spear at Fyd, "You dare to bring a bog before the king!" "This is Fyd of the tribe of Hathuruk by order of the King of Uruk. This is Mar-Dug, Senior Priest of the White Temple. He knows your High Priest well and will tell him that I speak the truth," Kalam-Bad argued. The corporal stepped back and, with spear still lowered ordered the party to proceed to the temple gate where the Captain of the Guard would decide what to do with them.

As they neared the temple yard the Qom-Tur watched with concern. The menacing appearance of the guards implied that the party was a threat and he dispatched the Captain of the Guard immediately to determine what was going on. As they came closer the king recognized Kalam-Bad and Mar-Dug and strode over to where they waited, "My friend, Kalam-Bad...and my friend, Mar-Dug. Welcome to Ur. What brings you to our city?" Kalam-Bad and Mar-Dug quickly explained their mission without mentioning their intent to move Akhuruk's academy to

Uruk. They commended the corporal's diligence but assured the king that their intent was entirely peaceful. Kalam-Bad pointed to Gahnya, "This is the daughter of Akhuruk and this is his grandson, Miqel who spent the past three years here at the academy. Is Akhuruk well?" "He is well. I think he may be at the temple now.", the king responded.

Kalam-Bad asked the Qom-Tur to step aside with him, "Before we go to find Akhuruk I have some sad news for the family of a young boy named Malil from Ur. He was a student at the academy with young Miqel and went to visit Miqel's family in Uruk two moons ago. A few weeks ago he was killed by a lion and we must tell his family. This bog you see killed the lion and saved Miqel from being attacked but Malil had already been mauled so badly he died almost instantly." The king was shocked, "Enlid is here. The boys went to Uruk with him and he knows Malil's family well. Tell him your story and he will take you to them. Akhuruk will be almost as upset as the boy's family; he thought of Malil as if he were his own grandson. The bog is your responsibility, Kalam-Bad. Do not let him out of the sight of your warriors while you are here. The people of Ur will not understand his presence even if I tell them."

The High Priest of Al-Ubaid came out to see what the commotion was about and recognizing Mar-Dug and Ifn-Lot rushed over to greet them warmly. Mar-Dug smiled, "My friend, Ghant-Ur. It is indeed a pleasure to see you again so soon. Perhaps you can help us." With that Mar-Dug explained the situation with Fyd and Miqel and how Fyd had tried unsuccessfully to save Malil. At his request Ghant-Ur told King Qom-Tur, "The bog, Fyd is welcome to stay with us in the temple for a few days. He will be safe there while the others visit Akhuruk. By the way Akhuruk is in the temple now. I will send for him for I know he has missed Miqel and will want to see his Gahnya."

While the others waited for Akhuruk Kalam-Bad went looking for Enlid since he knew him from their meeting at the campsite on their previous trip. Enlid was deeply moved at the news of Malil's death, "He was such a bright boy and so full of fun. I will take you to his family but let me tell them. I think it will be easier coming from a friend they know. Even so I could wish this lot did not fall to me; he was much loved at home."

When Akhuruk came out of the temple into the yard Miqel ran to him and hugging him began to cry, "Oh, Papa. Malil is dead. A lion killed him while we were at the far meadow." As Gahnya came up to him Akhuruk asked, "What is this? Malil is dead and all this company has come to Ur. Why?" "Father, I think we need to go home and talk to you and Mother. Yes, Malil was mauled by a lion and Miqel was spared only by Fyd's quick actions. Fyd, come here for a moment; I want you to meet my father."

Akhuruk was obviously confused and quite taken aback when Miqel grabbed Fyd's hand and brought him over to be introduced. Fyd, sensing his problem spoke before Akhuruk could say anything, "I Fyd. Miqel my friend. Papa my friend. I not hurt you." At last Akhuruk smiled and placed his hand on Fyd's shoulder, "Thank you for protecting Miqel. I am sure we will get to know each other better. For now this is all too much for me. You go with Ghant-Ur now and I will take my family to our home."

Kalam-Bad and Mar-Dug decided to explain at least part of their mission to Qom-Tur and approached him to request a further audience. The king listened carefully as they told him their plans to try to persuade Akhuruk to return to where his daughter could look after him and his wife. Mar-Dug told him that Ifn-Lot was prepared to assist in Miqel's education and that Miqel would be admitted as a priest in the White Temple service when he had completed his training under Akhuruk at Uruk.

Qom-Tur thought over what they were saying and asked, "Does Ghant-Ur know about this?

Have Ayn-Far and Men-Chad-Res agreed to it?" With that Kalam-Bad told him of the bogs' involvement in the capture of Eh-Buran's gang and Miqel's attachment to Fyd. He went on to explain what Men-Chad-Res had done for Oghud's tribe, even giving them lands near Uruk for their own and naming the tribe, Hathuruk. Qom-Tur was astonished, "Enlid told me of Eh-Buran's death and the capture and execution of his gang. But he did not mention anything about bogs. Is Men-Chad-Rez sure that his plan is safe for the people of Uruk...and for our people here in Ur?"

Mar-Dug answered him, "We had the same concerns, as did Men-Chad-Rez at first. But on investigation we found that there were so few bogs left in this tribe...and there are no others in this entire area insofar as we know...that they would not likely survive unless Uruk helped them. Men-Chad-Rez feared a rogue tribe would develop if their situation became any more desperate; they almost starved last summer. In fact their presence at the far meadow was a result of that desperation: a band had crossed the river to hunt. One of the hunters drowned in the crossing; you know the bogs never cross the river, at least they have not in my memory."

"I understand. I suppose the matter of transferring the academy to Uruk was just a matter of time. Either that or it would have been closed because of Akhuruk's age. I wish now I had placed him in the service of Al-Ubaid; he and Urunya have so little. Mar-Dug, from your recent visit I think you know how badly we have fared in the drought. Ur is far more dependent on game and naturally growing produce than Uruk. Actually we have been blessed by being closer to the sea, but that blessing has become a curse as we have come to rely too much on nature. It is my plan to send farmers to Uruk to learn of your methods and find how much land we need to put into cultivation to provide for our needs beyond the produce we get from garden plots and small farms devoted almost entirely to barley."

Kalam-Bad interjected, "They will be welcome of course. No, I do not think Men-Chad-Rez knew of your plight, beyond the shortages we have all experienced. We were generously fed when I was here with Mar-Dug; I suppose we never thought about where the food came from." Qom-Tur laughed, "Now that the rains have come there is more game and plenty of fish. I know Mar-Dug wants to be with Ghant-Ur while he is here. Kalam-Bad, why don't you and your daughter stay with us; I assure we have plenty to eat and will enjoy sharing it with you."

Urunya was ecstatic to see Gahnya and Miqel. Before she could begin to prepare the evening meal Gahnya informed her that Coban-Bul had been assigned to provide everything for them so they could visit without interruption. Akhuruk would wait no longer, "Gahnya, I want to know all...all about what has prompted your visit. You know we have wanted you to come for a long time and we want to know all about Baldag and Ette and Bodi too. But to be escorted here by a Prince and a Senior Priest and to have servants preparing our food is most unusual. Such things just do not happen." Gahnya put her hand on Akhuruk's arm, "Father, I think Miqel is going to burst if I do not let him tell you and Mother all that has happened since he and Malil left to come home for awhile. Baldag and Ette and Bodi are well; and they are very busy right now I suspect. As for Kalam-Bad and Mar-Dug I will explain their being here after Miqel is through."

Ghant-Ur wanted to know about things at the White Temple, Ayn-Far in particular so Mar-Dug began, "There is nothing new at the temple since I was last here. However Ayn-Far is failing fast. He has said little about it, but his limp has become more pronounced and the other day he said he did not think he has long to live. It is sad; he has been a great High Priest for all of us. You know it was Ayn-Far who obtained general agreement among the temples of Sumer for the exact order of the twenty-two steps in the Sacred Circle' construction." "Yes, I know. I was a Senior Priest then and there was a lot of opposition to the addition of the twelfth and eighteenth steps. Worse, there was a strong faction supporting the short, fractional version. I am not sure that that group will ever give up. I am distressed at the news of Ayn-Far, both as a friend and out of fear of what we face when he is gone. Do you think you can hold the temples to the agreement, Mar-Dug?"

Mar-Dug remained silent for a long time, staring at the floor. Then he looked up, "I do not know, Ghant-Ur. I plan eventually to send Ifn-Lot back to Kish to reinforce our position. Kmal-Dyl is widely respected for his work: it was his final argument that led to the adoption of the twenty-two step master construction. Nevertheless those fanatical people in Mari, perhaps with a displaced wizard from the Nile have recently established a following for the fractional shortcut. Aside from day to day usage they have a lot of right on their side if that solution is used only for dimensioning systems when working with the squared circle. I even support that. But the 'Sacred Circle' is sacred ground and should not be tampered with. To send Ifn-Lot to Kish right now could lead to open conflict."

Ghant-Ur responded, "Ayn-Far's authority will fall to you, Mar-Dug. I will support you and Ifn-Lot, as will all the priests of Al-Ubaid. And I believe you can count on Eridu. South Sumer is pretty much of one opinion now. If we become divided it could lead to war. The kings want accord, not discord and the chiefs and princes go the way of the temples. If Kish turns westward and follows Mari our southern priests and wizards will be isolated. War with Mari would be a fearful thing; their warriors are not easily defeated and they appear to have a lot of them."

Ghant-Ur continued, "Turning to a lighter subject, why should we not have Ifn-Lot take Miqel and the little girl, Ekhana through Al-Ubaid? They would enjoy it I think and if indeed Miqel does wish to become a wizard it might reinforce your standard construction position some day." Mar-Dug agreed and called for Ifn-Lot immediately. When Ifn-Lot came in Ghant-Ur rose and suggested, "Ifn-Lot, Mar-Dug and I think it would please Miqel and Ekhana if you gave them a tour of the temple tomorrow. I will advise our priests so there will be no interference and you are free to show them anything you think it is wise that they see. Our custom here is as it is at the White Temple, children do not address Senior Priests and answer only if they are spoken to."

Miqel and Ekhana were happy to be with Fyd again; Ghant-Ur had given permission for him to accompany them on their walk through the temple. The drawings and paintings were as much a mystery to Ekhana as they were to Fyd but she was fascinated with them and would have stayed all day for Ifn-Lot to answer her questions if he had not kept them moving. Miqel promised her, "I will teach you the Zodiac of the sky and how stars lead the way to the south." "Oh, would you? That would be wonderful, Miqel." Fyd seemed puzzled at what they were talking about and Miqel told him he could learn these things too. Ifn-Lot was amused at Miqel's presumption that everyone would fully comprehend anything he could understand but decided to say nothing as they returned to Mar-Dug and Ghant-Ur.

Things had not gone so well at Akhuruk's tent. When Gahnya told him of all the plans Baldag and the king had worked out and that Mar-Dug really did want him to set up his academy in the White Temple he rebelled at the idea. "I am not so old that I must be led by the hand, Gahnya. Urunya and I have done well enough all these years and I am quite sure I can provide for us here as I always have. Now that the rains have come we can find game easily enough and tuition will be more forthcoming from the farmers and shepherds who want their sons to be wizards." It was getting late and Urunya quietly told Gahnya to drop the subject until the next day.

After Gahnya and Miqel were asleep Urunya spoke to Akhuruk, "Papa, you and I are old. We

111

are not feeble and there have not been so many summers in our lives that there will not be more. But we cannot change the ways the years have dealt with us and times to come will be more harsh without any family to know our needs. If Miqel is as gifted as you and Mar-Dug think he is he deserves your teaching; with Malil dead there is no one else here among your scholars that you have mentioned as having the capacity to become a Senior Priest. For me it would be nice to be near our daughter and grandchildren and have a reed house to live in. And I think you would be pleased to know you could provide for us from your academy without resorting to handouts from Gahnya and Baldag. We might even have enough to give our grandchildren gifts. That will never happen here in Ur." Akhuruk merely snorted but it was obvious Urunya's argument had struck a chord as he settled fitfully into sleep.

While Miqel and Ekhana were seeing the temple Ghant-Ur called Akhuruk to meet with him before the shrine of Al-Ubaid. As the sun's rays streamed across the Altar of Sacrifice Ghant-Ur spoke, "Akhuruk, Qom-Tur and I have not been fair to you these past few years. Your academy has provided the young priests we have needed and they are excellently trained when we get them. The severe shortages we have all suffered were not sufficient cause for withholding fair payment for your services. I am sorry for that. If recompense were the only matter to deal with we could well provide for you and Urunya without your having to move to Uruk. However there is an overriding consideration here and that is Miqel. Unless he becomes the wizard we have looked for to stabilize the situation in the coming years all our work may come to nothing and kings and priests will spend all their time fighting futile wars over different constructions for the 'Sacred Circle' and the "Circle and Square'."

"I think I know that what you say is true. My own pride has been hurt, not only here at Ur but in Uruk as well. It is hard for one such as I am to forget the humiliation of grubbing for a living and depriving a wife of things that even an uneducated farmer provides. Urunya has convinced me that Men-Chad-Rez is offering a real position where I can actually contribute to the White Temple service and at the same time do what is right for Miqel. I will go to Uruk but first let me gather the priests I have trained and speak to them. Would you join me in that?" "Of course, Akhuruk. We will do it today and I think Qom-Tur would like to be included also."

During the time the Uruk party had been in Ur Kalam-Bad's warriors had been at the Ur landing negotiating for sails to be mounted on the reed boat they had arrived on. By the morning of the second day the boat was ready for trial and the warriors each took turns handling the sails and the long oars that would serve as rudders when they sailed back upstream to Uruk. The little tent they had brought was erected near the center of the skiff and would give shade for the journey. They were sure this was as close to a king's barge as they were going to get from the meager bartering goods available to them. And it was indeed comfortable and fairly fast in the water, even against the Euphrates current.

As the day neared its end Qom-Tur had a feast prepared for his guests from Uruk. Lambs and pigs were roasted on the spit and wine was plentiful. Qom-Tur rose to speak, "I am glad you have come here. Mar-Dug, we still do not have the means to assist you in the creation of the great henge in the far eastern country but we are grateful to be able to send you on your way with better fare than the last time you were here. Kalam-Bad, will you speak to Men-Chad-Rez regarding our discussions of increased farm production here in Ur?" Kalam-Bad assured him that he would and also invited him to send his farmers to Kalam-Bad's own lands whenever it was convenient. Qom-Tur continued, "We will miss Akhuruk and his academy here but we wish all of you every success, particularly you, young Miqel. Much can come of your mastery of the secrets of the circle. Apply yourself and listen carefully to your masters while you have time to learn. It will not be so long until you are a man like one of us and then there will be too many distractions for you to learn all these things." Miqel humbly lowered his head at such a compliment from a king but he smiled as Ekhana beamed at him and Gahnya pulled him close, still wondering at all that had transpired in so short a time. Qom-Tur told them he and Ghant-Ur would be at the gate in the morning when they would be leaving for Uruk and the different groups parted to bed down before the light was completely gone for the the day.

A light rain fell that night and the air was quite cool when the last star faded and the pink glow in the east served notice of another day. Fyd was permitted to accompany the warriors and Coban-Bul to the landing to wait for the rest of the group to arrive there. He marveled at the boat with its sails, "How boat go? No poles to push boat? How get Uruk?" The warriors explained that the wind would drive the boat upstream but though Fyd had seen sailing boats before he could not believe that the boat they had arrived on could be so easily converted to a wind-powered craft in so short a time.

With Akhuruk and Urunya and their modest possessions added to the load it was decided that three of the warriors would travel back to Uruk by land. Although a southeasterly wind had come up the boat would not reach Uruk landing before sometime the second day and this meant finding a site to pull into for one night. Kalam-Bad hoped they could make it to the place where his party had met Enlid's trading group since it had been an ideal spot for camping. Fyd was given one of the steering oars and placed alongside the one remaining warrior to help keep the boat faced into the current. Kalam-Bad took charge of the sails though no one asked if he knew anything about sails; as it turned out he knew very little about sailing.

Things went smoothly at first and the boat made slow headway upriver. The wind began to gust and Kalam-Bad was almost swept overboard attempting to hold the sails against the wind. In spite of all Fyd and the warrior could do the "barge" piled into a large mass of reeds and disturbed a couple of sleeping crocodiles. It was decided that the warrior would man the sails and Kalam-Bad and Fyd would tend to the oars, but only after the wind died down a bit. After a short while the wind settled to a steady breeze and the skiff was once more launched out into the Euphrates where it sailed straight up the middle and held course for several hours. Fyd was once more disappointed that he had to leave the crocodiles but there was nothing to do about it. Miqel was almost as disappointed as Fyd for he was determined to show Ekhana that Fyd could do 'everything'. Akhuruk was filled with dismay and certain that this was all an evil omen against his leaving Ur, however Urunya got him to talk to Miqel and Ekhana which proved to be a worthwhile distraction from his grumpiness.

Along about mid-afternoon Mar-Dug caught sight of the place where they had crossed the river two months before and pointed it out to Kalam-Bad. "I think your are right, Mar-Dug. It surely does look like the place, but the water level is so much higher we will have to find a different landing spot; the banks are too high here. A short way upstream they came to a small inlet and steered into it without mishap, beaching the prow of the skiff with the confidence of professionals. Fyd glowed with pride as Akhuruk patted him on the shoulder and said, "How glad I am we have a real boatman with us." Kalam-Bad chose to ignore the sarcasm but Mar-Dug called Coban-Bul over to see if there was any wine. There was and Mar-Dug walked over to Akhuruk, "Take a little of this with a crust of barley loaf. It will settle your stomach", (and your disposition he thought to himself).

Miqel and Ekhana insisted that Fyd go fishing with them and they happily set out for some shallows near the boat. In a short while they had taken enough fish for the whole party. Ekhana had caught more than Miqel and almost as many as Fyd and took them to Coban-Bul, strutting like a peacock. It was Miqel's turn to be disgruntled but Fyd motioned to him to come with him down river a little way. He had seen some geese feeding there and thought Miqel might bring one down with his sling to save his face from Ekhana's gloating. Miqel let fly with a stone and felled a large goose his first shot as Fyd's great club brought down another one almost simultaneously. Miqel strode triumphantly into camp but Ekhana did not want to believe he had killed the goose, "Fyd did it. Fyd did it." Urunya laughed and said, "Ekhana, I have seen Miqel's sling in action many times. I assure you he killed the goose. But enough of jealousy, you two. We are all glad to have what you and Fyd have provided. Am I not right, Coban-Bul?" Coban-Bul nodded enthusiastically, "Oh, yes, Madam. These will be much better than the meat I brought for us to eat. You rest now and we will have a meal very quickly."

At dawn Kalam-Dug was alarmed to find that Fyd was missing. Miqel was at as much a loss as any of the others to know what might have happened to him, "He was here when we went to sleep. He can't have just disappeared. He has gone hunting, don't you think? That must be it: he has gone hunting." Gahnya was upset, "But why, Miqel? He knows we will be in Uruk today and that we have plenty. He did not need to go hunting." Before there was any more speculation Fyd appeared with a crocodile skin, head and teeth still intact, "Fyd kill monster. Good hide. Fyd keep hide. Teeth make pretty things for mother, Miqel. I fix teeth for you." Kalam-Bad was almost doubled up with laughter but Ekhana was horrified, "Fyd, you could have been killed! Why would you do such a thing?" "Monster not hurt Fyd. Fyd kill monster." To him was the simple sum of it.

With a good breeze the party arrived at Uruk shortly after noon. They made their way to the temple yard and Men-Chad-Rez came to meet them, "Akhuruk. Urunya. I am so glad you came. Welcome to Uruk and we all hope you will be happy here." "Thank you, Men-Chad-Rez. I am rather looking forward to it now. The thought of moving has been unsettling to me, but it will be good for us to be back with our family. There is much to do to get the academy going as soon as I can and I would like to do that." Baldag came running with Ette and Bodi, and Akhuruk and Urunya took the girls into their arms, tears streaming down their faces. Baldag embraced Gahnya and Miqel, then turning to Akhuruk, "Papa, it is wonderful to have you here. We will make things as good as we can for you." "I will take care of myself and Urunya, Baldag." Akhuruk snapped and Gahnya shook her head at Baldag, signaling no response was in order. Poor Baldag was as bewildered as Men-Chad-Rez but it seemed better just to let the matter drop for the time being.

Mar-Dug walked over to Akhuruk and gently placed his hand on his arm, "Why don't you let Urunya go with Gahnya and Baldag and the children while you come to the temple with me for a little while? There are important things we need to do and you will have plenty of time to visit afterward." Akhuruk's face lighted up, "Of course. Of course, Mar-Dug. We must get on with what I came here to do. Urunya, you go on to the house and I will see you there later." He bent down and hugged Miqel, "We must get things ready for you to start working on the 'Sacred Circle' immediately. Is that not true, Ifn-Lot?" Ifn-Lot said that it was true and that Miqel should be ready to begin his studies the next morning. "Did you bring Miqel's square and compasses with you?" he asked Akhuruk. "Certainly. Of course I did. He must have them and there will be no time for the tedious process of making new ones, now will there?"

Akhuruk was happy for the time being, after having served notice that he was someone to be reckoned with. And after all the years of being ignored his importance as a teacher was appreciated, both in Ur and Uruk, kings and high priests alike.

At the reed house Baldag asked Gahnya what in the world was the matter with Akhuruk.

Urunya overheard him and sighed, "Baldag, Papa is an old man and with all the plans and commands from kings and High Priests I think he felt he was being taken for granted. I myself contributed to it when I talked him into coming here. We have all been thinking only of Miqel when it was Akhuruk who recognized Miqel's potential in the beginning. And it was Akhuruk who disciplined Miqel and Malil to where someone as eminent as Mar-Dug would see that potential in Miqel. He is not a vain man, nor is he just old and crotchety. He can have a great influence on Miqel for some time yet and I suspect he does not want any interference in his teaching methods. You must impart this to Ifn-Lot or we really will have a sour old man on our hands. Worse, we might even turn Miqel away from his promise of greatness."

CHAPTER TWELVE   'Chad-Mar, the High Priest'

Ayn-Far called Mar-Dug and Ifn-Lot to his bedside the morning after they returned from Uruk, "You were not gone long. Did all go as we planned?" "Yes, Ayn-Far. Things went well and Akhuruk is here at the temple this morning setting up his academy in the room you designated for him." Mar-Dug answered. "How are Ghant-Ur and Qom-Tur? Are things any better at Ur and Al-Ubaid now that the rains have come?" "Much better. In fact Qom-Tur gave a feast for us the night before we left. He and Ghant-Ur are fully in support of what we plan to do. Qom-Tur even apologized to Akhuruk for their lack of support of his academy during the years of the drought." Ayn-Far smiled weakly, "I never thought he would go that far. Qom-Tur has been a headstrong ruler, not always a good one for Ur. Ur has fallen behind Uruk over the years that he and his father have reigned there."

Mar-Dug agreed but went on, "He and Kalam-Bad worked out an agreement I am sure Men-Chad-Rez will support where farmers from Ur will come to Uruk to learn of our farming methods and allocation of lands to relieve their overdependence on game and wild produce." Ayn-Far coughed and lay back, "I know little of such things but it should strengthen our ties for the future. And that is essential. I hope we will be able to do as well with Eridu and Kish. Does Ghant-Ur comprehend the situation we face with the priests of Mari?" "He does indeed. He has offered the full support of the priests and wizards of Al-Ubaid but will not take any part in the leadership to hold the standards of the 'Sacred Circle'. That appears to fall squarely on our shoulders."

"Your shoulders, Mar-Dug. Yours and Miqel's if he turns out as we expect." Mar-Dug was alarmed at how weak Ayn-Far was, "Master, you must rest now. We will come back when you are feeling better. Can I get you anything?" "No, thank you. But stay. I fear I shall not have a time of 'feeling better', Mar-Dug. The past few days have been very hard for me and I have no strength to resist whatever it is that is taking the life out of me. There is much that I want to talk to you and Ifn-Lot about regarding the establishment of a standardized method for the application of the diagrams in our search for knowledge about the circle and how it relates to the square. There has to be a better way to communicate what we know than years of teaching aspiring young priests each step of the way." Ifn-Lot broke in, "I know all too well that that is true. By the time they have been trained to draw with precision many of the brightest youngsters have lost interest in contributing anything to advancing the level of knowledge we have already attained. But I do not know what is to be done about that."

Mar-Dug bent over Ayn-Far, then sat back, "Ayn-Far I think there is a way. And I believe someone with a fresh and uncluttered mind like Miqel's can help us to achieve it. We must somehow create a set of symbols that can be taught with rigid discipline so that wizards from anywhere can recognize the points of departure being addressed in future discussions relating to the circle and its resolution." Ayn-Far raised himself on one elbow, "Something that would insure the remembrance of the order of the constructions? None of us has ever known anyone who could tell us where the basic diagram came from. For all we know it just is. But everyone everywhere accepts these symbols without any really major differences in their order or how they are applied. Even the fractional people do not argue over it; they use it as their foundation the same as we do."

Ayn-Far's eyes glistened, "What will you use for a memory device to tie the symbols together so there is no variation in the order of application? We all know that the order is all important to reaching the conclusion." Mar-Dug went on, "Do you recall Kmal-Dyl's little story about the 'god's eye'? I think it could serve very well. It can even be expanded on to further insure there is no deviation in the order of the three constructions that produce the Sacred Circle." "That is a child's story, Mar-Dug. It is charming in its simplicity but I fear we would be laughed out of the temple by even our own senior wizards if we went around reciting it as a method of furthering research." "It would not be my intent to introduce it to the older geometers. Let the young boys learn it and tie it to a given set of descriptive ciphers so that it stays with them all their lives."

Ifn-Lot grinned, "I remember that story: 'An evil demon plucked out Horus' right eye. The messenger of God, Thetu found the pieces and put them back together for Horus. But it was Horus's better eye, the left one which became sacred and must be remembered if anyone wishes to find the secret of the Sacred Circle.' I learned it when I was very young. Mar-Dug, I recall you had been visiting with Kmal-Dyl and told it to me."

Mar-Dug mused, "Miqel talked about a serpent taking the eye away instead of Zeti; or perhaps that is what Akhuruk calls Zeti when he teaches. The Nile Priests claim a legendary figure took the right eye and divided it into symbols, each one representing a part of the eye. The symbols are assigned to fractions. When they add the fractions together they are one sixty-fourth short of totaling 'One'. They add an odd little cipher they call, 'Life' to make the whole. It looks somewhat like a fisherman's hand net. I am told priests from the Nile region have fashioned it in gold and wear it as an amulet...they call it 'ankh' and people worship it. Ayn-Far became agitated, "That is what I fear the most, Mar-Dug. People will worship anything. If we do not obtain widespread consensus soon kings will start fixing their rule to these geometric constructions and there will be holy wars before we know it." "That has not happened yet in Sumer, Ayn-Far, or to my knowledge in the Mari country. But the myth Ifn-Lot just recited has already been used for god-creatures in both the upper and lower kingdoms of the Nile area. They see the hawk as the embodiment of Horus, their 'god of gods'...not 'The God'...but the chief god of the earth divinities. 'Zeti' is supposed to be a mythical demon but they worship him just the same. And Thetu is 'Thoth' or 'Dahooty', something like that. Anyway it is their name for the Ibis which they have now endowed with supernatural powers of intellect. In the Upper Nile kingdom people would fight you if you challenged their practice of worshiping such idiotic fantasies. One of our wizards barely escaped with his life there a few years ago when he laughed at some people who prostrated themselves before an engraved Horus.

This was more than Ayn-Far could contend with. He became violently ill and began to vomit with flecks of blood visible on his white beard. "Ifn-Lot, summon Coban-Bul to come at once!" Mar-Dug shouted. Before Coban-Bul could get there Ayn-Far went into convulsions and began gasping for air. His eyes pleaded for help even though he knew there was no help to give. He was dying and all Mar-Dug could do was bathe his forehead.

Coban-Bul and Ifn-Lot entered the room running and Coban-Bul, after one look pulled Mar-Dug away from the bed, "Master, you are the High Priest now. Master Ayn-Far is dead." "I never should have let him get so upset. It is my fault, Ifn-Lot. It is my fault. I feel like a murderer." Mar-Dug was sobbing as he knelt beside the bed. "No, Master. Master Ayn-Far called me late in the night and I gave him some broth and washed his face and beard. He was spitting blood then and knew he would not last through this day. He made me promise to say nothing until he had talked to you about some matters that he said were more important to him than life." Coban-Bul spoke very softly, yet with authority and Mar-Dug knew he was telling the truth.

117

Men-Chad-Rez closed the temple yard and declared a week of mourning for the memory of Ayn-Far, High Priest, Emissary of God and Prince of Luhinlil, the god of the White Temple. Mar-Dug would officiate at all ceremonies and then his own official elevation would take place at the next new moon.

The long cortege of robed and hooded priests issued from the temple gate and wound its way toward the Euphrates where a pyre had been prepared on a palm log barge. The pall bearers carrying Ayn-Far's body on a woven-plank bier walked in front of Mar-Dug and came to a halt before Men-Chad-Rez and the assembled princes of Uruk. They stood silently in ankle deep water while the bier was lifted on to the pyre. As Mar-Dug struck the pyre three times with the funereal torch Men-Chad-Rez raised his arms toward the sky, threw his head back and shouted, "God, Most High, the inward being of your noble servant comes to you now. Let no wind or bird prevent the smoke of his breath from rising straight to where you dwell. Let this fire warm the heavens as the sun warms the earth. I, Men-Chad-Rez, King of Uruk, Chief Prince of Luhinlil and the White Temple have spoken it."

The flaming barge drifted slowly into the current of the river. There was silence on shore until it disappeared downstream. Then a shout was raised by the priests and the king's company, "God, Most High, let Mar-Dug rule your temple with wisdom. Let this people be glad for your grace. Let this people follow Mar-Dug with obedience." Mar-Dug fell prostrate before Men-Chad-Rez. When the king had lifted him to his feet Mar-Dug proclaimed, "To you I bow, Chief Prince of Luhinlil. To no other of earth's beings do I bow." Men-Chad-Rez concluded the service with, "It is good."

Miqel had watched all this with his family and wondered at what it meant to him and to them. On the way back to the reed house Akhuruk took him by the hand and looked down, speaking softly, "Miqel, it is well that you have known Ayn-Far even for so short a time. He was truly a great wizard before he became High Priest and he has done much to keep our standards from being violated by those less gifted. Mar-Dug will be even greater I think; he must be for change is shaking the beliefs of many of our number now. I will do all I can to give you a solid foundation in geometry but you must grow in it until you cannot be shaken from a position you know to be right and true." "I will, Papa. I will. Will I ever get to learn from Mar-Dug again now that he is the Chief Priest?" "I am sure you will, child. Mar-Dug loves you as your father and I do. Having no children of his own he has taken an interest in your education. That is one of the reasons your grandmother and I have moved to Uruk...Mar-Dug wants to advance your schedule of learning so that you will not spend years drawing the lines and circles for other, older priests when you become a wizard. He wishes for you to understand these works, not just master the drawings themselves."

As they neared the house Miqel ran to Fyd, "What will you and Coban-Bul be talking about, Fyd? I mean when all these rituals are over with, what will he teach you that you do not already know?" Fyd looked bewildered and Baldag told Miqel, "Miqel, you know perfectly well not to talk so fast to Fyd. You must talk plainly and slowly so that Fyd understands what you are saying at all times. Not only that you and Coban-Bul must teach Fyd to communicate in a manner similar to the way we do. I think he will pick it up rather quickly but not if you are going to speak so fast your mother and I can scarcely keep up with you." "Don't be too hard on him, Baldag. He and Fyd communicate very nicely until Miqel gets excited. Fyd, Miqel wants to know what Coban-Bul does that you will do." Urunya butted in.

Fyd smiled, "Coban-Bul make fire. Fyd not make fire. Coban-Bul show Fyd how make fire. Coban-Bul make bread. Bread good. Coban-Bul show Fyd how make bread." That did not sound like much to Miqel, but Fyd continued, "Fyd want talk like Miqel, like Uruk men. Fyd not talk like Miqel now." Miqel agreed they could work on that but he secretly hoped that there would be time for him and Fyd, and even Ekhana to hunt and fish. He scarcely knew anyone else in Uruk outside the temple and his family .

There was nothing Akhuruk could do at the temple for the next week or ten days and Urunya was glad, "Papa, Miqel must have some friends of his own before you close those doors behind him at that awful tomb of a temple. Let him play for a few days and then Gahnya and I will stand aside." "He has played for over two months, Urunya." But Akhuruk was stared down by two determined women and decided to lend a hand to Baldag with the flocks before fighting a losing battle at the house. He stalked off with Baldag and Gahnya asked, "Do you know where Ekhana lives, Miqel? Ette can take you over there if you would like to go." "I think I would like that. Can Fyd go too?" "No, Fyd wants to learn how the oven is built and I have promised to show him before he has to meet with Coban-Bul." There was a note of finality in Gahnya's voice and Miqel ran off with Ette to find Ekhana.

During the week of mourning there were many things requiring Mar-Dug's attention, things he had assumed would have been taken care of during a slow transition of power. Though Ayn-Far's death had been expected the suddenness of his demise caught the temple service unprepared. The funeral ritual was old and virtually automatic but the ascension to the high priesthood, though ritually confirmed required realignment of loyalties and assigned duties.

Immediately following the services for Ayn-Far Mar-Dug called the senior priests before the shrine of Luhinlil. "Before I am entitled Prince of Luhinlil I want to know if there are questions in your minds relating to the correctness of this act or the authority for it. None of you were present when Ayn-Far affirmed this with Men-Chad-Rez, nor do I know if he discussed it with any of you. You are my friends and I expect you to speak freely and openly now. You know that disobedience of the High Priest is punishable by death and there have been cases in the past where that has been applied to assumed disloyalty, proof in such events not being required. Like Ayn-Far you will find I am not a despotic person. Yet I am, before Luhinlil and God mandated to uphold the discipline of the temple service and I have every intention of doing so. Therefore open your hearts now while I am still one of
you. Speak what is on your minds."

Hel-Wyd was the oldest of the senior priests, a good many years older than Mar-Dug. The others waited respectfully for him to speak. "Mar-Dug, we are all bowed with grief from the loss of our beloved Ayn-Far. He was truly the Emissary of God. We have known for some years that you were the chosen one to succeed him and he has rigorously questioned me and some others here as to the rightness of his decision, even I think before he ever discussed it with you or with Men-Chad-Rez. As you have matured any doubts we might have had have long since been overcome by your wisdom and behavior as the most senior of our number. Like most of the other priests I have a family. You have none. I think it is fair to say that we have become your family and are as devoted to you as we have been to Ayn-Far."

"May you be blessed by Luhinlil and God, Himself for your kindness, Hel-Wyd, my brother. Are there others who will speak now?" Mar-Dug waited for a response but none was forthcoming so he continued, "It is my intention to elevate Ifn-Lot to senior priest as one of my first official acts. Does anyone here know factual cause that would prevent his appointment?" Again there was silence. Mar-Dug faced the altar and intoned, "Luhinlil of Uruk. Luhinlil of Uruk. Let the decision of these gathered be to your pleasure. If it pleases you, seek the approval of God, Most High that the service of this great White Temple will give honor and respect to

119

your name as it is enshrined here."

With that essential ritual concluded Mar-Dug became more relaxed and asked the priests to sit down with him while Coban-Bul brought them something to eat. When he had gone Mar-Dug again spoke, "There are matters Ayn-Far and I have planned recently that we were discussing when he died. I think you should know of them and I will ask for your complete support." He talked of the seriousness of the conflict that loomed over the 'Sacred Circle' and Ghant-Ur's pledge of continuing support. He pointed out the dangers of letting people, uneducated in the geometric arts worship parts of the diagrams as they were doing along the Nile. He noted the eagerness of those people to have something material to place their hopes on and the quickness of militaristic rulers to seize the opportunities afforded to exploit such misplaced fervor.

"In the past kings of Upper and Lower Nile declared themselves gods; they were fully backed by ambitious priests. That would be like enshrining Men-Chad-Rez in place of Luhinlil and letting him speak as if he were in daily contact with the god. It is cultism gone amok." The priests stirred uneasily and Mar-Dug asked whether anyone there was aware of such leanings in Sumer. Gurn-Thar spoke, "My grandfather told me his grandfather had warned the then king against these things but the king did not think the people would stand for such."

"Your grandfather, the High Priest was a strong and wise wizard, Gurn-Thar. Yet that is what we are: wizards. Few if any of us are trained to rule the people and kings, by custom do not practice wizardry. We do what we do well and leave the ruling in their more capable hands. The people respond to the king and leave us alone in our more esoteric pursuits which is the way it should be. No one is allowed in the temple except by permission of the High Priest. Even the king serves notice before he enters this shrine and he comes straight in and returns the same way. He does not go into the academies or the drawing rooms or our quarters...ever."

Hel-Wyd commented, "I do not recall this having ever been a real problem in Sumer. Though there have been some tombs that small cults surrounded at night for what I suppose are worship services, the tombs themselves contain nothing more than bones and the weapons and some sentimental items the families of the kings wanted to bury with them. Temple service dignitaries' bodies are burned just as Ayn-Far was so that there is nothing about us to worship."

After Coban-Bul had taken away the remaining food Mar-Dug changed the subject, "You are all aware of what Men-Chad-Rez and Kalam-Bad are doing for the bogs. In another generation they should be very much like we are in most of their habits and ways. It will take longer to change their thinking, particularly regarding community living and farming but I do not think we have anything to fear from the little Hathuruk tribe. The chief's son, Toq in particular seems to have the attributes for absorption into our society; he knows they cannot survive in their ancestral ways with villages springing up all over the country and cities expanding into their hunting grounds. Some of you have become aware of Fyd, the bog I have assigned to Miqel, son of Baldag. Do any of you have any misgivings about this?"

Gurn-Thar frowned, "You know we do, Mar-Dug. We need time to get used to all that is changing here in Uruk. I doubt that any of us has any real doubts about the wisdom of it, or the humaneness of the approach. But we were all raised to fear bogs, to consider that they are not people, at least not people like us. And with their fierce looks and the crude, smelly hides they wear they do reinforce that line of reasoning. Furthermore I believe the stories we have heard of their cannibalism during the drought."

Mar-Dug did not answer until he had studied the faces of the other senior priests and found that they were apparently sympathetic to Gurn-Thar's views. "I have shared these thoughts myself, even toward these men when I first met with them. Let me remind you, however that in our own culture the stories about the great floods that occurred in Sumer before our grandfathers were born tell also of the destitution that followed and how some of the people became so crazed with hunger they killed and ate newly born infants. Until a few weeks ago none of us was aware of the really desperate measures to survive the Hathuruks were experiencing. Except for the rains there would have been no bogs left in another year. They are less afraid of us than of our dogs but in Ur Ghant-Ur took Fyd into the temple while we were there to prevent the people from killing him. These are people, not animals. If we are the enlightened ones of Sumer then we must know that and set the example for the others to follow. Otherwise we might as well be like those along the Nile and resort to symbol worship." Mar-Dug was angry and showed it. Gurn-Thar hastened to turn his wrath away with well justified fear, "Master, I did not mean to offend you. You asked us to speak our minds and I have told you the truth."

"Forgive me, Gurn-Thar and all my brothers. It will take time as I know all too well. All I ask is your patient forbearance. There is an overriding matter that requires me to proceed with Fyd as Miqel's servant and protector. Ifn-Lot and I believe that Miqel possesses the mind and talents to become a wizard of the class of Kmal-Dyl, perhaps even more gifted than Kmal-Dyl himself. Ayn-Far came to share that view before he died. More importantly we face a situation in western Mari country where the fractional zealots are challenging the 'Sacred Circle'. This was part of the upsetting news that provoked Ayn-Far's anger which may have led to the seizure that resulted in his death.

"Miqel loves Fyd and cannot be easily persuaded to give him up. Even Men-Chad-Rez changed his mind when he learned of the sedition we face in Mari from some who were once numbered with us. My point is that we are simply not able to defend ourselves unless someone rises who is so intellectually endowed that any challenge to his authority cannot be sustained among reasonable men. And I hope that there are reasonable men left...even in that weird region along the Nile."

Hel-Wyd asked, "Mar-Dug, is it your intent to bring Fyd into the temple?" "He will be present at times, primarily to serve Akhuruk and Miqel at the room we have provided for Akhuruk's academy. No, of course he will not have free rein of the temple, nor do I think he would want such any more than Coban-Bul does. I have elected to assign Fyd to Coban-Bul for training as a temple servant and Coban-Bul enthusiastically supports the assignment. It will be up to him, as well as Miqel and Akhuruk to teach Fyd to communicate in our way of speaking instead of the short verbal phrases the bogs use. This is in essence an experiment. If we are successful then we will know that bogs are as we are except for the environment in which they have been reared. If we are unsuccessful, and I include the experiment with the Hathuruk tribe on the lands in Kalam-Bad's territory then I will have to concede that we are wrong. Even then we would have no right to let people kill them. Nevertheless I am convinced we will succeed. Fyd is quite bright as I discovered when traveling to Ur with him."

Miqel and Ekhana were surrounded by children near their ages, but it apparently had not occurred to Urunya that they would not be "on holiday" as Miqel was. Even Ekhana could play only an hour or two at a time; Methwyd had divided her schedule between education and tasks she was responsible for each day. Ekhana was delighted to have Miqel come over when he did for Methwyd relaxed a bit knowing the week of mourning would be over quickly. With the other children the chores were almost continuous and the boys also helped their fathers in the fields part of every day.

Running down to the river and searching for nuts and dates for the table served as play for all of them and Miqel was glad to take them into the water and teach them how Fyd fished, scooping and tossing with their hands. The rivalry between Miqel and Ekhana continued but it was a happy sort of thing now; Miqel no longer felt disgraced when she caught more than he did, which was often.

The ceremonies for Mar-Dug's assumption of the High Priesthood were long and arduous. They began in the early evening following the first glimpse of the rising new moon. A shout went up from the temple parapets and Hel-Wyd immediately plunged a special sword into the heart of an ox lying bound on the sacrificial altar in the Shrine of Luhinlil. As each senior priest stepped forward Hel-Wyd dipped two fingers in the blood and dragged them across the priest's forehead, forming two short, red lines. This was the sign of Luhinlil, god of husbandry and patron god of Uruk.

The senior priests were followed by the priests and finally trainees for the priesthood who then returned to their positions along the walls, holding torches. There they would stand until the sun broke through its gates on the parapet to the east. At last Mar-Dug walked to the altar and performed the ritual for Hel-Wyd who then dipped one finger into the blood and made a small circle with a long tail on Mar-Dug's forehead, the 'Sacred Circle'.

The king entered the shrine accompanied by his princes. In the eerie, flickering glow of torchlight Mar-Dug repeated the ritual for each of the princes, finally drawing a vertical line crossing the two lines of Luhinlil on Men-Chad-Rez's forehead, signifying his right as king to speak directly to Luhinlil without intercession by the High Priest . Men-Chad-Rez then drew the same symbol in blood on Mar-Dug's forehead, proclaiming, "I pronounce you Prince of Luhinlil. Let Luhinlil intercede with God, Most High for your wisdom and for your protection and for your long life." Again a roaring shout went up as the great assembly cheered Mar-Dug's entitlement as, "Prince".

The princes retired carrying the bull on poles provided for the purpose. It would be roasted along with other domestic animals and game for the people's feast in the temple yard that day. This was a day of celebration in which there could be no work in the fields. Every man brought of what he had: a sheep, a lamb, a goat or birds or fish. Every woman brought a loaf of bread and every child brought a cake of figs or raisins. Skins of wine were furnished by the princes. This would be a feast similar to the one when a new king was named and few of the people ever saw so much at any other time.

At the shout from the east parapet when the sun broke through the first child to be born after the old High Priest's death was brought to the shrine by Hel-Wyd and laid before the Luhinlil altar. As the sun penetrated the shrine casting a glow on the altar four doves were released, signifying the four cardinal points and the four seasons: the aborning of a new High Priest and the realms of earth and sky for which he would intercede with the gods.

Now Men-Chad-Rez reentered the shrine and calling Mar-Dug to follow him led the way to the Great Gate of the White Temple, the eastern gate where the people of Uruk were massed and waiting. At the center of the gate he stopped and Mar-Dug stood before him. Men-Chad-Rez draped a gold chain with a gold 'Symbol of the Bull' hung from it over Mar-Dug's shoulders, pronouncing, "Prince of Luhinlil, I name you, Chad-Mar, Emissary of God and High Priest of the White Temple of Luhinlil. Let no man live who dares dispute the authority I vest in you. May God Most High bear witness. May God Most High be gracious to his servants, the King and the High Priest for all their lives. I, Men-Chad-Rez have spoken it."

A deafening roar went up from the people and the priests. The ceremonial torches were thrown from the top of the temple walls and the newborn child was brought out and given back to its mother. Once more Men-Chad-Rez raised his voice, "The feast will now begin." and weeping openly clasped Chad-Mar by the shoulders and kissed him on the cheek. Mar-Dug, now Chad-Mar would never again have a time of his own as long as he would live.

CHAPTER THIRTEEN   'Miqel, the Wizard'

Miqel's training under Ifn-Lot and Akhuruk had been a phenomenal success. At first it was difficult for Akhuruk to relinquish total responsibility for Miqel for he wanted to make sure that he continued to polish Miqel's expertise as a drawing-scribe. Ifn-Lot was gentle at first but it soon became apparent that he knew he was a senior priest and the authority that carried with it. In time he began to take his meals with Akhuruk and Miqel as Fyd served them. During these opportunities he told them of his experiences as 'Davri' of Aff. Akhuruk bristled at the effrontery of the "fractional savages" attacking the Sacred Circle and its adherents.

Fyd, who could speak almost as well as Coban-Bul now could not help overhearing their conversations. He would exclaim, "Surely no priest would harm you, Master. These men like Eh-Buran and Ib-Seeg. They not priests. No, they not priests." Ifn-Lot would laugh, "Fyd, you are too kind toward them. They are very much priests and not only that, they are accomplished wizards. They just do not think the way we do here at the White Temple." "Then they wrong, Master. Are they not wrong, Master Akhuruk?"

Akhuruk would assure him they were and then ask Miqel to recite his learning for that day to Ifn-Lot. By now Miqel had mastered the Sacred Circle construction, both in practice and in theory. He understood its meaning and how it could be applied. He was sixteen and already more advanced than most of the senior wizards at Uruk.

Ifn-Lot went to talk to Chad-Mar one day and the High Priest wanted to know all about where Miqel was in his education. "It is astonishing, Chad-Mar. I doubt Kmal-Dyl can outthink Miqel on the things he knows now. He is getting into the square and circle process and has already figured out that the great henge is the only hope for resolving the difficulties with it." Chad-Mar smiled, "Then why have you not revived our plan for a henge east of the Tigris, Senior Priest, Ifn-Lot?"

"That is what I am here to talk to you about, Chad-Mar. I doubt that Ur and Eridu will ever offer much in the way of effective help for such a project.. Qom-Tur is too busy training his farmers in the Uruk methods and he is still niggardly in providing for the Al-Ubaid service from what I can learn. That leaves Kish as the only other large temple with an interest in building the henge. News from up that way indicates that they have about given up on the northwest ventures. They are too costly and the Mari bands are giving increasing amounts of trouble to anyone trying to travel from Kish through Hit to the Great Sea."

"There may be a possibility there, Ifn-Lot. Yet you of all people must remember that the king of Kish has taken very little interest in the affairs of the temple. He provides for them well but for two years now Abb-Oth has had to suspend all projects that involved manpower for construction; the king will not furnish the men. Too, there is a new chieftain who has declared himself King of Mari according to what we can learn of the goings on in that rats' nest of a country.

"The king of Kish has conscripted most of the young farm boys from the villages up and down the river and trained them as warriors. He lets them return to the fields for the growing season but they spend the rainy months in the desert east of Kish being hardened into troops. Have you not heard this news? One of Kalam-Bad's nephews was up there a few months ago with a trading party and when he returned he said it was if a war was going on."

"I talked to him, Chad-Mar. I am still trying to find something about Per-Qad; where he might be if he is still alive; what he might be doing. There has been no news from there that implies that he exists for over a year. Even if he described me to the Mari priests it was long enough ago that I have nothing to fear except meeting Per-Qad face to face. I doubt that he is anywhere near Kish. He has his own skin to protect and he cannot know whether there may be men looking for him there.

"Since the drought ended it appears Kish is producing more food than is needed there. The traders told me that bags of grain are being sent for barter as far as the Tigris and even on up to Ughada. Ughadan craft wares are showing up at the Kish trading stalls on a regular basis these days."

"Ifn-Lot, do you suppose Rem-Chakh might be willing to go in with you on the henge construction? I know he is no wizard but Urnath has a lot of influence with him according to Kmal-Dyl. Priests of the Ughada Temple spend all their time with the rituals for their 'Mother of Heaven' but they are a jolly lot for the most part and they might like to see their goddess laid out at a henge site. You have to begin with the basics and a little chalk stone sprinkled on the ground would suddenly turn into that weird figure before their eyes."

"It's a thought, Chad-Mar but I would not count very heavily on it. The only thing that would make Rem-Chakh enthusiastic about a project like this would be if he thought it would influence the King of Ughada to be more generous in his support of the temple. I was there a long time ago with Urnath and if the king had provided much more in the way of food and wine for Rem-Chakh's obese priests they would not have been able to move enough to tend to their duties." Chad-Mar laughed, "Do you think Ghant-Ur ought to try using the Mother of Heaven to keep Qom-Tur in line? Al-Ubaid could surely use some extra food and wool."

Ifn-Lot doubted that Qom-Tur would be interested in another god or goddess but wanted to continue the discussion regarding Kish, "It just might be that Abb-Oth can convince the king that henge building would be good training for the older farm boys he has conscripted. They would come back tough and strong after breaking rocks and digging the huge trench network we will need for an effective henge the size you and Kmal-Dyl say is required."

"You can go on up there and try to sell your idea, Ifn-Lot if you think your personal risk is small enough now to justify the exposure. Will you be taking Miqel and Fyd with you?" "Yes, Chad-Mar. But unless Men-Chad-Res will furnish a hundred men there is no use in our approaching the King of Kish. Can you get him to at least match what Kish will send with us?"

"I think he will. Kalam-Bad's Hathuruk area is giving the bogs all they could ever have dreamed of and the farms are producing well around Uruk now. Perhaps Oghud would assign three or four hunters to go with you to help provide game for the workers. Men-Chad-Res loaned Qom-Tur a large number of farmers' sons to help him get the Ur farms into efficient production and they are due to return any day now. By the way I am sure Kalam-Bad will want to go to Kish with you. He wants Ekhana to see the temple up there. When do you think you will leave?"

"If you can get Men-Chad-Res' assurances in about a week I will leave then. Miqel needs to talk to Kmal-Dyl before he gets any deeper into the square and circle and I believe he should thoroughly understand what Kmal-Dyl has done in the area of the invention of writing he keeps working on. That really is Miqel's promise in my opinion. He may be the one to do it." Chad-Mar rose and smiled, "With the way things are going in Kish and Mari I think Miqel had better invent it before we are all involved in a war."

Before Ifn-Lot could talk to Miqel about Kish he had to convince Akhuruk the trip was necessary and safe for Miqel. Akhuruk had heard the rumors of troubles with Mari and undoubtedly Baldag and Gahnya would know of them too. Fortunately Akhuruk had mellowed since the first few months when he moved his academy to Uruk. He was aware of what Miqel had been taught that he himself could not have given him. Still, he was Miqel's grandfather. Ifn-Lot decided to take Kalam-Bad with him to talk to Baldag first.

They found Baldag putting up some new reed mats on his house and he invited them in to talk. Gahnya was out in the garden with the girls so the three of them were alone. It took an hour for Ifn-Lot to give Baldag the details of what he was proposing to do and Baldag listened the whole time. He waited for Ifn-Lot to get to a break point, then said, "I am against it, Ifn-Lot, both for Miqel's safety and yours. There is no way I can talk Gahnya into agreeing, much less Urunya. However the truth is that Miqel is at the age that he can decide for himself. If I say he cannot go now in a year he will go anyway. This wizard business is a hard life but you and Chad-Mar told us it would be. What do you think, Kalam-Bad? Are you really going to take Ekhana with you?"

"Yes, Baldag, I am. Methwyd thinks she should go as long as I take six or eight warriors with us. I believe the stories about Mari are badly overdrawn insofar as Kish is concerned The king of Kish has a lot of problems keeping the town under his rule and his lack of involvement with the temple probably makes him resort to scaring the people there into line. Mari's gangs serve well for that purpose but I do not think they pose any real threat in Kish itself. We will not be going upriver from Kish anyway."

Baldag frowned, "Then let me handle the women and you talk to Akhuruk. Try to give me a little time before you talk to Miqel. He has never disobeyed me and I do not want to put him in the position of having to do that now."

The next day Baldag was at the temple gate calling for Ifn-Lot. When he came into the temple yard Baldag told him that he and Gahnya would not stand in Miqel's way. Ifn-Lot said, "Akhuruk agrees also but Urunya is dead set against it emotionally. I think all we can do is let Gahnya try to calm her mother. Do you concur, Baldag?" "I suppose it has to be. It will take a lot of calming I fear. Let us take care of that. When will you be leaving?" Ifn-Lot said he thought they could leave in two days if Chad-Mar had Men-Chad-Res's agreement by then.

Miqel was elated and Fyd was equally excited, "This is long way on river, Miqel. You and Ekhana and Fyd get to do much fishing, maybe we kill some birds. Fyd happy about that." Miqel became serious, "Poor Fyd. We have kept you so tied down here at the temple you do not get to hunt or fish much at all anymore do you?" "Fyd not unhappy here. Fyd likes temple. Fyd likes to fish too." Ifn-Lot burst out laughing, "Fyd, you can do all the fishing you want on this trip. And I will be glad to eat the fish you three experts catch."

There would be plenty of time on the journey to fill Miqel in on all that would be required of him in his discussions with Kmal-Dyl. But first he had to receive his final instructions from Chad-Mar who knew almost as much as Kmal-Dyl about the things they were going to Kish to find out.

The journey to Kish was enjoyable for Miqel. It was the first time he had been allowed to relax for more than a day in over two years. He and Ekhana vied with Fyd as to who could catch the most fish in the shortest time. Fyd was smart enough to insure that they usually won, protesting, "Fyd getting old. Not fast like Fyd used to be." Miqel and Ekhana would laugh, knowing it was not true. Fyd's hands and his club were still like lightning and they had seen it every day when he forgot to slow down for their benefit.

Kalam-Bad and Ifn-Lot were amused and at the same time having a good time relaxing. The strain of being a senior priest was wearing on Ifn-Lot and he was aware of it. Furthermore the responsibility for Miqel took so much time he could barely keep up with his other assigned duties at the White Temple. Nevertheless the time had come to stop playing. Miqel had to be ready for Kmal-Dyl.

Ifn-Lot took him to the stern of the boat where they could talk without interruption. "Miqel, how would you put sounds to the symbols of the Sacred Circle? And what kinds of symbols would you use?" Miqel reflected on the questions before he answered, "Let me respond to the last question first. I would make a complete new set of symbols, Ifn-Lot. Those we have are easy to make on clay tablets but the wizards I have seen have each adapted them a little bit for his own preference. Some of them are confusing to me and I am sure would be to anyone trying to read them if he did not know the particular wizard who made them. How then can they be called a standard?" "There is a lot of truth in that, Miqel. What would you do differently. Clay is just about all we have for tablets."

"Nevertheless I would design them for chiseling in stone I think. For the clay tablets I suppose they would have to be baked to get a permanent set that would be the standard for consensus. Just like the Sacred Circle itself I would make them sacred. Once they were accepted no one could change them, ever." "You would take on quite a task for yourself, young wizard. Why do you think other men would accept your symbols when you will not accept theirs?"

"My symbols will be taken directly from the construction of course, just as theirs are now. But I would make them take the shapes of things we can remember easily, even if they are harder to draw for writing. The important thing is that they must always be remembered in their exact order. Is that not true, Ifn-Lot?" "Yes." "I would have things like birds and animals and plants, maybe even a fish and a serpent." "For now, Miqel I will take your word that you can do that effectively. Remember, however that Kmal-Dyl is a brilliant man and has spent years on this type of thing. Be prepared to hear him out before you venture forth with your own ideas. Will you promise that?" "Certainly, Ifn-Lot. I did not mean to be presumptuous. I was just trying to answer your question." "And what is your answer to the first question?"

Miqel grinned, "If I tell you will you not scold me?" Ifn-Lot, who was used to Miqel by now shot right back, "Of course. But you must answer anyway." "All right then. My own feeling is that men have been talking to each other so long we cannot change their ideas of things that already sound like something to them. So if a symbol looks like a fish we should name it, 'Fish' and then take the part of that name that is best remembered and that will be the sound for that symbol." "Go on, Miqel. I am listening."

"Do you recall the little story of Kmal-Dyl's about the Hawk's eye and the serpent god who stole it?" Ifn-Lot laughed again, "You know I do." "Well, the story itself applies only to the Sacred Circle so the characters might as well also apply only to the the symbols of that construction. The Nile people claim it as their own and we use it here in Sumer so it is what I would call universal. Even the Kish and Mari people get their fractions from it from what Chad-Mar says.

"The serpent would be one of my symbols of course. And its name would be Zet I think. That will apply quite well in Nile or in Sumer, don't you think?" Ifn-Lot leaned forward, "I think you are on to something here, Miqel. Continue. What would the sound be for Zet?" "'zzz', or 'dj'. Like when you say, 'As yet'." "That is very good. Go on."

"Horus in Nile talk would be at the point where the hawk can be drawn on the diagram. I like that part for it is almost done then. It would be two sounds, each for a different symbol; the symbols will not look like a hawk, they just have to be at that point in the order. one sound would be 'rrr', or 'arrh'; the other would be 'ess', or 'sss', with the 'ess' following the 'arrh'. The same would apply to 'Thetu.' I think I would assign the 'thuh', or 'duh' to the top point on the diagram to start the triangle. It makes it easy to remember and that sound has to go

127

somewhere. It is also part of the little story. I might put the 'tuh', or 'tah' at the very end, the twenty-second and last symbol. With that I get sounds for five symbols out of that one story."

"Miqel, that is sheer genius. Keep thinking along those lines. I am sure Kmal-Dyl will want to follow all this up with what he has done. Perhaps the two of you can invent writing in a few years." "I hope so. May I fish now?"

When the Uruk party reached Kish Ifn-Lot and Kalam-Bad went first to pay their respects to Abb-Oth. Abb-Oth came to the gate and invited them in after being introduced to Kalam-Bad. "Welcome to Kish, Davri, or does anyone call you that now?" Kalam-Bad looked at Ifn-Lot, obviously confused until he replied, "No, Master. I am Ifn-Lot now and expect to remain so, perhaps as long as I live." "Then so shall it be here, Ifn-Lot. And I hope there will be no threats to your enjoying a long life. I think things are fairly well settled in the city; it is the country just west of here that is troubling us."

"So we hear in Uruk. Kalam-Bad's nephew was here with a group of traders a few months ago and brought us the news of the new, self-declared king of Mari. Is he anything to fear in reality, Abb-oth? Or is this just something the king is using to gain more authority here in Kish.?" Abb-Oth squirmed uneasily and Ifn-Lot hastened to reduce the tension, "I meant no insult to your king, Master. We have known for a long time that Mari would like to extend its sphere to Kish; in fact I suspect they would like Kish for their capital. I just supposed the factions that have always existed here were causing the king problems with all the unrest west of here, and wondered if the Mari gangs are really that threatening."

Abb-Oth relaxed, "Some of both I fear. Your assessment of Kish is essentially correct. The factions you refer to seem to be the same ones we have always had here. I do not think you need fear them if you are out among the people. But the Mari priests have become much more bold recently and I am watching our own priests very carefully to be sure we do not have any defections. "So far there have been none." "That is encouraging."

"What brings you back to Kish, Ifn-Lot? Since you are accompanied by a prince of Uruk you must have something quite serious in mind." Ifn-Lot was not ready to talk about the project yet; it would have been imprudent to do so without consulting with Kmal-Dyl first. "Chad-Mar has sent me here to introduce a young wizard to Kmal-Dyl. We think he may be the genius we have searched for for so long." "How old is he, Ifn-Lot?" "About sixteen years, Abb-Oth." Abb-Oth could not help laughing, "Surely you are not serious. I can conceive of one so young mastering Zodiac and even having some knowledge of the Sacred Circle, but to call him a wizard at that age is overreaching, don't you think?"

"I hope you will consent to meet him after Kmal-Dyl has talked to him, Master. This shepherd's son is no ordinary young man. Kalam-Bad can verify that." Abb-Oth turned to Kalam-Bad wondering what he could add. "Master Abb-Oth, Men-Chad-Res is fully in support of what Ifn-Lot is saying. I was with Chad-Mar and Ifn-Lot when they met this boy...he was only twelve years old then...and Chad-Mar went on down to Ur to explore his background at an academy there. He is a very precocious lad."

Kmal-Dyl was not prepared for Miqel. At first he would talk only to Ifn-Lot and Miqel remained respectfully silent. Kmal-Dyl referred to the so-called royal cubit he had been working on and Miqel's ears perked up as Kaml-Dyl said, "I think the cubit should be dropped for awhile, Ifn-Lot. The pyramid project is just too big a venture for anyone to consider anymore. I assume you are aware that all northwest exploration has been called off. Without a great henge there can be no pyramid."

Without stopping to think what company he was in Miqel blurted out, "Oh no, Master. They can be independent of each other. If we could build a great pyramid there would be no need for the great henge. We are being too conservative I think." The astonishment on Kmal-Dyl's face made both Ifn-Lot and Miqel think that he felt affronted until Kmal-Dyl responded, "That is an interesting comment, young man. Will you explain it please?"

"The Sumer Cubit is based on the Sacred Circle so there is no reason to believe it is not correct. What is known is that it will not yield a solution for the square and circle that we can check without a very, very large henge. Ifn-Lot has told me this is what you have said." "He told you correctly, Miqel. Did he tell you that we do not know what fraction to use in its construction?"

"Yes, but I do not think that henge fraction is essential anymore. There is a way to use the fractional circle for the other dimensional unit, the royal cubit...just as you have suggested I believe...and then build on an enormous scale, perhaps thousands-to-one for the pyramid. We could test that on a very large henge without having to put in all the gates I think. It would really be a huge circle with only enough stones to sight to the stars for the one construction to test the squared circle theory."

Kmal-Dyl motioned to Ifn-Lot to let him continue, "Miqel, go back to the beginning of what you are trying to say. I think you may have found something I have missed." "Yes, Master. You have said that the only way to square the circle that can ever be measured is to find the relation between the radius of a circle and the side of the square that has the same area. At least that is what Chad-Mar and Ifn-Lot taught me that you said." "Yes, I have said that and I believe it is true."

"I have been using a fraction that should be close enough to the dimension you are seeking to work with and if I use a large enough scale for the pyramid then I could have exact conversion into Sumer Feet very easily. Can I not?" "Yes, of course you can, Miqel. Continue." "If you build a trench circle at the henge to that scale you would need only one very large stone tto use for a socket base for the star-sighting pole at the top of the pyramid dimension."

Kmal-Dyl was following every word with rapt attention, "That is the size of the trench circle I suggested, Miqel. And the stone you mention is also part of the great henge. You are correct to this point. In fact the legend of the henge builders who traveled beyond the Great Sea has it that those are the dimensions they wanted to use. This is what our northwest ventures have been seeking: a place that will fit our requirements and be flat over a large enough area to take that size henge.

"That is where the henge and also the fractional Sacred circle comes in. I think the thing to do is convert the square of the fractional sacred circle as it relates to my little fraction...something we already know how to do...using a simple henge only for that purpose. This will give us a close approximation of the angle we are looking for. Then whenever the pyramid can be built we could build a structure with a set of dimensions that did indeed "Square the Circle"". Kmal-Dyl sat back, exhilarated by the exercise Miqel had just described, "Ifn-Lot, I declare this young man to be a Senior Wizard. I am sure Abb-Oth will confirm it and Chad-Mar must already agree. I do not think he will live to see the pyramid built to the scale he has described. But I believe he is correct that we could construct the minimum requirements to test it with a much simplified henge and it would be a fairly economical project. Miqel, I will talk to you more on this; and I want to discuss what you see in the Sacred Circle construction that could lead to writing. But that will have to wait until tomorrow.

CHAPTER FOURTEEN 'The Uneasy Border'

The war raged on in Upper Nile. Piracy was common in the stretches of river north of Nekhen, even past Aqqrem as loyalist generals resorted to murder and plunder to enforce their authority in the areas where they still had strong garrisons. Though they struck under the Standard of Upper Nile the people would have gladly garroted every one of them except for fear of their armies and roving bands of armed thugs carrying the local general's banner.

Trade was reduced to short runs between towns and villages within the control of a single garrison and shortages were mounting with each season of the unresolved warfare. Town by town north from Nekhen, Khafu and Ekhdur continued to decimate the remaining forces loyal to Djo-Aten's kingdom. The towns gradually were secured but renegades flocked to the next general down the river and the strengthening garrisons from Asyut north posed a serious problem of strategy for Menhes.

Menhes was lonely in Nekhen without MeriLyth but his time was taken with joining his troops for each battle farther down the Nile. The kingdom was fully secured to the second cataract and Sel-Abba's troops maintained law and order in that region. At length Menhes sent Seb back to Sel-Abba to arrange another meeting with Prince Addi-Hoda. The losses from the continuing battles were taking their toll on the effectiveness of his forces. It was more difficult to provision the farther ranging attacks even with the long boats.

It was arranged that Addi-Hoda would travel to the first cataract to meet Menhes during the high point of flood time of the Nile when effective military campaigns were out of the question. It had been almost four years since their last meeting and there was much to discuss. Sel-Abba and Addi-Hoda appeared in all their splendor with a full entourage of warriors and attendants. Menhes brought only Ekhdur and Ar-Chab and their aides with him.

"King Menhes of Upper Nile, I greet you, my friend." Addi-Hoda spoke with a beaming smile as he embraced Menhes. "Prince Addi-Hoda of Nubia, without whom there is no King of Upper Nile to meet with, my wise friend and benefactor." Menhes laughed in return. "You have learned that the crown is heavier than you would ever have thought, have you not, Menhes?" Addi-Hoda asked, noting how weary Menhes appeared.

"Yes, Lord Addi-Hoda, I have. And I have learned how lonely a warring king is. It has been nearly four years since I have seen my wife and longer than that since I have seen my father and mother. We have had great successes in the field but our losses can no longer be ignored. And the remaining Djo-Aten armies are gathering into a force so large that it will be difficult to defeat in a short assault such as we carried out at Edfu and Nekhen."

"I was not aware that this was the case, Menhes. How can we help? My sons are prepared to fight anywhere your own troops do and, if it will help you we can furnish thousands of men...all of them well trained...by the time the Nile has subsided." "That is most generous of you, Addi-Hoda but this is not your war to wage. Your own troops have had severe losses of life and there have been too many of them crippled by injuries for me to ask you to continue in that type of supportive role. Sel-Abba is a great general. You already know that but you would be proud to see his direction of his forces in battle. It is brilliant.

"No, what I am here to ask for is that you let me name Sel-Abba 'Regent of Nekhen and Edfu' while I move north and regroup the forces I have for the final campaign against the armies from Asyut to Aqqrem. I trust Sel-Abba as I do my own brothers. If you can give him the troops to maintain control in the area around the capital I will pull all my forces out and get on with winning the war before any more peaceable Upper Nile people are murdered."

"It will be done as you ask, Menhes. But let me do one more thing. When you are ready to strike let Sel-Abba detach his brother, Assi-Rah who is now a general in the Nubian army and the four thousand troops he has under him to fight with you. We have enjoyed peace in Nubia and are honored that you count us as your allies. Let us help you."

Menhes needed the men desperately but he knew the hardships this would pose for the young Nubians, facing hardened and seasoned veterans in the battles of the north as they would be doing for the first time. He bowed his head and thought a long time while Addi-Hoda waited.

Finally it was Sel-Abba who spoke, "Menhes, my Brother, do not fear for us. Assi-Rah was with you at Edfu: he commanded the archers there. Some of them will be the ones who go with you. These are not boys now and they are not afraid of battle or of dying. The young ones we will send will be the javelin throwers who move in quickly and fall back as you have seen. We had no losses at Edfu. It was only in the battle for Nekhen that we began to take the hurts of war. After that we pulled back to the first cataract except for the two thousand reserves you have used only in the last resort with each of your battles. It is time we committed ourselves to the security of Nubia and Upper Nile that your crown offers. There must never be a time when another 'scorpion' emerges to ravage our borders."

Menhes could only accept and Ekhdur and Ar-Chab felt like cheering. Addi-Hoda stepped forward and said, "Then it is done. Now there is a small formality I wish to attend to. You honored me with the armlets and ring of Djo-Aten. I want to return the ring of your great grandfather, King Ghum. It is rightfully yours and belongs on the hand of the King of Upper Nile." "Thank you, Prince Addi-Hoda. It is a priceless treasure for me. Now it is time for us to get back to our duties. I hope that when this war is over the crown will not be so heavy." "It will not grow lighter, my son. Only you will grow stronger so that it will not feel so heavy. May your gods give you success."

When Hev-Ri and his little group first told Menku of their Kish saga he was distraught, wondering what the world was coming to. Var-Lil managed to brighten his days and Bagh had ways of cooking game that none of the people at Crocodile Lake had ever tasted before. But as the war dragged on it became increasingly difficult to get any information on the situation at Nekhen and Menku began to fail. He could no longer leave his bed without being carried and could sit up only for brief periods before slumping back and dropping off to sleep.

It had been months since the last message from Menhes got through and Meri-Lyth had spent her time helping Hetti with Menku, leaving her mother to care for her sisters. Though she was a queen now there was nothing to be queen of at the lake camp. She was devoted to the Menku's who loved her as their own daughter but there was nothing she could do to ease Menku's pain beyond trying to make him as comfortable as possible while he simply wasted away. Hetti had been grieving for over a year sensing intuitively that he was not going to get well, her only solace being that when his memory left him he really did not know what was going on.

The pirate boats of the loyalists had come as far as Meidum on occasion but Hor-Amen's ships had chased them back up the river before they could land. The Lower Nile fleet of armed long boats patrolled to within a day's sailing of Aqqrem but always turned back to avoid confrontation with the massive Djo-Aten force that was now gathered below Asyut. It was good that Menhes could not know of the massacre at Asyut.

There had been only a few who escaped and eventually got to the lake with the news. The priests who were at the academy and their families had all been wiped out. Herdsmens' sons had been conscripted and their families forced to serve the menial tasks associated with caring for a garrisoned army. Small children were murdered outright. Other stations north of Asyut had not fared so badly but only because their herds and farms were needed to feed the army. Hev-Ri, with Vukhath and Shephset and the warriors who had gone to Kish with them could hope for no more than that perhaps their wives and older daughters might be still alive as servants. Since the warriors were herdsmen it was possible that some of their sons could be serving in the army or had escaped to a station down the Nile as herdsmen themselves. These were fragmentary hopes at best but they clung to them.

Menhes had wanted to bring his father to Nekhen when the Upper Nile kingdom was entirely under his rule but it was not to be. On a day when the Nile was at full flood Menku died quietly in his sleep. Hetti agreed to let Hev-Ri have a funeral barge built at Meidum. The body was placed on the pyre which was lighted with full royal honors being accorded to the grandson of a king and father of the new king of Upper Nile. The ceremony took place at night with the funeral cortege disappearing immediately into the darkness as they returned to Crocodile Lake.

Hetti asked Hev-Ri, "What do we do now? Menku is dead and only the gods know what is happening to my sons. When will this war be over, ever?" "These are things I cannot answer, Madam Hetti. We are safe here and the traders who brought us up from Pe can keep us concealed and supplied as long as is necessary I feel sure. They are very loyal to you as they were to Menku. I think all we can do is wait, hard as that may be." "Gentle Hev-Ri. You are such a blessing. Of course you are right. Forgive an old widow her mourning. I have depended on Menku for direction since I was a girl. You are the senior official here now, Hev-Ri; Meri-Lyth and I will have to rely on you from now on."

Khafu walked into Menhes' tent near Rafiza where he had regrouped the Army of Upper Nile and offered a proposal. "Menhes, it is time we took the Djo-Aten ships out of action. They are being used mainly for plunder but each one is loaded with armed warriors. We can't make a strong land attack on Asyut without complete control of the river. You know that." Ekhdur walked in with Assi-Rah as Menhes asked, "How do you propose to do that, Khafu? We cannot afford to take any losses of our long boats or the men who man them. And I suspect all we would do would be to chase them into Lower Nile which could lead Hor-Amen to retaliate. I do not intend to have a war with him."

"Remember how you got the long boats to Kom Ombo at night, Menhes? I think we can do the same thing to get past Asyut. It would take perhaps eight of the fast boats drifting single file along the far shore but we could do it quickly with the Nile at flood. We would be below Aqqrem before the loyalists even knew we were there." "I am willing to concede that, Khafu. But then I fear you would have an important part of our forces isolated, maybe even trapped down there. Do you intend to take their ships out one at a time by boarding? That costs men we do not have."

Khafu looked at Ekhdur and Assi-Rah, hoping for support. Assi-Rah grinned, "King Menhes, I believe you underestimate my archers and javelin throwers. The loyalist ships will not get close enough to our long boats to have a single man alive if you let me man Prince Khafu's ships. Will you not agree, Prince Ekhdur?" Ekhdur pressed the point, "Menhes, Assi-Rah is right. The Nubian archers are incredible and if the ships do get too close the javelin throwers are even more devastating. Each man will take his shield of course. I doubt we would lose a man if we can stay on the east side of the river, and it is wide enough now to be able to maneuver that wouldn't you say, Khafu?"

Khafu beamed, but it was Menhes who answered, "Of course you are right. Only one thing. You will strike and get back here as quickly as possible before the Asyut garrison can get its barges out in the stream with archers behind their shields. All I want out of action is their wooden boats; we can set fire to their reed skiffs and barges at any time. When can you do it?" "We will start down river before sundown today, Menhes, if Assi-Rah's warriors are ready. Eight long boats are moored at the landing now." Assi-Rah assured Khafu that his warriors would be on board well before sundown and Menhes silently blessed Addi-Hoda and Sel-Abba for their foresight. "Khafu." "Yes, Menhes?" I meant what I said about a quick strike and a quicker return here. You do understand that?" "It will be done, Menhes. I hope to be back in four days with every man alive and well...and with the Djo-Aten fleet reduced to rotten reeds."

On the Nile the Menku long boats floated swiftly past Asyut in almost complete silence as Khafu and the boat crews watched the town fires on the distant shore. Not even a dog barked and it was obvious that things were quiet at the army post. Any sentries they had were not looking for boats at that time of night since they felt secure with their own privateers tied up at points along the river. By dawn they were only a short distance above Aqqrem and the sails were already full with the wind. The ships were speeding along on top of the torrent when the lead ship caught sight of a large loyalist wooden boat lumbering upstream toward Asyut. There were perhaps fifty warriors on board, all of them of the mace variety used to subdue the villagers in their looting sorties. Khafu ordered the boat to the center of the Nile and as they got close enough thirty-five Nubian archers let fly with arrows from behind their great shields. Almost immediately another salvo of arrows flew across the water and the loyalist warriors lay in bleeding disarray in the bottom of their boat. Khafu ordered the second boat to close as his own sped on downstream. Within minutes the Djo-Aten craft was rammed and starting to sink without a single survivor.

The Menku boats then regrouped and sailed on past Aqqrem to a landing site Khafu had chosen. The second boat was inspected for damage from the ramming of the loyalist craft and when none was found, Khafu gave orders to put back out on the water. The ships would go in twos. The first two would go a short distance on down the Nile to be sure there were no other pirate boats that had gone into Lower Nile territory. If they found any they were to be destroyed. If they encountered any Lower Nile royal craft they were to turn and get south of Aqqrem without a fight.

The next two would sail abreast, still staying near the east banks while maintaining the best speed possible. If they came on a Djo-Aten ship near Aqqrem they would split and attack it from both sides. This routine was to be repeated by the next two ships until each pair had overtaken and sailed past the ones preceding them. At a designated point below Asyut the eight ships would regroup and approach the garrison base single file, figuring to get past it and come back down river at full speed to finish the job of taking out everything the loyalists had that could float. They were to stay out of range of shore archers in all circumstances; if they found the enemy was on the east banks they were to sail in midstream to save the lives of the Menhes forces.

There was only one small ship sunk below Aqqrem while the first couple that went upstream found two large wooden army craft but no reed skiffs. They did strand a few fishermen on the east bank as they were being passed by the next marauding vessels. About halfway to Asyut three of the large barges used to transport troops were caught well out from the shore. Each had over a hundred men on it, including fifteen or twenty archers. They were no match for the highly maneuverable Menku ships and the troops were dead or dying before the barges were rammed. There were some injuries on the two long boats from arrows that found their marks and three of the Nubians were killed.

Khafu was worried. Where were the wooden ships they must have had? With the Nile flooding over its banks it was possible that some of them might have been taken off the river but they had not seen any evidence of it down near Aqqrem. When the eight long boats got near Asyut he found his answer. The commanding general of the Asyut garrison was staging a review and there were fifteen, fully armed ships moving slowly down the Nile past the Asyut landing where the General stood with the whole town turned out to watch.

There was nothing to do but attack. With the wind favoring the Menku ships and blowing harder than it had all day they had a chance. Khafu lead his vessels straight up river near midstream, waiting to see if the review craft would break file and engage his little fleet. There was obvious confusion on the shore and in the loyalist ships as the crew frantically tried to get the decorative Nekhbet Banners down and full sails up for battle. Their ships were overloaded with spear and mace troops and could not turn fast enough to be effective in the swift current.

The Menku ships barely managed to get upriver from Asyut before the first four Djo-Aten vessels turned out into the Nile to face them. Khafu split his long boats into fours and sent the first contingent to straddle the oncoming ships. The effect was catastrophic for the slowed army ships with their warriors falling to the hail of arrows from both sides before they could throw a single spear. There was no time to ram now as the next five review ships got under sail and plowed in behind the drifting hulls of dead warriors. A few had jumped into the river and were desperately trying to get aboard any ship they could reach. They were beaten back without mercy as all the craft began to move into battle position.

The first four Menku ships turned back and sailed through the Djo-Aten force with arrows and javelins cutting down the enemy crews. This time however spears and clubs were frantically flung by the Asyut warriors, most of them being harmlessly deflected by the Nubian great shields. There were casualties and there would have been more if the four reserve boats had not swept down from above with their hail of arrows putting not only the five lead ships but two more behind them out of action. This left only the last four army ships to contend with and they were trying to make a run for the banks. Fortunately they were by now well below Asyut and the running shore troops could not get into position to defend them. Khafu maneuvered his four lead ships between them and the bank just in time for the second four midstream ships to sail up and pour their arrows and javelins into the helpless loyalist troops.

The whole engagement had taken less than an hour and the long boat casualties numbered only about fifty men. The long boats made one last sweep down the river ramming and sinking the drifting ships before turning and sailing back past Asyut. The garrison general had ordered as many archers as he could round up into the barges and sailing skiffs that had been tied up at the Asyut landing and they had begun to move out into the Nile to present a feeble line of craft to intercept the swift moving Menku ships.

It was a brave but foolish measure as the Nubians crouched below the gunwales of their boats protected by their shields and the Menhes force sailed straight through. Khafu regrouped and gave each long boat a target craft to take out. They were to move as single units and shoot to both sides, never allowing any of the troop craft to get close enough to attempt boarding. When they reached their target they were to ram it and head back toward Neckhen. Each vessel accomplished its task and some of the smaller skiffs which were not rammed drifted aimlessly with dead crews from the fierce volleys of Nubian arrows.

Before the sun set all eight ships were well within Menhes territory and turned into shore for the night. The casualties were heavier than Khafu had wanted to have to report back to Menhes. Thirty Nubian warriors were dead and another sixty sustained serious wounds, most of which would heal in time. But the effect on Asyut had been calamitous. Not only were the garrison's best ships sunk...and strong wooden ships could not built without going to the delta below Pe for wood...but hundreds of veteran troops were dead. Menhes was walking down by the Rafiza landing with Ekhdur and Assi-Rah when the eight long boats came into view riding up the river under full sail. The three broke into exultant shouting as they saw the erect Nubians lined along the gunwales with their shields on their arms. It was a beautiful sight.

Khafu stepped ashore and Menhes grabbed him by the shoulders, "Welcome back, Brother. Tell me, how did it go?" As Khafu started to speak the boats began to unload the dead and wounded Nubian warriors and Assi-Rah rushed to be with his troops. Menhes and his brothers followed. Menhes asked, "How bad were the losses, Khafu?" Khafu told him the numbers and expressed his regret to Assi-Rah. The Nubian warriors filed past Menhes until Assi-Rah ordered them to stand where they were, and then, "Tell me my brothers. Is the scorpion's fleet destroyed? Are his warrior crews dead." The captain of the operation stepped forward, "General Assi-Rah, the fleet is destroyed and the Scorpions's crews are dead. Lord Khafu has spared us in every way possible, yet we have lost some of our number. Such is war, my general." Assi-Rah turned to Menhes who had listened to the captain and said, "I think these men have done what they said they would do, King Menhes." Menhes smiled and nodded. Then he spoke, "May your gods bless you and those who have suffered and those who have died by your sides. This is a great moment. After you have conducted the rites of the dead there will be a feast to honor what you have done. I thank you."

Menhes called Ar-Chab and Assi-Rah into the meeting with Khafu, Ekhdur and Sel-Abba the next morning. "In spite of the Nile flood the time has come to attack the main loyalist army at Asyut before they can build enough reed barges to move effectively. This time I want to come in from above Aqqrem with a large enough force to preclude another renegade army forming down there. The main thrust will still be to the south of Asyut and I need your counsel as to how we will launch a sustained drive to be decisive once and for all."

Ekhdur waited until it became obvious the others were holding back for him to speak. He rose and faced the group, "I believe we should send our heaviest and strongest mace and spear warriors north of Asyut. If troops break away from their main force at Asyut it is going to take hand to hand combat to bring them down; a lot of of them will be in twos and threes I suspect. That has been our experience up to now at any rate. With the garrison ships out of action we should be able to get our men down there under cover of night, using only barges with the protection of two or three of the long boats. The long boats can come back and join the attack. Do you agree that that is feasible, Khafu?"

Khafu nodded and Menhes asked, "How many troops do you think there are at the Asyut garrison, Ekhdur. Have we been able to get any good information from there?" "Not much recently, Menhes. There were about five thousand men there before we took Nekhen; that is a good number. I would estimate another four or five thousand have moved north as we have driven down the river and then there are the conscripts from the towns and villages. They may not be very enthusiastic fighters once the battle begins, especially if we appear to be winning. I am sure you can count on the loyalty of the townspeople afterward but we cannot know how many of our old friends are left down there. All the Menku station people are gone. I am sure of that."

"Then you would count on as many as twelve or fifteen thousand warriors all told?" Ekhdur said that was a reasonable top number. He did not believe there were any replacements for those Khafu's expedition had killed. Menhes then asked, "Are there any forces left in any of the villages between here and Asyut? I am sure there are some small groups to hold authority but I refer to large numbers. What do you think?" Khafu interrupted, "We did not see any activity that looked like there were troops in the villages as we came upstream after the battle. They did not know we were coming so it is not reasonable to suppose they would have hidden anything from us." Ekhdur took up his discussion again, "I think Khafu is right. We need another pincers plan but I do not think we have to be concerned with any rear guard activity upriver from Asyut. For one thing they would be afraid we would pick them off one at a time, and I would if I thought they were there." Again Menhes spoke, "What do you mean by another pincers action, Ekhdur? Would you bring the spear men up from below Asyut as one jaw of the vise?"

"No, Menhes. I would keep them in reserve. There should be no more than twelve hundred of them there in my opinion: that is a force to be reckoned with but it will not take away too much from our main army. I believe we should do about what we did at Nekhen, bring the main spear and mace troops ashore just beyond Asyut as the army advances from the south by land. Use the Nubians on the west flank again to keep the garrison troops running back into the club and spear wielders, both north and south of the city. If they break through they will run into the reserves while the Nubians regroup with their hail of arrows."

Menhes thought a moment, "I think they have learned a lesson, Ekhdur. They will have their own archers and javelin men by now." Here Khafu broke in again, "There were a few archers in the main fleet, maybe fifteen or twenty in some of the boats. But I do not think they have very many. Furthermore they lost every one who rode in one of the review ships. There were spear men but no accurate javelin throwers that we saw. Incidentally Ekhdur, I would think you would want some of the sling men in the north reserve group. They are a great help in picking off stragglers." "That is a good suggestion, Khafu. We will do that. I should have thought of it."

Menhes had heard enough to know what he wanted to do. "Khafu, it will take six barges to get the reserve troops below Asyut. I want them at least far enough downriver to give the landing force room to maneuver. The long boats will be used for the first wave warriors attacking just beyond Asyut. They will use our old Menku station landing. We will march the entire army to Fudjad while you patrol the river between Rafiza and there. There must not be any further warning to the Asyut garrison. They surely know by now we are going to invade them but I calculate they will be expecting a river assault directly from here. Use no more than two or three long boats for your patrols at any one time but be absolutely sure no river craft escapes below Fudjad to get a message to their general. Chase them down if you have to. Ekhdur, is Alkhom the general of the Asyut garrison now, or do we know?"

"He was six months ago, Menhes. We hear there have been some attempts on his life but that they have failed so far. I think he is still in command." "Good. He had a lackluster record with Djo-Aten and is known for throwing line on line of club swingers into a fight without regard for casualties. Hadu was a far better field commander which is probably why Djo-Aten had him at Edfu. Alkhom's formations are completely exposed to flanking attacks; all he does is make an arc of his single main line. Arrows and javelins will cut his troops down the way sickles cut grass."

Ar-Chab asked how the two main attack forces would be divided. Menhes answered, "When we get to Fudjad we will split into three main groups: Ar-Chab, you will take the twelve hundred reserve troops. Ekhdur, you will take two forces of two thousand warriors each for the river assault. I will command the main army marching in from the southwest. My east flank will have two thousand javelin men and mace swingers. The central column will be made up of three thousand ax and spear men. The west flank of course will be Assi-Rah and his two thousand

Nubians. Behind the central column I will keep two thousand mace men in reserve to move toward whichever parts of the advancing columns appear to need them most.

"The final march from Fudjad will take place during the night. There is a good landing five miles this side of Asyut. You know the one I mean, Khafu?" "Yes, Menhes, the old grain landing." "Correct. It will be from there that you load Ar-Chab's force and tow the barges across the river from Asyut. Ekhdur's second wave will be ferried in the long boats to the same site and left on the banks until you return for them after landing the first wave at Menku landing. Then you will go back again and tow the barges to their landing point. Ar-Chab, you will have to work out where you want to land with Khafu."

Ekhdur asked, "When do we leave for Fudjad?" "Tomorrow at dawn. It is a two day march and we will rest the third day until mid afternoon. Then we will have a meal and start for the old grain landing with the rising of the moon. That should give us time to get the barges and long boat men into position under cover of darkness. I will begin the main thrust toward Asyut itself to arrive within sight of their outposts just before sunrise.

"I want to draw Alkhom out of Asyut toward the southwest if possible to give you time to get both waves landed before you engage any of his troops. We will still have a two hour march when you hit the banks with the first wave. That means I have got to close with him before he starts sending rear guard detachments back into the town. Khafu, that does not give you much time to get all the long boats back to this side of the river with the rest of Ekhdur's troops."

Khafu responded, "We will have enough time, Menhes. But I intend to leave the barges downriver from Asyut while I let the second wave force off about a mile upstream. Then when we

land the first wave I will take the wind against the current to pick up the second wave, letting them debark at Menku landing with the boats still moving with the current. From there we can move the first six long boats across to the lower point where the barges are tied up without fighting the current. It will be easy enough to get them back to the west bank four miles below Asyut."

Sel-Abba asked, "Will you need the forces I have at Nekhen, Menhes?" "Not initially, Sel-Abba. I need you there and Khafu will send a boat up there today to take you back. When we need your forces we will send the long boats to Nekhen for perhaps a thousand troops but I believe that will be when the main battle is over and we have to stabilize Asyut to be able to govern it...just as we did at Edfu and Nekhen. Is that acceptable to you?" "You know that I would rather be with you in the assault. However I will accept your judgment as being the wisest thing to do. May the gods bless you and these men who will follow you into battle. We will come when you are ready."

The main land column overran the first Asyut outpost shortly before daylight as the sentries sat around their fire. None escaped and one of the prisoners was forced to tell Menhes where the second outpost was located in exchange for his head. It was incredible that the next outpost was so close to the town. It seemed that most of the outposts were spread along the river. Menhes detached a small garrote squad to subdue the next two posts before they could give any signals back to the garrison. Then he force marched his troops within sight of the town just as the sun started to rise, daring Alkhom to come out and meet him in the open fields.

Horns sounded in Asyut as troops swarmed out of their tents and began to form a battle line in a wide arc at the outskirts of Asyut. Menhes central column advanced straight on the center of the arc as his right flank moved toward the river to try to join Ekhdur's forces there. The left flank of Nubians made a wide sweep and came in from the west just as the armies clashed.

Alkhom's forward line fell back against the heavier armed Menhes troops and as the secondary loyalist line began to move up a torch was thrown in a high arc from where Menhes stood.

It was the signal Assi-Rah had been waiting for. The Nubian javelin throwers ran forward toward Alkhom's wavering right flank and hundreds of his men fell where they stood. Immediately the air was filled with arrows, one volley following another less than a second apart. The entire right flank of the defenders broke in confused flight for the town only to be met by Ekhdur's right flank just coming up from the river. Assi-Rah's forces regrouped to the west as Menhes drove through the center of the arc, splitting the line.

This time Menhes' right flank javelins flew into the east side of Alkhom's lines and they fell in behind the crumbling center. Now two torches were thrown from Menhes' command point and simultaneously the Nubians and Ekhdur's second wave attacked the flanks. Alkhom's entire army was encircled. The javelins and archers were drawn back and the mace and spear men advanced in hand to hand combat. There was no escape. Every deserter was met with an arrow or a javelin. Now three torches sailed high into the air and Ar-Chab's force began moving to the west in a sweep to come in on Asyut from the northwest. Three hundred sling men advanced, taking out their targets singly with horrifying accuracy. They fell back and the north reserve spear men marched through the scattered rear guard of Alkhom's army toward his center column.

A Nubian javelin caught Alkhom between the ribs and he fell dead with his personal guards falling almost immediately after him. His army was in rout as the triple jaws of the King of Upper Nile continued to close. Surrounded clumps of warriors surrendered while others fought on to their deaths. By noon there were none left to fight. The people of the town had fled to the west, their only escape before Ekhdur's troops. Now they began to file back into Asyut with their hands on their heads, men women and children alike.

They were herded into a field near the Menku landing where they could be questioned regarding the fate of the Menku station people who had lived there. The prisoners were brought to them and identified. Some were sons of Menku shepherds, some of whom were still living. They would be spared of course. Women and children came forth to be recognized by their kin among Menhes' forces. There were few of them left and the remaining prisoners were executed.

The following morning Menhes sent Ar-Chab and his troops inland a short distance to begin a march north to the farming and herding communities. These were to be checked for any remnants of the old royal armies and the village elders were to be assured of the peaceful intentions of their new king. The Nubians were left in Asyut under Assi-Rah to restore order there and Menhes, with Khafu and Ekhdur loaded the long boats with troops to complete the takeover of Upper Nile as far as Aqqrem. The small outposts along both banks of the Nile surrendered with little resistance and word was received from Ar-Chab that there were no more pockets of loyalists inland from the west banks.

Under cover of night a long boat was dispatched with Ar-Chab to bring his family and MeriLyth and Hetti to Aqqrem. A skiff had already been sent to find the young traders from Crocodile Lake and prepare the camp there for abandonment. The long boat returned early one morning and MeriLyth, Queen of Upper Nile disembarked at the Aqqrem landing to the cheers of the armies gathered to greet her and her party. As Menhes rushed to take her into his arms she began to sob uncontrollably until Hetti quietly came and told Menhes of his father's death.

The royal procession returned to Asyut with mixed grief and joy; the rejoining of families was tempered with the losses to all of them in the slaughter that had occurred there years before. Menhes declared a week of mourning for Menku and those who died at Asyut Station and

Academy. At the end of the week he assembled his court and called for a victory celebration there. A few of the families had found sons and daughters still alive, among them Hev-Ri whose sons had been herdsmen for the Djo-Aten garrison.

Menhes elevated Hev-Ri to Royal Priest of Aten and directed him to reopen the academy with Seb-Seshat as Chief Wizard in Charge. Hetti decided to restore her home ar Asyut among familiar surroundings. Khafu would return and rule over a new Asyut Province extending to Meidum. Khafu's entire family had been murdered and he wanted to look after Hetti while restoring Asyut to its former importance as a herding station and main center of trade with the Lower Nile country.

Menhes and MeriLyth took Ekhdur and Assi-Rah and the troops from Kom Ombo with them to return to Nekhen for the coronation ceremonies. Arriving there Menhes called for a reunification of the families and a feast of gratitude for the Nubian Alliance. Sel-Abba and Assi-Rah were showered with gifts of gold and lapis lazuli before they returned to their own lands with the assurances of secure and peaceful borders.

Menhes bestowed the title of Prince of Upper Nile on Ar-Chab and placed him over the Province from Nekhen to Asyut. Ekhdur would rule from Edfu with his province including Kom Ombo and extending to the second cataract. With all these formalities done it was time for Menhes to begin his reign. The coronation was more a feast than a rite for it was a time of great happiness not only for the people but for Menhes and MeriLyth themselves. The years of their marriage had been spent almost entirely in separation and the responsibilities each had born made them seem much older than their years. Their love for each other had grown stronger with their longing for the war to end and yet now they would have little time for the normal joys of young lovers. As Addi-Hoda had said the crowns would weigh heavily on both of them for as long as they lived.

In Upper Nile Menhes was active with the consolidation of towns and villages into a kingdom. The strong garrison above Meidum was well settled with the troops from Kom Ombo and their families. He had Hev-Ri reopen the academy at Asyut and Khafu and Hetti would live there with the remnant of the families that survived the massacre. A large enough garrison was established to afford protection and govern the area as far as Aqqrem to the south and past Rafiza northward. It was not so far from Nekhen that Menhes could not visit on a regular basis and learn of the sentiments of the people there.

Things were slowly falling into place in the towns around Nekhen and whatever loyalty there may have been to Djo-Aten had faded sufficiently to preclude any real worry of continuing attacks by murderous gangs. Menhes had dealt severely with all attempts on his life and the people seemed to be genuinely affectionate toward him and his family. Loyal elders were in complete charge at El-Kab and miners were beginning to bring in gold from Ombos again. A rather large group of crafts people, both men and women had settled at Edfu, turning the gold and semiprecious stones into amulets, armbands and pectorals for trade, and weaving the abundant wool into garments and blankets, mostly for local use.

MeriLyth gave birth to a son and Menhes named him, Ki. The little time that Menhes and MeriLyth could spend together with Ki was the first real joy Menhes had known for years and he valued the moments as only a weary warrior could. He knew there would be no peace until the matter of the hostile relations with Lower Nile came to an end. Whether that meant war or an uneasy truce was not at all clear. He did not want war; in fact he did not want to conquer Lower Nile. The prospect of trying to govern a province that was scattered all over the delta was for added burdens with little reward. And any attempt to reconcile the Aten-Amen differences seemed out of the question.

The situation in Lower Nile had deteriorated even after the drought in the delta region had come to an end. The concessions to the moon priests Hor-Amen made during the dry years so strengthened their hold on the people that his authority was greatly curtailed even in the normal affairs of state. To equip the temples in a manner satisfactory to the priesthood demanded conscription of free men and forced levies on their crops and herds. More and more amulets were dispensed and icons for worship appeared in every tent and hovel. The mere shadow of a hawk was enough to drive humble fishermen into a frenzy of fear: Horus might be displeased with them and wreak his godly vengeance on their families. An eclipse of the moon brought a riot in Pe that almost unseated Hor-Amen while moon priests ran about wildly waving golden Ankhs at the heavens. In the ensuing melee between the royal troops and the community at large over a hundred men, women and children were killed, the blame for it all resting on a bewildered Hor-Amen.

The banishment of trade with Upper Nile continued even after that entire country was firmly under Menhes' rule. It worked to the detriment of both nations though somewhat moreso for Lower Nile which had had to resort to expanded trade with the ships from Crete to have an outlet for its surplus grains and wool. The Cretans drove hard bargains and were generally hated by the Pe traders who passed on their feelings to the farmers and herdsmen up the Nile as far as Meidum.

In an attempt to end the embargo Menhes sent Khafu as an emissary to Hor-Amen with plans for an open trade agreement. Taking the advice of Hev-Ri, Var-Lil was sent to ease the tensions with the moon priests since he was from Kish and had no association with Aten worship. Var-Lil had remained at the lake camp with no hope of getting home until there was peace along the entire length of the Nile. He had moved to Asyut and was teaching at the academy where he virtually worshiped Seb...to Seb's tolerant amusement. What did not amuse him was Var-Lil's lack of knowledge of what Seb considered the basics of wizardry. Still Var-Lil was a born ambassador and he eagerly welcomed the opportunity to go back to Pe with Khafu.

The royal barge of Upper Nile arrived at the Pe-Diph wharf with the Nekhbet Standard flowing and Khafu's own banner decorating the prow. Fifty Upper Nile warriors formed a guard of honor as Khafu and Var-Lil stepped ashore and asked to be taken to Hor-Amen. The corporal in charge of waterfront guards made them wait until he checked with the captain of the guard who came down to them after a couple of hours. He was accompanied by a senior priest of Amen who proceeded to question them at length, threatening them all the while.

At length Hor-Amen agreed to see them in two days and the Upper Nile party was ordered to remain on the barge until they were sent for. On the third day the captain returned with over a hundred, heavily armed guards and orders that the Upper Nile crew and warriors must stay aboard under guard as Khafu and Var-Lil were taken to the king. Although Var-Lil tried to make light of the insults Khafu was infuriated and except for their personal safety would have left for Nekhen immediately. Nevertheless there was nothing to do now but go along with whatever game Hor-Amen was playing, if indeed it was a game.

They came to the trade yard where Hor-Amen stood with his son, Amen-Kha at his side. Amen-Kha dismissed the guard and looking at the travelers with disdain asked, "What has your usurping master sent you to propose to the rightful King of Lower Nile? Has Aten deserted you?" Khafu smiled and replied, "King Menhes, Prince of Nekhbet and Lord of Nekhen sends greetings and wishes for peace between our great nations. Upper Nile is a rich country and wishes to enter into trade with Lower Nile to the benefit of both our peoples."

Hor-Amen continued to remain silent as Amen-Kha spoke again, "What have we to do with murderers of kings and their families? We have all the trade we need among ourselves and Hapi provides for us generously. It is not necessary for us to stoop to dealing with cutthroats and thieves." At this Hor-Amen stepped forward and said, "Perhaps my son is too severe in his judgment of your motives, Prince Khafu. Just what sort of trade agreement have you in mind?"

Khafu responded, "Nothing more than existed before the war in Upper Nile, My Lord. We would open our landings to your trading craft and expect you to reciprocate. My brother and the people of Upper Nile hold only friendly feelings toward your kingdom. Our whole family was born near Meidum and we were well treated by your father and by you during all the years we lived in Lower Nile. We have no desire for further territory and are willing to declare Aqqrem as a free zone, neither Upper nor Lower Nile in allegiance."

Hor-Amen, under the watchful eye of the Chief Priest of the Pe Temple asked, "Will your traders not bring amulets and icons from the Aten worship to corrupt our faithful people here? Where will our assurance come from that that will not happen?" Khafu was perplexed by the question, not knowing what it had to do with peace between the two countries but he answered, "We will insure that no such items of worship are brought to your people by our traders. Our temples are local and do not represent the King except the one at Nekhen where he himself worships. We of Upper Nile have no intention of trying to proselytize anyone, as Var-Lil of Kish will attest."

Amen-Kha thrust his finger in Khafu's chest, "Liar! You come here to commit sacrilege against our god, Amen just as you have denied the sacred spirit of Horus throughout Upper Nile. We know what you are doing. If it were mine to command I would have you and your entire party beheaded here and now." Hor-Amen restrained Amen-Kha and advised Khafu and Var-Lil, "I think it is better that you leave now. You may tell your brother that now is not the time to enter into such an agreement. I have spoken."

The astonished and dejected emissaries quickly reboarded their barge and made way for Nekhen as fast as the sails would carry them. When they got there and reported what had happened to Menhes he was furious but decided to hold off any action until time could soften the fanaticism of Lower Nile's moon priest cult. In a few weeks, however reports began to come in from Aqqrem that Upper Nile fishermen were being harassed and their boats seized by roving bands of Lower Nile royal guards. Menhes sent word to Khafu to strengthen the garrison at Aqqrem and place four armed long boats on the water to protect the local people there.

It was not long until the first skirmish between Upper and Lower Nile ships occurred resulting in the sinking of one of the Menku long boats with all hands aboard. At this affront to sovereignty Menhes sprang into action calling for Ekhdur and Ar-Chab to mobilize their troops and head for Asyut with him. There they joined Khafu to map out a plan to punish Lower Nile before total war would break out. It was decided to take all the towns and villages as far as Meidum and establish a large force at Crocodile Lake with Meidum being used as an armed port.

The Upper Nile armies sailed down the Nile in barges and long boats stopping at villages and towns to conquer them. At each a small troop was left to insure no further resistance and the main army moved on down the Nile. There were no Lower Nile ships in sight until they came almost to Meidum. Hor-Amen's main fleet came out to meet the overwhelming forces of Upper Nile and Khafu employed the same strategy that had been so effective against Alkhom's ships. The Menku long boats with shielded archers and javelin men straddled ship after ship of the enemy fleet with devastating effectiveness until what was left beat a quick retreat to Pe-Diph, leaving Meidum unprotected.

When the Lower Nile fleet got back to Pe with news of the rout above Meidum Hor-Amen was apoplectic. He called Amen-Kha and demanded to know what the fleet was doing there in the first place and why Upper Nile had been attacked at all. "Amen-Kha, you knew that King Menhes was still completely prepared for war and we have not even put together a standing army. What arrogant stupidity possessed you to push the forces from the south into a defensive posture and give them the excuse to come marauding into Lower Nile? We have lost Meidum and Crocodile Lake and Menhes will not stop there. Now we are the ones who must sue for peace at the best terms we can get."

Amen-Kha reddened at the scathing rebuke, "If you were not so frightened of a few common herdsmen from Kom Ombo I would have had a larger force at Meidum and victory against the infidels would be ours. You have sat here with your hands folded all these years, waiting for the Menku's to take the whole Nile country. You are a disgrace to the crown and an insult to the people of Lower Nile."

Hor-Amen leaped to his feet and ordered the captain of the guard to seize Amen-Kha. The captain and his guards stood in silent disobedience as Hor-Amen continued to scream, "Treason! Treason!" Amen-Kha slowly and deliberately approached his father and thrust his sword between his ribs again and again until there was no more sound from the dying king. He bent over and took the plumed crown of Lower Nile. Placing it on his head he exclaimed, "I am Amen-Kha, King of Lower Nile, Blessed of Horus and Lord of Pe. Let anyone who dares to challenge my authority know that death comes swiftly and with certainty. I have spoken."

The guards kneeled and the captain expressed their loyalty to the exulting new king. Amen-Kha ordered that the provincial generals be summoned immediately and then headed for the temple where he found the Chief Priest, Om-Diph, "Om-Diph, the King is dead. You will declare from the temple walls that I am the King of Lower Nile and you will add the blessing of Horus and Amen. You will declare that I am the Prince of Amen and Lord of Pe. Now!" Om-Diph started to ask what had prompted all this and how the king had died when he saw Amen-Kha begin to unsheathe his bloody sword. He ran for the walls and screamed the pronouncement at the top of his lungs, then returned and bowed to Amen-Kha, "My Lord, the King. The priests of Amen are yours to command. Tell us what you wish of us."

"Om-Diph, we are at war with Upper Nile. My father's weakness lead them to attack us between Aqqrem and Meidum; the King of Upper Nile now holds Meidum, Crocodile Lake and everything south of there along the Nile. I did not wish for this war but we must defend ourselves against all who would profane the sacred trust of Amen. I want the worship of Aten completely obliterated in Lower Nile. Any remaining temples will be razed immediately and priests of Aten will be tracked down and beheaded, wherever they are. That applies equally to any of the 'Sun Wizards' who came here to live in the time of Akh-Loh of El-Kab. We must purify the kingdom now. My father prevented you from being effective in this until now but I will not hold you blameless if you shirk your responsibilities even slightly. It will cost you your head. Do you understand me?"

"I understand, My Lord. And I thank you. Your commands will be carried out exactly as you gave them and as thoroughly as you will wish. Now if it please the King may I offer a word of advice?" Amen-Kha nodded assent and Om-Diph went on, "The people must be told the old king is dead, not how he died but that he is dead. It will serve you well to hold a state funeral and burn the body on a funeral barge with full honors as is the custom. May the priests of Amen take care of this for you?" "Yes, of course. Do it quickly but in good form, Om-Diph. I will light the pyre."

At Meidum as Menhes relaxed with Khafu, Ar-Chab and Ekhdur he asked of no one in particular, "What do you suppose prompted Hor-Amen to attack us? It makes no sense at all. Lower Nile, as far as we have seen is not in any way prepared for war. I would think we could probably capture Pe with little more resistance than we have had down to Meidum. But what would we want with Pe?" Khafu spoke first, "It is all the more unlikely when you consider that Hor-Amen is older than I am. This was a brash act: something a young hot-head might do. Do you suppose that Amen-Kha did this without Hor-Amen's knowledge? He is wild enough to be capable of anything from my one encounter with him."

Ekhdur thought that might be true but wondered, "Hor-Amen has been well respected throughout his long reign, particularly to the south of Pe. I do not see how Amen-Kha could have taken the fleet without his knowing it. Furthermore why would he have been so quick to do it? Do you suppose they are building ships in the delta to match our long boats? It would take years, not months to build a fleet of any effectiveness."

Menhes doubted that. "With no trade on the Nile the only thing such ships are good for is war. And Khafu says the fleet he saw was not much but small river craft with a few royal barges. Their slowness led to the rout they suffered. Surely if they had had faster ships they would have sent them against our long boats. They are well acquainted with our ships from the years we traded with Pe. No, I think there is something going on at Pe that we do not know about...perhaps something that we cannot know about."

Ar-Chab asked, "What do you think we should do now? We can't very well just withdraw from Meidum. That is too high a price to ask of our troops, some of whom have already died in these battles." Menhes responded, "You are right, Ar-Chab. Yet I do not relish having more to rule than I had before. It will take years to consolidate Upper Nile on a completely peaceful basis. There are bound to be pockets of people still loyal to Djo-Aten. Certainly a lot of the people know almost nothing about me. How can they know if they want to trust me or not? I suppose we will have to set up a sizable garrison here. But that is expensive and furthermore it is dangerous if someone like Amen-Kha comes into power in Lower Nile."

Ekhdur spoke again, "It is a risk we have to take, Menhes. But I have a suggestion. Let's move the herds and warrior-herdsmen, especially those at Kom Ombo down to Meidum with their families. We can protect the farmers around here and have a community army like the one you had at Kom Ombo. If Lower Nile starts to threaten, Khafu's ships will know it before they can get any great numbers of troops landed. And our own forces could retreat to Crocodile Lake where they could never be engaged effectively until we could get down with heavy support from Asyut and Edfu. That will take time of course but I suspect it is time we have and that if we do not threaten Lower Nile for awhile they may leave us alone."

"Then that is what we will do. Are we all agreed?" Menhes asked. The others said they were in agreement and Menhes then gave his orders, "I want every warrior south of Aqqrem who is not sent to Meidum to be in continual training while at the same time I want maximum production from the fields and from the herds. I believe Addi-Hoda will give us enough herdsmen to man the Kom Ombo and furnish plenty of meat for the people from Edfu south. All our warriors will be warrior-herdsmen and warrior-farmers but they will be drilled in the arts of war part of every week. I want the youngest to become as expert in archery and javelin throwing as the Nubians. They will be sent to Sel-Abba for that. In addition I want any of those who show skill with the sling to be sent to Sel-Abba for further training. That means I am going to have to have a meeting with Addi-Hoda and Sel-Abba but I do not think there will be any problems with Nubia."

143

"What about the ships, Menhes?" Khafu asked. Menhes was slow to answer, "I think we will have to keep the long boats south of Aqqrem, Khafu. Without acacia wood we cannot build anymore and we cannot afford any attrition from chance battles. As for patrol duty we will have to use the royal barges. Load them up with archers and javelin men who can work effectively behind their shields. Put on the maximum sails they will carry so you can get back upstream fast if you have to. These are not very maneuverable ships but they are the best I can offer now. Every ship will carry two pots of burning oil at all times. If the Lower Nile fleet threatens, our archers will shoot flaming arrows by the hundreds to at least burn their sails. We are going to have to sail the river on a purely defensive basis for some time to come."

Om-Diph was wise enough to know that to carry out Amen-Kha's directives would lead to a reign of terror throughout the country; and he knew he had brought about the downfall of Hor-Amen. What had begun as no more than seizing an opportunity to get added support for the Amen temples during a time of Hor-Amen's weakness had got out of hand. Some young radical priests fell in with the ambitious and headstrong Amen-Kha when his father gave him the delta province to rule after the drought brought unrest there. Om-Diph had stayed out of the way believing Amen-Kha would grow out of his wild ways and thinking he could control the priests at any time they appeared to threaten his own authority.

Amen-Kha had bypassed Pe and taken his zealots down the west bank of the Nile toward Meidum. Gathering strength in numbers as they went it was not long before the generals took note of their influence and demanded to know where their fortunes would rest with Amen-Kha himself. He promised several of the younger rulers provinces when he would succeed his father and soon every action by Hor-Amen was interpreted as being against the common good of Lower Nile and contrived to delay their elevation.

Hor-Amen had felt secure enough to ignore Amen-Kha's machinations. In fact he was glad to see his own son becoming so aggressive, feeling it would strengthen his own rule in the long run with such an obvious successor. After Khafu had appeared at Pe Hor-Amen had assumed that Menhes would himself return to open trade with Upper Nile and there would be plenty of time to soothe the tempers Amen-Kha had inflamed. Om-Diph was as surprised as Hor-Amen when Amen-Kha rebelled and obviously had no time to consider what to do to temper the actions spawned by the murder.

In secret Om-Diph called the senior and most trusted of his priests to him and told them of his concerns, asking if they knew any way to prevent the inexorable bloodshed that would come from Amen-Kha's plans. One of them, Badjut thought that if all wizards were required to take an oath of loyalty to Horus and Amen it would isolate the problems to the few Aten priests known to still be practicing their rites in Lower Nile. The wizards generally did not care very much what or whether they worshiped openly, preferring to take their work as ritual itself as each beseeched God, Himself on his own behalf during contemplation.

Om-Diph thought the idea worth trying and told Amen-Kha what he was going to do. Amen-Kha approved on the condition that his own loyal priests administer the oaths...with instant death for refusal to comply. Om-Diph could only accept the condition but resolved to get word to all the wizards in advance, risking his own head in the process. He fervently wished that he had a single wizard that all the others would listen to. But wizardry in Lower Nile had been neglected for years almost to the extent it had been in Mari. What was left was a lot of drawing-wizards with little if any research carried out beyond structural necessities. The wizards who remained dedicated to seeking the truths of the square and the circle kept their thoughts to themselves and had to eke out their living farming or herding sheep, though some still taught in the drawing

144

academies.

Amen-Kha had no time for rituals of any kind now. He conceived a plan of controlling the Nile past Meidum and isolating Menhes' forces there so that he could systematically destroy them at his own pace. He quickly mustered all the river craft available and loaded them with warriors, placing the reed skiffs in front to harass the Upper Nile ships, making them prey to the more heavily armed wooden ships remaining in his fleet.

Menhes was still at Meidum when Amen-Kha's first boats sailed up the Nile to challenge Khafu's barges. Khafu let them get almost within boarding range before ordering the fire-arrow storm. Eight skiffs were blazing in minutes and the barges plowed through them toward the slow wooden ships of Lower Nile.

The Menku long boats had been preparing to depart for Asyut, Nekhen and Edfu to take the main armies back to their garrisons and they were still just below Meidum. Menhes decided to risk them in a swift drive down the river and the Lower Nile fleet was trapped. The carnage was awful and this time not a single craft was allowed to escape, nor were any prisoners taken. Those who made shore were allowed to escape to tell Amen-Kha of the total defeat.

It was weeks before Amen-Kha learned the extent of his ruin. There could be no effective attack on Meidum or Crocodile Lake for years and all he could hope for was that Menhes would not move on Pe. To prevent a revolt of his senior generals Amen-Kha elevated his sycophants to provincial status and relieved all of Hor-Amen's most able field commanders of their posts.

Menhes departed for Nekhen secure in the belief that there would be years of freedom from any serious threats from Amen-Kha. And Meidum was a far better buffer than Aqqrem could ever be.

CHAPTER FIFTEEN   'Decline at Pe-Diph'

To keep the situation with the people from deteriorating Amen-Kha began a purge of the temples that made Akh-Loh's actions pale in comparison. When Om-Diph learned of this he submitted himself to Amen-Kha, addressing him, "My Lord, we have tried to obey your wishes. If I am not within your favor let me die now for I cannot direct death for my priests without cause."

Amen-Kha was surprised at the reaction but in one of his rare moments of reason he realized he could not take Om-Diph's life and retain any authority with the people. He had gained his own power through the temples and Om-Diph was High Priest of Lower Nile. "Prince of Horus, Emissary of Amen, how could you believe you are not in my highest favor? And that extends to the great numbers of your loyal and devout priests of Amen throughout all Lower Nile. No, it is only those who would commit heresy against our sacred Amen that I hate. If you tell me any priest is a true believer I will accept that and he will not be harmed. I have spoken."

With that Om-Diph responded, "We will search out our ranks, Amen-Kha. It will take time for our priests must travel by foot now and the distances are great. Any dissidents will be brought before you here in Pe." "Let it be done as you say, Om-Diph. But be diligent about it. We will restore the kingdom to its rightful boundaries in time but only if all the people and all the priests and wizards are loyal to us."

Amen-Kha sought to tighten his hold on the plumed crown with ever more despotic measures. He required the new warrior 'generals' to accompany Om-Diph's priests out to the small farms and villages in order to heighten the fears of retribution from the moon-god. The expropriation of cattle and sheep and the demand for 'gifts' of barley and lentils all came in the name of Amen. The drought had ended and this was further proof that Amen was pleased with Amen-Kha's rule if one could believe the priests. Hapi was behaving himself and the fishing was good so that although there was general resentment at the crude, high-handed ways of the officers of the Lower Nile army there was little danger of any uprising. The people remembered the quiet times of Hor-Amen's reign but only as being pretty muchly left alone. The drought had taken its toll on many families and now they had plenty to eat so the occasional bullying was tolerated as a fact of life; and life was hard in the best of times.

The story was altogether different at Pe. To keep his generals in line Amen-Kha followed the practices of Scorpion when he has king of Upper Nile. Of course he knew little of Djo-Aten except as a name his father had sometimes mentioned. But he kept the beer flowing and looked the other way, sometimes even participating in the orgiastic excesses outside the temple walls. Anyone who hinted at defiance was swiftly executed. His head was placed on his spear and mounted on the parapet for all to see; and to learn from. And learn they did. Amen-Kha became more and more self-assured.

In Upper Nile Menhes was active with the consolidation of towns and villages into a kingdom. The strong garrison above Meidum was well settled with the troops from Kom Ombo and their families. He had Hev-Ri reopen the academy at Asyut and Khafu and Hetti chose to live nearby with the remnant of the families that survived the massacre. A large enough garrison was established to afford protection and govern the area as far as Aqqrem to the south and past Rafiza northward. It was not so far from Nekhen that Menhes could not visit on a regular basis and learn of the sentiments of the people there.

Things were slowly falling into place in the towns around Nekhen and whatever loyalty there may have been to Djo-Aten had faded sufficiently to preclude any real worry of continuing attacks by murderous gangs. Menhes had dealt severely with all attempts on his life and the people seemed to be genuinely affectionate toward him and his family. Loyal elders were in completecharge at El-Kab and miners were beginning to bring in gold from Ombos again. A rather large group of crafts people, both men and women had settled at Edfu, turning the gold and semiprecious stones into amulets, armbands and pectorals for trade, and weaving the abundant wool into garments and blankets, mostly for local use.

MeriLyth gave birth to a son and Menhes named him, Ki. The little time that Menhes and MeriLyth could spend together with Ki was the only real joy Menhes had known for years and he valued the moments as only a weary warrior could. He knew there would be no peace until the matter of the hostile relations with Lower Nile came to an end. Whether that meant war or an uneasy truce was not at all clear. He did not want war; in fact he did not want to conquer Lower Nile. The prospect of trying to govern a province that was scattered all over the delta was for added burdens with little reward. And any attempt to reconcile the Aten-Amen differences seemed out of the question.

Menhes called in Assi-Rah and Sel-Abba to discuss the disposition of the remaining Nubian troops in Upper Nile. After reviewing their situation he asked, "Sel-Abba, you have been here a long time as have the members of your garrison. You and Assi-Rah have carried out everything Addi-Hoda promised with greater excellence than I could have ever dreamed of. You know of course that you have been free to go home for quite some time. I would be honored for you to stay in Upper Nile and join in our rebuilding the kingdom but I wonder why you have stayed. Is it your wish to live here permanently? If so you must know that I must obtain your father's approval and he must know it is your own wish and not some pressure I have applied."

Sel-Abba looked at Assi-Rah and decided to answer for himself and his troops, "Menhes, we are hunters first, warriors second...always. There is too much restriction for much hunting south of Edfu on this side of the Nile and I for one do not want my children raised as farmers or even shepherds. That is not the way of our ancestors. There is a vast land between the Kom Ombo and the first cataract on the other side of the river and I would like to settle there with such of my troops...and those of Assi-Rah as well if they care to join us...who wish to do so. I think many will make that choice. I agree that we must talk to Father. We will be guided by his wishes as well as yours." Assi-Rah thought for a bit and said that he would like to take his troops back to Nubia. They had been farther down the Nile and were not the rotated troops that Sel-Abba commanded.

Menhes asked the two brothers if they thought Addi-Hoda would come to Nekhen for a meeting with him and his brothers. He wanted MeriLyth and Khafu and Ekhdur to meet Addi-Hoda. Recalling his own arduous journeys to Nubia there was no likelihood he could take them past the second cataract with Ki still a baby. Sel-Abba spoke again, "I do not know, Menhes. He has not been in Upper Nile during my lifetime though I have heard him say that my grandfather came here when Ghum was king. What sort of meeting do you propose? Assi-Rah and I can take care of the matters we have been discussing when we leave here to see him."

"I was thinking of a feast in his honor lasting several days. Now that my great grandfather's murder has been avenged it is time to restore the friendships between our two countries." Both Sel-Abba and Assi-Rah grinned broadly and assured Menhes that they were certain that their father would come. "Then it is done. Will you make the arrangements and send a runner so that I can have the royal barge at the first cataract to bring him and his guests here as befits as king."

Pe was sinking deeper and deeper into a malaise; considering the soggy delta, a morass might be a better word. Amen-Kha became more suspicious with each new moon. He decided that the traders from along the coast were just thieves and began executing them for any pretended excuse. His real purpose was to seize their boats since most of those he had had been destroyed by the Upper Nile skirmish. The bartering trade was drying up and with no boats from south of Meidum coming to the Pe-Diph wharves some items were getting scarce, a fact that was all too obvious to the village people who relied on barter for their living. The occasional Cretan boat bringing wares from Cyprus, particularly knives and copper goods was about all there was. And the Cretan boat masters were finding they could do as well with less risk trading along the coast up toward the mouth of the Orontes.

The boat masters from Crete were furthermore looking for the worked gold items from Nekhen and Edfu which were no longer to be had in Pe. They were forbidden to sail farther up the Nile even if their boats could negotiate the river without grounding, and some of them could. Their grumbling reached Amen-Kha and he strolled down to the wharf where one boat crew was sitting idly, having failed to barter for anything of value. He walked over to where the master was sitting with his crew and the temple guards ordered them to prostrate themselves. Amen-Kha waved the guards off and addressed the master, "Stand up. You may speak. I will listen to what you have to say."

"The king should know that we have been coming here for many years, in my case since I was a boy. For all those years we brought goods to Pe that could not be had in Lower Nile, bartering for whatever your people had to exchange that we could use to trade with up the coast and in Cyprus or Crete. We used to get crocodile hides and teeth that would fetch much in the way of knives and pottery. Now we cannot take enough away to feed the crew much less barter with on the rest of our voyage. Can the king tell us what is wrong?" Amen-Kha answered in a voice loud enough for all to hear, "It is the Upper Nile usurper and murderer, Menhes who has cut us off from trade up the river. He destroyed our boats and threatens to make war on our poor, peaceful people. What am I to do?"

"My Lord, it would help us greatly if you would let us sail a little way up the river, only as far as Meidum. There I can get goods and hides from Crocodile Lake and bring some of the stuff back here, taking the rest home to let me get outfitted for another voyage. Meidum has never been Upper Nile; surely it is not now." "You are right, it is not. But how can I trust you not to go on up the river and bring Menhes' warriors back down here to attack us?" "I will make a bargain with you. There is nothing of any consequence for a great distance past Meidum. I will be back here in three, not more than four days. If I am longer than that you can say that I have broken our bargain and do with my crew and me whatever seems good to you. If there is not anything worth bartering for at Meidum we will just come back here and then head out to sea. If, on the other hand it is worth the trip it might ease things for the people of Lower Nile in the future. Are you willing to gamble on us?" "You have struck a bargain. I will wait for you no more than four days. After that my guards will seize your boat and you will be Lower Nile servants." "I am Agga. I keep my word. As you have said, so we do. We leave at sunup."

With a fair breeze Agga and his crew reached the Meidum landing by mid-afternoon. There were several craft along the shore though none of the Upper Nile long boats were there. Some guards and a few villagers were down by the water's edge and they were surprised to see a boat from Crete that far up the Nile. It was unusual for Cretan vessels to sail up the Nile at any time but with the tense situation between Pe and Nekhen no one had expected any craft to arrive from the south. The guard captain hailed Agga, "Who are you and what brings you to Meidum? I thought Amen-Kha had lost all his boats the last time they came up this way."

"I am Agga, a plain boat master from Crete. You can talk to my crew but they will not understand you; they do not speak the language of Nile. We are here to see if you have anything from Upper Nile or Crocodile Lake that is worth trading. I have knives and copper goods as well as some pottery from Cyprus. The people at Pe have nothing worth bartering my goods for and I have to have something to take back to Cyprus and Crete or I cannot outfit another boat. Are you from Upper Nile? If you are I cannot trade with your people here. Amen-Kha forbids me to do that."

A boat was pulled up on the shore near where Agga's boat anchored and a man sitting on the bow called, "I am Naan. I used to take Crocodile Lake goods down to Pe for barter but not of late. Yes, there is plenty here to trade. This is not Upper Nile. Hor-Amen knows that." "I remember Hor-Amen when trading was good at Pe. Now that they are driving away the small skiffs and boats from up the seacoast there is not much there worth the trip for. I talked to Amen-Kha...he is the new king...yesterday and he gave us a chance to see what there is in Meidum that we can barter at Pe or take home with us."

Naan got off his boat and walked toward Agga before the guard captain could say anything. "We don't get the news from Pe down here. I have been over at the lake all the time but even since I got to Meidum today I have not heard anybody saying anything about Hor-Amen being dead. Has he been dead long?" "A while. There is not much talk about it but there was a boat at Saqqut when we put in there last week and the master said he had been at Pe when it happened. He thought Amen-Kha killed Hor-Amen over some argument about a river fight with the Upper Nile boats. He told me not to say anything when I got to Pe if I wanted a head on my shoulders. There are priests all over the waterfront and I never saw so many guards there before."

Naan offered, "I have a few things here from Crocodile Lake but I can get just about anything you want if you will give me two or three days. Why don't you and your crew come ashore and get something to eat before the sun goes down. We can talk barter tomorrow." "We have to be back at the Pe-Diph landing before sundown three days from now or I will lose my boat and we will be conscripted into Amen-Kha's service. That is the bargain I made to be allowed to come here. I do not have time to waste. Still, you are right. We might as well get something to eat and see what tomorrow brings."

When Agga had provided his crew with food and beer Naan told him he would see him the next day or the day after. He said he had to check on some barter goods a little way out of Meidum and could go there that evening. As soon as he was out of sight he began to trot toward Crocodile Lake where Ar-Chab was repairing the old Menku station. Menhes wanted to have cattle and flocks there in case war with Pe should break out. It was after the moon had set when Naan arrived at the station and called out to the guard he knew would recognize him, asking him for a torch. "What brings you back at this awful hour, Naan?", the guard wanted to know. "I have to talk to Ar-Chab. There is a boat at the Meidum landing with some barter stuff from Cyprus I think he may be interested in, and the boat master is eager to get back on the river."

The guard told him Ar-Chab was nearby and woke his relief guard to take Naan to him. When Ar-Chab was awake enough to talk he dismissed the guard and asked, "Why in thunder would you be coming here to wake me in the middle of the night, Naan? Surely Pe is not sending boats up the river again." "No, my Lord. It is more interesting than that. And I do not think it can wait until morning." With that Naan told him of his conversation with Agga, including the rumor from Saqqut that Amen-Kha had murdered Hor-Amen.

Ar-Chab asked if Agga had given any evidence that would make him believe that was true. Naan went on to tell him of the chasing away of the small boats from up the coast so that all the real trade Pe had now was principally with Cretan masters and their boats that sailed the great sea. He also told him of the restrictions Agga was under in being allowed to sail up to Meidum. "Naan, do you think this Agga will be coming back to Meidum on future voyages?" "He told me he wants to make three more trips along the coast and on to Pe before the winter sea gets too rough for sailing. This is a trial side-trip and if he pleases Amen-Kha he thinks it can be a regular bartering place for the rest of the season."

"Then I need to get this information to Menhes. I think he should be at Aqqrem, or even Asyut by now; he planned to come there when I last talked to him. We are setting up the old stations along the river from here to Asyut. Does Agga feel there is unrest in Lower Nile?" "Not anything organized. He says there are guards and priests swarming all over the Pe-Diph landing area and the traders and common people there are mostly trying to protect their heads. No one talks at all. That is why he has had no luck in bartering at Pe. He claims it will be ruinous if he can't get something to take home so he can outfit another boat."

At dawn Naan was rushing around picking up whatever he could to take take back to Meidum for bartering with Agga. Fortunately there were a number of good pieces of worked copper; a few had gold hammered into them which had been carefully burnished to gleam in the sunlight. Most had been stripped from the dead troops of Scorpion's once powerful army but those he picked gave no trace of their origin. They might as well have come from the early days of Hor-Amen's reign in Lower Nile. And there were the ever desired arm bands, some expertly woven, others of copper. When he thought he had enough to entice Agga to return on his next voyage he set out for Meidum at a brisk walk.

As the day wore on so did his weariness from the dash to Crocodile Lake the night before. By late afternoon he was plodding along with each step feeling like his last. Finally he stopped at the edge of a little creek and slept until the brightness of the full moon woke him. At that he moved on toward the river's edge at Meidum where he was sure he would find Agga in the early morning.

Agga was out of sorts and ready to head back to Pe almost empty handed. The people were afraid to barter with him for fear that he might be a spy from Amen-Kha. After all Amen-Kha had threatened to level Meidum before he lost his fleet of boats. When Naan spread out his treasures Agga let out a shout, "The gods have looked on me with kindness this day, Naan. Where did all this stuff come from?" "In the old days there was a cattle station over toward Crocodile Lake and these are things that were left with the people around here when it was abandoned. There has been no trade with Pe so there was no place to barter it I suppose". Agga and Naan worked oout a barter deal for the goods Agga had brought with him.

"It looks pretty good to me; reminds me of things we used to get from Pe.""So it does. So it does. Is there more of it out there, Naan?" "I think so, Agga. It will take time to collect enough to be worth your while though. When do you think you will be coming to Meidum again? Soon?" "It depends on whether Amen-Kha will let me keep coming to Pe and then Meidum. With this batch of goods I think he will and if so I will be back by the next full moon." Naan noted that it would take more of the same kind of goods Agga had brought for the people at Meidum to have something to trade with. They had virtually nothing for so long they would be elated to get back to bartering.

Agga and his crew were in Pe before sundown the third day after he left for Meidum. Amen-Kha was off hunting so Agga kept his barter material covered and he and his crew stayed with the boat overnight. Early the next morning Amen-Kha showed up at the landing and called, "Well, Agga, I see you got back as you said you would. Did you find anything more than

150

worthless trash up there?"

"My Lord, we have brought back good stuff. I think you will agree and if it pleases my Lord I would like to get about trading and head back out to sea not later than tomorrow morning." "Show me what you have. It had better be as good as you say it is...and I had better not find any Upper Nile things to offend our god, Amen in there!" Agga grinned, "I did not see anything that would have even suggested that those people worship any other god, my Lord. It is so quiet up there I was ready to come back here with nothing until some fellow came in from somewhere between Meidum and Crocodile Lake with these things. Aren't they beautiful?"

Amen-Kha let out a soft whistle of delight, "That is good stuff, Agga. We have not seen anything like it here in Pe for several years. Where did the man think it came from?" "He said it was stuff that probably came from Pe years ago when there was a shepherd's station at Crocodile Lake. Since it was abandoned these things show up when the village people give them up to be able to barter for things they need." "Yes, there was a station there a long time ago. A shepherd named, Menku from up toward Asyut kept it for trade with Pe during my father's time as king. You say it is quiet up there; did you see any Upper Nile people or their boats there?"

"No, my Lord. The only boats I saw were small and there were a few reed skiffs and a reed barge or two. Nothing more that I saw anywhere between here and Meidum." "I am glad to hear that. You may proceed to barter and leave whenever it suits you. Neither I nor my guards will interfere." With that Amen-Kha directed his guards to keep the priests from harassing Agga and his crew. Having finished his trading Agga shoved off to sail down the river, but not before sending word to Amen-Kha that he expected to be back by the next full moon.

Ar-Chab walked cross country and up river to about twelve miles south of Meidum where a small inlet secreted the boats used to provision the station from passing traffic on the Nile. He got a fast boat into the water and headed for Asyut as fast as the sails would take him there; fortunately there was a southward breeze and he reached Asyut by noon of the following day. Menhes had arrived there only the day before and was surprised to see Ar-Chab, "What brings you here, Ar-Chab. Is anything wrong at Crocodile Lake?"

"No, Menhes, everything is going well at the station. It should be in full operation before another new moon rises. Tell me, how are MeriLyth and Ki?" "They are well. MeriLyth is busy of course and there is a lot of preparation going on for Addi-Hoda's visit. I presume he will come for the feast in about two or three weeks. You have not answered why you are here."

With that Ar-Chab told Menhes all Naan had revealed about the situation in Pe and the expected establishment of limited trade with the Cretan boat traveling to Meidum from there. "That is most interesting, Ar-Chab. I did not know that Amen-Kha had murdered Hor-Amen, though I should have expected it I suppose. This puts an entirely different light on the relations between our two kingdoms and I am not sure I can predict how Amen-Kha will deal with Upper Nile. My best guess is unpredictably based on our past experiences with him. He is a hothead, no doubt about that, but he is also stupid when it comes to fighting. Hor-Amen could be intractable, particularly regarding his fanatic zeal for his god, 'Amen' but otherwise he was generally peaceable enough for me not to worry very much about him."

"From what Naan said, Menhes, I suspect Amen-Kha has a problem with his tyrannical suppression of bartering with the boats from the coast up past Saqqut. According to Naan's new friend, Agga about all Pe is getting is coming from what the Cretan boats bring in; and most Cretan boats are too deep hulled to negotiate the Nile successfully."

"Ar-Chab, how do we know that this Agga is not one of Amen-Kha's spies sent up to be sure we are not up to anything that far north?" "I asked Naan that, fearing that Amen-Kha might have heard about the reopening of the station at Crocodile Lake. He said that he doubted it. Naan picked up a little of the Cretan tongue...just a few words and phrases...while he was going back and forth between Pe and Crocodile Lake. He would hang around the wharves at Pe-Diph and talk to the boat masters there, some of whom were Cretan. He says that Agga's crew spoke only Cretan, that they were totally oblivious to his conversations with Agga and could not even ask for food from the villagers. When are you going back to Nekhen, Menhes?"

"I will be leaving in a couple of days. I came down to get Khafu to bring Mother and Hev-Ri to Nekhen before the Addi-Hoda visit. Djo-Aten's royal barge will come for them and I must have it back in time to send it to the first cataract to bring Addi-Hoda down the Nile in keeping with his royal station." "Do you think Hetti will come, Menhes? She was pretty adamant that Asyut was as far south as she ever intended to go when we moved her here." Menhes laughed, "That was before she had a grandson, Ar-Chab. that also applies to you. I want you to be there during the time Addi-Hoda is there." "And when will that be, Menhes?" "I have planned it for the week after the next full moon."

"That will be perfect. If all goes well Agga will have been back at Meidum before I leave for Nekhen and I can report on anything he brings of interest to you then." "Good. I want to talk to Addi-Hoda and seek his advice on how to keep peace with Lower Nile. i am beginning to have my doubts that there is any way to avoid continuing skirmishes along the river. I think Amen-Kha has bragged so much that he will have to back his claims up with some kind of action against what he imagines we control. I would not be too surprised if he sends small expeditions up toward Meidum to harass andmurder the local farmers and village people just to show he can win some fights. Whether it is something we have to respond to to keep our cover at Crocodile Lake requires knowledge of the situation. I will need all the information I can get."

CHAPTER SIXTEEN   'Assault at Kish'

In the early morning Abb-Oth arranged a tour of the temple at Kish for the party from Uruk and included Fyd. Kalam-Bad had a meeting with King Thar-Mes but insisted that Ekhana accompany the tour. Miqel was elated that Ifn-Lot agreed to go along and he was amazed at the number of devices Kmal-Dyl had designed for sighting the stars and observing the times of the sun's path across the sky throughout the year. Otherwise he felt that the work at Uruk's White Temple was more advanced, at least from the standpoint of the academy and its teaching methods.

The following day Kmal-Dyl summoned Miqel and Ifn-Lot to his apartment to continue their discussions. "Miqel, I would like to discuss my work with you as it relates to the Sacred Circle and writing. Hear me out for I have invested years of my life in this work and hope I can save you some of the frustrations I have had." "I will listen and am honored that you will take Ifn-Lot and me into your confidence."

"I have concluded that in my lifetime I will be unable to design an acceptable set of symbols restricted to the twenty-two steps of the construction alone, acceptable in the sense that scribes in general could be taught to use it. I think there are a few wizards who could master a set of ciphers, each one standing for a single consonantal sound; such a set would use up almost all of the twenty-two steps. However I have worked out thirteen vowel sounds that have to be somehow accounted for and this is where the complication comes in. I count nineteen distinct consonantal sounds we all use in our speech regularly and that would require thirty-two symbols to accommodate all the sounds the writing would have to convey.

"We already have hundreds of ciphers in use in Sumer, not all of them in any one place of course. Some of them are based on old petroglyphs and a large number of the most widely used ones represent in some way things that are familiar, not only to the wizards but to people in general...signs that can be made in clay with a reed. I think we could make little tablets that could be sun baked, or even fired for our records. We have nothing else to work with that is generally available between Kish and the Gulf. Would you not agree, Ifn-Lot?" Ifn-Lot concurred and Miqel continued to remain silent.

Kmal Dyl went on, "I have been working with a reed with one end cut to a sharp point and the other left in its natural circular state. By using first one end of the reed and then the other I can make symbols in clay that look enough like the ciphers extant today to be recognizable to anyone who would take the time to learn them. To be effective they will all have to be basically horizontal and point to the left since most people are right handed. I would prefer for writing to progress from left to right; and if we could somehow produce an easily reproducible smooth, flat surface and a brush for illustration that would be the way it would naturally go. But one must push with the reed as contrasted to pulling with a brush so right to left is the way I would design a system of writing. Furthermore if one uses a chisel in this left hand it is also necessary to move from right to left."

Miqel commented that he had come to the same conclusion though he had not tried a reed such as Kmal-Dyl described. He made some motions with his hand and observed, "Master one could use a reed the way you are talking about very quickly I think. What sounds will you employ?"

"I am coming to that. I think I will have to encode vowel sounds with each of the principal consonants so that a single symbol stands for a single syllable. I will set up a square matrix so that, for example the consonant, 'Buh' would also become part of separate ciphers for 'Bah, Bee, Beh, Bay, Boo'; and so on for the other consonants. Do you follow what I am saying?" Miqel answered, "Yes, Master. I follow your line of reasoning. But will that not make a very large number of symbols to memorize? And to use it won't it make an awkward sounding method of transliteration when anyone is attempting to read it?"

"Granted on both counts, Miqel. What I am telling you is that in order to achieve writing that will be useful at all as a record of thoughts and events and names of places and people this is the only thing I have devised that will actually work. It is admittedly cumbersome, but for drawing scribes it would not take an inordinate amount of time to learn and put into use. That means only trained scribes will perform writing, however I think for a very, very long time that will be true in any system of writing anyone can come up with. I do not see that as a problem.

"I am already testing a quite short version of such a syllable based system at the academy here. It permits limited description of names and places with sounds that are familiar enough to be understandable. The complete system will take me another four or five years if my health holds. Though it is less than a desirable solution it affords some facility in the art of communication that will not exist I fear unless I use my remaining days to introduce it. It is a bitter disappointment to me to give up on the 'Sacred Circle' based system. There has to be a way to do it; it has simply not been given to me to be the one to come up with it.

"I must ask two things of you. First you will not reveal this conversation to anyone. I have enough doubters now that it will be impossible to accomplish anything if anyone even suspects I am doubtful of the effectiveness of such writing myself. Second, I will not show it to you. I believe you are young enough and bright enough to possibly invent a simpler system that uses a minimum number of single, distinct sounds. It will be of no help to you if you have the syllable based system as a crutch to fall back on. Your system must not be derivative from anything that exists today. It must be wholly original to be as useful as I envision it can be."

Grieved, Ifn-Lot replied, "Master, I am sorry to hear what you have to say. What you are doing is beyond anything anyone else I have ever heard of who is alive today is doing and it will revolutionize our means of communication. All of us wish you long and healthy years of contributing to our knowledge. However if this is your wish we will comply. What Miqel is working on is completely different of course. But as he will tell you his point of departure is based on your own teachings. We all hope your confidence in his ability to find this most elusive of all answers will be proved correct, even if it is after my time and yours."

Miqel's disappointment was so clearly written on his face that Kmal-Dyl turned away without speaking. Miqel rose and walked over to where Kmal-Dyl was sitting and putting his hand on his arm softly spoke, "Master, I will try as hard as I can to do what you say. My confidence has not had the trials yours has had. If I have any success it will be because you gave me the bases to work from. If I fail I will be gratified to know that you have left a form of writing where none exists now."

Kmal-Dyl smiled warmly and then changed the subject, "Ifn-Lot, I want you to proceed with the limited henge we discussed. I have mentioned it to Abb-Oth without giving him any details except to say I believe such a henge can be constructed not far from here. Northeast of Kish there is a fairly large area of stone and gravel and it is generally flat. Not the kind of place we have looked for for so many years but it should suffice for your purposes. Are you familiar with the Nur-Bikh wilderness?" "I am indeed. A forsaken plot if ever there was one. Yet you may be right; I had never thought of it as serving any useful purpose. The only question I would have is where we can get enough water to keep those of us working there alive over any extended

154

period."

"I have thought of that also. Some hunters came back from there recently and reported that they found plentiful water less that a day's walk from that area of Nur-Bikh: one of those freak turns where the Tigris broke through its banks and formed a new steam. You would have to have pack animals going back and forth daily during the digging and erection of the stones but I do not see that that is so unusual anywhere we would be building a henge of any size. That will be the case almost anywhere in Sumer.

"How long do you think it will take you to get the design work completed? Everything possible should be done here in Kish or in Uruk before setting out for the desert with men and tools." Ifn-Lot pondered the question then gave his answer, "I would expect it will take close to two years before we will actually be up there digging. That includes surveys of the site to find the best specific area for the henge. Travel back and forth between Uruk and Kish will take time and there is the matter of convincing not only Thar-Mes but Men-Chad-Rez as well that this is worth the effort in men and provisions. I doubt that we can count on any help at all from Eridu, though Temple Al-Ubaid in Ur might lend us a few drawing scribes. Then of course there is the actual design itself. I think we have the dimensions fairly well framed in but they will have to be refined and for anything that large we will need some good copper plates and stakes to inscribe for star-sighting from the upright stones, much the same as you do here at the temple. For such a scale we cannot rely on ropes of any kind to measure the distances between points: they would stretch so much as to be useless.

"I am not attempting to make this appear more difficult than it is but it is a daunting exercise and will require great care to gain the most advantage for our effort. Assuming that we can start in about two years we should be finished by the time six or eight new moons have risen. That is my best estimate for the time being,"

Kmal-Dyl sighed and responded, "It is a huge effort, Ifn–Lot but I do believe it should be done, even if it will produce knowledge that will benefit only those who follow after us many years from now; perhaps it will be many generations from now. First things first. It would be my opinion that it is time for you and your party to get back to Uruk. I will take care of the work that needs to be done here, including getting Abb-Oth to obtain the support of Thar-Mes. I think he will give it without too much reservation. Furthermore I need to get back to work on my system of writing. I will get no more years than I have left and it will get no easier as time passes."

Thar-Mes and Abb-Oth came down to the river to see the Uruk party off and Fyd took the tiller with no complaint from Kalam-Bad. Miqel and Ekhana took turns trying to bring down a bird or two with their slings but had no luck so they decided to wait until they turned in downstream and the movement of the barge would not affect their aim.

The days passed quickly and things were quiet at Uruk. Fyd went to visit Oghud and Toq at the new Hathuruk station and found them peacefully tending the goats. With hunting and gathering no longer their only means of survival the women were able to make the camp more livable and the tribe seemed happy enough with this new life.

Men-Chad-Rez and Chad-Mar insisted that Miqel complete his work at the White Temple academy under Ifn-Lot and Akhuruk before he could participate in any henge design. Ifn-Lot was able to devote enough time to the henge design with his confidence in Akhuruk's teaching and the design progressed well. After a few months however Akhuruk's health began to fail and he became more and more confined to the reed house with Urunya frantically hovering over him. At first he resented it but as time wore on he simply gave up. By early winter it was obvious he would not live to see the spring and Baldag and Ghanya tried to prepare Miqel for the inevitable.

Miqel would not believe that Akhuruk was going to die and became withdrawn; not even Fyd could cheer him up.

Finally one morning Akhuruk could not be awakened and Urunya summoned Baldag and Ghanya to the house. It was decided to bury his remains in a field near the reed house he had lived in and Baldag agreed to take care of it quickly. He and Fyd dug a shallow grave and placed the body in it, covering it with gravel and such stones as they could bring up from the riverside. Then Baldag went to the academy to tell Ifn-Lot and Miqel what had happened.

Although Baldag was gentle with Miqel it was of little comfort. He had suffered the loss of Malil without understanding the reality of it but this was the first time in his life he had to face the death of someone he loved as deeply as he had Akhuruk. Ifn-Lot remained silent as Miqel wept inconsolably.

It was weeks before Miqel turned back to his work and when he did he plunged headlong into it, savagely attacking every aspect of the symbolic representation of the 'Sacred Circle' construction. He ate little and slept less, to such an extent that Ifn-Lot shared Baldag's alarm for his health. The results of his work were not promising at all. Sumerian phonics and the thirteen vowel problem articulated by Kmal-Dyl seemed intractable.

At length it was Miqel who came to the conclusion that he would have to ignore all the Sumerian symbols and create new signs for the consonants before proceeding to the vowels. Beyond that was the necessity to group the consonantal sounds and array them in order, assigning a "sounds-
like" name drawn from objects familiar to everyone.

He hit upon an idea that really was from his earliest thoughts on the subject: to keep looking at the construction diagram itself until he could "see" things that resembled animals, fish, eyes or other parts of the body; serpents, household objects, anything at all that could be described by a simple cipher. He arranged these items in the order of the construction itself, often having more than one object for each step. Over time he began to associate these things until they consumed his entire conscious thought.

Ifn-Lot decided that it was time for Miqel to put these studies away for awhile to avoid the pitfalls of endless repetition without any real progress, a common occurrence in such circumstances when one is attempting creation. The henge work was at a point where it required a journey to Kish, perhaps the final journey before setting out for the Nur-Bikh wilderness to lay out the site for digging.

Though Miqel was past eighteen years of age and as such capable of making his own decisions Ifn-Lot felt he should obtain Chad-Mar's support before taking Miqel with him to Kish. Ghant-Ur at Al-Ubaid could offer neither men nor provisions and Eridu was no better. Men-Chad-Rez had agreed to assign shifts of forty men to be relieved at each new moon. Each new party would carry enough food for the entire time they would be away but the tools and any other requirements would have to come from Kish.

Chad-Mar thought it would be a good diversion for Miqel and convinced Men-Chad-Rez to let Kalam-Bad accompany them with an armed guard, at least as far as Kish. Again Methwyd wanted to go and take Ekhana to learn the weaving methods practiced at Kish. While hides and furs suited the men quite well in their official capacities as warriors and chiefs woven tunics were more comfortable and far more practical for the climate of Sumer.

Everything went as well as could be expected as they sailed upstream to Kish. Fyd did manage to kill one crocodile on the way and skinned it to barter its tough covering as a shield. At the Kish landing the party was met by Rom-Sha who promptly escorted them to Thar-Mes.

156

After exchanging greetings with Kalam-Bad, Thar-Mes spoke to Miqel and Ifn-Lot, "Abb-Oth will be glad to see you. I think Kmal-Dyl feels everything here is ready for your henge at Nur-Bikh except gathering the pack animals for the expedition and of course assigning the men to do the heavy work." Ifn-Lot told him of Men-Chad-Rez's offer of men and provisions and Thar-Mes said, "Then it is time to get the party together. I will wait to hear from you and Kmal-Dyl as to when you wish to leave."

After they had been at Kish for three days the courtyard came alive one morning with a great commotion surrounding a bedraggled and badly battered hunting party that limped in from somewhere upriver. One of the men was obviously not a typical hunter and from the way he spoke, Rom-Sha estimated he was from very far away, perhaps as far as Nile. The hunters claimed to have been attacked by a marauding band from Mari and told him that the outsider escaped from the band when they ran for their boat and headed down the river. They made no judgment as to whether he was one of the Mari gang or, as he insisted their prisoner. He had helped them get away and that is all they knew.

Thar-Mes had had enough of Mari infiltration into the temple and the countryside surrounding Kish. He was prepared to disbelieve anything any of these foreigners had to say and was at the point of ordering their executions when Ifn-Lot came into the yard and immediately recognized Per-Qad. He begged Thar-Mes to be allowed to talk to Per-Qad and Thar-Mes allowed Per-Qad to stand, "You will be given a brief moment to talk to the Senior Priest from Uruk. Unless there is compelling reason to spare you, you will be executed this day."

"Per-Qad waited for Ifn-Lot to speak. "Per-Qad, do you wish to explain why you deserted us so long ago, and why we have never heard from you since?" "Davri, I beg of you, please believe me. That night I twisted my knee so badly I could not move. I was afraid if I called out you would attempt to rescue me and we would all die. That is truth. What happened afterward will take too long to tell you now but I was tortured until another Mari party made me travel with them to act as a servant and explain the constructions to young drawing scribes. In a raid similar to the one you experienced one hunter had stayed with the boat and those of us here managed to jump in before the raiding party killed all of us. They did kill seven of these hunters, who incidentally are from up around Salbat, according to them. I believe their story." Ifn-Lot bent over and whispered, "Per-Qad, I am Ifn-Lot, not Davri. Do not ever mention that name again."

Ifn-Lot then turned to Thar-Mes, "If you will release this man to me I will promise you to guard him with my life until we can be convinced there is nothing to fear from him. I do believe what he is saying is true." Thar-Mes thought a moment, then called Rom-Sha over and ordered him to assign a guard to Ifn-Lot until he, Thar-Mes relieved him. Turning to Ifn-Lot he continued, "I think you and your friend will both be safer with a guard until we are absolutely sure he is not a spy from Mari. There has been an increasing number of people from far up the river happening to stumble into Kish of late."

A single figure wandered away from the crowd that had gathered and slowly walked down to the landing where he began to talk to a couple of fishermen in low tones. He and the others had recently arrived from Huta; that was what he told the guards. They had stayed busy fishing and planned to return to Huta in a few more days, hoping to do a little hunting for crocodiles on the way. He had been in earshot of Per-Qad when he addressed Ifn-Lot as, 'Davri'.

The henge party was at last ready to depart for the Nur-Bikh wilderness and Kalam-Bad decided to tramp along with them, taking Ekhana with him. They would return as soon as the campsite was made and then head back for Uruk. Since Thar-Mes had sent the hunting party that arrived with Per-Qad back up the river several days before he decided to let Per-Qad go with

Kalam-Bad and then return to Uruk with him. He was not sure what to do with Per-Qad if the Uruk party was not there to provide for and protect him. Thar-Mes ordered Rom-Sha to conscript laborers and burden bearers from among the men who chanced to be at the landing and in the general yard area, whether they belonged to Kish or not, preferably not. A motley crowd of traders, hunters and fishermen was rounded up in the early morning hours before the sun had risen above the plain and herded into line for the trek to the wilderness. Among them were the three "fishermen from Huta".

Fyd, along with Miqel and Ekhana set out ahead of the party, looking for anything they might find in the way of game for the first evening meal. The party moved slowly to allow the heavily loaded goats to make their way. The Kish armed guard and Kalam-Bad's spearmen stayed near the front of the group to insure against attacks by desert bandits and to keep their eyes on Miqel and Ekhana. That was not really necessary for they soon tired of their fruitless hunting and rejoined the party. Ifn-Lot carried the plans, drawn on sheep-skin and talked to Per-Qad about what could be done to get him back to Asyut.

Shortly before noon on the third day there was murmuring in the ranks of the laborers and Ifn-Lot walked back to see what it was about. Suddenly the fisherman who heard him called, 'Davri' screamed, "So you are Davri. You will guide no more enemies of Mari and the sacred goddess, Ushtur." With that he lunged at Ifn-Lot and drove a flint knife through his heart. The other fishermen started to run but they and the assassin were felled immediately by Kalam-Bad's spearmen.

With Ifn-Lot dead there was nothing to do but turn around and head for Kish. Miqel and Fyd buried Ifn-Lot's body and placed a marker above a pile of stones covering it. The sad walk back left the leaders wondering who else could not be trusted. It was decided to send the Kish guards back with the laborers on a forced march to reach Kish as quickly as possible. Upon their arrival a runner would be sent to inform the remainder of the party if it was safe for them there.

Thar-Mes was enraged. He ordered the execution of the entire labor party and closed down the bartering yard. For a week no one would be allowed to enter the city, nor would anyone be allowed to leave except on the express orders of Thar-Mes. This of course was a severe hardship for anyone who came to barter without enough provisions to last a week. Whatever they could find as fish or handouts would have to keep them alive but Thar-Mes was unyielding.

Thar-Mes waited for Per-Qad to return with Kalam-Bad and then called for him to meet him in the courtyard. "Per-Qad, if that is your real name, I want to know all you know about Mari from your wanderings up there during the past year. Be assured that your life is worth nothing to me with Ifn-Lot dead. Nevertheless you can be of use to me if you reveal the distribution of the Mari bands and tell me whether they have an organized army or not."

"I will tell you all I know, my Lord. Yes, my name is Per-Qad. My master, a man named, Menku from Nile sent me with my friend and Senior Wizard, Hev-Ri to learn from Kmal-Dyl what could be done to prevent the same divisiveness that exists in Sumer and Akkad from developing in our academy in Upper Nile. I am sure you are aware that we were attacked by a gang of Mari zealots and one of our number, a sun-wizard named Rabul was killed. I started to run and fell with a badly twisted knee. I kept silent fearing the others would try to rescue me and we all would be killed. This is what I told Ifn-Lot and it is true. I knew him only as a mysterious man named, Davri. Fortunately for me the gang did not know he was one of the party they attacked. I was told he had been targeted for death for years in Mari for his role in acting as a guide to people traveling from the upper Euphrates down to Kish and Uruk. No one in Mari knew what he looked like, nor did they know the identity of his friend, a man named, Malbu who

158

provided a boat from Huta southward, or northward for returning travelers."

Thar-Mes listened intently and was inclined to believe him, particularly since his reference to Hev-Ri agreed with the stories Hev-Ri and Shephset told of their journey. "Continue." "I traveled over a rather limited part of the Mari kingdom, if one can call it a kingdom. The bands I was with were almost entirely in the eastern part of the land along the Euphrates from about Leb to Quri, a distance of perhaps thirty thousand Sumer cubits, and west of the Euphrates no more than twenty thousand cubits.

"The Mari kingdom is a loose confederation of bands of shepherds and farmers with their villages scattered over a vast area: picture a rough circle two hundred thousand cubits across. The city of Mari, in the eastern part...I was there only briefly...is not much of a prize; it is really a town where there is an academy devoted to teaching drawing scribes and a few priests. All priests in Mari worship Ushtur, their 'Mother of Heaven' and all priests and scribes are convinced that the fractional Sacred Circle is a true gift from Ushtur. I, myself support the fractional persuasion, not because it is more accurate...it isn't...but because it is simpler to use and we cannot measure the difference anyway. That is why I was sent to hear what Kmal-Dyl had to say."

"May I continue?" Thar-Mes was fascinated, "Continue". "Their king is Qad-Rab and he lives at a large station called, Ham-Bal about twenty or twenty-five thousand cubits northwest of Mari. His forces loosely connected to Ham-Bal number perhaps a thousand men, but not many of them are there at any given time: water and food are simply not available to support a large garrison type army anywhere in Mari...if I am to believe my captors, and I do. If it were not for their fanatic zeal in preserving the signs in the heavens and the fractional Sacred Circle constructions there would be nothing more than tribal groups of farmers and shepherds with no central authority at all. At least that is my opinion. I suspect there are no real wizards as such in all of Mari, just a few trainees and drawing scribes captured from Kish and Uruk, maybe even some from Ur.

"That is all very interesting, Per-Qad but I have more urgent reasons for wanting to know about the whereabouts of the Mari marauders. As far as I am concerned this act of murder is an act of war. Nevertheless I do not want to risk avenging Ifn-Lot's death with a reckless expenditure of my own warriors and chieftains in a country that far away. Do you have any thoughts on how they might be effectively punished and how we could put an end to their terrorizing everyone who travels the Euphrates?"

"I am no warrior but I think it would take a very long war to overcome Mari in any sense of a total and lasting defeat. They have command of every watering place in their territory and can move bands of fierce fighting men in and out of battle with nothing more than a quick strike-and-run tactical scheme. Since their warriors always live off the land, taking what they need or want and killing if opposed they can fight a war of attrition, striking at any point of their own choosing, then vanishing into that desolate wilderness they call home. I never saw their king, Qad-Rab even though I wandered for a long time with Mari warriors. It would seem to me the only way to hurt them is to fight them in a manner similar to their own ways."

Thar-Mes was taken aback at the suggestion, "Do you expect me to send our men to Mari to starve or be murdered in their wilderness?" "No, of course not, my Lord. What I was thinking of would be to establish several supportable garrisons along the west bank of the Euphrates across from towns on the east bank we already know are not loyal to the Mari king, such towns as Leb and Bav. A provisioning station could be set up at Huta...the elders there would welcome such I imagine...and your troops could be rotated at the end of each of the seasons. That way no warrior would be up there for a very long period and there would always be fresh troops. That is what Qad-Rab uses; the same party seldom strikes twice at the same village. I would guess a garrison would have a hundred and fifty warriors and no war-party would number over forty.

"Your garrison troops can form war-parties and move into Mari country, westward two or three days walk from the Euphrates, killing everything in their path; picking off stragglers in the process and retreating to safety if met with really effective resistance. They would then return to the station and regroup to move out in another direction in a few days. Repeating this over a period of time would establish a wide area west of the Euphrates that would be effectively rid of the Mari bands."

"And what if Qad-Rab decides to drive my troops into the Euphrates with a large force such as you describe at Ham-Bal?", Thar-Mes asked. "Your troops would have to constantly take the Mari boats off the west bank of the river and sink them or convert them to their own use. That way Qad-Rab's forces would be stopped at the water's edge while your warriors escaped to the friendlier towns on the other side. Qad-Rab cannot support a large army in the field for more than a few days before he has to go back inland for provisions. You would be abandoning only one station, and that for a rather short time. Qad-Rab will find nothing moving northwest which is why he has never roamed up there according to the bands I was with. Up toward the Orontes there isn't anything worth a supply line that long."

Thar-Mes thought for a bit and told Per-Qad, "This will take a lot of planning and a lot of thinking about. You have been helpful and you are free to do as you wish. Where do you want to go now?" "I would like to go to Uruk with Kalam-Bad's party and then I hope I can somehow arrange to get back up the Euphrates and return to Upper Nile. It may be that Miqel will want to go there with me. My master can provide anything he will ever need there and he could be the greatest wizard in all of Nile. Perhaps he will even invent writing there.

FIGURE FROM THE STANDARD OF UR

Dated circa 2,700 BC

Illustrated by W. C. Cawthon

Figure 12: Standard of Ur Figure

CHAPTER SEVENTEEN 'The Shadow Over Uruk'

Kalam-Bad had been present when Thar-Mes questioned Per-Qad and was as sure as he ever would be that Per-Qad told the truth. "Per-Qad, there was no way for you to know Davri had taken the name of Ifn-Lot, anymore than I ever knew he was Davri though I had heard of Davri for years. All of us in Sumer knew the legends of his rescues and the seeming impossibility of anyone beyond his most trusted friends identifying him . It was only after you were captured that the mysterious Davri simply disappeared for all anyone knew. It was an unfortunate happening that lead to his death but that is done and it cannot be undone. He thought little of the incident. I doubt that he ever really feared for his life...he was an extraordinarily brave man. You owe him your life, but then so do your friends, Hev-Ri and the other sun wizards from Nile; and a lot of ordinary souls from Akkad who wanted nothing more than to visit Kish or Uruk or Ur."

At that point Abb-Oth walked into the yard and came over to where Per-Qad and Kalam-Bad were standing. "Thar-Mes has told me that you were one of the wizards who came wanting to see Kmal-Dyl. I think it would be regrettable if you left without meeting him. He can see you now and I would like to sit with you while you visit with him." "I am greatly honored, Master. I wonder what you will do now that Ifn-Lot is gone and the expedition to Nuhr-Bikh is at best delayed for a long time."

Kmal-Dyl was grave as he spoke to Per-Qad, "I think this is the end of our hopes for building the great triangle anywhere in Sumer. Ifn-Lot was our only hope since he had effectively steered Miqel toward that goal after we discussed the possibility of it. Miqel is most likely to develop a system of writing, probably after I am gone; yet the ultimate goal of squaring the circle must also take his time and attention sometime in the future. I think he, and only he among our wizards can do it, or set up a method whereby it can be done. From talking to Hev-Ri I do not think you people from Nile have anyone who will come up with a solution or even seek one with much purpose. It may be that you can take Miqel to Nile where he would be free to pursue these things without the threat of the war with Mari hanging as a shadow over everything we do." "Master, I can assure you Menku will give him all he needs and there would be no interference with his studies there. Beyond that I am in no position to judge.I scarcely know Miqel, though I do regard him as brilliant."

"Those of us who have listened to him as he expounds his thoughts on a variety of subjects deem him to be beyond simple genius. It is almost as if he were a messenger from the gods, or from God, Himself for that matter. He quickly takes whatever you have to say and projects it beyond what you are thinking; at least he does with me. Would you not say so, Abb-Oth?" Abb-Oth nodded and Kmal-Dyl continued, "The henge in the wilderness is of no use now to us here in Kish...or in Uruk either I suspect. That leaves only the matter of writing...and that in itself is certainly enough...to be dealt with for the next few years. Yes, I do believe we will have writing of some sort in my lifetime. But Miqel's approach might produce the ultimate form of writing, something we have never dreamed of doing heretofore."

"Master, I fear I do not understand what you are saying." "Of course you don't. How could you? Still, when Ifn-Lot came to me with Miqel I was not prepared for his line of thinking. Enough. If you can convince him to go with you to the land of the Nile you will have many long days to hear whatever he is willing to reveal to you. I wish you well,"

Kalam–Bad was ready to be off for Uruk and Per-Qad joined the party at the landing where Thar-Mes and Abb-Oth came to see them off. They were downstream a fair distance by the time the sun began to beat down on them. Miqel looked forward to seeing his family, wondering how Urunya was getting along without Akhuruk and when Ette and Bodi would find husbands. After all, Ette was fifteen and Bodi would soon be fourteen, none too young to start families of their own. Ekhana was eager to show her friends in Uruk the new ways of weaving she had learned at Kish and Methwyd beamed over the samples she brought with her.

On arriving at Uruk Kalam-Bad took Miqel and Fyd with him to break the news of Ifn-Lot's death to Chad-Mar. Before they got to the White Temple they were met by Rom-Sha who asked them to wait until he could inform Men-Chad-Rez who was at his house by the river. Men-Chad-Rez came to the temple yard wanting to know how it was that they were back so quickly. "Is something wrong, Kalam-Bad? I expected you to be gone for at least three more weeks." "Yes, my Lord, it is very bad. The henge expedition is ended. A crazed murderer from Mari stabbed Ifn-Lot when we were not three days out of Kish. He died instantly."

"Why did your spearmen not protect him, Kalam-Bad? Did they not know that none of the people from Mari is to be trusted; surely Ifn-Lot had reason enough to know that." "We all know that all too well, Men-Chad-Rez. But when Thar-Mes rounded up laborers to be conscripted for the henge work there were these three men who claimed to be fishermen from up the river...they had been at Kish for some days and seemed harmless...and they were conscripted with the rest of the men in the yard and from down by the river. Ifn-Lot was walking back to the pack animals which were just behind the labor gang, perhaps he was going to get something he wanted there and suddenly this Mari assassin screamed a curse and whipped out a knife. It was over before the spearmen could save him. The man and his companions were all dead by the time Ifn-Lot's body fell to the ground but that is no consolation for the loss we have sustained."

"But why Ifn-Lot? He was as gentle a man as you could find. Why would they go all the way out in the wilderness to kill him?" "You know of course that before he came here to live he was called Davri and lived far above Kish at Aff most of the time. It seems that he had been hunted for years by the king of Mari, yet no one knew how to identify him. This thug from Mari just happened to overhear a chance remark and realized that this was the Davri they were all looking for. I think it is as simple as that. Abb-Oth and Thar-mes have worried about the Mari infiltration of Kish. Abb-Oth even fears there may be some of their zealots in the temple as servants. They can serve well and quietly for years without being detected I am told. In the meantime they send messages back to Mari by such men as fishermen and hunters, all of whom claim to have come from places like Leb and Salbat, too far away for anyone to know anything about them or who they might be. Just as we see here in Uruk there are always farmers coming in to offer their gifts to the temple; hunters and traders coming to barter their hides and goods and the fishermen who pick up whatever there is in the trade yard in exchange for their fish. But there has never been anything like this before."

"What does Thar-Mes plan to do about it? He cannot just hope it will not happen again; surely he knows he cannot think that?" "Thar-Mes has declared that Kish is at war with Mari. I have brought one of the sun wizards from Nile with me and he can tell you about that. He was with the others who came before Ifn-Lot came here to join the temple service. He is the one who was captured and escaped only a few days before we left for the Nur-Bikh wilderness. He wandered with the Mari bands for a long time. I think you will wish to talk to him at some length."

"I will indeed. But now you must tell all this to Chad-Mar. This will be the heaviest burden he has ever had to bear I fear. Miqel, I think you and Fyd had better be off to see your family. Let Kalam-Bad take the news to Chad-Mar. Rom-Sha, take Methwyd and Ekhana to their home

163

and tell the guards they can go home too."

Miqel plodded his way home, glad to be coming home but dreading to answer the questions that would surely arise. His fears were well founded. Gahnya was at Urunya's house helping her soften some hides and Ette was baking bread when he got there. "Miqel, we were not expecting you. Are you all right? Let me tell you what has happened. I am going to be Ny-Su's wife. Father has arranged it with his father and it will be at the next new moon. Isn't that exciting?" "O, Ette I am so glad for you. Ny-Su is a good man and he will be a good husband. We will have much to talk about I think." "Fyd will you go down to the goat pens and see if Father is there? Ette, where is Mother and where is Bodi?"

Ette ran to Urunya's house and she and Ghanya and Urunya returned as fast as Urunya could move. Before they could begin to talk Baldag came trotting home with Fyd. Then everyone talked at once. Miqel raised his hand and, laughing asked for enough quiet to answer some of their questions, "Yes, I am fine. The trip up and back was easy compared to other journeys we have made, particularly since it was all by boat. Kalam-Bad and Methwyd and Ekhana are fine. The expedition had to be called 133 off; but before I get into all that let me find out how you are. Ette has told me that she will soon be Ni-Su's wife. Other than that I do not know anything about what has gone on here."

Baldag spoke first, "Things are much the same as when you left; you really haven't been gone that long of course. Bodi has gone to the yard to try to barter some lentils for some wool; I haven't started shearing yet and she wants Ekhana to teach her what she learned about the weaving at Kish. She should be home shortly I think. I hope she finds the wool. Fyd has been very quiet. Is something wrong?"

Miqel darkened, "Ifn-Lot is dead, stabbed by a Mari assassin." He spoke without emotion and the silence was unbroken for a few moments except for Gahnya's sobbing. Baldag began softly, "Miqel, Ifn-Lot meant so much to you as a friend and as your mentor after Akhuruk died. I cannot know your grief, nor can I understand the awfulness of all this. Why don't you sit down with your mother and me while Fyd roasts a lamb. Ette and Urunya can get a meal together and we can talk after we have eaten. I think it will be better that way."

Miqel nodded and slumped to a reed mat with his eyes searching the distance. He said nothing. Gahnya asked, "Miqel, do you want to tell us about it?" "No, Mother, I don't. But I know that I must; it is not fair to you and Father. Ifn-Lot was your friend too. Let me begin a few days before we set out on the trek to the Nur-Bikh wilderness. A sun-wizard from Nile appeared at the Kish landing and Ifn-Lot recognized him as the one who was captured when he and Hev-Ri's party were attacked far north of Kish, up near Huta. Ifn-Lot was their guide. The sun wizard's name is Per-Qad and he has been wandering all this time with Mari war parties. He managed to escape and get to Kish and there it was Ifn-Lot who saved his life: Thar-Mes suspected he was a Mari spy. Per-Qad called Ifn-Lot, Davri, the only name he knew.. A Mari spy overheard the conversation and was conscripted into the labor gang. He killed Ifn-Lot when we had walked less than three days into the wilderness. That ended the henge expedition, forever I suppose. Without Ifn-Lot there can be no henge for years to come, if anyone wants to try it even then."

Baldag asked, "Do you know what you will do now? Will you continue in the temple service? Have you seen Chad-Mar?" "No, Father, I have not seen Chad-Mar; Kalam-Bad went alone to tell him. And no I do not know what I will do. I suppose I will go back to my work on writing since there is nothing to do now on the great triangle studies without the henge. Chad-Mar knows that. Kmal-Dyl wants me to finish my system of writing and for his own reasons...and I think they are good reasons...will not help me in that. As soon as I have talked to Chad-Mar I wish to have some time alone with Per-Qad to learn all I can about the country, Nile and his home in Upper Nile. Perhaps after that I can get back to work. Right now I do not much care. Could we discuss this tomorrow?"

Kalam-Bad walked into Chad-Mar's apartment with Coban-Bul at his side. "Kalam-Bad! What has brought you here?" Kalam-Bad shifted uneasily and looked at the floor until Chad-Mar dismissed Coban-Bul. "I have news I wish I did not have to bring you, Chad-Mar. Ifn-Lot has been murdered in the wilderness east of Kish." Chad-Mar remained silent, too stunned to utter a word. Kalam-Bad waited for him to speak and the moments seemed to drag on longer that the actual time that elapsed. Then Chad-Mar took a deep breath and asked, "Can you tell me if he was alone? Did he say anything before he died? Who would murder Ifn-Lot?"

"He died instantly, Chad-Mar, and we were with him; even Miqel and Ekhana had accompanied us as we began walking toward the site in Nur-Bikh. Three of the conscript laborers turned out to be spies from Mari. One of them overheard a man named Per-Qad call Ifn-Lot, Davri and a few days later he killed him." 'Who is this Per-Qad? Surely you have executed him for such a breach of confidence." "He is the sun wizard from Asyut in Nile who was captured and taken to Mari where he was held until a short time ago. I think Ifn-Lot told you about him."

"Yes, of course he did. He...we all were concerned for him and I certainly wondered if, being a fractional priest he had deserted to Mari. Did he have a believable story to explain his long absence?" "Yes, he did and it was Ifn-Lot who believed him when Thar-Mes would have executed him. He never knew Ifn-Lot by any other name except, Davri. He has been most helpful to Thar-Mes in his plans to punish Mari by describing what he has seen of Mari territory, and he has seen a lot. Thar-Mes has stated that a state of war now exists between Kish and Mari."

"I suppose this ends the work that we thought would lead to Miqel's great triangle project. This is just too much for me to comprehend. What effect do you think it has had on Miqel? Do you know if he met more than casually with Kmal-Dyl?" " Ifn-Lot told me about their meeting, not what they discussed but that Kmal-Dyl insisted that Miqel be elevated to Senior Priest, or rather Senior Wizard I believe is what he said. Miqel himself will have to tell you all about those meetings. This appears to have affected Miqel very deeply, probably more than he is willing to reveal. I want to talk to Baldag tomorrow and see how he regards Miqel's outlook for the future now."

"Kalam-Bad, leave me to try to absorb the calamity of this terrible thing. I am sure by tomorrow I will be better able to deal with it but I will ask that you return to me after you talk to Baldad. I would prefer to know of your conversation before I see Miqel."

Men-Chad-Rez walked into Baldag's house as the family was finishing the evening meal. He did not intend to stay; he just wanted to offer his own personal sympathy and any assistance that might be needed in dealing with the great loss Miqel had sustained. Indeed he felt it was a loss that would affect Uruk in ways he could not really understand. He was proud of the work that emanated from the White Temple and in fact felt certain that except for Kmal-Dyl there was no match for the White Temple service anywhere in Sumer. In that he was right.

"Welcome, My Lord. Have you eaten? We have plenty to share and there is wine left if you would care for it." "No, Baldag, I have eaten. Before the night descends on us I just wanted to tell you of my grief and sorrow for you, and particularly you, Miqel over the death of Ifn-Lot." "It is kind of you to come, my Lord. I believe we will be all right. Do you not think so, Miqel?"

"Of course, Father. My Lord, Men-Chad-Rez I thank you."

Kalam-Bad's visit with Baldag was a disappointment. Baldag was sure that Miqel would overcome his grief and bitterness over all that had occurred but he did not convince Kalam-Bad that that was true...or even that he really believed it was true. Kalam-Bad left meaning to report back to Chad-Mar that it would be for him to work things out for Miqel's future, if indeed he was the master wizard everyone seemed to think he was.

Kalam-Bad told Methwyd, "I wish I had never heard of all this wizardry business. It cannot bring anyone any happiness or joy in life. Miqel is a fine young man now. He ought to have a wife and enter the king's service. I think Men-Chad-Rez would restore the prince's title he rightly should have and he could have a good life with children and grandchildren to enjoy before he rots away in some cold temple trying to find out things God never intended for man to know. That is what I think." "The gods give to whom they will, Kalam-Bad. You know that. You are a powerful warrior and I am grateful for your gifts, so is Ekhana. Our lives are full and we have plenty of life's things to make us content. But what if God gave Miqel this great gift of insight into the secrets no one has ever known? Would you oppose God Himself?" "No, Methwyd I would not. I am just sad and weary and wish it all had not happened. A few weeks ago it seemed that everything was going to work out so well and those of us here in Uruk were witnesses to the coming of age of the greatest wizard ever known in Sumer. That is what Kmal-Dyl and Chad-Mar think.

"Maybe Ghanya is right. Maybe we are all selfish and have never given much thought to Miqel as anything but a mind. I have been with him on these trips since he was just an overgrown boy and he is still boyish when he and Fyd and Ekhana compete for the fish in the Euphrates. He is a man now. But what is a man who has no life but the dreary repetition of endless seeking for things no one knows. And if he finds his answers how will he know he has found them? There is no one to tell him. And our tools are not such that he can prove them. It is the same thing with the fractional Sacred Circle people and the true believers in the real 'Sacred Circle'. I fear it would take a structure much bigger than Miqel's pyramid, however big that is to prove one is better than the other. Even if they did prove it who could use it for anything except talking about in the academies?" Methwyd smiled, "Kalam-Bad, you are just tired and out of sorts I think. Go to sleep now. Tomorrow will come and things will not be so bad as you imagine they are tonight."

Chad-Mar was upset that Kalam-Bad had not come to see him after he left Baldag; still he waited for his explanation. "Of a truth, Chad-Mar it was better that I did not talk to you yesterday. I felt a weight I couldn't carry had settled on my shoulders after I talked to Baldag. And you have the greater burden in all of this messy business we have got ourselves busy with. Yet that is the messy business that is ours, really yours to deal with; and it must be dealt with soon if Miqel is not to be split in two."

"Once again you alarm me, Kalam-Bad. Can I in any way set your mind at ease?" "I am not sure, Chad-Mar. My problem, or what I think is my problem is that I know a little of what you wizards do but not enough to understand why it is so important to you or anyone else. Forgive my ignorance of your domain. I think it is better for you to talk to Miqel now. He wants to spend a few days talking to Per-Qad and I urge you to let him do that. I do think you should talk to Per-Qad before you permit it however. No, I do not think Per-Qad has any desire except to get back to his family in Nile, but I would not wish him to affect Miqel in some negative way."

"Thank you, Kalam-Bad. I think I do grasp what you are saying and am grateful for your saying it. We who have lived our lives apart, always within the walls of the temple do not have a very good understanding of the needs of men as men. We are inured to the hardships of a life of our choosing, and as strange as it may seem we come to take satisfaction in that very life itself, apart from whatever accomplishments we may achieve in our work. I guess we mostly just wish to be left alone. That is certainly not the way of your life. Is it?"

"No, Master, it is not. Yet that does not make my life better or more meaningful. Just different. I cannot know your life and you cannot know mine. Otherwise neither of us would be fit for the responsibilities we accept in our places of being. I have never really thought on these things much until all this happened. Not just Ifn-Lot's death: these great undertakings, the henge, writing, resolving the 'Sacred Circle' dilemma. Most of the people in Sumer are only a little ahead of Oghud and the bogs; they somehow survive until they die and that is about the sum of life for them. A few of us are allowed to enjoy the years we are given, not many though. I will leave now before I wear you out with my meanderings into such deep things, about which I can do absolutely nothing." For the first time Kalam-Bad laughed as he waved goodbye.

Chad-Mar called for Miqel but not until the following morning. Kalam-Bad's conversation had disturbed him more that he wanted to admit. And there were no answers he could give either. At last he decided that there were no answers and he resolved to put it out of his mind for now.

"Good morning, Master. I thank you for seeing me. I wish I could say something to ease your consciousness of these last few days and the disaster they have brought. I do not know what could possibly serve to do that however. I would think it would be better if I could answer what questions you may have since I am sure Kalam-Bad has told you the particulars of Ifn-Lot's death." "Yes, Miqel, he has and they are sorrowful pieces of such a string of chance happenings that lead to the end of a life so dedicated and gifted. We cannot undo the random flow and its damage any more than we can reverse the swelling flood of the Euphrates.

"I have wrestled these nights away with questions for which I must accept there are no answers; it is not given to me to seek such. Nor to you. What must be answered however is what you will do now. I presume you will continue in the temple service. I think it would be wise that you did, for a time anyway. I must tell you that we will close the academy Akhuruk founded here; it would be too great a burden for you to take it over and it would not further your work to be tutoring drawing scribes. We have ample means of doing that with our other priests.

"When you have accustomed yourself to living with this grief I wonder if it might not be the thing to do for you to attach yourself to Kmal-Dyl, eventually to take his place, whether there or here at the White Temple. Can you tell me your reaction to this?" "It is not my reaction to consider, Master. Kmal-Dyl has already decided that. For his own reasons he does not want me to work under his guidance, or alongside him either." "Did he tell you why, Miqel? I have been told of his high regard for your work and your promise. Why would he not want to guide you toward fulfillment of that promise?"

"He did tell Ifn-Lot and me that. But he made us swear not to reveal what lead him to make that decision. And the decision is final. What I can tell you is that it is not for selfish reasons on his part. Quite the contrary he deems it best for me that I pursue my studies and my work entirely alone with no one to fall back on or use as a crippled man would a crutch. He wants me to learn from my own errors, not to repeat his or anyone else's experience. I have not had much time to think about it though I am sure it is wise, he is a wise person."

"Then where does that take you now? Kalam-Bad tells me you wish to spend some time alone with Per-Qad, and that surely can be allowed for. I do, however wish to talk to Per-Qad before then. I must review with him what Hev-Ri and the other sun-wizards took back to Nile with them, assuming of course that they got back to their academy there. And I would like to know how advanced the Mari priests are in anything other than the fractional Sacred Circle. I will call him here now and after that you and he can take whatever time you want together." "Thank you, Master. I am in no hurry, no hurry at all. My mind does not want to function very well right now."

Chad-Mar sent for Per-Qad and when they were alone he told him, "I should hate you, Per-Qad. Ifn-Lot was like a brother to me and I cannot help holding you responsible for his death. Yet I know it was circumstance and I believe what I am told regarding your involvement in all these tragic events." "Thank you, Master. I will live with this all my days, wishing I had never left Asyut at all. But things are as they are. We cannot change them to fit our own desires however much we may pray the gods to reverse the course of life."

Chad-Mar reflected for a moment on what Per-Qad had said and his own questioning of the meaning of it all. "Per-Qad, let's look at what is to come; the past is there and we cannot alter it. I want to talk to you about what your own plans are. Do you think you are up to the rigors of attempting to get back to Nile; you cannot do that alone you know. Even if it were not for Mari there are too many days and too many pitfalls between here and your country for a lone traveler to reach his destination." "I do wish to return to Kemet, Master, and I am prepared for the hardships that entails. Had there not been any skirmish with the Mari raiders the journey here was harder than I would have imagined possible but we did undertake it and except for Rabul and me the entire party got to Sumer as we set out to do. I am aware that I will need help and that I have nothing to offer in return unless someone wants to visit Upper Nile and the academy at Asyut. I can be of help there. I also think I can help Miqel regain his perspective, though I do not think I can contribute to his work in any meaningful way."

"Kmal-Dyl has said he cannot contribute to Miqel's dream of inventing writing and I know I cannot. As for the square and the circle that has been an almost mythical goal from the times of legend. Men have dreamed and died only to be replaced by more men who dreamed and died. I for one would not pursue it since it brings only disappointment and disillusion. But this Miqel is different from us; it is almost as if he was not born of this world we live in. I don't think it is just extraordinary brighness or cleverness, there is something apart from our realm of thinking that he seems to go through when he is creating new ideas that no one ever thought of before. I would not bring up the subject to him but I wonder at times if he 'sees' things with his mind that we ordinary creatures do not."

Per-Qad was not prepared for such an astonishing confidence from Chad-Mar. Nor was he a particularly deep thinker, though he was a thoroughly grounded and rather creative wizard, whether such a one of the 'sun' or the 'moon' or the 'mother of heaven'. "I suppose we simply will not know the answers to those things and I truly doubt that Miqel himself knows. He says he wants to know about Upper Nile and the Asyut academy and I accept that as a lively curiosity and nothing more. If he would like to come to Asyut and do his work there I can assure you and him that he will have complete freedom to study, create or simply teach others what he already knows so well. My master, Menku is a kind and generous man and a tolerant one at that. He wants someone who can see through the petty arguments we have and settle them before we get into the distracting quibbling that has dominated much of the work in Sumer and Akkad. Miqel certainly would satisfy his wishes in that respect and I suspect in all respects."

"I would think he could, indeed I would think so. I would wish that he would remain here in the temple service and I think that is the thing for him to do. We can provide for all his needs relating to his work but that may not be enough. While we have been setting our own goals for him he has become a man and now must decide for himself what it is he will do. We knew that when we started this program for Miqel but little did we expect the extent of the powers of his mind then. You are free to visit with him and I hope you can satisfy his curiosity about Nile without it involving his leaving us to accompany you there. Yet if he does I will not interfere, as much as I will regret having to stand aside."

"I can only assure you, Master that I will not attempt to unduly influence him either way. What I will do is listen to him and let him ask whatever he wishes of me. If I can I will answer; if not I will be honest enough to tell him so." "So be it, Per-Qad. I will have to await the outcome. One thing more: give him time. Give him time."

Miqel and Fyd had wandered up the Euphrates a short distance in search of game. Fyd looked straight at Miqel and said, "Miqel, you are man now. I watch you and Ekhana. She is woman now. Do you want Ekhana for your wife?" "Fyd, I do not know. Yes I do. But that is not all there is to it. As it has been planned my life leaves no room for a woman and she could not find any happiness if I choose to become a senior priest at some temple. Right now I don't know what I want to do for the rest of my life. Until Ifn-Lot died learning all the constructions and the secrets of the temples seemed to be everything I could ever wish for. It was, and is exciting and I intend to continue working with these areas of study. But now there are other things too that are exciting and interesting and I feel they do not have to take away from my principal works. I have learned a lot from you; someday I believe I will be able to throw a club almost as well as you can." 'You throw club good as Fyd now, Miqel. You sling stone better than Fyd." "Thank you, Fyd. You are a kind man. It is just that I think that is an important thing to know.

"And then there is Ekhana. I never really knew any girls except my sisters until Kalam-Bad brought Ekhana along on that first trip. She was a lot like Malil to me then. We tried to outdo each other in everything, and in a great many things she could outdo me. It was fun and I was happy to be with her and always glad when she was included on our journeys. Now that I am a man I am sure there is the strongest desire in me to be a whole man, not only to try to unlock the secrets of the gods, but to live like other men. I do not want to disappoint my father or Chad-Mar; as long as I had Ifn-Lot this was something I could put off until another day when the work and studies would be finished to the point I could decide. Now it is that time and I am simply not prepared for it. Do you understand at all what I am saying?"

"Fyd understand most of it. Being man brings hard times for the head. Miqel, you know things. Man must know what man he is. Things not all there is. There is more. Bogs must live. Living hard. Takes all man can do. You do more. Living not hard for you. You not hunt. Still eat. Bogs not hunt. Bogs not eat. You talk to Per-Qad. Maybe he tell you that Fyd watch priests with Coban-Bul. Priests lonely. Priests not talk to other priests much."

"Fyd, I tell you what I do think. I think Father is not going to be happy with you and me if we do not find some game to roast. He would probably be as happy with fish but we must take something home."

Per-Qad arrived at Baldag's house the next morning and Ghanya told him Baldag was shearing sheep up the river a way. Per-Qad told her he was actually looking for Miqel, that they had a lot to talk about before he started making plans to get back to Nile. "Per-Qad, I don't want you to make it any more difficult for Miqel than it is already. Let him put Ifn-Lot and these worries over henges and such out of his mind for a while." "I do agree with you, Ghanya and I have no knowledge of or desire to discuss henges with Miqel. It is my thought that he wants to know what things in Kemet are like, more 138 specifically Upper Nile where I come from." "That is interesting. Perhaps Baldag and I can hear some of those things too, after you and Miqel have worn each other out talking. Incidentally, why did you come here to Uruk, Per-Qad?"

"I could not stay in Kish. Unlike Ifn-Lot the Mari people know what I look like and my life would not last very long there I fear. Worse, they might seize me and take me back to Mari for torture. And this is likely to be the only chance I ever have to see Uruk. I wanted to go to Ur also but I must be past the Orontes before winter, preferably before the rains begin and the Euphrates starts to rise. If Men-Chad-Rez and Chad-Mar will help me get by Kish to Huta I believe I can get to Upper Nile from there." "Why do you think they will help you, Per-Qad?"

"I think I was of considerable help to Thar-Mes and he sent that message to Men-Chad-Rez through Kalam-Bad. I talked to Chad-Mar about it. I do not think there is great danger to Kish from Mari...they cannot provide for any force of size that far down the river. But there is great danger to Mari from Kish and Thar-Mes aims to punish them severely for infiltrating Kish and for murdering Ifn-Lot. If Kalam-Bad can take a boat and a few guards as far as Huta I know a friend of Ifn-Lot's there who I feel sure will take me safely up the river to Aff. That means I will not be here for more than three or four weeks at most."

At that point Miqel walked in and was surprised to find Per-Qad there. "Per-Qad, I have been down at the temple yard looking for you. Have you been here long?" "Miqel, it is good that you have come. No, I have been visiting with Ghanya only a short time. I had hoped you and I might spend some time together before I start planning my journey home." "Will you be leaving us soon, Per-Qad? I had assumed you might wish to join the White Temple service; you have much to offer the academy there I think."

"That is good of you to say, Miqel but I really doubt that I can teach your young priests very much; and you must remember that though I am no fanatic like the Mari priests I am an advocate of the fractional Sacred Circle construction." "Chad-Mar knows that, doesn't he? Why does your academy at Asyut permit you to teach the priests there?" "These are not priests, Miqel. We are called 'Sun Wizards' at Asyut and most of the trainees are scribes who are overseen by a Nubian named Seb Seshat." "That is such an odd name. Was it his name in Nubia?" "I do not think I have ever heard what he was called in Nubia. He had been with the Menku academy long before I came there; furthermore that is not his real name. It is a title he took for a name many years ago. It just means, 'teaching scribe'. Things are very different in Upper Nile from the way they are in Uruk, in all of Sumer for that matter. The academy is not associated with any temple."

CHAPTER EIGHTEEN   'The Marriage'

Miqel and Per-Qad walked past the temple down to the river with Fyd trailing along behind. There they turned and strolled southward with no particular destination in mind, chatting as the time passed. Miqel asked, "Per-Qad, I am interested in what you said regarding the academy at Asyut. What purpose is served by teaching the fractional Sacred Circle there when Hev-Ri is a master of the real Sacred Circle? After all, the fractional version is little more than a simple construction that does not require much to train drawing scribes to use it."

"That is all very true, Miqel. But the Nile is not like the Euphrates in many ways. And, for practical considerations Kemet is only the land on either side of the Nile below what we designate as the 'first cataract'. There is Upper Nile and Lower Nile but, except for different kingdoms there is no difference. All people of the Nile country are dependent on the yearly flooding of the Nile. It happens every year for years but the flood occasionally fails to come. Then there is a disastrous loss of the capacity to provide food for all the towns and villages throughout Kemet, much like the drought you have recently experienced here in Sumer and Akkad. At flood the Nile leaves a rich silt spread over the land for about fourteen thousand Sumer cubits on either side of the river. It provides growing land for the crops the farmers produce and grazing land for cattle and sheep and goats. That is what Kemet means, the 'black land'."

"I understand what you say but do not follow the association with the fractional Sacred Circle." "Forgive me. I did not explain that the Nile washes out all land boundaries every year. Some of the boundaries are simple enough to measure but others have a circular section to them and must be measured to insure that the people have a fair approximation of the amount of land they hold and farm or graze. Using the square and circle construction based on the fractional Sacred Circle is accurate beyond anyone's needs for such measurements of property. And it is so much simpler and quicker to apply than the real Sacred Circle that we use it consistently for these purposes. It has nothing to do with priests or sacred things at all."

"I never knew any of that, Per-Qad. It makes such good sense I wonder why there is any controversy." "The holding of the truth of the real Sacred Circle will probably be extremely important some day to all of us, or to those who come after us. If the construction is lost...and there is no way to communicate it except word of mouth...it may pass into the mists of legend, forgotten except as something someone once knew. Kmal-Dyl has explained that is the reason for the 'Consensus of Sumer' he and Ayn-Far obtained agreement to. I understand perfectly why it is so essential to keep it from being set aside here and hope it remains that way until someone can invent a system of writing that lets us choose which we want without destroying one or the other."

Miqel looked puzzled, "There seems to be no trouble at Asyut. Why would your master send you to Kish with Hev-Ri if he is content with what you and the other wizards do?" "He knows of the problems here in Sumer and is even aware of Kmal-Dyl's twenty-two step construction. Hev-Ri has told him of that, and with his large fleet of trading boats constantly in contact with people coming down the seacoast he stays rather well informed of general happenings outside Kemet. He is getting old and is afraid that after he is gone we will all begin squabbling over the advantages of one system over the other until the academy will be split and lose its value to Upper Nile. He wanted to bring Kmal-Dyl to Asyut to live; in Menku's mind it will take someone of his stature and mental powers to put down division and keep peace there."

Miqel's silence was broken by a shout from Fyd and the swish of his club which was followed by a dull thud when it broke a wild pig's neck. "We eat tonight, Miqel! You like pig, Per-Qad?" "Of course I do but I haven't had one since I left Mari. This will make a feast for all of us. I don't think I have ever seen anyone quite so quick and accurate with a club as you are, Fyd. Where did you learn that?" "Miqel knows. Bogs not throw good, bogs not eat. You watch Miqel, Per-Qad. He throws good like Fyd." "Another of your talents, Miqel?" Per-Qad asked. "I have been using a sling as long as I can remember and, yes, I think I am rather good with one. Ekhana is just as good, maybe even better, is she not, Fyd?" "Ekhana sling stone good. Sling stone like bog. Ekhana not better than Miqel."

The three of them laughed and Fyd set about drawing the pig and cutting off the feet to make it lighter to carry back to Baldag's house where he would roast it. As they walked along Per-Qad turned to Miqel and asked, "Do you not ever intend to have a family, Miqel? In my country wizards have families like anyone else; so do priests. I do not see the priests in Sumer as being any more dedicated to the search for truth than those in Nile. They do subject themselves to more privation here but I think that is of their own choosing. Of course it depends on whether the king, or in our case someone like Menku provides enough for the academies and temple services."

"It is one of those things I have not thought much about until now, Per-Qad. Before my grandfather moved to Uruk and set up his academy in the White Temple my family resigned itself to my becoming a senior priest. I would live at either the White Temple or some other temple my entire life, always alone and always removed from family life. I was just a boy and it was so exciting that I never considered there was any other choice. That is the way it is done here. I am sure Hev-Ri has told you that." "Yes, he has but he did not try to convince me it was the right way for priests, much less wizards to live. You do seem to be fond of, even affectionate toward Ekhana. Do you love her, Miqel?"

"I do not know if I know what that means, Per-Qad. If I had a wife I cannot imagine anyone but Ekhana being that wife. She may not feel the same way about me of course. Our fathers would have decided that for us a good many years ago; perhaps they still should. It is my decision as to whether I have a wife; but it is not my decision to have a wife if I wish to become a senior priest at the White Temple. That is the decision of Chad-Mar and that decision is already made as it was before him. It is a subject I had rather not discuss right now. Perhaps I can think about it again later and we can talk of it then."

Kalam-Bad approached Men-Chad-Rez as he was watching some traders bartering wool and grain in the stalls outside the temple walls, "May we talk, my Lord?" "Kalam-Bad, you are always welcome to come and talk, you know that. Is there something in particular on your mind?" "Well yes, there is, Men-Chad-Rez but I would rather go sit in the shade; it is hotter than usual out in this sun I think." Men- Chad-Rez smiled, noting the glistening sweat pouring from the huge man's body as they moved beneath a nearby palm. Rom-Sha sent a guard to bring a skin of water and they settled comfortably on a reed mat.

"It is about Per-Qad. I promised him I would help him get on his way back to Nile and it is fast approaching the time he needs to leave for there if he is going before the rains come. The winter current will make it too difficult to get up the Euphrates and he would have a hard time getting a guide across the desert past Salbat; it will be cold and wet from there to the Orontes. That means fewer hunting parties or boats heading for the sea." "That is all true. What do you want from me, Kalam-Bad?"

"I would like your approval for me to take him with a few guards and a boat to Kish where I think we can negotiate with Thar-Mes for his safe travel to Huta. There is a boatman named Malbu there according to Per-Qad who will help him get on up to Salbat and he believes Malbu can persuade the elders at Salbat to guide him to Aff, Aff is where Ifn-Lot lived for so long. It should be easy to get from there to Thurn's and there is a young man there who will likely guide him all the way to Ugarit." "What makes you think Thar-Mes will help you, or him?" "Per-Qad thinks Thar-Mes should by now be sending rotational troops as far as Bav, maybe even Quri to punish the Mari people for Ifn-Lot's murder and to clear the Euphrates from marauding bands of Mari priests. He should be safe from them anyway by the time he gets past Bav."

"Kalam–Bad, suppose things do not work at Kish the way you expect what are your plans then? I will not approve your taking Per-Qad as far as Huta. You were on the trek to the wilderness with Ifn-Lot and could be recognized by an infiltrator from Mari. I will not allow that risk." "In that case I would bring him back here. I am sure he can join the temple service here or in Ur." "Then make your plans. I approve."

After the roast pig was out of the way Miqel asked Baldag if he could talk to him. "Of course, Miqel. I need to go down to the goat pens and we can talk there. Fyd can bring the goats up for Bodi to milk." After Fyd left Miqel began, "Father, I think you know these days have pressed hard on me and I have done a lot of searching into the course of the life I have accepted for the past several years. I have every confidence in my ability to continue the works I am engaged in now. I am vain enough to think I will not only invent writing, that is close now I think; but I also think I may be able to set up the design basis for the pyramid for someone to build at some time in the distant future. That in itself will require writing; I do not believe it can be done otherwise. Still it does not seem likely I can do it here...ever."

"Why, Miqel?" "The lack of support for a project like that was most evident when Ifn-Lot was designing the henge for the Nur-Bikh wilderness; and that was a poor choice of a site to accomplish much. There just is no likely place to proceed in Sumer and that is not from lack of searching. But for me the most difficult problem is Kmal-Dyl's refusal to allow me to work with him. Oh, I know why and respect him all the more for it. That does not ease the disappointment though. Chad-Mar wishes for me to continue in the White Temple service but that seems somewhat hollow now. Father, I am a man and that is simply no life for a man. It will become more and more restraining as I get older. Until recently there were the diversions of hunting and fishing and the trips up to Kish; no more however. Those are all things of the past if I stay at the White Temple."

"I begin to understand what you are saying, Miqel. I had thought time would have taken away most of these doubts by now but I see it has not done so. When I reluctantly agreed to turn you over to the priests your mother and I concurred that it would be up to you to decide the way of life you chose when you became a man. And you are a man. I am glad you are determined to continue to employ the gifts you have been given, though for the life of me I do not know how you can do it if you are not provided for by the temple."

"I think Per-Qad can take me to his academy at Asyut where I will be free to work as I choose and live a life like other men. He says his master, a man named, Menku will welcome me there. I would like to go there and see it and I want to take Fyd with me." "How long do you think you would be gone, Miqel?" "I do not know, Father, perhaps two or three years. It is a long and difficult journey and I would need help to get back to Uruk, something I can only assume would be forthcoming." "I will support your decision, Miqel. I am sure Men-Chad-Rez and Chad-Mar will not stand in your way though they will be extremely disappointed. Your mother is another matter and I will have to deal with that, and I will."

"There is something else, Father. I want Ekhana for my wife and I want to take her with me. Do you think Kalam-Bad will agree that?" "I will talk to him the first thing tomorrow, Miqel.

My own guess is that he will agree; he is very fond of you and so is Methwyd. I cannot speak for Ekhana of course, yet you and Ekhana have been friends for a long time. She is fine young woman and will make you a good wife. You know I am sure that I think she is a very fortunate woman to have you to want her for a wife."

When Kalam-Bad returned home Methwyd was waiting for him, "Kalam-Bad, it is time Ekhana had a husband." Kalam-Bad blinked, "Is that not a little sudden, Methwyd? I know she is old enough but I have not heard a word about it until now." "I suppose it would not have come up right now except for the tragic events that Miqel has been exposed to. He is a man now and must make his decision to have a wife or go into the White Temple service. I think you and Baldag should arrange for Ekhana to be that wife. We all like Miqel and I agree with Gahnya that it is just awful to see a fine young man like that wasting away in the temple." "Has Ekhana put you up to this or have you and Gahnya been scheming together? I want to know, Methwyd." "Yes in answer to both questions if that will satisfy your curiosity. Kalam-Bad, surely you must have felt the sadness of Miqel and seen how much he has changed since we set out for Kish so many weeks ago." "Yes, I suppose I have but there are so many things to think about I did not pay that much attention to it.

"I have been over talking to Men-Chad-Rez today and he has approved my setting up another trip to Kish, this time to take Per-Qad up there and start him on his journey home to Nile." "Will it be soon, Kalam-Bad?" "Yes, though I cannot say exactly when we will leave; I must talk to Per-Qadbefore completing my plans. I will talk to Baldag tomorrow regarding Ekhana and Miqel. Leave that to us; and you and Gahnya stay out of it for the time being."

Per-Qad had been given a small alcove in the temple with only a reed mat and a skin of water for furnishings while he was in Uruk. He ate the scant fare of the priests, which suited him well enough. Each day at sunup he was down in the temple yard, fascinated with the lively bartering and squabbling that went on there constantly. Miqel found him squatted off to the side of a couple of deal-making traders from Eridu and Ur who were attempting to barter shells and crocodile teeth necklaces for pigskins and wool.

"Good morning, Miqel. What brings you to the yard so early? I would have thought Baldag would have things for you to be doing." "No, not today. I came to talk to you again, Per-Qad. Shall we walk over to those trees and sit down for a bit?" "Certainly, Miqel. You seem grave this morning. Is there something I have said to offend you?" "No, not at all. The truth is I am even more interested in what you have told me about Upper Nile, and especially about the Asyut academy. I want to go there with you when you are ready to leave. There is more. I hope to take Ekhana with me as my wife, and of course Fyd accompanies me anywhere I go. Do you think your master will object; and do you, yourself agree that this is the thing to do?"

"I agree. Surely I agree and am very happy you have chosen to go with me. As for Menku and Hev-Ri they will be delighted beyond their greatest expectations. You will see when we get there. That may be some time of course. It is a very long and very hard journey. Do you think Ekhana will be up to it?" "Of that much I am sure, Per-Qad. She is a strong woman and she can handle a sling like the best of men. She has also been learning weaving, here and at Kish. She will be able to contribute if we have to eke out a living along the way. I am prepared for that." "Well then. It is all in Kalam-Bad's hands now. I am waiting to hear from him as to when we can leave for Kish. Soon I hope."

The same morning Kalam-Bad and Baldag met, each on the way to the other's house. After perfunctory greetings they both started to talk at the same time. Baldag yielded, laughing, "Kalam-Bad, you were on the way to see me and I am on the way to see you. Why don't you tell me what is on your mind first, then I will talk." "I will come straight to the point, Baldag. I want Ekhana to be Miqel's wife. Methwyd and I have talked this over and we think she will make him a good wife and we like Miqel so much we want them to be together." Now Baldag could not help laughing and Kalam-Bad took offense, "I think this is a good thing to do, Baldag. I do not see anything funny about it at all." "No, my good friend, there is nothing funny about what you are saying. What is funny is that that is what I was coming to talk to you about. Miqel wants Ekhana to be his wife. He has asked me to talk to you, and if you agree there is no more to be done except for him to take her for his wife."

Baldag came back to the house and told Gahnya what had taken place and they both chortled over it. Then Baldag went in search of Miqel to tell him the news. Miqel was on the way to the house when he met Baldag and left him immediately to see Ekhana. She was at home weaving when he arrived and ran out to join him in the garden. He spoke first, "Ekhana, I have talked to my father and he has discussed you and me with your father. I want you to be my wife; our fathers and mothers agree that this should be but I want to know if you want me for a husband." Ekhana lowered her eyes and tears began to creep down on her cheeks. She spoke so softly Miqel had to lean toward her to catch what she was saying, "Yes, Miqel. I have wanted to be your wife for a long time. I did not think it could ever happen with your plans to live your life out in the White Temple. But now all that has changed and it seems only natural that you and I should live together always. I love you so very much."

Miqel pulled her close to him, "I love you and always have, Ekhana. I've wondered if this could ever come true. There is something else however. I hope it will not change your mind. I have talked to Per-Qad...my father knows this...and I plan to go to Nile with him and join the academy at Asyut where I will not be a priest. There I will be what they call a 'Sun Wizard'. They have families and are supported while they carry out their studies and search for truth as thoroughly as we do here in the temples of Sumer. His master is a very rich man; Per-Qad thinks I am the person he and Hev-Ri and the other sun wizards came to Kish to find. Will you be willing to go with me? I fear it will be a very hard trek but once there I believe our lives will be better."

Ekhana was not prepared for this. She turned away and looked back at the reed house she lived in with Kalam-Bad and Methwyd, "I have never thought of leaving Uruk, Miqel; I have not been away from my parents more than a few days at a time. Of course I will go with you wherever you go; I could not bear to have you leave without me. Will we never come back to Uruk? Never?" "I do not think we will be back here for at least three years, Ekhana. I know that is a long time but the travel between Sumer and Nile is so difficult I do not think we would want to attempt it until Thar-Mes has established a safe corridor along the Euphrates where it flows past Mari. Then there is the matter of writing. I think I can complete a workable system of writing in two or three years of uninterrupted work. Then if the chief wizard at Asyut accepts it and the king of Upper Nile will decree its adoption I would like to bring it back to Kmal-Dyl and the temple services of Sumer."

"It sounds exciting, Miqel. When will be be leaving? Father is making plans but has not told me when he expects Per-Qad will be ready to go to Kish and then on to Nile." "I do not know that any better than you right now, Ekhana. I do know that we must be going soon or we will run into winter in the north. Not only would that make it too hard to get through the wilderness to the great sea; it would make sailing on the sea too great a risk, even if we were able to find boats going down the coast toward Nile."

Ekhana nestled back into his arms and her eyes searched his, "It shall be so. Let me talk to

Father and Mother. Then we have so much to do before we leave." "Of course, Ekhana. I think we will need some items for barter, enough to get us to Asyut I suspect. And we will need provisions; we can't live entirely on fish and game, even if it is plentiful, which it may not be in some places along the way. I will be back later today. Per-Qad and I have to talk to your father about travel to Kish. One other thing: I am sure Fyd will go with us."

Baldag had had a difficult time with Gahnya when he told her of Miqel's decision to go to Nile with Per-Qad and he wondered how Kalam-Bad and Methwyd would take the news. Up till now no one had considered whether Men-Chad-Rez would permit Miqel and Ekhana to go to live in Nile; or whether Chad-Mar could be counted on to concur in Miqel's decision, essential for Men-Chad-Rez's support. Baldag went looking for Miqel to insist that he go immediately to Chad-Mar and tell him the entire story before all this would come crashing down on his head. Although Chad-Mar was extremely fond of Miqel he was easily offended and this might be considered as effrontery if left unaddressed too long.

When he found Miqel he was talking to Per-Qad outside the temple, "Miqel, I must talk to you alone for a moment." "Surely, Father. Is anything wrong?" "Not yet, Miqel but it may be if you do not get to Chad-Mar quickly and inform him of your plans, all of them including taking Ekhana with you." "I will go now. This is something I have dreaded and I shudder to think what will happen if Chad-Mar is offended by all this. He is a powerful man in Uruk, the most powerful except for Men-Chad-Rez and he is Prince of Luhinlil. I had better get to him before Kalam-Bad talks to Men-Chad-Rez again about the journey."

Chad-Mar invited Miqel to pull up a stool, noting the seriousness of his expression, "Miqel, I sense that you have something to tell me I do not want to hear. Speak your mind." "Master, I am afraid you will not be happy with my decisions. I have wrestled hard with my mind to come to some reasoning that would satisfy the plans you and Ifn-Lot and Papa had for me. I have come to conclusions that I feel will not please you and I am here to beg your acceptance of my decisions."

"Continue, Miqel." "First, I am going to take Ekhana for my wife." Miqel took a deep breath as Chad-Mar's gaze turned cold and hard, "Second, I wish to finish my system of writing at the Asyut Academy where the wizards have wives and as I understand it are able to devote themselves to the same disciplines of work we have here in the White Temple." At that Chad-Mar wryly smiled, "I wish I could blame you for my deep disappointment, Miqel but I cannot. I do not deny my selfishness in that, yet the stirrings of memories of my own youth tell me that you are guided by Luhinlil, perhaps God. Tell me, has Kmal-Dyl's seeming rejection caused you to make these plans?"

"At first I think that made me more determined than ever to rush to invent writing here, to devote myself to that to the exclusion of all else. But, as you have said, time does heal and I now accept both Kmal-Dyl's reasoning and Ifn-Lot's death as things over which no one had any control, any part in directing at all. If the gods decreed it it would be no more real than if chance or circumstance simply placed me in the way of a fate I did not choose any more than I can reject it. I think I shall not know if Luhinlil, or God, Himself is in any way involved in any of this."

"Well said, Miqel. Well said. When you have completed your work on writing will you bring it back to Sumer?" "I would certainly hope so, Master. Ekhana wanted to know the same thing and as I told her that will depend on the King of Upper Nile's acceptance of it and willingness to decree its usage throughout his kingdom. All this of course presumes I will be successful." "I think that is not so much a presumption, Miqel. I will talk to Men-Chad-Rez; I think I can prevail upon him not to interfere with your plans. My heart does not rejoice at those   plans but I do earnestly wish you godspeed." "Thank you, Master. I could not ask for more and I will never forget all the things you have done for me."

Miqel told Fyd of his plans, including his desire for Fyd to accompany him and Ekhana to live in Asyut. "Fyd go with you and Ekhana. Fyd go to Nile. Fyd glad you take him with you. Fyd go and tell Toq and Oghud first." "Of course, Fyd. You must tell Toq and Oghud and wish them well for me and Ekhana while your are there. But you must be quick to return. I think we will be leaving soon for Kish." "Fyd come back quick. Be ready to go with Miqel and Ekhana."

After a tempestuous scene between Ekhana and Kalam-Bad and a weeping Methwyd they settled into exhausted, grudging acceptance of what seemed inevitable. Then Kalam-Bad took Ekhana into his arms, "We are glad for you, Ekhana. I think you would not expect us to be glad you are leaving us, yet we have always known that would come one way or another. And I think this is the best way for you and Miqel. I have no doubt he will be the greatest wizard there has ever 147 been and if he can best carry out his mission under the gods in Nile so be it. We will not oppose him or you, child." "Thank you, Father. Miqel plans to return to Uruk when he has complete acceptance of his work in Nile and we can decide then where we will live."

Kalam-Bad left to take Per-Qad to Men-Chad-Rez and obtain his full cooperation in the preparations for making the trip up the Euphrates as far as Kish. Chad-Mar was already in the yard with Men-Chad-Rez when Kalam-Bad arrived. He had just told Men-Chad-Rez of Miqel's plans and before he could get a reaction Kalam-Bad asked, "Chad-Mar, have you talked to Miqel?" "Yes, Kalam-Bad. That is what Men-Chad-Rez and I had just started to discuss when you walked up. Men-Chad-Rez, I would like to know how you feel about Miqel's plans to go to Nile and take Ekhana and Fyd with him."

"I suppose astonishment might be my first feeling. I could not have expected this outcome and am not prepared to accept it. Perhaps the two of you can enlighten me on why I should or should not permit this to develop any further." Chad-Mar answered, "I have not had time to talk to Kalam-Bad since Miqel left me today. Frankly, I am in favor of his going if it will, as I think it will get Miqel back to his normal, creative self again. He has convinced me he is going there to be able to have a wife and do his work at the same time; I also think he is fascinated with what Per-Qad has told him about this strange place of legends and myth." Men-Chad-Rez turned and asked, "Kalam-Bad, how do you stand?"

"I am I suspect in the same mood as Chad-Mar. As a father and sometime mentor I wish they would not go. But I do recognize that Miqel is a marvelously gifted young man and to that end I must believe it is the thing for him to do. Of course I am selfish enough to want him for Ekhana's husband and that may affect my judgment too." Men-Chad-Rez roared with laughter, "I never thought I would hear either one of you turning soft in the heart, not in my lifetime did I expect that. I do not see any problem; however I wish to think about this tonight. I will give my answer tomorrow morning."

Kalam-Bad was in the yard when Men-Chad-Rez appeared the next day. He waited for Men-Chad-Rez to speak. "Kalam-Bad, I will tell Chad-Mar that I approve of your plans to take Per-Qad...and Miqel, Ekhana and Fyd with him...only as far as Kish. If Thar-Mes will not provide escort guards for them you are to bring them back here and we will make our plans from there as to what to do about Per-Qad. If I did not think Thar-Mes would provide guards I would not approve your trip at all.

"One thing will be essential. You must gather up enough barter goods, things they can wear on their arms or legs or about their necks for them to get to Nile. Per-Qad has nothing; I will provide for him. You and Baldag can take care of the others. You will take six of your best guards with you, but they are to return here when you do. I have spoken." "Thank you, my Lord. It will be done as you have said."

Fyd returned from Hathuruk with a prize goat for Men-Chad-Rez, a gift from Oghud. He proudly presented it with a message he had been told to deliver, "King make gift to Oghud. Oghud make gift to King. Oghud obey King. Oghud like Hathuruk. Hathuruk good place." Men-Chad-Rez accepted the gift, smiling at the beaming Fyd, "Fyd this is a fine goat. I am grateful to you and Oghud for it. Do you think Baldag would keep it with his goats for me? Why don't you ask him?" "I take goat to Baldag. Baldag take good care of goat till King needs goat. Baldag is good man."

A week passed quickly. Urunya let Miqel and Ekhana have the tent she and Akhuruk lived in at Ur and they made a temporary home of it next to her reed house. It was the happiest week of their lives but it was over so quickly and whether parting is supposed to be sweet sorrow it was not to be the case this time. There was genuine heartbreak for Gahnya and Urunya and the same applied to Methwyd. It was all Baldag and Kalam-Bad could do to get them to let the party head up the river. But they did leave, and in great style. Men-Chad-Rez furnished the royal barge and a full crew to go with it.

Arriving at Kish the party was welcomed to the temple yard, Men-Chad-Rez's barge having been immediately recognized by the captain of the guards. Thar-Mes stepped forward with his arm raised, "Welcome to Kish, Kalam-Bad. I see you have brought Per-Qad with you. But what is the meaning of the royal barge?" "Men-Chad-Rez was kind enough to provide it for our trip up the river. My guards and I will take it back when we leave.

"I come to ask your help in getting Per-Qad and those with him at least as far as Huta, Thar-Mes." "I think that will be no problem, but what do you mean by 'those with him'?" "You know Miqel and my daughter, Ekhana, Thar-Mes. Miqel has taken her for his wife and they plan to accompany Per-Qad to his academy in Upper Nile. Miqel's servant, Fyd will also go with them." Thar-Mes frowned, "What does Chad-Mar think of this, Kalam-Bad? Kmal-Dyl and Abb-Oth were convinced that Miqel was going to continue his work on writing and the henge when you left here several weeks ago."

"Chad-Mar and Men-Chad-Rez gave their approval to Miqel's proposal to finish his work in Nile and later on to bring the results back to present to Kmal-Dyl and the other temples here in Sumer. Per-Qad believes his academy will allow Miqel complete freedom to work and to have a wife. That is about the sum of it. How is your state of war with Mari affecting life here in Kish?"

"Not so bad as I would have thought, Kalam-Bad. Per-Qad's advice regarding the garrisons along the Euphrates has been followed with good results on our first trial. We have lost a few warriors in the first skirmishes a short distance into the countryside there but the reports of the wounded who were brought here have been encouraging. The resistance has been fragmented and the Mari marauders seem to be poorly equipped to fight defensively. They are fierce when they attack small parties of hunters and other travelers on the Euphrates. But I do not think they have the stomach for fighting a well lead force of trained, experienced warriors."

"That is good to hear, Thar-Mes. How far up the river have your troops settled?" "Almost to Bav, and sixty more garrison troops are on the way there now. The villages north of Leb have been very helpful, and well they should. They have always had problems with the Mari warriors, particularly the village fishermen. The Mari warriors would take their boats and usually throw them in the river afterward; they are a scurrilous lot. As for your party I think we can get them to Huta very easily. I am sending replacements for the casualties at Leb and thirty or forty more warriors to set up a small station at Quri sometime in the next two weeks. By the way I plan to send a few goats up there to carry provisions and furnish a little milk for the troops as they go farther inland. The boats will be somewhat crowded but if your party can obtain a boat at Huta I think they can fit in all right."

"That will be better than we could have hoped for, Thar-Mes. In the meantime I know Miqel and Per-Qad want to see Kmal-Dyl and Abb-Oth while they are here. Do you think they will be favorably received, based on what I have told you?" "That they will have to find out. I really do not know how hard Abb-Oth will take the news. I doubt that it will bother Kmal-Dyl as long as Miqel plans to return to Sumer in a few years. They both will want to send messages to Hev-Ri I imagine. One more thing during your stay in Kish: be extremely careful what you say. It could be disastrous for our boats and for your party as well if the plans for these troops to travel to Quri are overheard before they actually leave."

"We will take your warning and keep our mouths shut. You can count on that. Is have all our own food." "You can set up within shouting distance of my place, Kalam-Bad. There are some trees up there and there is no better security anywhere in Kish."

CHAPTER NINETEEN   'The Clouds of War'

True to his word Agga was back at the Pe landing two days before the full moon would light the night sky almost as if it were daybreak. He had stopped at Edhemet and Saqqut on the way down and had a full cargo of excellent articles for bartering. There were woven goods from the Jerusalem-Jericho area, some with threads of gold worked into them; the usual heavily decorated pottery and some new hammer-hardened copper bladed knives; even a pair of lion skins for the king's warriors. He knew there would not be much to barter for at Pe but hoped there might be some gold or copper nuggets he could pick up to take back to Cyprus and Crete.

Amen-Kha was in the yard and seeing Agga's boat came down to the river to see what was to be had. He was delighted at all the things Agga brought and scorned the local traders for having so little to offer in exchange. "Do you plan to go back up to Meidum, Agga?" "Yes, my Lord, that is if my Lord will allow me to travel there again." "I will insist that you get up there, Agga. Did you not tell me that there were some weapons up there? Where did the young man you talked to say they came from?"

"He said when this Menhes fellow drove the other king's troops north from Aqqrem and on down the river past Asyut there was a big battle and the old king's troops were slaughtered. A lot of them drowned in the Nile trying to escape and they left their weapons strewn all over he place. The villagers went in and picked up whatever there was that looked good to them and some of it found its way down to Meidum and Crocodile Lake. I suspect your warriors already have most of the stuff from Meidum but my friend says there is more at the lake. Does my Lord not have enough weapons? The guards I see around the landing seem pretty well armed to me."

"That murderer, Menhes will not stop at anything. I have begun training the herdsmen and farmers north of here to be able to defend our kingdom. Clubs and pikes they have but those do good against spearmen and archers. I do not expect to find good bows...they are too fragile to last long...but good obsidian or copper tipped arrows are of considerable value and good spears, even spearheads would be worth something to my generals."

"My Lord, I do not like to bring my boat up the Nile if there is going to be war between these two kingdoms. We are boatmen and traders, not warriors and I would be ruined if I lost my boat." "If it comes, it comes, Agga; but I don't think you have anything to worry about. If Menhes gets too threatening I will march my forces up to Meidum and from there get them out on the plains where we can stop any of his overreaching schemes. He has too many of the long boats my father foolishly provided for Menku years ago to engage him on the river again. I have started construction of that type boat down in the delta region but they will not be ready for use for another year at best."

"I am relieved to know that, my Lord. If it please my Lord I and my crew will be off for Meidum this afternoon. I would like to have enough daylight left tomorrow to get goods brought over from Crocodile Lake before I have to leave on the third day. Who knows, they may have exactly what you are looking for up there."

Agga turned in at the Meidum landing a little before noon the next day and looked around for Naan. One of the villagers told him he expected Naan could be found in a grove of trees only a stone's throw from the town. He directed Agga there and they found Naan idly sorting a large variety of barter articles, tying some together, wrapping others in woolen cloth. "Ho, Naan. What have you got for me?" "I see you came back, Agga. I was so sure of it I have collected this stuff for you. You might as well look it over out here where there will be nobody to try to grab it before you have the chance."

"I will, Naan. But I have a question for you. Can you get any of the spears of arrows that were left over from the war in Upper Nile?" "I think so, Agga. Why do you want those? You don't look like a warrior to me." "That is certain, my friend. No, it is Amen-Kha who wants them. He says he may have to march up the Nile past Meidum to keep this man, Menhes in his place. Says he cannot wait for boats to be constructed, even though he is having some long boats built down in the delta country."

"People around here will be glad to know that they will be protected but I don't think there is anything at Meidum worth fighting over, do you?" Agga leaned back and laughed, "I think if Amen-Kha sent three of his spearmen up here the whole town would run for cover, Naan. Is there anything at Crocodile Lake anyone would want?" "Unless you are talking a few cows and some sheep and goats, nothing. This is poor country, Agga." "It does look like it. How long will it take you to check on those weapons?" "I will be back before noon tomorrow, if that is good enough."

Three of Naan's boatmen stayed with the stuff and Agga sifted through it while Naan set off to find Ar-Chab. Ar-Chab was getting ready to bed down when Naan walked up, "What have you to tell me now, Naan?" Naan related Agga's gossip and asked Ar-Chab if he could have twenty or thirty spears and perhaps a hundred or so arrows for Amen-Kha's warrior trainees. There are plenty of them here; take what you want. Are you sure this is anything more than gossip; Agga seems to be a very talkative man for a boat master." "I suppose that is something you have to take into account, Ar-Chab but I would tend to believe what he has to say. None of this is of any possible interest to him in his business except to make better deals at the bartering yards. I think he just talks to pass the time of day without attaching any significance to what he is saying."

"What is your guess as to when Agga will be heading back to Pe, Naan?" "With these weapons I imagine he will leave tomorrow afternoon, in fact I am sure of it. I am going back to Meidum now; I can make good way with the moon tonight and get there fairly early in the morning without being as exhausted as I was the last time."

Ar-Chab stopped at Asyut to take one of the long boats and a full crew for greater speed on the Nile. He arrived at Nekhen on the fourth day after the full moon first rose to find the town bustling with activity in preparation for Addi-Hoda's appearance. The royal barge was expected in Nekhen the next day. Ar-Chab went immediately to find MeriLyth and Ki and he was happily playing with the baby when Menhes walked up to the house. "Ar-Chab, I have been expecting you...glad to know who counts for something around here, eh, MeriLyth?" "I was going to look for you, Menhes but grandfathers have to be good for something, isn't that right, Ki?"

The toddler grinned and climbed up into Ar-Chab's arms as he and Menhes sat down to talk. Ar-Chab told him of Agga's return and of his search for weapons for the trainee army Amen-Kha was building north of Pe. "What do you suppose Amen-Kha is up to, Ar-Chab? I wonder if he has any of Hor-Amen's generals still in power or if he has deposed all of them. A trainee army suggests he is pretty desperate or just plain dumb. In spite of wanting spears and arrows they will not be able to use them any more effectively than their clubs and pikes if we ever meet in the field. I am glad to know he has not got any long boats built yet; maybe he does not want to take us on on the water again."

"Menhes, the talk of a march on Meidum may not be just talk. Do you not imagine that Amen-Kha needs to do something heroic to offset his past humiliation before his people?" "There is a lot of credence to what you say, Ar-Chab, but I do not care too much if he takes over

181

Meidum: it is Crocodile Lake that worries me. If he finds your work nearly complete with the cattle station there he may feel pushed into war; and I do not want that. I still hold out hope that he will settle down and we can reopen trade with Pe. Go on enjoying your grandson; I want to wait and discuss this with Ekhdur and Addi-Hoda before I decide what, if anything to do about all these threats ."

The royal barge floated into the landing at Nekhen with plumes and pennants waving in the breeze and the standard of Nubia standing high above the mast. Prince Addi-Hoda waited for Menhes to come aboard so that they would step ashore together, followed closely by Sel-Abba and Assi-Rah. They walked between the raised spears of Nubia's finest warriors, tall and glistening in the bright sun of Upper Nile. Seb-Seshat kneeled before the two princes and Addi-Hoda touched his head and spoke, "My good friend and emissary, Seb. I had hoped you would come for my visit. You must join us at the feast Menhes tells me he has prepared for us."

At that moment Addi-Hoda caught sight of MeriLyth, wearing her crown and holding Ki in her arms. He strode over to her and smiled, "Can this be our beautiful queen and our young prince?" He bowed and held his arms out to Ki who instinctively reached out to be held. Addi-Hoda turned to Menhes, "Such a fine son. May the gods bless him and make him as brave and wise as his father and his father's fathers." Menhes bowed in humble pride not knowing what to say. It was MeriLyth who spoke, "Prince Addi-Hoda, you have given us life and our people peace. May the gods give you the long life you have earned so well and may your sons and their sons keep the greatness of your rule alive to all generations."

The next day while the feast continued Menhes brought Khafu, Ekhdur and Ar-Chab to a specially created tent to confer with Addi-Hoda and his sons. Menhes spoke, "Before we talk about the future of our two kingdoms I want to ask the Prince to help guide me in this difficult situation we have facing us with Lower Nile."

Addi-Hoda was surprised, "Is there trouble down there, Menhes? I had supposed Hor-Amen was getting too old to be stirring up strife." "I have good reason to believe Hor-Amen's son, Amen-Kha has assassinated him, Addi-Hoda. After the disastrous defeat of the Lower Nile fleet when they attacked our boats south of Pe I am told Hor-Amen was so outraged that he berated Amen-Kha for his stupidity. It was then that Amen-Kha killed him." "That is unfortunate, Menhes. But does it mean that Upper Nile has to get involved? I would think there can never be a reconciliation between Upper and Lower Nile as long as there is no tolerance for the worship of different gods in either kingdom."

"I do not want to have any part in the governing of Lower Nile, Addi-Hoda. Upper Nile is stretched for such a long distance along the river I have great difficulty keeping communications up to date now. Beyond that there is nothing in Lower Nile we could conceivably want. What I do want is peace there and the reopening of trade between the nations. We do not need to trade with Pe so much as we need access to the great sea and the traders from there without having to risk a battle every time one of our boats gets below Meidum. Added to that I have begun to reestablish the old cattle stations where my father had them, all the way down to Crocodile Lake. I need them to furnish information from and to the outreaches of Upper Nile as well as to assure the well being of the people who have lived in those areas so long."

"Have you tried to reason with Amen-Kha?" "Not so long ago I sent Khafu and Hev-Ri to Pe to attempt to open bartering with them. Amen-Kha personally humiliated them, calling me a usurper and murderer. I have known that Amen-Kha is a hothead and not very bright...I mean that quite literally...but I fear now he is trying to secure his own rule by making Upper Nile, especially me the enemy of the people of Lower Nile. He is the only son Hor-Amen had and I understand he has replaced all of Hor-Amen's able generals with equally hotheaded young warriors who are loyal to him. As a result I suspect that Lower Nile has become much as Djo-Aten's Upper Nile was: drunken henchmen killing and looting the villages at will."

"That is sad, Menhes. Hor-Amen was known as a rather benevolent king from all I ever heard. Do you think Amen-Kha would be foolish enough to attack Upper Nile directly?" "Foolish enough, yes. That however does not mean I would attack him to forestall the possibility of a war 151 of his making. Rather I fear that he will start harassing the northernmost villages and outposts of Upper Nile as a way to appear heroic in defense of his god, 'Amen'. Information as recent as last week indicates that is what he plans to do, beginning with Meidum and Crocodile Lake and progressing southward from there."

"What do you want from me, Menhes. Ask and it is yours; you should know that." Menhes laughed, "Wisdom, Lord Addi-Hoda, wisdom. I feel I cannot just sit and wait until our countrymen and friends are murdered, yet I am perplexed as to what I can do that will not bring on out and out war."

Addi-Hoda smiled, "I think you have all the wisdom you need, Menhes and you are backed up with Khafu and Ekhdur in that area. Yes, I do think you cannot simply stand by and wait for a war that does not have to break out. I would strengthen all my stations down near Crocodile Lake and keep the long boat fleet no farther away than Asyut in case Amen-Kha does begin to move south. That would mean a very large force no farther south of Meidum than Pe is north of it. And I think I would risk building a large garrison at the Crocodile Lake station. If he learns about it so be it; it might sober him up enough to keep him in Pe regardless of how angry he may become. Will you need more warriors from Nubia?"

"What you say is what I will do for it does make the best sense of anything I have considered. As for Nubian troops I think we can handle this entirely with the Upper Nile troops Ekhdur and Ar-Chab have now. I would like to keep enough of Assi-Rah's warriors here at Nekhen and Edfu to prevent Djo-Aten's remaining renegades from getting out of hand. There are still some of them out toward Ombos. They do not bother anyone and I want to keep it that way." Assi-Rah broke in, "My Lord, Menhes, that will be done. I would feel more at ease if you would let me and Sel-Abba also send at least three hundred Nubian archers to Crocodile Lake for the next few months, or until you are sure this Amen-Kha will stay in Pe. Would you not agree, Father?" "Yes, Assi-Rah I do agree. Menhes, this is not a time to reduce the effectiveness of your forces, and I think our archers have been effective. I urge you to accept Assi-Rah's offer."

Once more Menhes could only accept. With that he proclaimed, "Let the beer and the wine be brought and let us get on with the feast." Turning aside he spoke to Addi-Hoda, "Thank you, Lord Addi-Hoda. I am grateful."

Agga eased his boat up to the Pe landing and began offloading his barter stuff. Amen-Kha chuckled, "I think the god, 'Amen' must like to be able to keep an eye on you, Agga. You come here only with the full moon." "That may be so, my Lord. He has been good to me and my crew. We have had smooth water ever since we left Crete ten days ago." Agga had never seen so many armed warriors around Pe before. They were visible as he came up the river and there must have been three hundred or more up toward the temple yard. Young shepherds were clumsily shooting arrows at bundles of straw in a stand of trees off to his right and guardsmen were denouncing them for every arrow that went sailing into the trees, "Do you think those arrows are looking for their mothers? The trees don't want them back; we need them. Now get moving and find them or you will get the butt of a spear to your head."

Amen-Kha looked at Agga, "They are right. We do need them. I need a thousand arrows with good tips. Do you think you can get them for me? We are making arrows as fast as we can but they have chips and shells for heads, not good for fighting. We do not find any obsidian around Pe and what we have is running out. I will take copper heads if you can get them; we can fit them on arrows, spears and lances. Those spears you brought last time are good. I think we have about enough of those though."

"You sound urgent, my Lord. Do you think it is safe for me to take my boat up to

Meidum?" "Oh, I don't think you will have any problems up there, Agga. I would not send one of my boats up of course; they know my boats." "Who, my Lord?" "The Upper Nile people of course. Some hunters from Gemset wandered out to Crocodile Lake and found cattle stalls being built. There is not much cattle out there anymore and it seemed to be a curious thing until some armed warriors chased them off. I think this Menhes is preparing to invade Lower Nile and I aim to head off such an attack before he gets any more troops and provisions in there." "Does my Lord wish me to go up to Meidum today?" "Yes, I need what you can barter for. If you see anything unusual I will expect to know about it."

Agga was in no mood to chat when he arrived at Meidum. He told Naan, "I need a thousand arrows or good arrowheads for Amen-Kha and I want all the trade goods I can get for myself. I do not know whether I can make one last trip up here this year or not the way he is talking." "What has come over you, Agga? Sure, I will get what I can. But a thousand arrows, or just arrowheads is more than I think you could find in this whole area, even if you went searching the fields for strays. I can perhaps get you some more spears if you want them." "No, he said he had enough spears, though he liked what you got me last month."

Naan started to leave then turned back, "Agga, surely you must know what has set Amen-Kha off to build up weapons like this. Is he mad at us up here in Meidum?" "No, I don't think he is mad at Meidum. He says Upper Nile's Menhes' guards chased some hunters away from cattle stalls out at the lake last week. Says Menhes is getting ready to attack Pe." "There are no troops out at the lake, Agga. You can walk out there if you want to. A few guards are out there to keep thieves away. I will be off now. Amen-Kha sure seems excitable, doesn't he?" "That is none of my business, Naan. I am just a trader."

Ar-Chab left for Asyut immediately, giving instructions to Naan to get enough barter goods together to lure Agga back up to Meidum one more time. And he told the guards to find several hundred broken arrows along with two hundred good ones. At Asyut Menhes was already in the process of amassing troops and provisions to sail down the Nile in the fleet of long boats; twenty-five of them were ready to leave. When Ar-Chab walked in he told Menhes what he had learned of the activity at Pe. "It sounds like another fool's venture to me, Menhes. Amen-Kha can't make archers our of farmers and shepherds in a week of years, much less in the space of two moons. My guess he thinks he can shoot a hail of arrows into the air and scare warriors off the field. Do you suppose he has never heard of shields?" "I don't know, Ar-Chab. I do know though that we will have to move up and challenge him, and quicker than I had hoped. I want the troops moved in at Crocodile Lake and be prepared to move to Gemset at any hour of the day or night. As for the long boats we will not show them past the inlet you use above Meidum. If he gets word they are there I will have to chance that. I doubt that he has any good informants up that way however."

As the guardsmen from Pe continued to round up increasing numbers of herdsmen, fishermen and farmers from the provinces in the delta area life became more frenetic in the capital city itself. Om-Diph worried about Amen-Kha's sanity. His long bouts of drinking with the troops and constant stuffing himself with food had left his face puffy, his body hanging with fat. He lashed out at anything that in even a slight way offended him, and everything seemed to offend him. His toadying generals were themselves becoming worried: their own heads seemed no more secure than those of suspected thieves and miscreants.

Om-Diph began to call his senior priests into the temple and keep them busy there, meditating, worshiping and training scribes day and night. Young priests were forbidden to go into the yard or down to the wharves except to barter for needed provisions which they had to bring immediately back inside the temple walls. Om-Diph came to rely on the younger senior priest, Badjut, seeking his advice on almost every matter he had to deal with. Badjut was a herdsman who had at an early age been admitted to the temple service where his quick grasp of the scribes'

training brought him to Om-Diph's attention.

Om-Diph hated himself for remaining silent and switching his loyalty to Amen-Kha after he had murdered Hor-Amen. He confided in Badjut, "I wonder if I had been as strong as the Prince of Amen as I was weak before Amen-Kha's savagery whether he would have had the courage to kill me. And if he had I think I were better dead than living this accursed life that is no life at all. I am ashamed before the priests of Amen, even ashamed to pray to Amen for what I have done." Badjut was dumbfounded at the confession, "My Lord, surely this is not of your doing. If it were not for you we would all have our heads spiked on the parapets by now. Amen must have kept you for another day, a day to turn the king's mind back to worship."

"Perhaps so, Badjut. I do hope so but for the life of me I do not see how that will ever come about. I fear greatly for the king's well being; his mind is not with him most days. If he carries out his boasts and attacks Upper Nile, from what I have heard of their forces he will slaughter all the young men we have in Lower Nile. And for what? Some imagined effrontery? Tell me, are there any of Hor-Amen's generals still loyal to his name? I have a reason for asking and it is not to stage an uprising I assure you."

"Yes, my Lord, I think so. I am certain Urba andThuyi are still loyal to Amen and to the service as they knew it under Hor-Amen. May I ask your reason for wanting to know?" "I am concerned for Hor-Amen's widow, Queen Qettrah. Amen-Kha would kill his mother as soon as anyone else when he is in one of his mad moods; further I am not sure she has enough for her servants and herself to eat." "I was not aware of that, Master. However I think I can take the necessary steps to provide for her without Amen-Kha knowing it. Urba has gone back to herding cattle two hours' walk down the river; I go down there on moonlit nights to visit with him. I can bring back enough for the Queen and leave it in a safe place where a trusted servant can take it to her." Om-Diph was relieved, "Do that, Badjut. Say nothing, absolutely nothing about our conversation this night. Swear to me!" "I swear before Amen that I will remain silent, Master."

Ekhdur set up the Rafiza landing as a staging area. Cattle, sheep, goats and grains sufficient for a long siege were brought there by barge leaving the faster long boats to take troops to the landing above Meidum from which they could walk to Crocodile Lake in a matter of hours. Each long boat also carried enough food and weapons to sustain its load of troops for three or four weeks.

After a long boat unloaded it headed back up the river for another group of warriors. Assi-Rah managed the Meidum transfer and Ar-Chab took charge at Crocodile Lake. On average the buildup was moving at the rate of a thousand to twelve hundred warriors every three days. Before the next full moon, Menhes estimated he would have about fifteen thousand troops in place, including two thousand Nubians, eight hundred of them archers. At that point he would bring twenty of the long boats to within about twelve miles of Meidum and hold them there. At that distance a runner could alert them and they could move down with shielded spear men and archers if needed to harass a force attempting to come up the Nile at water's edge.

Naan was given the task of identifying the villagers of Meidum and their fishing boats. He sailed along the river front with two other fishermen he could trust in small skiffs looking for any craft that might come up from Pe. On spotting such a boat he would alert a runner to bring guards and impound the alien crew and their boat. They were well treated but would stay upriver until it was decided what to do with them, or until either war came or it didn't. Guards between the lake and Gemset patrolled for hunters or anyone else not known to be a settler. They were also placed under guard and sent to the west end of the lake where the warriors of Upper Nile under Ar-Chab could question them regarding the situation in and around Pe.

CHAPTER TWENTY   'The Ibis at Pe'

Miqel walked into Abb-Oth's apartment with his head bowed, expecting the worst. Abb-Oth, his voice hard and with a cruel edge to it, spoke, "Miqel, you are not of the Kingdom of Kish. If you were I would have you exiled to the wilderness. I am not empowered to do that as you know so well, nor do I wish to create a rift between us and Uruk, or worse to lose the friendship of Chad-Mar. That said I have considered the long apprenticeship you have undergone and the terrible effects of the recent events on us all. I can only assume that these have lead in some way to this incredible decision you have made. Because of my respect for you, your gifts really, I will permit to you to speak in your defense, if you have any."

"Master, I offer no defense. I am a man and I have made my own plans. My decision has caused me pain from knowing I would disappoint those like you who have trusted in me to carry out the works for which you have contributed to my education. I have every intention, and I believe the capacity to carry out those works. After that I hope to return to Sumer and report to you and Chad-Mar and Kmal-Dyl the results. If you will not have me return there is nothing I know to say that will change your mind."

"I did not know that that was part of your plan, Miqel. Why do you think you will be better able to work in Nile than at the White Temple or here in Kish?" "Have you talked to Kmal-Dyl since I left, Master?" "Not about you, Miqel. Is there something I need to know regarding your relation with Kmal-Dyl?" "Only that he and I would not be working together, nor could I continue my studies under his supervision. Let me hasten to say that I do understand his motives and his reasoning. It just had not occurred to me that that would be the outcome of my revealing to him what I have been doing with regard to writing and the henge. Ifn-Lot was with me when we discussed this so I cannot fall back on his death as an excuse."

"Miqel, I think I have misjudged you, and wrongfully so since I allowed in my mind no room to consider anything but my own disappointment to see you taking a wife and turning away from the temple service. Tell me, what will you be in Nile? Do they allow senior priests to have wives and families there?" "I do not know that, Master. Hev-Ri and Per-Qad are called 'wizards', whether 'Sun Wizards' or not makes no difference to me. I know nothing of the worship of their god, 'Aten' and I do not expect that to enter into my work there. The Asyut Academy is not a temple nor is it associated with a temple. In its purest sense, as I understand it, it is a place where the search for the truths of the circle, the circle and the square and the heavenly signs is all that matters. If that is not true I suppose I will return to Sumer and become a shepherd like my father."

"That is an interesting concept. I do not recall discussing it with Hev-Ri when he was here, yet I know he had a family there. And he did refer to himself and the others only as 'Sun Wizards'. If you find it as you expect it to be how long do you think it will take you to complete your work on say, writing?" "Taking into account where I am now in my progress toward a usable system of writing, I would say two, at most three years. After that it must obviously be accepted and I think it will require the king of Upper Nile to mandate it for usage in all recording of events and correspondence between people and kingdoms. I do not think it will be a thing like the Sacred Circle with its endless battles to achieve consensus."

"And you have told Kmal-Dyl this?" "Only the part about my progress toward a system of writing, Master." "And what did he say?" "Only that I am on the correct course in his opinion, and that I am to pursue it alone." "Miqel, I think I begin to comprehend what has happened here.

I think you and Kmal-Dyl are both right. I do not know his reasoning and will not ask you to explain any further. I can talk to him about that later. I regret what I said to you and can only wish you and Ekhana well and look forward to the time you return to Kish to show us what it is you have done. May the gods be with you on your journey and all the moreso in your work." "And may the gods be with you, Master. I am very grateful."

Kmal-Dyl called Per-Qad to his room. When he arrived he told him, "I wish to send a message to Hev-Ri, presuming that you arrive at Asyut without any more serious encounters with the Mari people. Tell him you have brought to him the man who may be the greatest wizard in the world of thinking and that it is his responsibility to see that he is given every opportunity to perform his work. If Miqel is able to do all of which I think he is capable Hev-Ri must prevail upon his master to take his work to the king of Upper Nile. It will not do for the results of his studies to become some rote training exercise for young hopeful scribes to slave over and squabble over until it is lost forever. Will you tell him that for me?"

"I will indeed, Master. I think I can assure you that was Hev-Ri's intent when he came to you so many months ago. May I ask a question of you?" "You may." "Why will you not see Miqel while he is in Kish?" "I think, no I know Miqel knows the answer to that and it will have to remain between him and me, now that Ifn-Lot is dead. He also knew that answer and was satisfied with it. Did Miqel request that you ask me that?"

"He did not, Master. I feel I have been presumptuous in pressing the matter. I regret that I did so and ask your forgiveness." "It is nothing to forgive. Your question is a natural one. I simply do not choose to answer it. One thing however, if Miqel is able to return to Sumer with a successful system of writing I shall be among those who most gladly welcome him and will do all I can to support him in getting it accepted here. That of course presumes that the gods will spare me even that long. I am not well, Per-Qad. I believe I can finish my life's most important work before I die, but it will be a close race I think."

Ekhana had taken one last round of weaving instruction and carefully brought her samples to Kalam-Bad to take to her mother. She kept a couple of small samples to take on the journey in case she would be able to continue with her weaving in Asyut. She was aware of the long hours of work without respite Miqel habitually put in, and though she enthusiastically supported him in what he was doing, with Fyd to do the most arduous tasks she felt she must be able to contribute something besides chewing on hides and raising garden produce. Miqel took great pride in her accomplishments, whether in weaving or, as he put it as a huntress. She was equally good at both.

"Miqel, what have we to take with us besides the things we brought from Uruk? Do you think we will need more bartering goods?" "I haven't any idea. Perhaps we should ask Per-Qad. After all he has made the journey." "I know, but do you think we should try to carry some sort of shelter with us? It would be heavy and we certainly could not take one of these tents Father brought up here for us. But there must be something we could throw over our backs to keep the rain away." Miqel laughed and said, "Maybe Fyd ought to bring some crocodile hides along. Truth is that might not be a bad idea."

Per-Qad had spent most of his time with Fyd trying to learn the art of club-throwing. It was of no use. Fyd was able to teach him to throw a spear with credible accuracy, not to bring down a fleeing deer, but enough to defend himself if that was needed. Kalam-Bad presented him with a fine spear with a hard hammered copper point. It was well balanced and became Per-Qad's most prized possession. It was actually one of the few possessions he had of any kind. He was, like all of Menku's people a herdsman and shepherd, a skill Fyd much admired. He and Fyd agreed to take care of the goats that Thar-Mes was sending to Leb, at least as far as Huta where they would have to arrange their own transport up the Euphrates.

Finally the day came when the boats would get on the river and start moving against the slow current, north toward Huta. Kalam-Bad hugged Ekhana and told her, "My daughter, be a good wife and may the gods be with you and protect you on this long journey. We will miss you, child." "And I you, Father. Tell Mother I love her very much." And then they were gone.

A week later they came in sight of Huta and the first boat pulled up on the sand at the landing and immediately sent guards to the village to alert the town that they were on a friendly mission. As the other two boats came ashore the elders came to the water's edge and asked the passengers to come into the town yard where the usual trading of produce, hides and whatever anyone had was proceeding at a noisy babble. As was the custom the senior guardsman explained who they were and where they were headed.

As the elders nodded approval the guardsman assured them that they had food for all the people in their boats. But the elders insisted that they would have fish enough for everyone and sent young boys to build up the fires for the feast. Standing silently behind the other elders and watching the troops splashing in from the water, Malbu gave an audible gasp, "Per-Qad!" "What is it, Malbu?", one of the elders asked. Before he could answer Per-Qad stepped forward and spoke, "Yes, Malbu, I am Per-Qad and I have much to tell you and much to ask from you. May I talk to you alone for a moment?"

All eyes were on the two men standing and staring at other, one in shocked disbelief, the other in almost pleading humiliation. At last Malbu motioned for Per-Qad to follow him as he walked toward his house by the river. It was mid-afternoon and neither said a word until they rested beneath a palm. Malbu spoke first, "I suppose I have offended you, Per-Qad but after all this time to have you suddenly appear is a stunning surprise to me. I am not prepared for it. You wanted to talk. I will listen."

With that Per-Qad began the narrative of his capture and escape; of Ifn-Lot saving his life and of Ifn-Lot, as Davri in the last day of his life. At that point Malbu wept, "He was the most loyal friend I have ever known, Per-Qad. I am glad to know the missing elements of the story you have provided, the things I have laid awake at night pondering. I am sorry that we have lost Davri. I suppose I must have known he was dead when we did not see him for so long. But I have hoped I was wrong; that he would arrive here one day on the way back to Aff as he always did before. You said you had much to ask from me. Tell me what it is I can do for you now." "There is a young man and his wife with me who are going to Asyut where he will join the academy, the same academy Hev-Ri and I belong to. His servant is a domesticated bog...that in itself is a long story and I won't go into it now...and a very reliable and fascinating person. Thar-Mes could give us passage only as far as Huta. From here we must get to Salbat and then obtain a guide to Thurn's where I expect to get Nura to take us to the Orontes and Gelvi and his father. Can you take us to Salbat?"

"That is a very long way, Per-Qad and most of it is passing by Mari country. You know that." "According to Thar-Mes his garrisons control the Euphrates almost all the way between Leb and Bav. Part of the guards, two boat loads are to provide reinforcements to Leb and a new station across the river from Bav. The remainder in the last boat will go on to Quri and your boat can travel that far with their protection. From my wanderings with the Mari bands I do not think we will find any of them as far north as Quri. They have their hands full trying to escape the Kish forces south of there. They have been driven some distance inland according to Thar-Mes when I talked to him last week."

"I have not been up that way for almost three months and what he says may be true now. How does he know?" "The wounded from Leb were brought back to Kish to recover only three weeks ago. That is where Thar-Mes got his information. So far he has lost only a small number of troops up there but he cannot leave the wounded to interfere with the warriors' first responsibility, which is to continue to punish Mari for Davri's death."

"The gods work things out in their own way, don't they? Yes, I will take you and your party to Salbat. Now let us return to the town feast before the elders begin to worry about us. Luckily I brought in a large catch today or they might have a problem feeding this many people. What did you say were the names of your young couple and their servant?" "Miqel and Ekhana. Fyd is their servant. Miqel is a great wizard and Ekhana is the daughter of a prince of Uruk."

Ekhana gave Malbu's wife a beautiful gold and shell necklace she had worn for the purpose of bartering. It was more than enough to repay Malbu for taking them as far as Salbat and he was happy to find his wife so delighted. Fyd had found a shallow inlet a short distance up the river and returned with three crocodile skins, grinning with pride as Ekhana gently hugged him. "These will serve us well when the rains come, don't you think so, Fyd?" "These tough hides, Ekhana. They keep out rain; they keep out wind too. Maybe they scare off thieves." Ekhana laughed at the picture of the three of them dancing around under the hideous looking skins to frighten away thieves, or maybe evil-spirits she thought.

Miqel and Per-Qad were surprised to find Leb a rather prosperous little place. There were some reed houses along with the ubiquitous tents; and the stock pens were all well constructed, some of the walls were even based on sun-dried bricks. There appeared to be adequate flocks and the animals looked well fed. Across the river the replacement troops were being dropped off along with the goats Thar-Mes had sent. Malbu wanted to visit with friends at Leb but his boat was ready as soon as the Kish boats put out on the water for Bav.

The Kish boats were now lighter in the water and moved much more rapidly upstream making it more difficult for Malbu's boat to keep them in sight. Each of the passengers took turns at rowing...Ekhana took her turn along with the men...to add to the tug of the sails; even so, they were barely able to keep up. By the time they turned into a landing or inlet of some sort they were completely exhausted.

At Bav Malbu followed the troops to the landing across the river where the Kish station was located. He listened as the guards captain gave an up to date accounting of what had been going on for the boatmen to take back to Thar-Mes. "There are five wounded warriors here and we have lost three of our best spearmen, all dead; none captured. I think we have the Mari bands moved about thirty thousand Sumer Cubits from the Euphrates by now. We have not seen any of their boats on the river at all. Did you find the same experience at Leb?" The senior guard from the boat answered that things appeared to be about the same but wondered if there was any news from hunters down from the Quri area. "We had some hunters from Salbat through here about a week ago. They landed at Bav and I sent a boat over to find what they had observed up the river. The man I sent reported back that they had seen nothing much except local fishermen in small skiffs. He is familiar with the Mari people and is confident that these hunters were telling the truth. We can never be to sure of course."

Malbu decided to cross over to Bav and ask the elders what they knew, being acquainted with them from his years with Davri. He asked if the Kish boats would be spending the night at the station and was told, no but that they would be there for a few hours while they checked the provisions at the station. At Bav the elders were in good spirits and related how much more peaceful it had been since the Kish troops arrived. One man told him he was no longer afraid to

190

go upriver for fish and game. Malbu asked Per-Qad and Miqel, "What do you think? Do you want to risk going ahead of the guards' boats and letting them catch up with us? It will surely save our arms from all the rowing until they do." Per-Qad and Miqel both felt the risk was worth taking.

They had been gone no more than an hour when they saw an armed group of warriors in a small boat ahead of them. Fearing they were from Mari Malbu turned his boat and made a run for Bav as fast as the wind and oars could take them. The warrior boat was running rather deep in the water and although it kept them in sight did not appear able to overtake Malbu's boat. At about the time when the newly commissioned 'oarsmen' felt that the cramps in their muscles were more that they could bear the Kish guards' boat swung into sight.

Malbu grounded his boat and waved them down only to watch as they greeted the other boatload of warriors. They were also from Kish and were out scouring the river banks to be sure there were no Mari boats to be seen. Malbu told the Kish guardsmen to go on without them, he would try to sail up to where they turned in for the night but his 'crew' just could not row any more for awhile.

This was enough to sober Per-Qad and he had little to say until they arrived at Quri late in the afternoon of the next day. They were received with a friendly invitation to share the evening meal with one of the village elders and his family. "What do you hear from Salbat?", Malbu asked. "Not much different from what we always hear from Salbat, nothing.", the elder laughed, "Is that where you are heading? If you are would you like some company?" "What kind of company?", Malbu cautiously inquired, not knowing exactly what he might be getting into in this lonely place so far up the Euphrates from Huta. "My son wants to go up to Thurn's to see his friend Nura and I would feel better if he was with some more mature people; it is only fifteen years since he was born and I do not want to lose him." "Does he know the way to Thurn's? That is quite a distance for a young lad to be going on his own." "Oh, yes, he has been up with me a few times when I have hunted up that way. He knows all the landmarks and watering places in the wilderness. I figure he will have no trouble once he gets to Salbat.", the elder responded.

"Actually I will be going only to Salbat but my friends are going on to Thurn's and they hope to prevail on Thurn to let Nura guide them over to the Orontes. Nura has a friend called Gelvi who lives near Ugarit and sometimes he goes there to see him." "You know Gelvi? He has been here with Nura once." "Yes, Gelvi went all the way to Kish with a friend of mine, but that was a couple of years ago." Malbu was intrigued with the man's questions. "Do you happen to know a man named, Davri, Malbu?"

"Davri was my friend. What do you know about Davri?" "Sometimes he came here from Aff...that was where he lived. We liked him very much, but he was hard to get to know; such a quiet man." "I am sorry to tell you that Davri is dead. He died earlier this year out a ways from Kish." "I am so sad to know that. Will you take my son with you?", he asked, addressing Per-Qad. "I will be glad to have him join us, providing he knows the way well enough to act as our guide. I have been there only once and do not pretend to recall all the turns and landmarks."

The son's name was Tanis and he was large for his years, a big strapping boy with bright eyes and a grin that seemed to cross his entire face. He had been watching Fyd the whole time Malbu and his party had been at his father's place. Finally Fyd asked him, "You ever see bog before, Tanis?" "Are you a hithabog?", Tanis's eyes widened, half frightened. Fyd laughed, "Tanis not be afraid of bogs. Bogs not harm Tanis. Fyd teach Tanis to hunt like bog." "Would you really?" At this Miqel interrupted, "Fyd is a great hunter, better than any I have ever seen. He is also as kind a man as you will ever see, Tanis. You will get to know him better on our

191

journey."

Fyd spoke to Tanis' father, "Tanis know how to use spear?" "Why yes, Fyd he does. He is very good with a spear, even killed a small pig at about sixty feet last month. Why do you ask?" "Fyd teach Tanis to hunt, Tanis need spear. Per-Qad carry spear. Fyd take club. Miqel, Ekhana take slings. We hunt anything that way." Tanis' father walked back into his tent and brought out a beautifully decorated spear with a long copper head and skillfully wrapped thongs for gripping, "Tanis, you take your grandfather's spear with you. Be careful with it and bring it back; it is the only possession of his I have to remember him."

Tanis was overwhelmed; he had never been permitted to even hold that spear before. He carried it to the boat as Malbu called everyone to climb in for the trip to Salbat. It was late afternoon when they landed at Salbat. Tanis, who was known by the elders there leaped out of the boat and ran to the village, returning in a few minutes with several townsmen who invited Malbu to bring his party ashore. They wanted news from Quri and the other towns farther south, but mainly they wanted to know if the Mari bands had bothered them on the way up. "No troubles with Mari people from what we saw. I think the Kish stations are taking their toll on the marauders." Malbu went on to explain the Kish war to punish Mari for Davri's death. At that news one of the men interrupted him, "Did you say Davri is dead? When? How?" Malbu and Per-Qad told him what had happened at Kish and that they were going on to Aff the next day. "I don't think Davri had any family in Aff, Malbu. He used to talk about his family in Eridu and friends in Ur and Uruk, but he never said anything about a family up here." Malbu responded, "There was much we did not know about Davri. He was a close friend of mine but we never talked of anything relating to him personally, just what he was doing when he came to Huta."

Malbu left for Huta as soon as the aura of the sun gave enough light to see. Miqel told him, "I hope we will be back and see you in three or four years, Malbu. Ekhana and I thank you for all you have done for us." "I will be in Huta if the gods keep me. I wish you well on the remainder of your journey to Nile."

At Aff Per-Qad told the elders what had happened to Davri since he was last there. They were grave but did not hold any animosity toward Per-Qad. They wanted him to tell Hev-Ri they were well. Aff was aroused over the damage to flocks a young lion had been inflicting and Fyd wanted to know where the lion roamed. He was told that the lion seemed to come in toward Aff from the northwest, killing mostly at night and never getting very close to the village. One of the men said, "We have never seen him. Some have heard his roar but he kills and eats and disappears before we can get a hunting party out to where he has been. We cannot track him on this gravelly soil in the daytime and no one wants to hunt him at night."

Fyd had an idea and he spoke privately to Miqel, "Miqel, you take armbands, trade for goat. We let goat carry water, carry food. Lion smell goat. We kill lion. Maybe Tanis kill Lion. Tanis be man if he kill lion." It was such an obvious idea Miqel wondered why none of them had thought of a goat to carry their water over the desert to the Orontes. He promptly offered one of his silver armbands to one of the townsmen who was more than happy to make the trade. Tanis had overheard Fyd's comment, "Fyd, do you really think I can kill a lion? A grown lion?" Fyd said he hoped so, that he was sure Tanis could do it if they found the lion. Miqel was less than enthusiastic: the memory of Malil left him wanting nothing to do with lions. "Fyd, we have to get to Thurn's and I would rather we walked the whole way in a day if we can. We can hunt lions another time."

By noon the next day Ekhana was feeling ill; something, perhaps a piece of tainted meat at Aff caused nausea. She became weaker as the afternoon hours wore away and finally told Miqel they had better stop and let her rest until morning. They found a place with a few trees to set up camp for the night. Tanis told them they could dig for water but they did not need it. They had brought fire from Aff and soon Fyd was cooking a hare he had killed.

When the moon came out bright, reflecting off the whitened gravel and sand Fyd woke Tanis and motioned to him to keep silent. As they walked over to where the goat was tied near the fire Fyd told him, "Maybe we kill lion tonight." He carefully put the water and provisions in a neat pile and lead the goat about half a mile out to some bushes where he and Tanis could be hidden. He tethered the goat to a low bush and they lay down to see what would happen. A slight breeze came from behind them, "Lion smell goat. Not smell us if Tanis keep head down low."

In about an hour a low growling could be heard, Fyd estimated it was about two hundred feet, off to the left from where they lay. "Tanis not move now. Fyd tell Tanis when throw spear. We kill lion tonight." The sound hushed as the lion caught wind of the goat and a soft rustle in the bushes told Fyd he was charging. He lifted his head to see the lion only thirty feet from the goat. At that he jumped to his feet with his club swinging over his head and shouted for Tanis to throw. The spear missed the lion but before it could get out of range Fyd's club crippled its hind legs and it lay writhing on the ground. Tanis was frightened out of his wits but he quickly retrieved his spear and thrust it into the lions chest. He had killed a lion. Fyd took the hide off the carcass in a matter of minutes, grinning the whole time. He did not have to tell the others anything except the truth, Tanis had killed the lion. Fyd gave the hide to Tanis to prove to Nura that he was a lion hunter and a man. Miqel knew better than to ask Fyd anything about the night's activity.

Ekhana was all right the next morning, a bit weak from losing all she had eaten but otherwise set to get on to Thurn's. They arrived at Thurn's well before noon. Nura was there and excited at the prospect of getting to see Gelvi. He liked Tanis, though he considered him too young for a man of his years to pay much attention to, that is until Tanis showed him the lion skin and Fyd vouched for the fact that Tanis had killed it.

They would need all the water and bread they could load on the goat for the three day tramp to Rud. This was the hardest leg of the journey for anyone traveling in either direction. By the second day they were glad for the goat's milk; they took fire but found only enough wood to ward off animals the first night. The second day Miqel and Ekhana killed a couple of hares and Per-Qad managed to spear a wild pig. Miqel told him, "That will make a fine gift for the people at Rud. Let's eat the hares and take the pig with us."

Gelvi and his father had brought a band of hunters to Rud two days before and had taken them up the Orontes, south toward the hills. The boat was expected back the next day. When it arrived Nura and Tanis ran down to the water and, jabbering gave Gelvi all the news before he and his father could get up to the village. His father told Per-Qad, "It is good to see you again. Your friends thought you were dead. I am going on back to Ikruth tomorrow; the hunting party wants me to pick them up in two weeks so I will not stay and wait for them here. You are welcome to sail down to Ikruth with us."

Gelvi wanted to take Tanis and Nura to Ugarit so that they could say they had seen the great sea. His father was willing to take them to the mouth of the Orontes but they would have to walk on down to Ugarit. That suited them fine; they might join up with Zuv and do some hunting, that is if he was there. Per-Qad asked if he and his party could join them as far as Ugarit and was told they were welcome. Gelvi's father even agreed they could take the goat with them in his boat.

At Ugarit Ekhana told Miqel, "Soon enough it will be the time for rains in Lower Nile, is that not true, Per-Qad?" "Yes, that is so, Ekhana." "Then I think it is time we bartered for a small tent, one the goat can carry. We must have something to protect our provisions and I think we will be glad to have a tent over our heads when the cold rain starts to fall." Per-Qad wondered why Ekhana was worried, "I think we will find a boat somewhere along the coast that will take us to Pe, Ekhana. Once there I have no concerns for our travel on up the Nile to Asyut; there are always boats going up that way. We might need a tent though if we have any problem getting passage from the coastal villages to Pe."

"Crocodile hides are fine. But they are not enough. A tent will let us keep fire for the journey down the coast and I for one like my food cooked; and I like to sleep without worrying about snakes and animals all night." Miqel spoke up, "Well put, Ekhana. I think we all agree with that. We will find a small shelter of hides perhaps that we can set into the side of any slight rise in the land, just like the one my father had at the far meadow. I do not reckon it will take any more bartering than it did for the goat." Fyd thought for a moment, "Miqel and Ekhana right. Baldag had good place at far meadow. Kept fire. Kept food. Kept dry." Per-Qad laughed, "This then will be the wizards' expedition. We will take our comforts with us. Who knows what lies before us."

There were no seaworthy boats at Ugarit, only small craft for local fishing. Per-Qad thought it better that they walk down to Tylfar than wait since in six or seven weeks it would be past the season of the larger craft from Cypress and Crete. They set out with the goat and newly acquired tent, reaching Tylfar by late afternoon to find that there was a small seagoing craft there. Better yet the boat master was leaving the following morning for Qumrif, over a hundred miles south of them. A beautiful silver amulet bought passage for calm water sailing toward Qumrif.

While they were on the water Per-Qad struck up a conversation with the boat master who had visited Pe many times. "What is the news from Nile, my friend?", he asked. "If you are a trader it is all bad. We cannot go into Pe now. All we can do is barter up and down the coast from here to Saqqut." "Why is that?" "The new king of Lower Nile...he is a murderous one that one...he's driven everyone but the boats sailing out of Cypress and Crete away. He has even put some of the crews under guard and threatened to kill them. He says we are all thieves but he is the thief. He takes our stuff for nothing when he hasn't got anything to barter and those who protest are liable to lose their boats...or their heads. We all stay out of there now."

Per-Qad asked, "What happened to Hor-Amen?" "They say his son, this Amen-Kha killed him. I know he is hot tempered enough to do it and I believe he did it. Now he keeps talking about this new king of Upper Nile as being a murderer. I don't know anything about that other than that he is old Menku, the herdsman-trader's son and the Upper Nile boats don't come to Pe now." "I thought the Menku traders got along well enough with Lower Nile, even below Meidum and Crocodile Lake. What happened?" "You seem to know a lot about Nile. Are you from the river country?"

Per-Qad told him only that he was returning there after a journey to Sumer. "You a trader? Where did you live?" Per-Qad answered cautiously, "I did live at Crocodile Lake. Used to work for Menku's cattle station there. I am no trader, just a herdsman. My friends are shepherds and the big fellow is a hunter from a way down the Euphrates." "Don't mention Menku in Pe, whatever you do. He is dead anyway. They say there was a war in Upper Nile and everybody at the Menku station at Asyut was killed, families and all. They called their king Scorpion before Menku's son...they call him Menhes...drove a peg into his skull. Anyway there was a lot of fighting and old Scorpion's troops did a lot of killing before this Menhes finally killed them."

Per-Qad was shocked and so was Miqel for he had heard all these names before. Per-Qad could only assume that his family was dead, and how many others of the sun wizards were left he could not guess. He wondered when all this happened but did not feel like asking. He and Miqel had to get further passage down the coast and he could not be sure that they would be welcome if anyone knew they were wizards and he was loyal to the Menku family. He also remembered the close call he had had at Pe when Hev-Ri had to bail him out of trouble. And that was when Hor-Amen was still ruling there.

When they got to Qumrif there were no boats sailing south so they set up their tent on a grassy slope and waited. They all fished and were able to barter some fish for bread and lentils, keeping them busy and well fed. Per-Qad told Miqel, "You have heard what the boat master said. This is unlike anything I could have imagined, Miqel. Whatever comes I think we need to establish ourselves as simple people trying to eke out a living. You know enough about flocks to be a shepherd and I have herded cattle in my earlier days. Fyd is a born hunter and Ekhana can hunt and she can weave too. "That may be important to us until we can get to the part of the Nile Menhes now controls. I do not know where that begins however. If he has Meidum we can walk that far easily and get over to Crocodile Lake and safety. If not I do not know what we will do. Our first goal is to get to Pe. Then I think we will set up Ekhana's tent in some secluded place and work out of there. It may be that you and I can get on with the temple service, training drawing scribes while Ekhana weaves and Fyd hunts to keep us supplied with food. All this is just a guess of course. We will just have to wait until we get there and find out how bad it really is.

"One other thing. Your name is obviously not one heard in Nile. Fyd is all right, as is Ekhana. I think you need a name that signifies a bird or an animal." "Like what, Per-Qad?" "Let's see. Miqel..."M"...'Gem', that will do it." "What is a 'gem'?" "Gem is the black ibis in Kemet. Using that for a name will not call attention to your foreign origins." "But we are foreign, Per-Qad." "When we get to Asyut that is correct. Until then we are returning to Nile from a trip up to the Orontes for hunting.

"I will give you all you need to know about Crocodile Lake in case anyone gets too curious. Those crocodile skins may come in handy as an example of what we traded for; we can tell anyone who asks that we killed only one lion and traded that and the game we took for these armlets and amulets we are wearing. I know this sounds threatening and we may have no cause for such defensive worries. But Pe was a very sensitive place when I was there last and I think we can not afford to take chances. I want my head on my shoulders when this is over so I can use it to laugh at our fears."

After two weeks a Cretan boat appeared at Qumrif and unloaded a cargo of pottery. Per-Qad talked to the boat master, a man named, Agga regarding passage to Pe. "I am going to stop at Edhemet and Saqqut to see if I can barter this stuff I got here for something I can trade at Pe. We will be moving fast for I have to be in Pe by the full moon. You are in luck for this is my last voyage this season. What are you doing up here?" Per-Qad told him his concocted story and it seemed to satisfy him well enough.

Agga asked, "How long have you been gone, Per-Qad...that is your name, isn't it?" "Many months, Agga. We went up to the bend of the Orontes to hunt and planned to barter our way back to Nile with the game we took. We did fairly well until we got stranded at Ugarit, just as we did on the way up. We were there a month then. Mighty glad we had this goat; we have walked most of the places we have been." "I do not think you will get back to Crocodile Lake very soon, Per-Qad." "Why, Agga?"

"The king lets me go up there to pick up things he can use for weapons but I seem to be the only boat master allowed to go to Meidum...that is as far as I am allowed to go...and I do not think he will let me take anyone other than my crew with me. He is certain everyone is an Upper Nile spy; even flew into a rage when some people building cattle stalls drove a few hunters away from Crocodile Lake just three weeks ago. A friend of mine at Meidum says they thought the hunters were thieves. Who knows, maybe they were." Agga burst out laughing at the thought of what he had just said.

"Do you think there will be war between Upper and Lower Nile, Agga? Is that what you are telling me?" "What I am telling you, Per-Qad is that you do not ask questions of any kind at Pe. Keep your head down and your mouth shut and you will live."

Agga was too busy sorting his goods to talk on the way to Edhemet; as he had said he wanted to get in each harbor and out as quickly as possible. By the time they reached Saqqut he had done well enough with his bartering to feel good about getting to Pe. At Saqqut he picked up some very well made leather articles, especially sword and quiver belts that he was sure Amen-Kha would want. He wished this trip was over and he could get on back home; maybe things would be better in Lower Nile in the spring.

Agga walked back to the stern and sat on a coil of rope as he began to talk, "You know, Per-Qad it might be better if you and your friends did not go to Pe at all." "Where would we go, Agga? There is no easy way around Pe from what you tell me." "That's right, there isn't. And the delta is not a place to start walking around either. But I could let you off a short distance north of Pe at a place I know. It is an easy walk up to Pe any time you feel inclined to go there, and I think you can get enough work to provide for your needs until these war clouds blow over."

"Is this a place belonging to someone you know?" "The owner's name is Urba; I scarcely know him but I do know that his herdsmen and shepherds have been conscripted by Amen-Kha's guardsmen. He was one of Hor-Amen's generals and I am told he was very loyal to the old king. After he was stripped of his authority he disappeared down the river to this place of his and began tending his cattle. He also has a small flock and the usual goats but it is more than one man can handle; at least that is what they tell me down at the Pe-Diph landing when Amen-Kha is not listening."

"Do you think he would take us in, Agga? After all we came from up at the lake and you say Amen-Kha gets pretty frenzied at the thought of anyone from up there." "Amen-Kha, yes. Urba, maybe not. I doubt that he cares very much. You had been gone a good while when the old king was murdered. Before that I don't think Hor-Amen worried much about Crocodile Lake. There has been no Menku station there for years and what was left of the settlers were probably looking out for their own paltry living, not caring whether Amen or Aten was somewhere up there watching them."

"We can only rely on what you tell us, Agga. So much has happened I really don't know which way to turn. I told Gem the other day that I just wanted to keep my head on my shoulders so I can still be able to laugh at all this when it is over." At that Agga roared with laughter. "I think you are a wise man, Per-Qad. Maybe you should have been one of those wizards."

Urba was a large, powerful man with huge hands. He was watering his cattle when Agga's boat pulled into an inlet and beached. He seemed glad to have help of any kind and was not particularly interested in knowing much about where it came from. "I am glad you thought of me Agga. We must get to know each other better when things settle down. I am surprised that you continue to come to Pe, what with all that goes on up there." "It is the only way I know to make a living, General. And so far I am still living." "There is something to be said for that, isn't there? Would you and your crew like something to eat?"

"No. I thank you, but we have to get to Pe today so I can get permission to sail up to Meidum tomorrow. There is good barter stuff still up there and this is my last voyage until next spring." "I am sure there is plenty of work for your passengers; I will have to get to know them well enough to find what they do best. Good luck in Meidum. Perhaps I will see you next year when you come back. Stop by and I will give you whatever I know before you go to Pe. It will probably be worth your while."

Urba was taken with Fyd. He had never seen anyone handle a club the way he did, not even his best mace men could have approached Fyd's skill. He could not figure out exactly what Fyd was however. He was not like any men he had known, not even like foreigners who came to Pe.

Amen-Kha was becoming more suspicious each day that passed. He doubted the loyalty of even his most trusted friends including most of his new generals. He cut the provisions to the temple to bare survival rations, leaving that much as a sop to his wavering belief in the providence of Amen. Om-Diph pleaded with him, assuring him of the continuing fealty of the temple staff but it was to no avail. He turned to Badjut for help from Urba hoping that he might be able to feed the younger priests and keep them from being conscripted as warrior trainees. Urba gave Badjut food but having lost his own herdsmen could not see how he would be any help in protecting the temple servants. Urba introduced Badjut to Per-Qad who agreed to deliver food to Queen Qettrah at night.

Fyd was assigned as watchman for the tent which was well hidden in a small grove of trees back a little way from the water. He kept a fire going but knew that it would have to be put out if he saw any of the king's guards in the area. Fortunately there were none who came that way; all of them were busy training the new recruits at a camp south of Pe. He also fished and hunted for game to feed Miqel and Ekhana and Per-Qad. Ekhana would have nothing to do with calling Miqel, 'Gem'. She said it was not natural and he was her husband and that was the way it was going to be while they were there.

Badjut was walking along with Miqel while he tended the goats and asked him, "You seem to be different from other shepherds I have known who lived up at Crocodile Lake. Did you ever do any temple service, Gem?" "Yes, Badjut I did." "Where?" "Several years ago I went to Uruk in Sumer and served there for a fairly short time, learning what I could about the work the scribes did." "That is a long way from here isn't it?" "A very long way but it was an exciting trip. That is where I took Ekhana for my wife and where Fyd joined us."

"That explains a lot. Urba is fascinated with Fyd and so am I. What sort of man is he?" "They call his race Hithabogs there. They are a wild people but there are not many of them left anymore. Fyd and his tiny tribe were rewarded for being of service to the king of Uruk by being given an area of their own. They tend the king's flocks now but they continue to hunt as they always have. Fyd is no threat to anyone; he is as gentle as any man you have ever known."

Per-Qad was aggravated that Miqel had taken Badjut into his confidence in spite of his warnings to the contrary. Miqel told him, "Per-Qad, we are going to have to rely on someone here. There is no way we can keep on pretending we are what we are not. Urba can't be kept wondering how we can be such simple Crocodile Lake settlers; you and I are not really that good at tending the animals and I believe he knows it. I think we have to risk being found out just as you are at great risk taking food to the the old king's widow."

"I suppose you are right, Miqel. What do you plan to do, tell Urba and Badjut the whole truth?" "The truth, yes. But only what we think they need to know. I don't think you and I need to talk about your having been a sun wizard, or my plans to become one. That might offend

Urba, I assume he worships Amen. Nevertheless I think he needs to know that I have never been to Crocodile Lake any more than Ekhana or Fyd have. And Badjut may need to be able to trust us as much as we have to trust him. From what Agga and Urba have told us he could lose his head for coming down here. So could we."

One night as they lay in the tent Ekhana asked, "Miqel, have you given up any plans to work on your system of writing?" "No, Ekhana, I have continued to work on it ever since we came here. I don't have my scribe's pots and squares but that does not preclude my keeping my mind active. In fact I have already accounted for relating a good many of the twenty-two steps in the 'Sacred Circle' construction to the consonants that have to be accounted for, even three of the vowels." "How in the world did you do that?"

"Before we left Uruk I had pretty much decided what the objects I would choose for consonantal sounds would look like, based on where they fit in the construction diagram. The Nile names for articles that would be easily recognized and remembered are shorter and simpler than the same things in Sumer for the most part." "Give me some examples, Miqel. I am having a hard time following you."

"The last step cipher I have chosen looks just like a loaf of bread mother used to bake in her oven. Here bread is called, 'ta' so that will be the tuh sound and it goes to step twenty-two. Then there is the foot and leg figure; in Kemet foot is 'ba'. That means the buh sound will be at step two. Do you see how it works now?" "I think so. Are there others?" Just this morning Urba was building a little altar to his god, Amen and when I asked him what it was he said, "It is my own 'gu'; now that I can't go up to the temple I want to be able to worship here." "Well, the altar looks so much like what I have for step three it is almost uncanny. So the guh sound will be the third cipher." "What about the vowels, Miqel. We can"t talk using only consonants."

"This is what Kmal-Dyl was up against. He wanted to use a syllabary, you know, 'Bah, Boo, Bee' and so on. He and I agree that that is too cumbersome but he felt he had to proceed with it. There are thirteen vowels that he and I can count. Most of them are made up of two vowel sounds but five are basic, their sounds are: 'EE, AH, UH, OO, and EH'. Step sixteen looks like a lasso; that is what Urba calls, 'wa' so it will do for the wuh sound and the lasso will be the sixteenth cipher." "But that is a consonant, Miqel."

"True. But it also is the way I have worked out the dilemma of fitting thirty-two sounds into twenty-two ciphers. Wuh backward is 'UH-OO' which is the vowel, 'O'. It will depend on the usage when it is written...what anyone would expect. Obviously my sister's name is not Bwuhdi so when she writes her name in my system it will be read as 'Bodi'. Does this make sense to you, Ekhana? I hope it will to the wizards at Asyut." "I think so, Miqel. Right now though I'm sleepy."

A full moon turned the Nile into a pale ribbon bordered with deathly white sands. It had been a month since Agga's boat landed at Urba's place and things there were quiet. The daily routines kept Miqel and Per-Qad busy while Urba went hunting with Fyd almost everyday. Ekhana wished she had some wool and even a makeshift loom so she could weave and make some garments; those she had were getting tattered and, unlike the men she did not fancy wearing skins.

At Pe during one of Amen–Kha's more than usually violent orgies he skewered a young priest with his spear and left him writhing, crawling toward the temple. Om-Diph witnessed it and came running out, "You beast! You murderer! Haven't you done enough to turn this peaceful kingdom into savagery? I denounce you in the name of our god, Amen. May he do so to you as you have done."

He got no further. Amen-Kha seized a spear from a guard and drove it through Om-Diph's heart. There was bedlam as guards rushed to drag priests into the temple yard, killing some on the way. Badjut barely escaped by leaping off the wall and running for the woods behind the temple. Knowing nowhere else to go he headed for Urba's with a king's guard in close pursuit. By dodging through the trees on a path he had come to know so well he eluded capture and never presented himself as a target for a thrown spear.

Finally he came to the clearing near Urba's, gasping for mercy, "Amen, help me now! Amen save me now!" Fyd looked up to see the guard raise his spear and lunge forward. He never made the thrust; as Fyd's club broke his neck he fell dead where he had stood. Fyd rushed to Badjut, "Badjut hurt?" "No, bless you, Fyd. I am exhausted, that is all. But we had better get rid of this body before anyone else comes down here." "Fyd feed him to crocodiles. Nobody find him. Badjut keep spear. Badjut hide in tent. Fyd watch for guards."

At the tent Badjut told Per-Qad and Miqel what had happened. Ekhana asked, "What will happen to Queen Qettrah, Badjut? Should not Per-Qad bring her here? It may not be completely safe but it has to be safer than where she is." Per-Qad left without saying a word, returning with Qettrah in about three hours to find everything at Urba's quiet. Qettrah asked, "Who are these people, Per-Qad. I know Badjut and Urba of course but who are these other two?"

Urba sat silently as Per-Qad told her, "Queen Qettrah, Urba, you may as well know the truth about us, and you too, Badjut. I am a sun wizard from Asyut and Miqel...yes that is his name...is a great wizard from Sumer. We did not come here to harm anyone; I was just trying to return home, if I have a home or a family anymore,and these three were going with me. I have been gone for almost two years and know almost nothing about what has happened since I left. We were stranded here weeks ago and Urba has treated us with kindness as did a boat master from Crete named Agga. Badjut told us of your needs and I agreed to bring food to you to keep him from being detected in coming down the river to Urba's place so often. That is really about all there is to tell. We will do all we can to help you until you can return to your own home. We ask only that you stay hidden here until that time."

'WADJET', THE STANDARD OF LOWER NILE

The Cobra as portrayed on a gold relief in the tomb room of
Hetepheres, mother of Khufu, c. 2700 BC. Found beneath
the Great Pyramid, Khufu in Giza.

Illustrated by W. C. Cawthon

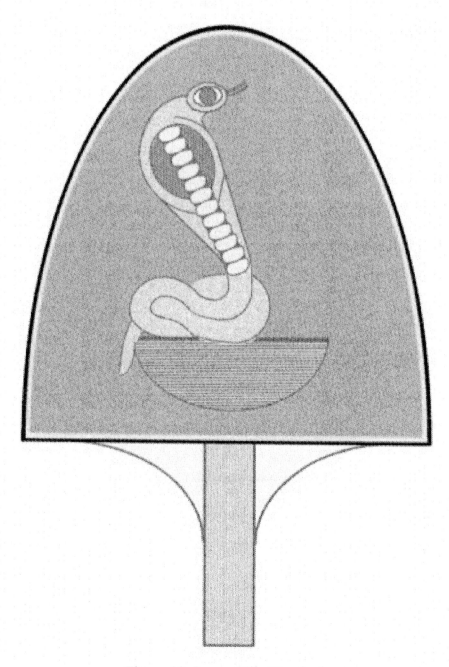

Figure 13: Lower Nile Standard

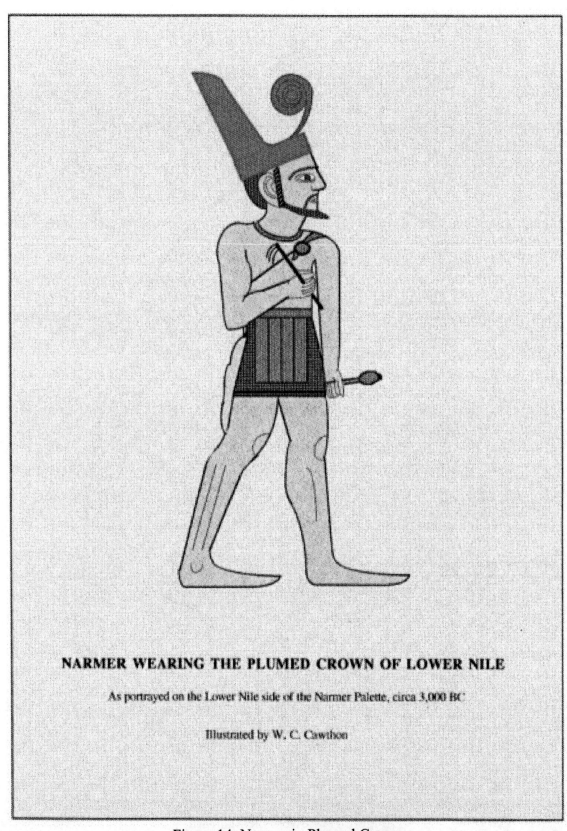

NARMER WEARING THE PLUMED CROWN OF LOWER NILE

As portrayed on the Lower Nile side of the Narmer Palette, circa 3,000 BC

Illustrated by W. C. Cawthon

Figure 14: Narmer in Plumed Crown

CHAPTER TWENTY ONE   'The Plumed Crown'

To regain control Amen-Kha called his generals and ordered the march on Meidum, via Suph and Gemset to begin at daybreak. Every able bodied man, warrior or not would join in, "We will teach those Upper Nile vultures to stay away from our homeland. The Nile will run red with settler's blood before the sun sets three days from now. I swear that by Amen!"

At sunrise a bedraggled swarm of warriors, farmers, shepherds, herdsmen and fishermen, armed with anything each could find set out for Zuph. The host totaled perhaps eight thousand men and boys. Arriving there they drove the villagers in front of them, killing a number in the process. A fleet footed boy outran the column and headed up river for Meidum. There he fell at Naan's feet pleading for help. When Naan found that an force of of such size was headed for Meidum and the lake he sent runners to Ar-Chab and Assi–Rah. Menhes had arrived from Rafiza two days before and was with Assi-Rah at the transfer station.

Menhes immediately sent another runner to order all long boats to the landing to pick up full loads of shielded warriors...spearmen and archers...and head down river past Meidum. They were to beach there and he, himself would lead them toward Gemset. Assi-Rah would take his Nubian archers and bring them in from the northwest side of Crocodile Lake while Ar-Chab moved the main force toward Gemset. In all fourteen thousand troops were moving within hours of the time the first runners arrived.

The swords and spears of Pe began devouring the unsuspecting settlers south of Gemset like a ravening lion the afternoon of the second day. Amen-Kha planned to head back toward the river from Gemset and take Meidum by surprise the third day, moving on from there to Crocodile Lake to complete his planned assault before camping and deciding how far to go up the Nile. He camped a few miles below Gemset to give his troops a rest before the next forced march attack. At dawn he and his generals moved the warriors out with Amen-Kha and his personal guards at the head of the column bearing the Wadjet Standard of Lower Nile. They moved toward Meidum expecting to reach the banks of the Nile before noon and take Meidum before sundown.

About three hours after sunrise Ar-Chab's main column appeared before Amen-Kha's southwestern flank forcing the troops to move westward, not knowing they would walking straight into Assi-Rah's warriors. The central body met Ar-Chab head on and the eastern flank tried to swing and set the trap they thought they would have with the western flank coming in on Ar-Chab's left. In doing so they presented their exposed rear to Menhes who was driving his forces directly up from the river south of Meidum.

Amen-Kha's trained warriors, macemen and spearmen forming the front line of his army fought fiercely and Ar-Chab drew his forces back to let Assi-Rah's archers inflict their awful damage. The Lower Nile archers in the eastern flank as inept as most of them were could only return a rain of arrows in the direction of Menhes troops. Most of the arrows glanced harmlessly off the Upper Nile shields, though a few found their marks. Menhes' warriors ripped into the Lower Nile trainee corps, the dead heaping up faster than the poor bewildered souls could escape.

On the western front the carnage was even worse as the generals of Lower Nile tried to counter attack. Ar-Chab now moved his main column forward, felling everything in its path with the maces and spears of trained and seasoned warriors. As Menhes' force came in sight of the his main army Amen-Kha realized he was trapped and began to pull his troops back toward Gemset.

The jaws of the vise began to close.

At that point Amen-Kha threw down his crown and waving to his personal guards to follow, cut and ran for the rear as fast as his fat legs could carry him, leaving his astonished generals to do such fighting they could manage to save whatever they could. Menhes ordered Amen-Kha taken alive and to be brought to him along with his personal guards and the Lower Nile generals, whether they were living or dead.

As Amen-Kha was flung to the ground at his feet Menhes picked up the plumed red crown of Lower Nile and put it on his head. Menhes was enraged and turned to Ar-Chab, "Take off his head and have it erected on a spike at the Meidum landing. Dump his besotted corpse in the river. As for his so-called generals I want their corpses in two rows: arms tied to their bodies and heads placed between their legs. Let their families retrieve their remains."

He then called Assi-Rah and Ar-Chab to the Meidum landing where he told the settlers there that there was one kingdom now. They and what people who were left from Zuph and Gemset would be free to strip the dead of the Lower Nile army. Then they were to burn the remains before sundown of the next day. Ar-Chab and Assi-Rah would tend to their wounded and do what they could for the wounded of the Lower Nile forces, allowing them to return to their homes afterward. The Lower Nile venture had been so frenetically organized and the battle was over so quickly it seemed impossible to contemplate what it meant to have 'One Kingdom". Menhes knew he had to put the pieces of Lower Nile back together immediately and somehow get some form of government into effect before the entire northern realm that had been Hor-Amen's collapsed into chaos, murder and starvation.

"Ar-Chab, I would like for you to take a long boat up to Asyut and bring Khafu and Ekhdur to Pe as soon as you can reach there. I will be at Pe tomorrow and I want Ekhdur to take over the government of Lower Nile if he is willing; I think he will do it. Assi-Rah, my friend, I thank you and your father and your brother for your support. I believe there are less dead than there would have been had we waited and experienced an extended war. It is over. When you have treated your wounded and set the pyres for your dead why don't you go on back to Nekhen and begin to implement the plans you and Sel-Abba had before this lunatic brought us to this battle. I will visit with you and your father when I get back up there, whenever that will be. Tell MeriLyth I am all right and give her and my son loving hugs for me."

At Pe there was no news from the battle. No one knew what had happened around Gemset; all that was known was that a few deserters had showed up and told of the massacre of the settlers at Zuph two days before. The yard was deserted as was the temple and most of the town. What priests had survived had fled many miles down the river or had gone inland, northwest toward the rocky plain at the edge of the desert.

At Urba's Badjut took turns with Fyd watching the river and the its banks to warn of any warriors who might stray that way. They were unaware that Amen-Kha had moved the entire army south to its ultimate end outside of Gemset. Urba and Miqel tended the animals and cautiously hunted for game while Ekhana stayed with Qettrah. As the days went by quietly Fyd approached Urba, "I go up to Pe. King will not see me. Fyd hide in bushes. Nobody see Fyd. I find out things, bring back to Urba."

"I don't know, Fyd. It may be quiet up there now but there have been a lot of people running down the river banks until two days ago. Perhaps the rest of them are dead and things are just as bad as they were when Badjut got here the other night. Are you sure you can get there and back without anyone seeing you?" At that Miqel broke in, "Urba, if anyone can watch without being seen it is Fyd. It has been his way of living all his life. I think I would let him go. We are not very secure down here if the turmoil is continuing there. If it is not I suspect Queen Qettrah would like to go home."

Fyd crept through the trees and beneath the lower bushes to within sight of the the temple and looked at the deserted yard. Litter was strewn everywhere but there were only a few men down by the water and they seemed to be peacefully fishing with nobody to interfere with them. There were no guards he could see. Suddenly long boats appeared coming down to the Pe-Diph landing and a king wearing the plumed crown waded ashore. Fyd had never seen Amen-Kha of course and assumed that was who it was. He had also never seen boats like those. The warriors with the king simply looked around, asking a few questions of the fishermen but Fyd could not overhear what was said.

He returned to Urba and told him what he had seen and Urba was unbelieving at first. "Fyd, I know you are telling the truth but maybe you just do not know what you actually saw. There are no boats like you describe in Lower Nile, not since Menhes destroyed our fleet. The ones we are building will not be ready for another year or more and we would have seen them coming up the river for they are being built a long way north of here. The man you saw with the crown. What did he look like?" "Man tall, not fat. Man look strong like Urba. Man have sword and carry club." "That is not a description of Amen-Kha. He is not very tall and he was very fat the last I time saw him a couple of months ago."

Per-Qad had been listening, "Urba, Fyd's account sounds exactly like Menhes and his boats to me. I know him well. He is tall and lean and muscular and his boats are over a hundred feet long with the prows riding high in the water...they are the old Menku trading vessels...you have seen them I know." "Of course I have, Per-Qad. They came here for years. But what could Menhes possibly be doing with Amen-Kha's crown? As far as I know he vowed never to come back here after Amen-Kha insulted his brother when he tried to reopen trade with Pe."

"I think it is time for me to go to Pe, Urba. I know Menhes well; after all his father was my master at the academy at Asyut. I will take Fyd with me and wait a short distance from the temple in the trees until he tells me it is as he saw it earlier. If it is Menhes we need to know what is going on and I think he will tell me. If things have changed I will return here and we can decide what to do next. This is all most perplexing. I cannot imagine Menhes wanting Lower Nile; he is not an ambitious person. I know he could conquer Lower Nile. I just don't think he would want to do it."

Urba was so confused by now he could not object, "Go ahead, Per-Qad. These are such strange reports I don't know what to make of them." Per-Qad took Fyd and headed for Pe, leaving Badjut to wonder if he had lost his mind. From cover Fyd whispered, "King still there. More boats come. More warriors come. Not many men in yard. All down at water. Same king as before." Per-Qad stood and saw Menhes at the temple. At the sight he motioned to Fyd to follow him and approached the yard, carefully pacing his steps to avoid alarming the warriors with Menhes. He raised his right hand and Menhes beckoned him to come forward.

"Per-Qad, what in Aten's name are you doing here?" "I have been stranded a short distance down the river from here, my Lord. I am just trying to get back to Asyut from Kish and it is a long story. But right now I have some people who are afraid for their lives and need to know what has happened." "I thought you were dead. Hev-Ri said you were captured by the outlaws from Mari." "I was, Menhes but I escaped. I will tell you the whole story, but I have brought the greatest wizard in Sumer, probably the world to Nile...I believe that is what your father wanted...and now all I want to do is get back to Asyut. I know about the massacre there but I have to start my life over somewhere."

Menhes was silent for a moment, "Per-Qad, do you know that my father is dead and that I am king of Upper Nile?" Yes, my Lord, a Cretan boatmaster brought us here and told me that." "There has been a disastrous battle, disastrous for Lower Nile and I am king of all Kemet now. I will let you make your peace with Hev-Ri in due time. But can you tell me, where are all the people?" Per-Qad proceeded to relay what Badjut had told him about the orgy that led to Badjut's fleeing to Urba's, "That is all I know about what has gone on here, Menhes."

"Who is this Urba?" "He was one of Hor-Amen's most loyal generals who went down the river to tend a small herd he owned after he was thrown out by Amen-Kha. That was after Amen-Kha murdered Hor-Amen and Om-Diph. A man named Agga, the Cretan boatmaster I told you about knew Urba well enough to get him to take us in when things got so bad at Pe. We have come to know him and trust him." "Are there other Hor-Amen generals like him still around, Per-Qad?"

"I am sure Badjut would know but I do not. I suspect there are however. Urba remains loyal to Hor-Amen's widow; she is with us at his place and we have been protecting her there. She was destitute after Hor-Amen's death. Amen-Kha cut off the provisions for the temple and the old Chief Priest, Om-Diph had provided for her before that." Are you referring to Qettrah?" "Yes, Menhes, she is a fine woman." "What happened to Om-Diph; I knew of him and my father spoke well of him." "Another one of those Amen-Kha personally murdered. That started the desertion of Pe. I do not know what happened here after that."

Menhes called Naan to him, "Naan, I want to take one of the boats down the river a short distance. Get the warriors back on board and I will want three of the other boats, complete with troops to accompany me. They can follow; Per-Qad will lead us to where we are going." As Per-Qad began to wade out to the boat Menhes saw Fyd, "Who might this be, Per-Qad?" "Menhes, this is Fyd. Fyd, this is the king of all Nile. Fyd is a Sumerian of the Hathuruk tribe who goes everywhere the wizard from Uruk goes and acts as a servant, guard and hunter for him."

As the boat beached below Urba's house Per-Qad jumped into the water and rushed up the bank to prevent Urba from running away. The sight of such a force of warriors would be enough to frighten anyone and all the more with what had been happening in Pe. Menhes walked ashore and strode up to Urba, "Are you Urba?" "Yes, my Lord, I am Urba." "I am Menhes, king of Nile. I have heard of what you have done for our friends and for Qettrah. I am prepared to reward you, but first tell me, are there other generals like yourself who were loyal to Hor-Amen?"

"Yes, my Lord. There is Thuyi who lives near here and there are three or four others I could locate if you have need of them." "I may well need them, Urba. Where is Qettrah? I wish to see her." At that Qettrah appeared with Ekhana just behind her, "Who calls my name? Urba, who is this man?" "Queen Qettrah, this is Menhes, King of Upper and Lower Nile and now our lord and master." Qettrah looked straight into Menhes' eyes, "Then my son is dead." Menhes answered softly, "Yes, madam, he died in battle. I am sorry to have to tell you that but you need not fear me. I wish you no harm. My father, Menku respected your husband and I will see that you are provided for and can live peacefully and respectably."

"It is as well I suppose. Amen-Kha was a bad son, my Lord. I knew he would come to a bad end but I never thought he would hurt so many people as he did. Still he was my son. Let me have a time to grieve for him as I did for his father." "It will be as you wish, Madam."

Urba called Ekhana and Miqel over to meet Menhes, "My Lord, this is the Sumerian wizard, Miqel and his wife, Ekhana. They have lived with me for several weeks and been a great help to me after Amen-Kha conscripted all my herdsmen." Miqel raised his right hand and spoke, "My Lord is the son of Menku. He was the one who sent Hev-Ri to Kish and Uruk. That is where I

205

leasrned of him and it is to his academy that I desire to go with my wife and Fyd."

"My father would be glad, Miqel. And I will be happy to send you there as soon as I can get things in order here at Pe. I wish to talk to you later on about what you do. I am not a wizard but I was trained at the academy and am familiar with the constructions. I am sure Hev-Ri will welcome you at Asyut. And my mother will be delighted to have one so young as your wife to mother. Ekhana, you will have to watch Hetti. She will smother you I fear." Ekhana blushed and laughed at the thought, "Thank you, my Lord. I look forward to meeting her."

Menhes then turned to Urba, "I want you to come back to Pe with me. Naan will bring the others up when they are ready. We must set up a government here and I want order before my brother, Ekhdur arrives. I will furnish whatever guards you need though I doubt you will need many. I have released the survivors of the slaughter at Gemset... you will be told about that later...and stragglers should already be reaching Pe by now. Some of them fought very well but as for the boys from the farms, send the poor devils home. They were not meant to be warriors and I have been told how badly the herds and farms need tending."

Per-Qad asked to speak to Menhes before he went back to Pe and Menhes stepped aside with him, "What is it, Per-Qad?" "Menhes, now that you are king of Lower Nile I think one of the first questions that will come into the minds of almost everybody down here will be, 'Will the new king make us put away the worship of Amen?'. They do not know any other god here and Amen-Kha forced the senior priests to go out into the villages and exact pledges of loyalty to Amen, using you as a threat. He told everyone that you were going to attack Lower Nile and install Aten as their god."

"I have never given that a thought and certainly do not intend to do it, Per-Qad. Still I can understand such concerns. I do hope that Hev-Ri along with the senior priests of Upper Nile can convert people to the worship of Aten but I do not think this is the time to even mention such a thing. These people will be distraught when they discover the extent of the catastrophe Amen-Kha has brought upon them." "I saw no priests at Pe today and we have Badjut with us. The people have no leaders from among themselves other than the ones you appoint, just as you have been discussing with Urba.

"Badjut was much relied upon by Om-Diph in the weeks before he died. We have come to trust him as much as we do Urba...entrusting him with our lives...and he has been selfless in his devotion to Qettrah. Would he not be a good choice for Chief Priest, even on an acting basis while all these changes are put into effect? I am quite sure a Chief Priest will be a necessity in Pe. Om-Diph was almost as powerful as Hor-Amen, by Hor-Amen's own choice." Menhes agreed to talk to Badjut about it and called, "Badjut, you come with Urba and me."

As they got into the boat Menhes asked, "Where do you think this Thuyi is today, Urba?" "Not more than a few moments from where we are in your boat." "If you were to choose someone to share in the authority at Pe would it be Thuyi?" "My Lord, Thuyi is my friend just as he was one of Hor-Amen's closest friends and advisers. I could choose no better man." Menhes spoke to Naan, "Head down the river to where Urba tells you to turn in. I want Thuyi to go to Pe with us today. Urba, you must convince him to come with us; we will not harm him. He can find out what has gone on here on the way back up the river to Pe."

Ekhana told Miqel, "When we get to Pe I am going to take Fyd and go to Qettrah's house. Do you think the king will give us a few guards for her until we are sure she will be safe there? After what Amen-Kha has done to these people who knows what some of them may do for revenge." "I think he will, Ekhana and I am glad you thought of it. I do not expect we will be at Pe many days before Menhes sends us on to Asyut."

What was left of Lower Nile's ragtag army began drifting into Pe late that afternoon. Some, seeing the long boats ran for the wooded areas; others put their hands on their heads and silently kneeled in submission expecting to be killed. Urba told them to get up and line up in the temple yard. He assured the warriors he knew that the Upper Nile troops were not going to kill them and sent them off to round up the rest of the stragglers.

Thuyi was still too confused to say anything so it was left to Urba to address them, "Warriors of Lower Nile you and I have a new king. His name is Menhes and he is now king of all Nile. What has happened to our army is over and done with. We cannot bring back the dead and we must now begin to rebuild our nation, returning to our peaceful ways of years gone by. If we will do that we have no cause for fear; Thuyi and I can assure you of that. The lands and our herds and flocks need all our efforts and our families need reassuring that the glory of Lower Nile will be no less than it was before. Amen is still in the heavens and I think and hope that we will know his blessings, just as I am sure Hapi will continue to provide our living. Go to your homes."

"That was well done, Urba. You and Thuyi must select warriors you can trust and establish law and order throughout the provinces. I will not tolerate vengeful mobs or thieves turning to looting and killing. You will need others of the generals you mentioned to me to help you. I leave it to you to find them and bring them here to me so I can authorize them before I leave. I intend to be here for no more than a week, less than that if my brother arrives sooner."

With that Menhes turned to Badjut, "I would imagine the temple is a foul mess, Badjut, if the yard is any indication. I do not intend to enter your temple at this time; perhaps at some time in the future you will invite me there but not now. All these men are watching everything I am doing to see if what Amen-Kha said was true. I intend for him to remain the liar that brought him to his death. There will be no remembrance of him here, none! His head hangs as an example of his treachery at Meidum, but for Pe I want him forgotten.

"For now you will be Chief Priest with whatever temporal authority Urba and Thuyi choose to give you, and I urge them to be generous to the temple. You must rebuild some sort of academy for training scribes and drawing scribes. As for your priestly duties I leave that to you. There will be no ceremony to elevate you to the Chief Priesthood until you have proved yourself to Urba and to my brother, Ekhdur who will be governor of Lower Nile in a few days." "My, Lord, I am grateful to you and will do all I can to build a temple service that the people can be proud of and have faith in. Right now I do not know how many, if any of the senior priests escaped the massacre. I am sure there are some younger priests who, as I were able to elude the guards and I will search for them and start over here at Pe. I am going to need help from Urba and Thuyi and I will help them in any way I can."

"Another thing, Badjut. I will hold you responsible for the safety and well being of Qettrah. My queen's name is MeriLyth and I have a son who is named, Ki. Nevertheless Qettrah is to be treated with the same respect and consideration she received before Amen-Kha became mad. I will hold you accountable for that. You will swear to me by your god, Amen. I have spoken." "I so swear, my Lord. It will be done as you have spoken."

While all this was going on, Miqel and Fyd had gone down to the river and caught enough fish to make a meal for Thuyi and all of those who had been at Urba's house. Fyd immediately set about cooking them and brought them to Menhes, "King needs to eat now. King must not go hungry." Menhes laughed, "Fyd, I think I am going to like having you around. Urba, our warriors will share what they have with those of your troops left in the yard. Let's eat."

The next morning Menhes called Naan over and told him, "I want you to take a boat and get over to Saqqut. Tell the elders there that all has changed at Pe and they are welcome to return to trading here. I will rely on them to get the message up the coast to places like Edhemet where our boats used to go. It is going to be necessary for these people to have an outlet for their goods before they can provide enough barter stuff to trade effectively with Upper Nile and with the boats from Crete that will be coming in here next year. Our crafts people at Edfu turn out more articles than we need in Upper Nile and we are going to have a lot of cattle left over at Rafiza and Crocodile Lake that I do not want to take back up the river. There will plentiful leather goods to barter at Meidum."

Miqel approached Menhes, "My Lord, may I make a request?" "You may." Per-Qad has told me of a rocky plain not far north of here and I would like to visit it before we set out for Upper Nile." "I will furnish a boat for you, Miqel. It is not far at all. What is important to you about the Gidjeh plain?" "In Sumer our wizards have searched for many years for a large, flat area to build a henge to carry out some research into the circle and the square enigma. I was working on this when war broke out between Kish and Mari, that was just before we left to come here. It may be that Hev-Ri and I can come up with something my Lord would find interesting as a proposal. For now I just want to see this plain."

Early the next day Miqel took Per-Qad and Fyd and left for Gidjeh. When they walked out on the vast area Miqel could scarcely believe what his eyes revealed. "Isn't it odd, Per-Qad that our ancestors all turned to the north side of the sea searching for a place to build their henges when this nearly perfect place lay within easy travel from the mouth of the Orontes. It appears they just made a wrong decision as to which way to turn; and after I would guess a thousand years no one seems to have ever come here from there." "That is odd, Miqel. Is it your thought that the pyramid you talk about might be built here some day?" "I would think so, Per-Qad. This is all I wanted to see. Let's go back to Pe."

Naan's visit to Saqqut was at first greeted with suspicion bordering on derision. But his quiet persistence eventually won the confidence of the elders and he closed his case with a reference to his friendship with Agga. Agga had told one of the elders about this friend of his at Meidum who made his trips profitable and when he found out that Naan was that friend he talked the others into giving Pe one more trial. If it worked out well they would gain from it. If not they stood to lose little they had not already lost. Naan sailed back to Pe, arriving there three days later.

Pe began to be repopulated, slowly at first but by the end of five days things took on a near normal appearance, normal as compared to the days before Amen-Kha brought so many young men there to make up his army. Ekhdur and Ar-Chab's boat arrived and Menhes went down to meet them, "Welcome to the newest part of the kingdom. Where is Khafu, Ekhdur? I wanted him to come with you."

"Khafu is gravely ill, Menhes. The right side of his body is paralyzed and he suffers fainting spells. He scarcely eats anything and Hetti is very disturbed about him, as are we all. I do not know that he is going to get any better, but then he might pull out of this. Khafu is a strong man and he wants to live." "When did this illness come on, Ekhdur? He was fine when I came down the river from Asyut two weeks ago." "He lost consciousness early one morning right after you left. When we aroused him he could not move his right leg. By nightfall he could not feel anything on his right side and he lapsed back into unconsciousness again."

Menhes brought Ekhdur and Ar-Chab to the temple yard where Urba and Thuyi were and introduced them, "These are my brother, Ekhdur and the father of my wife, Ar-Chab. Urba and Thuyi are in authority over the Lower Nile guardsmen to keep order here and in the provinces." After they were acquainted he took Ekhdur and Ar-Chab aside, Ekhdur, I would like for you to be the governor of Lower Nile. Are you willing?"

"You know I am willing to do anything you ask, Menhes. But I think I am going to be needed in Upper Nile now that Khafu is unable to help there, even if he lives. Ar-Chab would be better suited to the job anyway, for one thing he is younger than I am. I think you sometimes forget how much older Khafu and I are than you." Ar-Chab interrupted, "While I agree with your need for Ekhdur in Upper Nile I question his worries about his age, Menhes. Ekhdur is as strong as I have ever been and I am only a few years younger than he is. However if you want me to govern Lower Nile I will accept the responsibility for as long as you think it is necessary."

Menhes seemed lost in thought. At last he spoke, "In so few years so much has changed. The time when I went to Nubia to make an alliance with Addi-Hoda was not so long ago, but with the fury of the events that have transpired since then it seems like only a few moons have passed. I know you are right, Ekhdur. Forgive me for not taking all these things into account. Of course you will be governor, Ar-Chab. And I trust you will find Urba and Thuyi able and loyal to you. I will tell you more about them later today after I meet with the other four generals who served Hor-Amen before they were deposed by Amen-Kha. There is so much to tell you both."

The three of them talked long after the moon had set. "Ar-Chab, Ekhdur and I will leave for Asyut at first light. I think you understand our fears for our brother. There is one last matter I must attend to before we go. Ekhdur, Per-Qad has returned...Ar-Chab may have told you about it...and he has brought a man he considers to be the greatest wizard in Sumer and Akkad with him, along with his wife. I want Naan to bring them to Asyut where I will introduce them to Hev-Ri. And I want their servant and guard, a man named, Fyd to accompany them. You may have to steal him away from Urba who hunts with him and will hate to see him leave Pe. They can come up there when they are ready but I think the sooner they can get to Asyut the better it will be for them and for the work this young wizard is doing."

After Menhes and Ekhdur had left Ar-Chab called Naan to the yard and relayed Menhes instructions to him, "When you get back from Asyut I want you to help me get things settled down in Meidum and Gemset. You can live at Crocodile Lake and run the station there, Naan. But I want you to spend enough time at Meidum to get trading back up to the old standards there. Now, get down to Urba's place and see how soon Per-Qad and his party can reasonably be ready to depart for Asyut."

Urba was fishing with Fyd, planning to take the catch to Ar-Chab when Naan's crew dragged his boat up on the bank. "Any luck, Urba?" "With Fyd I always have luck, Naan. I think he knows how to talk to the fish." Naan and Fyd had a good laugh and Urba asked, "What brings you down here, Naan?" Naan told him that Menhes and Ekhdur had left for Asyut and Ar-Chab had sent him to make arrangements to take Per-Qad and Miqel, Ekhana and Fyd there.

Urba smiled, "I suppose I knew this would not last. They have been good company; are you sure they will be needing Fyd up there? I can give him a good home here." Naan laughed again, "Ar-Chab told me you wouldn't want to let Fyd go. No, Urba, this is the king's orders and besides you know Fyd is devoted to Miqel. By the way, what do you call him? I understood he was named for the black ibis but I keep hearing him called, Miqel. Which is right?

"Both are right, really. Gem was a Nile name he assumed to keep us from thinking he was a foreigner, Per-Qad put him up to it. He never liked the deception...didn't mind the name...and when he got to know me he told me the truth: he is a Sumerian wizard. I already knew he had not made his living as a shepherd. I like him and his wife. She is a very bright young woman and I think she can outhunt me three days out of five."

Per-Qad saw them walking up from the river and called Miqel and Ekhana to join them. "What is going on at Pe, Naan?" Naan told them of Menhes instructions and asked, "When do you think you can be ready to leave for Asyut?" Miqel spoke up, "If Urba can get along without Fyd we can leave today. I do think there are enough herdsmen around now that you don't need us so much, Urba. I realize I am not much of a shepherd and I don't think Per-Qad is the finest cattleman you have ever had either. Still, we have enjoyed our stay here and we certainly have benefited from your trust in us and the protection of this sanctuary."

Ekhana looked at Urba with a sly smile, "Urba, we have few possessions but what we have we would like to give you. Our goat has been invaluable to us and she is a good one. We want you to have her. You may call her what you will but I have named her, 'Perfydy'. I think the name is obvious and it seems to fit her." Fyd grinned but Per-Qad did not think it was very funny, particularly when Urba insisted that every time he called the goat he would think of Per-Qad.

Ekhana came to his rescue, "We are teasing poor Per-Qad. But we do want you to have the goat, Urba, and you are welcome to our tent and the crocodile hides we have dragged all over the country. They should make good shields for your guards, don't you think?" Urba put his arm around Ekhana's shoulders, "The very best, Ekhana and I thank you for them. I hope you and Miqel...and Fyd...will come back to Pe. And when you do, come stay with me."

Urba rode with them as Naan turned the boat toward Pe-Diph landing. They stopped only long enough to find if Ar-Chab had any messages for Asyut and then sailed on up the Nile."I will put in for the night at Meidum, Per-Qad. I want to see my family and be sure things are all right with them before we leave. Furthermore I will be glad to get a good hot meal before we head out toward Asyut. It will take us two, maybe three days sailing to get there. This breeze may hold but I don't count on it this time of year."

The situation was uneasy at Meidum, nothing alarming, just a general feeling of confusion seemed to prevail. Naan talked to the elders and told them he would be back to carry out Menhes' orders, that they had nothing to fear. With the troops leaving so soon after the battle nothing had had time to settle down there. Naan ordered the head of Amen-Kha taken off its pike and thrown into the river to remove the last threatening reminder of what could have happened to Meidum and its people.

After a comfortable night Naan roused the Pe sojourners before first light and they all headed down to the boat and turned upriver to what at last would be a permanent home. Ekhana wondered how the daughter of a prince of Uruk would be received.

'NBTY', THE STANDARD OF KEMET

The Cobra and Vulture from the Great Pyramid, Khufu in Giza.

Illustrated by W. C. Cawthon

Figure 15: NBTY, Combined Egypt

211

CHAPTER TWENTYTWO   'Speech of the Gods'

It was late in the morning of the third day when Naan's boat arrived at Asyut. The captain of the guards at the landing welcomed the party, "Asyut and all Upper Nile is in mourning for Prince Khafu, Naan. He died yesterday before sunrise and his body was placed on a pyre on a funeral barge last night. The period of mourning will be for six more days.

"I am to take care of your party during that time and already have a house set up for them. You of course are free to stay where you will. Do not try to see the family unless they call you; they desire to be alone. Queen MeriLyth is here with Ki and they are with Menhes at the king's compound." Naan wondered if a boat had been sent to inform Ar-Chab and was told one had left early the day before to sail without stopping until it reached Pe. "They probably passed you during the night, Naan. They would stop only to eat, spelling each other at the tiller the rest of the way."

Per-Qad knew the captain, a man named, Ahnpy from his days at the academy. He introduced Miqel, Ekhana and Fyd to him and asked if he might try to find out if any of his family had survived the massacre. Ahnpy answered, "Of course Per-Qad. I do not know but Hev-Ri is waiting to see you and he can tell you what he has found. Why don't you go on over to the academy and talk to him; I will take the rest of your party to their temporary home."

When Per-Qad reached the academy Hev-Ri was with Seb Seshat and some new scribe-trainees. When he heard that Per-Qad had come he rushed over and greeted him, "Per-Qad, I am so glad to see you, to see with my eyes that you are alive and well. I had hoped, and continued to believe that somehow you would escape but as time went by I began to doubt it. I know some of the story...I was sitting with Khafu when Menhes and Ekhdur arrived; and later Menhes told me he had seen you and that you were coming home.

"Per-Qad, it grieves me greatly to have to tell you that, like most of us your family did not escape the massacre here. Just as is the case for most of my own family I do not know how they died, I can only hope that it was quick and they did not suffer. I wish I could take the awful sting out of it but I can't." "I think I knew, Hev-Ri. It was like having a spear thrust into my heart when I first heard of it but when no one from up here said anything more I had to assume that my family perished with the others. I am prepared to accept that. I am sorry it came as your lot to be the one to confirm it though. I wish you could have been spared that. Do I still have a room to go to, Hev-Ri? I would like to be alone for a little while. We can talk tomorrow." "Your old apartment is ready for you, Per-Qad; it has been kept that way."

Ahnpy took Miqel, Ekhana and Fyd to a walled compound near the academy and showed Miqel and Ekhana to their apartment in the main house. Fyd would have his own room in the guards' house. Fyd, who had never lived in a room in his life found a bed and chair and a low table waiting for his use. He rushed to get Miqel and show it to him, "Miqel, Ahnpy make mistake. This a priest's room. Fyd is not a priest. Fyd will go stay outside." "No, Fyd, you are a guard and must stay here near us. This is Nile and this is your own room. You will get used to it and I hope you come to like it here." Fyd beamed, "Fyd have a room. Fyd is going to like that."

There was little for Miqel and Ekhana to do except tour the academy and its facilities which were so rich compared to anything he had seen in Sumer he could scarcely believe what he saw. The actual work stations were about equal to the White Temple but the quarters and work rooms were light and well ventilated, in no way the simple cells of Kish and Uruk.

Vukhath saw them and rushed over to introduce himself, "I am Vukhath. Hev-Ri and

Shephset and I visited Kish and Uruk. I am sorry I did not get to meet you then but we are all glad you are here now. We are thankful to Per-Qad for bringing you with him; it would have pleased Menku and I am sure you will find this a good place to continue your studies." "I am Miqel and this is my wife, Ekhana, Vukhath. Per-Qad has spoken to us of you and we are glad to be here. You met Ekhana's father I think. He is Kalam-Bad, Prince of Uruk." "Yes, of course. He and his guards were most helpful and reassuring when we were there. Is there anything you especially want to see before I take you to Hev-Ri?"

Miqel hesitated, "Vukhath, I would like to meet the man, Seb Seshat. I have heard so much about him I would like to see him." "That is easy. He is right down this corridor. Be prepared though, he does not talk much, not even to those he has always known." Just then Fyd caught up with them and Miqel introduced him and asked if he could join them. "Surely. Fyd, you can come with us."

They found Seb who looked up and smiled. Vukhath told Seb, "Seb, I want you to know Miqel and Ekhana and this is Fyd who came with them." Seb said nothing. He stared intently at Fyd, and Fyd stared equally intently at him. Neither knew exactly what sort of man the other was and neither felt very easy about it. Miqel spoke, "Seb, Per-Qad has told us about you and your work and the long years you have been at the academy. Fyd belongs to the Hathuruk nation in Uruk. His tribe is in the king's service there. He is our guard and also hunts and fishes with us."

Seb nodded and addressed Fyd, "Do you hunt much, Fyd?" "Fyd hunts a lot. Fyd likes to hunt. Fyd likes to fish. Seb like to hunt? Seb like to fish?" "Yes, I do. I hope we can hunt together. I know the country around here well and will be your guide if you will join me." "Fyd would like that. Fyd and Seb will hunt. Fyd and Seb will fish. Take game, fish to king maybe. King likes fish." "Then you know Menhes?" "King come to Pe. Fyd cook fish. Give fish to king. King liked fish." "Fyd, I think we are going to be great friends." At last he spoke to Miqel, "Master, I am your servant. Anything I can do to help you I will do."

Vukhath laughed as they left Seb, "Fyd, I do not think Seb talked that much to his prince in Nubia. You will find he is a good friend to have here." "Fyd likes Seb." Taking Ekhana by the arm he smiled, "I fear you will find all this rather boring, Ekhana but we are most happy you have come. When mourning is over Hetti will welcome you personally. She has been looking forward to your arrival since Menhes told her about you." "My lord, the king told me about her. I want so much to meet her. But I am fascinated with the things you do here. Miqel was allowed to take me with him when he was shown the temples in Sumer...I do not know so much about the constructions as he does...but he explained a lot of it to me."

"What do you like to do, Ekhana?" "I have taken up weaving and was given instruction in the new ways of weaving at Kish. Do you have looms here in Asyut?" Vukhath raised his eyebrows, "Do you know the patterns they have developed at Kish? I saw some of them when I was there and wished I could have brought some of them back to show Hetti. She is an expert weaver and has her own looms." "I know a good many of them, Vukhath and I think I can produce others that I saw there."

They reached Hev-Ri's apartment and he rushed out to meet them. After they were introduced he said, "I have been over to your house looking for you, Miqel. I did not know you were at the academy. Has Vukhath shown you our place?" "He has indeed, Master." Vukhath informed Hev-Ri of their meeting with Seb and Hev-Ri laughed, "I marvel at that, Fyd. I am so glad you came too." "Fyd likes Seb. Fyd likes room. Fyd is going to like Asyut."

"Tell me, Miqel, what did you and Kmal-Dyl decide to do about the square and the circle and a system of writing when you were with him in Kish?" "Master, that is a long story and I would like to discuss it with you when Per-Qad is with us, if you are willing to wait. By the way, do you know where Per-Qad is?" "I had to tell him that he had lost his entire family, Miqel. He wanted to be alone for awhile and has gone to his apartment. He and I will meet in the morning and it would be good to have you join us, particularly since I think you are involved in most of his story of what has transpired since I last saw him. Can you tell me one thing? How did you two get together?"

Miqel told him of the henge expedition and the coincidental escape of Per-Qad. He also told him how Per-Qad had unwittingly identified Davri/Ifn-Lot at Kish. "Master, I am telling you this for it is a terrible burden Per-Qad carries. He feels he was responsible for Davri's murder. He knows as well as we do that there was no way he could have known: Davri was the only name he had ever heard him called; Per-Qad's life was threatened by Thar-Mes who thought he might be another Mari spy. Davri stepped forward to save Per-Qad and Per-Qad, in surprise spoke his name. I think it would be better if we do not go back over that with him. He has suffered enough." "Thank you, Miqel. Let's talk in the morning."

Miqel walked over to Per-Qad's apartment early the next morning and found him sitting outside alone watching the sun come into full view over the trees across the Nile. "The memories are hard for you aren't they, Per-Qad?" "Yes, they are, Miqel. My oldest son would have been your age now and my wife of twenty years was a good mother and a loving woman. I will never know how they died, I think I do not want to know and I do not want to know who killed them. I must get back to work and put this horrible massacre out of my mind."

"You can help me, Per-Qad." "Miqel, what can I bring to your work? I am just an estimator, using the fractional construction for quickly determining the rough areas of lands for people who need to know. I have not explored the far reaches of the enigmas that fill your mind and I doubt that I would know what I had found if I did learn the answers to such questions as those that arise when we try to plumb the depths of the the square and the circle."

"I think you underestimate your gifts, Per-Qad but these are not the things that I need now. I am almost through with matching the 'Sacred Circle' construction with the ciphers that I want to use for the twenty-two steps. I can change them of course and have already changed some of them to fit new sounds of Nile words that describe them which I have learned since coming to Nile. The more I learn the more difficult it becomes to find the places for the sounds we can utter so that I can account for all the consonants and at the same time deal with the vowels in a way that will have meaning to those who read what is written when they are far away in either distance or time from the writer.

"You have helped me, perhaps without knowing it to place the buh and guh and tuh sounds in the order. I need someone who understands what I am doing who will listen while I try to put my thoughts in order. I think if we keep going over the steps together you will begin to recognize and picture in your mind something that will define a single sound, and that also looks enough like the images that seem to jump out at you from the construction diagram at the points in the ordered steps." "I can do that, Miqel. We can get the construction down on smooth stone. Slate is plentiful here and soft enough to scribe lines on."

"It is time to get over to Hev-Ri's place now, Per-Qad. I talked to him briefly yesterday and I think we can fill him in enough on what has happened to satisfy him for now. He will want to know more as time goes on but we need to have him understand at least the basic elements of the events that have shaped your life and mine during the past several months."

Hev-Ri was in good spirits, "This is a beautiful morning, isn't it? I hope you both slept well; my mind is racing with questions that require slower answers. Per-Qad, Miqel has brought me up to date on how you met each other, but I am not clear at all on what the henge expedition was for. Perhaps we could start there. You and I can talk about your long captivity by the Mari gangs at some later time. I want to know all about it and about the war between Kish and Mari but that can wait."

"As you wish, Hev-Ri. I think Miqel will have to tell you about the henge. I know very little about it." Miqel went into enough detail for Hev-Ri to understand the relation of the henge and the pyramid he envisioned. "That is not my real purpose for coming to Asyut however, Hev-Ri. I do think the henge and pyramid could be built on the Gidjeh plain northwest of Pe but that is a long, long way off and I fear too big a project to propose now. I came here to to complete my work on a system of writing that I have been studying."

"Did you discuss this with Kmal-Dyl, Miqel?" "Yes, I did." "Was this just before you left Sumer to come here?" "Not long before, Hev-Ri." "Miqel, you seem to not want to talk about meeting with Kmal-Dyl. Is there something wrong?" "Not so much wrong as painful, Hev-Ri. Ifn-Lot...Davri...was my mentor and he took me to see Kmal-Dyl. We listened to what he had to say about what he was working on and then he asked me to explain my approaches to the square and the circle and to the invention of a system of writing.

"At the end of our meeting he required us to swear we would never reveal what he was doing, which we did of course. Then he told me he would not allow me to work with him on my own studies. I fully understand his reasons but it was devastating to me. I am young and have never been completely on my own before, there have always been experienced and knowledgeable wizards to guide me. "I think Kmal-Dyl will succeed in what he is doing and that it will be of great importance. He thinks I will succeed in what I am doing and that it will be of great importance. He just feels that if I have him to fall back on I will never complete the work I have set out to do. He is probably right in that but it stings all the same to have the greatest known wizard to tell you he will never see you again."

"I must admit I do not understand what you are talking about, Miqel. This writing you mention, it has been sought for long before anyone can recall. Do you really think you have solved the problems related to communicating with written or engraved symbols?" "Not completely, Hev-Ri. But I am close enough to believe I will have a fully usable system within a year, possibly much less than that. It should be relatively easy to remember and the symbols, or ciphers if you prefer will be simple enough to duplicate and clearly indicate the sounds of speech so that someone reading them will speak the same sounds as the person who formed the ciphers." "What do you want from us, Miqel?"

"That is a question I can answer easily in one sense: I wanted the freedom to create in an environment such as your academy and still be able to have a wife and live away from a temple or academy. That is not possible in Sumer for only priests are allowed to be provided for by the temple service. One would starve otherwise. However that is not the only thing I wanted here. Although I am aware that he is dead now I believed that your master, Menku would see to it that the writing system I hope to develop here is used and adhered to. It is based on the Sacred Circle construction and I was told that he believed in that and the Sumer Consensus relating to it."

"I think Menhes will see to the last part of your wishes, Miqel. As for Ekhana we are even more pleased that she entered into your decision to come here. We aim to insure that she is glad she did and that you are too. What else?" "I think after all the excitement we have been through in the last several weeks I could use a quiet time alone with Ekhana at the apartment you have furnished us. I would like to take the remaining days of mourning and think these things through. I can use a square and scribe's equipment. I left all mine in Uruk." He and Ekhana left and Per-

Qad remained to talk to Hev-Ri.

Per-Qad spoke first, "Hev-Ri, after you escaped I learned that Rabul had been killed in the melee at the boats. I am sorry; he was a good friend and a fine man". "Yes he was, Per-Qad. Fortunately he died instantly and in the confusion all we could do was leave his body. I suppose it would be too much to hope that the Mari gang buried him there". "No, Hev-Ri; they just dragged the body into the river and it sank".

When the period of mourning for Khafu ended Hev-Ri sent for Miqel and Ekhana. When they got there he told them, "I must take you to meet Hetti before she comes after you. She is a delightful woman, albeit a forceful one as I know all too well." He laughed and continued, "She is most beloved and gives more love than she receives if that were possible. You will see. You will see."

Hetti greeted Miqel and called Ekhana over to be hugged, "Do you miss your mother, child? What is her name?" "Methwyd, Madam Hetti." "Oh, what a lovely name, almost as beautiful as Ekhana I think. And you must call me, Hetti," she laughed, "and why not? Everyone else does. Miqel, you and Hev-Ri will be talking things I do not understand, even Menku could not explain them to me. Why don't you leave this charming young woman with me? Ekhana, Vukhath says you weave and know methods and patterns from Sumer we have never seen. You must teach me these things. Have you ever woven with flax?" "No, I haven't. But I have seen some of the cloth since we came to Nile. It must be much cooler than wool." "Much, child. Much."

As they talked MeriLyth walked in with Ki. Hetti held out her arms and Ki, giggling, "Etti, Etti," climbed into her lap. "MeriLyth this is Ekhana. She is the wife of this great wizard Per-Qad has brought us from Sumer. Ekhana, MeriLyth is the queen." Ekhana immediately fell to her knees and MeriLyth laughed, "Oh please, Ekhana, get up. Here I am only the mother of Ki. Menhes told me about you and your husband...I must meet him too...and I cannot begin to tell you how much it means to him that you are here. His father had dreamed of this."

Hetti's compound was a marvelous place to Miqel and Ekhana. They had never seen anything like it, even around Pe. It was brick and surrounded by a low brick wall and there was a garden for the kitchen which itself was separated from the main house. Animals were kept in pens, which like the kitchen were downwind from the house. Servants and guards lived in their own quarters by the back wall, convenient to the house, garden, pens and kitchen. And a neat walk led to a small covered shrine to Aten. The house was roomy and oriented to catch the breeze and seemed grander than the temples of Sumer, certainly it was more comfortable.

Miqel and Hev-Ri went on back to the academy where Per-Qad was with Seb. Per-Qad called them over and said, "Miqel, look at what Seb is doing with this piece of slate." Seb had already scribed the basic diagram for the Sacred Circle construction and wiped the slate with chalk to make the lines easier to follow. It was so much superior to working with the smooth sand Miqel was used to that he was startled for a moment. "Seb, that is beautiful. Look, Per-Qad, there is the 'eye'."

He was pointing to the part of the diagram that was the basis for the beginning of Kmal-Dyl's little training mnemonic about the eye that was stolen and broken in pieces to make the fractions. In Upper Nile this had become a legend, the story of the wicked god, Zeti who stole the eye of Horus. "We call the eye, 'Oudjet', Miqel," Hev-Ri told him. "'Oozyet'?" "Yes, they say it is the mythical right eye of our hawk-god, Horus." "'Ahrus'?" "That is right. His left eye is the one that is sacred. It is right down here; see the Sacred Circle. That is the pupil of Horus' left eye."

Miqel thought for a moment and exclaimed, "Per-Qad, this is what I was talking about!" Per-Qad was confused, "What, Miqel?" "'Oozyet'! That contains the 'oo', 'dj', 'eh' and 'th' sounds, all in one word. Do you see the cobra that carries the little viper's head on its back?" "No,

I don't, Miqel." "Here." and Miqel took the stylus and sketched in a small asp with horns. "You mean, 'Uph', Miqel." "Is that what it is called?" "Uph is a horned viper in Nile." "Then it comes after 'U'," then he sketched in a quail chick he had previously decided would be one of his ciphers.

"That makes up sounds for more of the steps and I already have the ciphers for them. And look down here." He pointed to a pointed ellipse that looked like a mouth, "That is where you say the left eye of Horus is, isn't it?" Hev-Ri said, "Well, yes, if you are talking about the god. Actually the hawk is 'horu'." "'ur'? 'ruh'? That's the ruh sound, it will be step twenty. And it is followed by the pool of water: that will be 's'. See, 'ahr-hes', Horus. Six new sounds assigned to ciphers in just these few moments. This is wonderful, Hev-Ri. Seb, I thank you." Seb smiled and nodded, then without a word went back to scribing in the sketches Miqel had made.

Menhes called for Hev-Ri to bring Miqel to his house next to Hetti's place. "I am sorry you and Ekhana had to arrive during the mourning for Khafu, Miqel. But I hear you have made acquaintances at the academy during that time. I hope you have not lost a wife in the process. Hetti will move her in with her if you don't watch out." He and Hev-Ri laughed, then Menhes spoke to Hev-Ri, "Before we get into anything else, Hev-Ri, I want Seb to design a new standard for the combined kingdom of Nile.

"I envision it as combining the Upper and Lower Nile standards with Nekhbet and Wadjet side by side on their nests. And I think we should have the sun and the wings of Horus at the top. I want to reassure the people of Lower Nile that they are equals in the kingdom but I will not promote the worship of Amen. I won't proscribe it but I will not promote it either." Hev-Ri smiled, "Nebuty?" Menhes grinned, "Of course, the two ladies. Nebuty it is."

Menhes leaned back in his chair, an elegantly simple masterpiece of acacia wood overlaid with gold and lapis, "Now Miqel, tell me about your work. I am especially interested in the system of writing you are developing. How far have you progressed?" Miqel glanced at Hev-Ri, "My Lord, as Hev-Ri knows, a lot farther as of today. With Seb's drawing and Hev-Ri's descriptions I found six more of the ciphers I will use just this morning. This has narrowed the number of missing characters to so few that I think the complete system will be ready for testing within weeks, perhaps even days. The language of Nile is so sound oriented it is almost as if the gods had given it for the purpose of being written."

"That is amazing, Miqel! I think we will test it as soon as you tell me it is time. I want the first writing ever done to record these last two wars we have just been through. Now we will be able to keep the count of time and tell the names of people who are involved in events to be remembered. You might even say that the story of mankind's being will begin that day." He reflected a moment and added, "It is like saying that people, as living, communicating, identifiable beings are as of that day created. Created by the word of God, Himself.

"Miqel, do what you have to do to complete this work, but do be as quick about it as you possibly can. I need to get back to Nekhen and I have a lot to talk to Ekhdur about before I go. Hev-Ri, spare nothing to insure that Miqel is not interfered with. Never has any invention been so important. This is truly awesome isn't it, as if the gods...or God, Himself...had visited us."

Miqel returned to his rooms and found that Ekhana was there. "I thought you were with Hetti, Ekhana." Ekhana laughed, "It was Ki's nap time and MeriLyth insisted that Hetti must take a nap too. She put up such a fuss MeriLyth finally had to get her to lie down with Ki so he would go to sleep and that worked. So I came home. Oh, Miqel, these are wonderful people. I love it here."

"I am so glad, Ekhana. I have to begin working day and night now. The king wants my work on writing finished before they leave for Nekhen, if of course I can do it. He understands that. That means I have days to wind it up. He wants the first test to be a record of the wars that combined Upper and Lower Nile into a single kingdom. It is what I've always wanted, that the king would order its usage. Yet I do not think I have given a thought to the time when this would be finished. The creation of it has been my whole purpose. It frightens me a little to think that that part is almost over. Now it is time to apply what I have only worked on up until now."

Menhes and Ekhdur went over to Hetti's to find that she and Ki were just rousing from their naps. MeriLyth whispered, "Ekhdur, I don't know how you are going to get Hetti to take her rest when Ki is not here." "With a fight every day, MeriLyth. Even Khafu battled with her over it. But she does eventually give up. I have to order the servants not to ever mention it to her and doctors to her are worse than thieves and charlatans."

Menhes looked out and saw Ahnpy and Fyd standing at the gateway. "Fyd, come here." Ahnpy told him it was all right to go in to where Menhes was. "Mother, this is Fyd, guardian of our wizard and your Ekhana and the greatest fisherman in Nile." Ahnpy explained that Fyd wanted to know if the king would like fish that evening. "Now, Ahnpy, you must not have ever eaten any of the fish Fyd cooks or you wouldn't be asking. Of course we would like your fish, Fyd. Mother, MeriLyth, you have a feast coming."

Hetti was astonished. "What is Fyd, Menhes? I have never seen anyone like him before." "He is a wild tribesman of Sumer the king of Uruk made guardian for Miqel and Ekhana for life. When I was a child one of the oldest wizards told of a legend of a race of people who once lived in the land far above the great sea, a place no one knows. These were brutally powerful men who hunted and lived off whatever they could find to eat. Nobody has ever seen one of them in Nile so it was just another of the fabulous stories that claim to have originated thousands of years ago. I have wondered since I first met Fyd if he might be one descended from those men. He is powerful enough but the gentlest creature you will ever come to know, Mother. And I do want you to know him. He absolutely adores Miqel and Ekhana." "I will tell you what I think after I have tasted the fish, Menhes."

Miqel and Per-Qad were watching the children climbing up a small hill near the academy, then running back down and tumbling head over heels into the soft sand. Per-Qad commented, "If that hill was any higher they could get hurt doing that." "What did you just call that hill, Per-Qad?" "Do you mean the 'kaa'? It is a word we still use sometimes, Miqel. I have no idea where it came from."

"That is it! That is the uhk sound I have been looking for. Come on. I want to get to the academy and put it on the slate." "That's good, Miqel but what is your hurry?" "That is the last cipher, Per-Qad. My 'ATHYAT' is finished." "That is wonderful, Miqel! Now tell me why you call it, 'athyat'?"

"You know the construction, Per-Qad. It progresses from step one through step nine based on the square root of three. From step nine through step twenty-two it is based on the square root of two. In my system that is 'A' to 'Th', then 'Y' to 'T', 'Athyat'. It is just a descriptive memory device for me."

"How do you write that?" "Just a tether and a loaf of bread, Per-Qad. That is all one needs to know what I just said, 'Th-T'. I will show it to you at the academy. Let's pick up Ekhana on the way. I want her to see it."

The following morning Miqel, accompanied by Hev-Ri, Per-Qad, Seb and Ekhana took his slate to Menhes. After studying it for a few moments Menhes was ecstatic. "You have done it!

Yes, I see how it all fits together now. Seb, make another slate. I want to take it with me. Miqel, show Hev-Ri his name. I want to talk to you about your name and mine, the way they are to be recorded so that others may know about what they have read."

Miqel drew a room and a quail, a mouth and two reed flowers and said, " There it is, Hev-Ri. that is your name. My Lord, Menhes, I thank you. Could we talk while Seb prepares your slate?" "Of course, Miqel. Let's go over to the house. I want MeriLyth to see this."

Menhes settled down in the shade of the trees by the garden and let Ki climb over him. "Miqel, you were called the black ibis at one time. I name you, 'Th-T.'" He sketched a tether and a loaf of bread in the sand. "That is who you are now, my great wizard. In our land you will be Tehuti, the sacred ibis.

"And I will be what my father used to call me when I was a little boy, 'Catfish'. Write my name with the picture of a catfish and put a chisel below it, the kind you would use to engrave these ciphers of yours in stone: the fish that writes. A thousand, five thousand years from now people will wonder what your name and mine mean. That will be our little joke I think. They will call me, 'Narmer', maybe 'Kingfish'." And he laughed.

"Seriously, there is the matter of the slate to record the wars, Miqel. You and Seb work that out and then bring it to me in Nekhen. I want my picture and my name engraved on both sides. And I want Seb's picture on both sides, standing behind me and half the size of mine with his title, 'Seb Seshat' above his head. On the front side show Scorpion as he is conquered. There will be no king of Lower Nile on the back side. He should be forgotten forever. I also want a picture of you, half the size of mine on the Lower Nile side. Your new name should be written above your head, 'Th-T'."

This was 'Thoth of Egypt'.

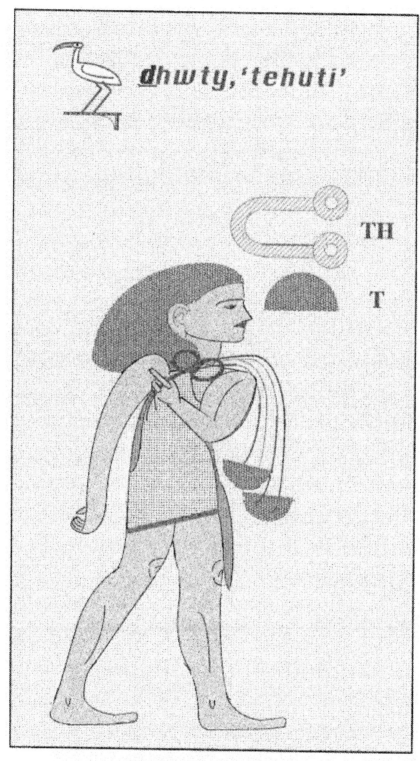

'Th-T', Thoth of Egypt

As portrayed on the Narmer Palette, c. 3,000 BC

Illustrated by W. C. Cawthon

Figure 16: Th-T

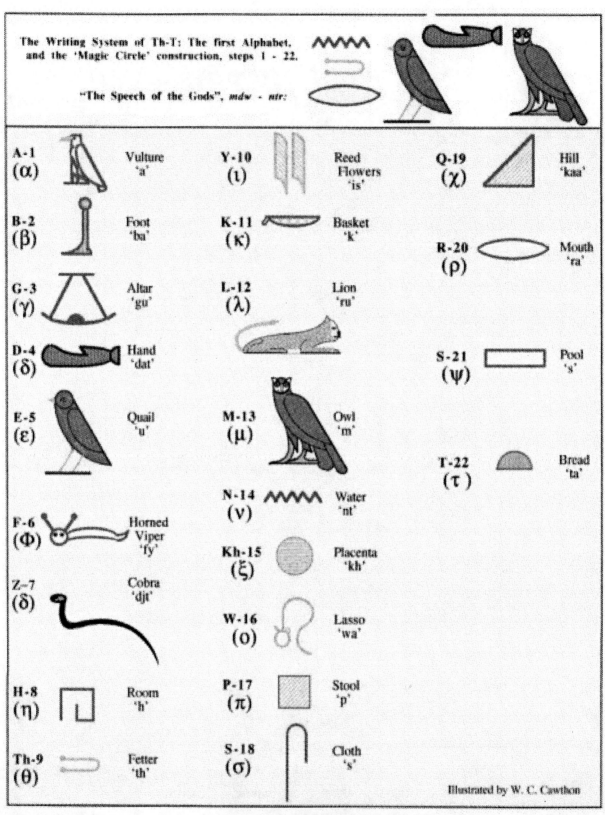

The Writing System of Th-T: The first Alphabet, and the 'Magic Circle' construction, steps 1 - 22.

"The Speech of the Gods", *mdw - ntr:*

A-1 (α)	Vulture 'a'	
B-2 (β)	Foot 'ba'	
G-3 (γ)	Altar 'gu'	
D-4 (δ)	Hand 'dat'	
E-5 (ε)	Quail 'u'	
F-6 (Φ)	Horned Viper 'fy'	
Z-7 (δ)	Cobra 'djt'	
H-8 (η)	Room 'h'	
Th-9 (θ)	Fetter 'th'	
Y-10 (ι)	Reed Flowers 'is'	
K-11 (κ)	Basket 'k'	
L-12 (λ)	Lion 'ru'	
M-13 (μ)	Owl 'm'	
N-14 (ν)	Water 'nt'	
Kh-15 (ξ)	Placenta 'kh'	
W-16 (O)	Lasso 'wa'	
P-17 (π)	Stool 'p'	
S-18 (σ)	Cloth 's'	
Q-19 (χ)	Hill 'kaa'	
R-20 (ρ)	Mouth 'ra'	
S-21 (ψ)	Pool 's'	
T-22 (τ)	Bread 'ta'	

Illustrated by W. C. Cawthon

Figure 17: Hieroglyphic Alphabet

Figure 18: Narmer Palette, Lower Nile Side

222

Acknowledgments

The following sources of information have been used extensively in the gathering of such facts as are known about this period in the ancient world before writing was invented. Although none are quoted directly each has in some way contributed to my research which has covered over twenty-seven years, beginning in 1971.

Clark, Adam, "The Holy Bible, A Commentary and Critical Notes".
   New York, Nashville: Abingdon-Cokesbury Press.
Diringer, David, "The Alphabet, a Key to the History of Mankind".
   London: Hutchinson, 1968.
Diringer, David, "A History of the Alphabet".
   London: Unwin Brothers Ltd., 1977.
Diringer, David, "Writing".
   New York: Frederick A. Praegger, 1967.
Casson, Lionel, "Ancient Egypt".
   Alexandria, Virginia: Time-Life Books, 1978.
Gardiner, Sir Alan, "Egyptian Grammar".
   London: Oxford University Press, Third Edition, 1957.
Hall, Manly P., "An Encyclopedic Outline Of Masonic, Hermetic,
      Qabbalistic And Rosicrucian Symbolical Philosophy".
   San Francisco: H. S. Crocker Company, 1928
Hoffman, Michael A., "Egypt Before the Pharaohs".
   New York: Dorset Press, 1990
National Geographic Society, "Peoples and Places of the Past".
   Washington: National Geographic Book Service, 1983.
National Geographic Society, "Ancient Egypt, Discovering its Splendors".
   Washington: National Geographic Society, 1978.
National Geographic Society, "Splendors of the Past: Lost Cities of the Ancient
      World". Washington: National Geographic Society, 1981.
Stewart, Desmond, "The Pyramids and Sphynx".
   New York: Newsweek Books, 1981.

About the Author

The author is a Texan now living in Nashville, Tennessee. He retired as a senior international manufacturing operations executive and is listed in Who's Who in the World. In World War II, he was an officer in the United States Navy with the SeaBees in the Pacific and later in the Korean Police Action, serving as Lieutenant Commander. He has been married 51 years, with three children and seven grandchildren.